THE
UNDEAD
MR.
TENPENNY

Book one
of
The Cassie Black Trilogy

TAMMIE PAINTER

ALSO BY TAMMIE PAINTER

Early Praise for
The Undead Mr. Tenpenny

The Undead Mr. Tenpenny is a clever, hilarious romp through a new magical universe that can be accessed through the closet of a hole-in-the-wall apartment in Portland, Oregon.

—Sarah Angleton, author of *Gentleman of Misfortune*

Man oh man, did I love this book! …The plot was great, and got even better as things progressed…. I think the biggest pro of this book is the characters.

—Jonathan Pongratz, author of *Reaper*

…suffused with dark humor and witty dialogue, of the sort that Painter excels at…a fun read for anyone who enjoys fast-paced, somewhat snarky, somewhat twisted, fantasy adventures.

—Berthold Gambrel, author of *Vespasian Moon's Fabulous Autumn Carnival*

…a fun and entertaining read. Great wit too.

—Carrie Rubin, author of *The Bone Curse*

Wow and wow again! I absolutely loved this book! You get such a feel for the characters and the story is so fast paced you don't want to put it down.

—Goodreads Reviewer

The Undead Mr. Tenpenny
Book One of The Cassie Black Trilogy

You may contact the author by email at
Tammie@tammiepainter.com
Mailing Address:
Daisy Dog Media
P.O. Box 165
Netarts, Oregon 97143, USA

ISBN: 979 8568 526 032
First Edition, February 2021
also available as an ebook

This book is dedicated to my grandmother, Martha. I can truly say without your having passed into the Great Beyond, this story would never have come to life. And a million thanks go out to my review team for giving me the confidence to publish this thing!

THE
UNDEAD
MR.
TENPENNY

THE UNEXPECTED

I work in a funeral home. I'm used to seeing all manner of dead bodies. I'm used to bodies ranging from young to old, fat to thin, dark to pale. I'm used to the peacefully deceased and the horrifically killed. I'm used to them lying there still, silent, and slowly decomposing.

What I am not used to is them getting up and walking away.

Which is why when Mr. Boswick — he of the untimely coronary embolism — started drumming his fingers against the cold surface of the metal work table as I added the final touches to his makeup job, well I'd like to tell you I kept my cool, that I maintained my composure, but that'd be a lie.

Nope, I screamed like a baby boomer who's just lost every dime in her 401K, then promptly upended my tray of cosmetics as I jumped several feet backward. Five weeks and two walking bodies later, and I'm still scraping beige powder out of the oddest places.

As the cloud of talcum-soft haze filled the chilly workroom, Mr. Boswick sat up with a grunt, put his hands to his ears, and gave me the dirtiest would-you-shut-the-hell-up look I've ever seen on a guy — dead or alive.

Still giving me The Look and moving with uncertain slowness, Mr. Boswick eased himself off the table. His legs trembled a little as his feet and legs took their owner's weight for the first time in several days. I could have taken him then. I could have just pushed him over and hogtied him, but let me tell you, no matter how many zombie movies you've seen or novels you've read, no matter how well you can suspend belief, you still go around living your life assuming the Zombie Apocalypse is something that happens to other people.

And so, rather than attack, double tap, or run, I stood there getting coated in Dewy Chiffon dust while Mr. Boswick took two clumsy steps with his hands held out like an unsteady toddler.

He looked back and forth between the two doorways in his line of sight. First one, then the other, then back to the first, then he headed toward Door Number Two. Unfortunately, this first effort at post-mortem decision making landed him in our storage closet, but we here at Wood's Funeral Home don't deduct points for guessing. Standing amongst a year's supply of paper towels and bottles of extra-strength cleaning solution, Mr. Boswick turned to me with a question on his heavily made-up face.

I suppose I should have rushed over, slammed the closet door, locked him in, and burned the place down to save humanity, but at this point my neurons were more than a little numb with shock and were refusing to chat with one another. Instead of being the hero, I pointed to Door Number One above which shone the green glow of an exit sign. Mr. Boswick gave a little nod of thanks before shuffling to and out the door.

With my brain operating about as quickly as a dial-up modem from 1992, I glanced down at the metal work table. To all appearances it was empty, but I reached out and patted it just to make sure all the chemicals I work around weren't giving me hallucinations. With a grimace, my hand landed on a cold, smooth surface that was definitely lacking the corporeal remains of Mr. Boswick. Then my eyes caught the photo of him I'd been working from. The photo his family had loaned us.

His family! If he tried to get to his family—

And there we have it, folks. Miracle of all miracles, Cassie Black's brain is functioning once again.

CHAPTER ONE

MR. BOSWICK'S LETTER

Yes, it really took me that long to register that I had just released a dead guy to wander the streets of Southeast Portland, but you've no room to judge until you see how well your brain operates when you encounter your first walking corpse.

It was up to me to bring in Mr. ZomBoswick. And thanks to my love of zombie movies, I knew that required weaponry. We didn't have anything useful like a machete or crossbow or rifle in the funeral home — again, much like the Spanish Inquisition, nobody expects the Zombie Apocalypse. What we did have was a baseball bat. The neighborhood Mr. Wood's place is in isn't the worst in Portland, but some strange people had been lingering around lately and it was comforting to know I had a blunt object at hand.

I grabbed my zombie-whacking, maplewood slugger and raced out the door expecting to see hundreds of former humans shuffling along with herd mentality, drooling over brains, and doing their best to spread the zombie virus as the non-infected dashed about in sheer pandemonium. But when I kicked open the door, leapt over the threshold, and held my bat at the ready, it turned out to be a completely normal spring day outside. Birds were singing, dogs were pooping, and people were ignoring each other to stare at their phones.

I scanned the area. The few people who did glance up with glassy eyes from their Twitter feeds gave me odd stares, but I couldn't blame them. I was standing outside a funeral parlor covered in Dewy Chiffon powder, dressed in my mad scientist lab coat and purple nitrile gloves, and brandishing a bat.

"Where's the zombie?" some oh-so-clever kid in a black hoodie asked.

"You tell me," I muttered as my gaze darted over the area, trying to spot my quarry and hoping he wasn't satisfying any brain-based munchies.

I was expecting to see a guy lumbering awkwardly forward, maybe dragging a half-shod foot as he went along. Again, in the space of less than three minutes, zombie movies and apocalyptic novels had done me wrong, and it took me several agonizing moments to locate Mr. Boswick. In his navy blue suit and his anchorman makeup, he stood about halfway down the block at the nearest Trimet stop, craning his head as people do to see if their bus is on its way.

I pulled off my gloves and approached him with extreme caution. And I mean Extreme with a capital E. I've seen *Shaun of the Dead*. I know what happens if you get bit by the undead: You end up locked away in your best mate's garden shed. Oh, sorry, spoiler alert.

"Mr. Boswick?" He glanced up and, possibly recognizing me as the screeching lunatic from his resurrection, he rolled his eyes then looked past me to check for his bus. "Are you going somewhere?"

He shrugged his shoulders and raised his eyebrows with exaggerated resignation.

"I know. Today's schedule for this line sucks, but that's what you get for returning from the dead on a Sunday." After a pause I tentatively asked, "Are you trying to get home?"

13

He nodded and his heavily made-up chin started quavering.

By this point, passersby were starting to give us some strange looks and I could tell at any second they'd be doing that I'm-just-holding-my-phone-at-an-unnaturally-odd-angle-for-the-fun-of-it thing people do when trying to sneak a photo of someone or something they shouldn't be taking a picture of.

"Maybe we should talk about this elsewhere." I indicated the park behind us with a tilt of my head. Mr. Boswick looked again for his bus. "It's not coming," I said as I slipped off my lab coat. Mr. B's shoulders slumped, but he shuffled toward the park where we found a bench that was surprisingly free of any homeless person's clutter.

"You can't go home," I told him. After shaking another layer of the spilled powder from my lab coat, I took a seat next to my client. "You do know you're dead, right?"

Was I really having this conversation?

Mr. Boswick nodded.

"Can you speak, or do you enjoy making me ask a bunch of yes or no questions?"

Mr. Boswick put his hands to his belly. "Speak hard," he said, literally pushing the words out. It took that push for me to realize he couldn't speak because to speak you need to breathe in air then use your diaphragm to move that air over your vocal cords in just the right way to make the sounds we modern humans call words. Granted, normally you also need to breathe in order to jump off work tables and wait for buses, but I guess speaking was a higher-order thing.

Anyway, setting the evolutionary anatomy lesson aside, to utter those two words Mr. B had to press his gut to push the air out. How did he know to do that? I mean, who'd have thought the dead would have instincts? Still, it looked uncomfortable, so I dug my phone out of my back pocket, turned it on, and opened

14

the Notes app. I handed the device to Mr. Boswick and hoped he wouldn't run off with it because how do you explain to your carrier that the really nice dead guy made off with your phone?

"Why do you want to go home?" I asked. His pale thumbs danced over the tiny keypad, then he stopped and showed me the screen.

Fight with wife.

"You want to go home to fight with your wife?"

He rolled his eyes again. Seriously, he was giving off a lot of attitude for someone whose current claim to fame was a death certificate. He tapped away, then showed me the phone.

Had fight with wife then died. Said bad things.

"And you want to make amends?"

He gave me a well-duh face. It was like having a surly emoji brought to life. Mr. Boswick thumb-drummed a few more characters.

Want to tell her I'm sorry.

Okay, I know I let him go wandering out into the streets without fully considering the potential havoc he might wreak, but now that I had my senses back I had to show a little responsibility.

"Nope. No way." Mr. Boswick scowled and stuck out his lower lip, his thick makeup creasing as he pouted. "I know that's not what you want to hear, but most living people aren't as cool as I am about dead people strolling up to them." The pout turned into a sidelong look and I just knew he was recalling my earlier banshee impersonation. "That was a rare moment of uncool on my part, but look at me now. If you showed up on your wife's doorstep, you'd scare her. I think that would be harder on her than a fight she's probably long forgotten."

Jenny good at holding grudges.

Ah, one of those. I paused for a moment during which an off-leash St. Bernard charged over, slobbery tongue lolling with doggy glee. He sniffed Mr. Boswick, whined, then, with hackles raised and tail tucked, scurried back to his owner's side.

I knew no wife would believe me if I went up to her door and announced that her husband was sorry. She'd probably call the police thinking I was some tarot-card-reading con artist. I shifted my lab coat on my lap and felt the spiral coils of the notebook I always carried with me. I squeezed the pocket. Yep, the pen was in there too. Surely, Mrs. B would recognize her husband's handwriting.

I slipped the pad and pen out of the pocket and, trading them for my phone, handed them over to my new zombie buddy.

"Write out what you want to say to her."

Mr. Boswick flipped the cover open and started adding his words to the top sheet. The sheet that already had the beginnings of my grocery list. Zombies, they have instincts, but no common sense.

"No, start a new one." I grabbed for the pad, but Mr. B held tight to it. After a couple pulls back and forth, Team Cassie won the tug-of-war competition. I ignored Mr. Boswick's grumpy huff over his loss, turned to a blank page, and handed the pad back to him. When he began to write, I added, "And use proper grammar, not Zombie Speak."

So, Mr. B wrote out his apology. It must have been a doozy of a fight because he was pouring his heart and soul onto sheet after sheet of my notepad. When he stopped, I took the pad, tore out his note, folded it in half, then handed it back to him. "Put her name on it."

It wasn't "Jenny" he wrote, but a word that must have been her pet name. It was so ridiculous that to this day I refuse to repeat it.

What now, I wondered. If I left him in the park, he would

wander off. If I left him in my workroom, he'd wander off. The only solution was to take him with me, but first we had to return to the funeral home. Mr. Wood, my boss, had caught the casino shuttle that morning and wouldn't be back until evening. I didn't own a car, but he always said I could use his Prius whenever I needed it. Well, today I needed it.

I slipped the keys off the ring by the door that led up to Mr. Wood's living quarters, told Mr. Boswick to hop in and buckle up, then drove to the Westmoreland address I recalled from his paperwork. When I pulled up to the tidy, pale grey colonial with impossibly white trim, Mr. Boswick stared wistfully at the façade then gave me a pleading puppy dog look.

"No way. You're staying here. This is going to be hard enough without a dead husband trailing after me. Now, scooch down so she doesn't see you."

Heading up the ruler-straight walkway lined with color-coordinated yellow and white primroses and pansies, I questioned my suitability for this line of work. I got into the trade of funereal cosmetics because I didn't want to interact with people, but here I was about to do some serious interacting. Maybe I should consider a job stocking shelves in a grocery store. I mean, if the canned peas started walking down the aisles it might be weird, but who would complain? Well, besides the two people in the world who willingly eat canned peas. Still, I wouldn't have to approach grieving widows with messages from their not-quite-dead husbands.

I lifted the heavy brass knocker and self-consciously tapped it on the door. In little time, a woman, slim with a pixie haircut as tidy as her garden, answered. Her eyes were swollen and ringed with red. Although not in full black, her skirt and sweater were a somber shade of dark grey. From inside the house wafted the rich scent of sandalwood.

"Mrs. Boswick?"

"I don't need Jesus and I don't need new windows."

Good line. I reminded myself to jot it down when I got back to the car.

"No," I stammered before she could slam the door in my face, "I'm Cassie Black. I work at Wood's Funeral Home."

"I'm so sorry." Flustered, she shook her head as if chastising herself. "But why are you here? Does the suit not fit?"

Thinking how dapper Mr. Boswick looked despite the whole "being dead" thing, I shook my head.

"No, the suit's fine, but I found this note. It seemed personal." I held out the folded sheets. Mrs. B looked at them skeptically until she saw her pet name on the front. She bit her lip, then her hand flew up to stifle a cry. Once she'd taken a shaky breath, she snatched the note from me. After several fumbling attempts to get the pages open, she began to read. Big fat teardrops plopped from her eyes when she looked up.

"How did—? That suit was—"

Before I had time to come up with an explanation for the inexplicable, Mrs. B lunged forward, pulled me into an unwanted hug, and blubbered out her gratitude. My entire body tensed. I like the dead. Not in a perverted, illegal-in-most-states way, but in an easy-to-be-around, no-pressure kind of way. I'm not good with the living. Never have been. And hugging strangers was way out of my comfort zone.

"Come in. Have tea."

"I really need to get back to work."

"Of course. I— It's just— This is so—" Yes, folks, you too can master Zombie Speak in only ten minutes of practice a day. "It's just what I needed."

I don't like it when things get emotional. I know I work at a funeral home, but it's pretty much just one emotion there:

sadness. Mrs. Boswick's reaction to the letter was unexpected relief mixed into a heap of loving joy with a rippling undercurrent of grief. I didn't know how to handle such a melange and, telling my legs it would be rude to run, I slowly backed away from the widow while offering my condolences.

When I returned to the car, Mr. Boswick had slumped down in the passenger's seat.

Dead.

Again.

But this time he had a smile on his face.

CHAPTER TWO

THE CHARMING MR. MORELLI

I won't go into details of how I got Mr. Boswick out of the car and back onto his table. Let's just suffice it to say that you get pretty strong working in my profession and really good at handling awkward packages. Cleaning up the cast away cosmetics was no easy feat, but there's worse things to clean up in a funeral home. By the time Mr. Wood got back from his casino outing, he was sixty-four dollars richer and none the wiser of how I'd spent my day.

After bidding Mr. Wood goodnight, I delayed my departure by passing through my work area to check on Mr. Boswick who, thankfully, was still not dancing the cha cha, nor writing apology letters to any other family members. With no further excuses to linger, I hoisted my satchel over my shoulder, and stepped outside.

The instant the heavy door latched behind me, a prickling sensation latched onto the back of my neck. I told it to go away, but no one listens to me, not even my own body, so the feeling stuck with me as I headed home and hoped my landlord was too busy watching reruns of *Gilligan's Island*, breeding cockroaches, shaving his back hair, or whatever it was he did in his apartment all day to notice my return.

I lived only five blocks from Mr. Wood's and had never felt unsafe walking home alone whether it was dawn, evening, or the dark of night. But for the past several weeks, whenever I made my commute, the hairs of my neck tingled and my nose involuntarily wrinkled at something in the air.

I say "something" because I honestly couldn't pick out any particular scent. Sure there was dog poop, human pee, fried food from the nearby food carts, and sometimes a stench wafting up from the Willamette River, but I was used to those as normal smells of the city. I had no idea what the "something" was, maybe just toxins in the exhaust I inhaled as Portland traffic crawled along beside me. Nevertheless, it put me on high alert whenever I caught wind of it.

As for the tingling sensation, I didn't want to appear skittish by constantly glancing over my shoulder. Instead, I watched the reflections in the shop windows I passed to make sure no one was following me. Only five blocks, I told myself as my ears tried to pick out any approaching footsteps over the overheating engines and bass-thumping car speakers.

Once to my apartment building, my eyes darted as usual to the chubby-cheeked garden gnome that resided in the sad strip of weedy grass stretching along the front walkway. I suppose it drew my attention because no matter how little maintenance was done on the two-story quadplex, that damn gnome always looked like it had been freshly scrubbed. Wish I could say the same about the windows.

Working from muscle memory alone, my fingers drummed across the building's security keypad. As soon as the code unlatched the lock, I whipped the door open and scurried over the threshold. Only then did I take the chance to look back and scan my surroundings.

No one lurked in the parking lot, but a white man wearing a maroon hoodie was passing by on the sidewalk. With his shoulders hunched and his hands crammed into the pockets of his skinny jeans, he peered out from his hood. He smirked when he saw me watching, then continued on his way without breaking his stride. Chilly fingers raked along my spine.

"Oy!" The shout sent me jumping half out of my skin and I jerked so hard I hit myself in the forehead with the door. "Close the door, Black!"

Everyone, meet my landlord, Morelli. I'm sure he must have a first name, but he's never told it to me and I'm not the kind of person to ask.

Right then, he was looming in the open doorway of his ground-floor apartment, handily located so he could keep an eye on my comings and goings. Morelli's got all the charm of a sewer rat (I'm convinced he eats them for breakfast) and the fashion sense of a troll. This evening, he had dressed in the finest cargo shorts you can get for under ten dollars at Costco; and to avoid staining his shirt, he'd opted not to wear one at all. Unless, of course, you want to count his thick patches of chest and back hair as upper body apparel.

"Your rent's due this Wednesday. You know that, right?"

This was our little game. The goal was for me to do my best to avoid him. If I succeeded, I had a peaceful evening. If I failed, he'd punish me by treating me to an announcement of when rent was due. First it would be weeks, then it would be days, and by Tuesday it would be an hourly countdown, as in, "Black, rent's due in eight hours. You know that, right?"

If Morelli wasn't such a slovenly jerk, I might almost be understanding of his reminders. See, until I landed my job with Mr. Wood, I hadn't exactly been timely in my rent payments. In fact, I'd missed several months in a row.

But Morelli *was* a slovenly jerk who obsessively observed my every entry and departure as if I was going to sneak off with the drywall one day, so my sympathy toward him was in short supply.

I kept telling myself I'd find another place one day, but so far that day hadn't dawned. After all, the apartment was conveniently close to work. More importantly, it was insanely cheap. Despite being in Portland where rent hikes were a raging pastime, and despite my being his only tenant for as long as I'd lived there, Morelli's rent had remained the same for years.

"Thanks for the reminder," I said with a casual salute. "I don't know what I'd do without you."

"You'd be on the street. Who'd rent to you? You should just be glad I let you stay."

I squeezed my way past him to the stairs that led up to my second-floor apartment. "You truly are a prince among men, Morelli. I have no doubt that humanitarian awards will one day be named in your honor."

Because I took being an introvert to a whole new level, Mr. Wood was always encouraging me to interact with other humans — living humans, that is. He'd probably be impressed at my current attempt at conversation, I thought, as I raced up the stairs before Morelli could lunge his hairy bulk at me.

"I'm watching you, Black. Don't think I ain't."

I mumbled various insults relating to him, his mother, and a herd of dimwitted sheep as I fumbled my keys into the lock.

"What did you say?" he grunted, but I'd already darted into my humble abode, tucking myself into a cocoon of space where there were no other humans to deal with.

CHAPTER THREE

SHOW TIME

The next couple days went by without incident, but I couldn't shake off my own questions about Mr. Boswick. Had that really happened? Was I losing it? Should I start eating fewer donuts?

But what really had me losing sleep — besides hearing the theme music for *The Brady Bunch* every half hour as Morelli binged his way through an all-night Brady marathon — was the worry of what might happen at Mr. Boswick's funeral.

When the day arrived I was as on edge as a cat in a room full of rattlesnakes. Would Mr. Boswick stay dead? Would he wake? Would he start pushing out queries, apologies, or requests? Would Mr. Wood let me remain in the back room, away from the messy intricacies of human interaction?

I had my answer to that fourth question soon after I arrived to work. As for the other three, well, I'd just have to wait with my gut twisting in nervous knots to see about those.

"Sorry, Cassie," Mr. Wood said, hurrying down the stairs from his living quarters and still adjusting his tie. "I'm running late, so I'll need you out there."

Mr. Wood had owned and operated Wood's Funeral Home for over thirty years. He was a warm, jovial, avuncular kind of guy who normally wanted to be the meeter and greeter at each funeral. It's like if things had turned out differently for him, he would have been an events planner and would have been at the head of Portland's most memorable shindigs. But having learned the trade from his father, who learned it from his father before him, Mr. Wood had literally been grandfathered into being the host of only the most somber parties.

Because I wasn't licensed to work with the dead, as far as the county officials were concerned, I was supposed to be nothing more than Mr. Wood's office manager. Although fully trained and educated, I didn't quite make it to the stage of being certified to practice desairology. Don't worry, I can't pronounce it either, but it basically means "your final beautician." My lack of certification meant I occasionally had to make the pretense of having nothing to do with handling anyone's final remains, only their loved ones' paperwork. This also meant I was expected to face the public now and then.

And I'll be honest, I'd prefer dealing with a corpse rising from the dead over interacting with living people, grieving or not.

"Look at you," I said brightly, "you're almost ready. They don't need me strolling through."

"But I think you'll like the younger people. They're just like you." What? Perpetual cynics? Lovers of IPA? Wakers of the dead? "Mr. and Mrs. Boswick spent many years being foster parents." I flinched involuntarily. Mr. Wood couldn't help but notice the reaction. "They weren't like that. Look out there. Those are the kids he helped raise. They loved him."

I tried, and completely failed, not to allow bitter thoughts such as, "Lucky for them," to snipe through my brain.

I peered out the viewing window from the kitchenette of the funeral home where I would have been happy to remain tending to my preferred funeral day duty of making coffee and arranging Swedish butter cookies on a tray. (And yes, more than a few of the treats may have ended up in my mouth, but it's important to make sure they're fresh, right?)

Besides the fear of him deciding an eternal nap wasn't in his plans, Mr. Boswick's funeral was odd because most of the attendees were people about my own age — mid- to late twenties. Normally, unless there's grandkids being dragged along, funerals are attended mostly by older people or at least by those who've already had their Over the Hill birthday party, whether that's the hill of forty, fifty, or even sixty if you're really optimistic about the definition of mid-life.

Mr. Boswick's "kids" were greeting each other, hugging the slim and prim Mrs. Boswick, and acting very much like an oversized happy family.

"No, I don't think they're like me," I muttered. I then busied myself with rearranging the cookies and checking very closely for any broken ones that I might need to remove from service.

"Cassie, you are the only other employee here. Some days you will have to interact with the clients. The living clients," he added when I opened my mouth to protest.

"You know I'm not good at it."

"Practice, my dear. After all, you interact with me splendidly."

My throat tightened. Sure, we get along great now, but we both know I didn't interact with him at all when I first started working at the funeral home. Back then, I kept my head down, mumbled my responses, and avoided Mr. Wood as much as I could. I even resorted to never taking a break because I didn't want to risk a conversation with him at the kitchenette's little table.

"Consider it payback for borrowing my car the other day."

I grumbled out the word, "Fine," sucked in a big lungful of air through my nostrils and blew it out through my mouth while thinking Zen-filled thoughts. I then picked up the tray of cookies and carried it out to the receiving lobby where most of the members of this unusual family were gathered, looking at photos that showed Mr. and Mrs. Boswick with a rainbow of children.

Keeping my head down, I moved as quickly as possible to the refreshment stand then kept my back turned as I fussed with some napkins and made sure the coffee pots were still full. All the while I ticked down the seconds until the funeral ended.

There being only so much fussing one can do over two pots and a tray, I scooped up a pile of the programs for the funeral and went to stand by the door to hand them out with what I hoped was a sympathetic look on my face, but probably resembled something more like the face of a woman with an uncomfortable bout of gas.

Just take one and move along, take one and move along, I mentally chanted as I handed a sheet to each person who passed from the receiving room into the chapel.

But, proof positive that this was not my lucky day, one of the attendees stopped and said hello. I muttered a condolence and looked dismissively past him, begging someone else to come along and be in desperate need of one of the papers my palms were beginning to sweat all over.

He was still there. Why couldn't the building do me a favor and catch on fire?

"I'm supposed to be a pallbearer," he said. "Could you show me what I need to do or where I should wait after the funeral?"

"You'll just wait at that door there," I said as quickly as my tongue, which was already tying into knots, would allow, then pointed to the double doors where the hearse would pull up. "Mr. Wood will instruct you when the time comes."

Do the cookies need refilling? I glanced over his shoulder. Nope. Damn it.

"So you work here?" he asked.

No, I crash funerals as a clever way to hand out advertising flyers. Here's your program for today's service. Oh, and don't forget your coupon for ten percent off your next car wash at Tidy Clean.

"Um, yeah," I said, demonstrating my fine oratory skills.

Thankfully, just then the pastor came in the main door.

"I have to go," I mumbled and hurried over to the pastor. He'd done plenty of services here before and likely knew exactly where to go, but since I couldn't telepathically induce an arson attack and none of the attendees had suddenly developed a craving for cookies, escorting the pastor into the chapel seemed like an excellent escape plan.

The moment I left the pastor at the podium to organize his notes, I realized my mistake. I was right next to Mr. Boswick. Granted, in his open casket he gave every appearance of still doing an excellent job of playing his role as Lead Corpse, but who knew when he'd decide he kind of liked roaming around and might want to do it again.

I backed away from the body as if, well, as if it might come to life, but also as if my being near it might wake him up. Unfortunately, in my retreat I backed straight into someone. Okay, I admit, I may have screamed, but only because I had an image of Mr. Boswick having jumped out of his coffin and stealthily sneaking up behind me.

My clammy grip on the programs faltered, and the sheets went flying as I tried to keep from tumbling over what turned out to be, not a zombified Mr. Boswick, but the very much still alive Mrs. Boswick. My face burned as I muttered my apologies to her and stooped down to gather up the mess of papers. I swear if my cheeks had gotten any hotter from my distressed embarrassment, you might have smelled roasting flesh.

Mrs. Boswick helped me gather the flyers. Figuring these people didn't need me handing them pieces of paper, I placed the collected sheets on the chapel's side table. I'd just been about to make a break for the kitchenette when Mrs. Boswick started thanking me profusely for helping her. Mr. Wood stood at the kitchenette door, ready to make an appearance, but came to an abrupt stop at the sight of this woman telling me how much she appreciated what I had done for her.

Given my past anti-social behavior, this was probably like seeing a giraffe pirouetting across the Hawthorne Bridge. Just not one of those things you see every day. Or ever. Unless the circus is in town and the animals got loose. Which does happen.

After an uncomfortable amount of hand-clutching and me saying it was no big deal, she wiped her eyes and returned to greeting her loved ones. I knew a chance when I saw one and made my escape by dashing into the kitchenette.

Where Mr. Wood was waiting with a very curious expression on his face.

"What was that about?" he asked.

"I found a note in Mr. B's suit and took it to her."

"You? *You* made an effort to speak to someone you don't know?" He paused. "But that suit was brand new. She added the expense to the funeral. How could anything have gotten in the pocket?"

I shrugged my shoulders and twisted my face into my best gosh-I-sure-don't-know contortion. I don't think Mr. Wood bought it. When the organ started playing, he gave me a knowing look then left to tend to the grieving widow.

With his easy-going nature, Mr. Wood let the matter slide. In fact, he might have written it off completely if it hadn't been for the Strange Case of Mrs. Escobar a couple weeks later.

CHAPTER FOUR

MRS. ESCOBAR'S CAT

The moment I began working on Mrs. Escobar, a wary feeling churned in my gut that had nothing to do with the two apple fritters and double espresso chaser I'd had for breakfast.

My two previous clients over the past couple weeks had been well-behaved without even the tiniest hint of reanimation tendencies. To be fair, they had both been in their nineties. Maybe they'd had enough of life and saw no need to jump back into it. But, at fifty-three years old, Mrs. Escobar was about Mr. Boswick's age and that sent alarm bells clanging across my nerves as I lined her eyes and livened up her cheeks. Would she wake? If she did, would she exert true zombie behavior and try to nosh on my brain? I then wondered if Mr. Wood would question the expense of a machete. Or perhaps a crossbow?

"No headphones today?"

I jumped back from the body, knocked my makeup tray to the floor, and screeched. Literally screeched. A 1950s horror movie's damsel-in-distress would have seethed in envy over my innate screeching skills. I whipped around, brandishing a very deadly foundation brush.

Mr. Wood raised his pudgy hands in mock defense. "Did I frighten you?"

I lowered my weapon and, while clutching my chest to keep

my heart from exploding out of it, stooped down to pick up the tray. Thankfully, all my jars and cases had been closed, but I did find the ragged edge of another chunk of the Dewy Chiffon I'd spilled during Mr. Boswick's waking.

"No, just too much coffee this morning."

"You're not getting the jitters, are you? People do sometimes start this work then later discover they're too — what's the word? — *weirded out* by it. I know it's a special arrangement we have, but if you ever change your mind about these duties…"

"I'm fine. I'm really fine. You just startled me. And I'm keeping my ears open."

"Unfortunately, that's probably for the best. Perhaps we should consider an update to the security system. Such a world now. I remember—"

Something groaned.

I barely held back a curse. In truth, I'd been hoping Mr. Boswick's waking had been a fluke. One of those mysteries of the unexplained that would one day find its way onto the pages of *Ripley's Believe It or Not*. My gaze instantly flicked to Mrs. Escobar. Then, remembering I was trying to hide this whole living-dead issue from Mr. Wood, I jerked my focus back to him and put my hand to my stomach.

"Bad tacos," I said, but Mr. Wood, normally so open-faced and trusting, trained an impressively skeptical squint on me.

"My old ears are still in top form, Cassie. That didn't come from you. Is Mrs. Escobar still gassing?" he asked, referring to the rude noises the dead make as everything relaxes and settles. He stepped closer to the body. "She should've cleared out by—"

Mrs. Escobar chose that moment to sit up, her curled hair ringing her head like a black halo. I looked to Mr. Wood, looked to Mrs. Escobar, then back to Mr. Wood. So much for flukes of nature and keeping things under wraps.

"I can explain—"

"What in the—?"

I could see what was about to happen even before my head fully registered it. Reacting the instant Mr. Wood's knees went watery, I dashed over and caught his round frame as he slumped, then supported him so he wouldn't hit his head on anything. I eased him to the floor just as Mrs. Escobar scooted off the table and shuffled toward the door. Unlike Mr. Boswick, she had no problem selecting the correct doorway on the first try.

I felt bad about leaving Mr. Wood there on the tiles without even a pillow, but I figured I had more pressing matters to tend to. Plus, it was already pretty warm out for an April morning, and I'd be damned if I'd let Mrs. Escobar sweat off all the makeup I'd just applied. Really, you can't believe the things that go through your mind when you're chasing down zombies.

My target wasn't difficult to spot. Wearing a bright pink dress, Mrs. Escobar stood out like a walking piece of Mexican pastry. As with Mr. Boswick, it didn't take much to catch up to a very disoriented Mrs. Escobar. I fell in alongside her and, as with Mr. Boswick, I found it curiously easy to chat with the not-so-dead.

"Hey, Mrs. Escobar, where are you headed?"

"*Casa*," she said, making the word with the gut push that seemed to be instinctive in roaming corpses.

When her family had dropped by to make arrangements, I was certain they had all spoken in completely unaccented English, but perhaps Mrs. Escobar's dead-awake mind was reverting back to her ancestral tongue.

"What for?" I was already pulling out my notepad from my pocket, but Mrs. Escobar turned to face me and came lightning quick with a huffing answer.

"*Gato*." Her heavy chin trembled with worry. "*Mi gato.*"

"Your son said your sister would take your cat."

Mrs. Escobar's eyes went wide and I have to say I'd done an excellent job on her eyeliner.

"No!" She gave her gut a good punch to make this as emphatic as possible for a dead person. Then she yanked the pad from my hand and scrawled out a message. Thankfully, when she turned it around for me to read, the note was mostly in English since my Spanish is a bit rusty.

Hermina hates cats. Send to die.

"She wouldn't," I assured her, but Mrs. Escobar was having none of it. She stabbed the pad, made a series of vicious lines under the word *hates*, then drew her index finger across her throat. I thought of Mr. Wood on the floor; he might be uncomfortable, but he wasn't going anywhere.

Mrs. Escobar, however, was.

Moving down the street in her bare feet, she began heading, I assumed, to her cat-hating sister's home. I recalled Mrs. Escobar's paperwork and knew she and her sister lived not far away, a couple blocks at the most. Despite the unseasonably warm morning, it was as good a day as any for a walk. I caught up with Mrs. Escobar again. She earned some strange looks, but that was mostly because she kept pushing on her belly and repeatedly grunting, "*Perra,*" which I knew wasn't in reference to the cat.

When we neared her address, I grabbed Mrs. Escobar's arm — desperately hoping it wouldn't come detached — and pulled her behind the neighbor's overgrown laurel hedge.

"Look, Mrs. Escobar, you stay put and I promise I'll get your cat. Your *gato,* okay?"

She nodded. Her gut was probably too sore at this point to push out *Gracias, Bueno,* or even *Sí.*

Looking sort of official in my lab coat (if you ignored the

faint streaks of Creamy Fawn powder I'd used to highlight Mrs. E's cheeks, I marched up to a small bungalow painted white with trim the same color as Mrs. Escobar's dress. Out front, sitting directly in the sun was a small pet carrier. I stooped down so I was face to face with a latched door made of metal grating.

My jaw gave a little twitch of angry tension. I may not like people much, but I adore animals and do not like seeing them in distress. Inside, there was no water dish, but there was an orange tabby resting on its side and panting steadily. I stood up. I was about to grab the carrier and rescue the cat when the front door whipped open.

"You're the pest control?" a long-nosed, short-statured woman snapped as she scanned me up and down with a sneer on her face. She had the look of an evil parakeet that would bite your finger off if given half a chance.

Besides just walking off with the carrier, I hadn't formed any real plan of how to save Mrs. Escobar's cat. However, if Parakeet Woman was going to be kind enough to provide me with a ruse, I was more than willing to play along.

"Yes," I said confidently. I held up the carrier and, with a vile taste in my mouth, told her, "Glad to get this thing out of your way."

"No van?" She lit a cigarette and blew most of the smoke up and away from her face, which meant it went straight into mine.

"Around the corner at another call."

"Whatever, just get rid of it. What do I owe you for the disposal?"

Since I'd recently had to send Louise, my old lady cat, to the Great Scratching Post in the sky, I was painfully aware of the hefty fee for euthanasia — it was one of the reasons I'd been late on my rent a few months ago. What I was about to do might technically be construed as misrepresentation, but this woman was not only blowing smoke in my face, she was also torturing and willingly asking for the execution of a perfectly good pet. So, I quoted what I'd paid for my cat's farewell shot, then complained that my company hadn't gotten around to being able to handle mobile payments and I could only take cash.

The woman balked, but as she grabbed her purse from one of the coat hooks lining the entry hall, she said, "It's worth knowing I'm rid of it."

I shoved the wad of twenties in my pocket and turned away with the carrier in hand. Just as I thought I'd pulled it off, Parakeet Woman said, "Wait, don't I know you from somewhere?"

My gut did a nice little somersault. "Doubt it. New to the area," I mumbled then hurried away as fast as my legs could take me with my awkward cargo. When I found Mrs. Escobar peering from the cover of the laurel hedge, she glanced at the carrier and clapped her hands together with delight. Her eyes glistened with joy until she saw the state of her cat. She then scowled at the house and made a couple rude and very emphatic hand gestures.

"*Perra*, indeed," I said. Mrs. Escobar gave me a conspirator's grin.

Yep, she was still grinning, still standing, and still my problem. Mr. Boswick had been polite enough to go back to being fully dead after I'd satisfied his final wish by delivering his note. I'd gotten Mrs. Escobar's cat. Job done, right?

But there she was, still perfectly capable of walking alongside me back to the funeral home. On the one hand, I was thankful for this. It would have been nearly impossible to lug her and the carrier back to Mr. Wood's. On the other hand, I had no idea how I was going to ensure she was ready to take center stage in her final show the next day.

I was still pondering what it was going to take to kill off Mrs.

Escobar when we slipped back through the rear door of the funeral home. Mr. Wood wasn't where I'd left him, but I'd already learned you can't expect prone bodies to stay put.

I set down the carrier and got the poor creature inside a dish of water. Mrs. Escobar, still in possession of my notepad wrote, *You take. Se llama Pablo.*

"No, I can't have a cat," I said, watching the tabby and hoping he would respond to the water.

At this, Mrs. Escobar's eyes welled up with tears.

"No, don't cry." I wasn't being kind, I just didn't want her to ruin the work I'd done on her eyes. "I'll take him to the adoption center. He'll find a good home."

Pablo's nose twitched at the smell of the water. I couldn't help but smile as he pulled himself onto unsteady legs and began lapping up his drink like a drunkard on two-dollar beer day. Mrs. Escobar smiled at him, smiled at me, and spread her hands in a way that said, "See, look how well you two get along."

I'd had a hard enough time hiding Louise from Morelli who had a strict no-pets policy, but I had a feeling there was only one way to make sure Mrs. Escobar was good and dead for her funeral.

"If I give Pablo a home, will you be happy?"

Mrs. Escobar nodded.

"I guess I have a cat, then." I reached in to pet him, but our introduction would have to wait because Mrs. Escobar chose that moment to pass into the great beyond a second time. Luckily, when she slumped forward, she landed mostly across my work table, saving me from having to hoist her back onto it. I had to appreciate such an unexpected level of courtesy.

CHAPTER FIVE

BOTTOMS UP

Once Pablo had his fill of water, he curled up in the carrier and fell asleep. I had been hoping he might need more attention, because now that he was okay, I had to face the music and check on Mr. Wood.

I peered into the carrier once more to see if the cat was still content. Unfortunately, he was. I wouldn't say I was wishing for a relapse, but his resilience was a little inconvenient. After all, tending to a feline emergency would obviously preclude having a chitchat with my boss.

Since I'd gotten accustomed to things like feeding myself and paying Morelli his rent, as I passed through the kitchenette and to the front of the funeral home to Mr. Wood's office, I crossed my fingers that he wouldn't fire me.

But what would his reaction be? Would he be fuming? Would he have called the police? Would he be cowering behind his desk in fear of the Zombie Apocalypse I'd warned him about time and time again?

About a month ago I'd lectured Mr. Wood on the many benefits of being eco-friendly. As a result, he'd traded his oversized sedan for a Prius and he'd installed LED lights that only came on when a room was occupied. His office door was closed, but light shone through the gap at the bottom of the door, signaling that Mr. Wood was inside. Granted, with my recent experiences, what waited inside could have been another dead person roaming around, but Mrs. Escobar was the only client we had at the time, and since the local news had yet to sensationalize any local zombie activity, I was beginning to suspect these wakings were unique to Wood's Funeral Home. Lucky us.

I took a deep breath, inhaling the spicy scent of the reception area's bouquet of lilies, then drummed my fingertips on the office door before cautiously stepping in.

Mr. Wood is a round man. He's got a round belly, round face, and wears round wire-frame glasses over round hazel eyes. His hair has gone grey and what remains forms a nice round ring around his head. He normally looks like a white Buddha in a three-piece suit, complete with an honest, welcoming smile that speaks of someone who opens the windows to let flies out rather than whacking them with a newspaper.

When I entered the office, however, all trace of his usual beatific calm had vanished. Mr. Wood sat hunched at his desk, his face scrunched into a resolute scowl, and his hands had a white-knuckled grip on my baseball bat. The moment the door opened, he leapt up from the chair so fast it rolled back, smacked into the rear wall with a thud, then rebounded right into Mr. Wood's legs. He ignored the chair, choosing instead to swing the bat up, fully ready to hit a zombie-skull home run.

"What was that, Cassie? Why didn't you run from it? What's going on?"

I note those questions as if they were three coherent and separate sentences, but Mr. Wood sputtered them with such haste they all jumbled on top of one another.

"I– Well," I stammered, as I deciphered his tangle of words. "First, could you lower the bat?" He paused a moment, looked at me, looked at the bat, and lowered it to his side, but I noticed he kept a firm hold of the wooden weapon. "You see, the past few weeks—"

"Weeks!?"

I nodded. "The dead — just a couple of the dead, not all of them — have been sort of waking up."

The bat fell from Mr. Wood's hands as his legs gave out and he dropped into his plush, leather chair. His round head shook off the swoon. He then plunked his elbows on the desk, pulled off his glasses, and pressed the heels of his palms into his eyes. He stayed like that for several moments, like someone fighting through the worst of a headache. Finally, he looked up.

"Is this a joke, Cassie? Are you trying to be funny? I know you have a dark sense of humor, but—"

"No, I swear it. It really does happen. You saw it."

"How many?"

"Mrs. Escobar was the second," I paused, thinking that if he knew how few that actually was, it might ease his mind. "But that is over nearly a three-week period."

"Three weeks? This is been going on three weeks? Why?"

"They both seemed to have had unfinished business to do. Like they had one final chore to clear up."

Mr. Wood, clearly biding his time to gather his scrambled thoughts, used his shirt to wipe his lenses, then readjusted his glasses onto his face.

"Did you help them?" he asked. I nodded. "So that's what Mrs. Boswick meant. You didn't find that note in her husband's pocket."

"As far as she knows, I did."

"You went to her because of him? But you avoid people like you think we all have leprosy."

I shrugged one shoulder, my cheeks uncomfortably hot.

"Sometimes it's easier with the dead."

"That sounds so wrong, so very wrong. If the OMCB found out—" That's the Oregon Mortuary and Cemetery Board, for those not up on their Pacific Northwest funeral home lingo. Mr. Wood slumped back in his chair. The bat rolled out from under the desk. "But you've been handling this?"

"So far it's been straightforward."

"How is it happening? Is it you? Did this happen in school?"

"No, but then again, I never finished the program," I said with a deprecatory laugh. Mr. Wood was not amused. "Look, I don't know how it happens or what made it start now. I thought maybe it was something with this location."

"Wood's Funeral Home has been here for three generations. We have a very good track record of keeping our dead people dead. There has to be something we can do to stop this."

"I could rent *The Exorcist*. Maybe it'd have some tips." Mr. Wood closed his eyes and began rubbing his temples. Okay, so now wasn't the time for jokes. Got it.

I watched Mr. Wood's fingers make circular motions for a minute before finally asking, "Am I fired?" My throat tightened as the question came out.

His fingers stopped and his eyes slowly opened. "No," he sighed, then added, "I'm not firing you," but he was clearly holding back the word *yet*. "You're handling these, these..." He waved his hand as if summoning a word from the air. "Cases?"

"Yes."

"You really do have to take care of this, Cassie. And I don't mean just continuing on as you have been doing. I'm already running a great risk by letting you work on the clients without the proper licensing."

"I know."

"You need to find a solution. I can't put my livelihood, my

family business—"

"I'll figure it out," I interrupted, even though I had no idea how I was going to figure this out. I knew how to get the dead back to being dead, but I didn't know what was causing them to wake in the first place. If I didn't know that or why the problem had started, how was I to stop it? And if I was causing it, which Mr. Wood was implying, why was it happening now?

"I'm putting a great deal of trust in you, Cassie. I have since the day you came here." I stared at the floor, blinking as hard as possible to force any tears to go the hell away. The leather of Mr. Wood's chair squeaked as he shifted, and I heard the hollow, rolling sound of his desk drawer being opened. "I need a whiskey." He pulled out a bottle, spun off the cap, and tipped a large portion into his black mug with the Wood's Funeral Home name written in gold lettering. Just as he lifted the mug to his lips, he paused. "Is Mrs. Escobar...?"

"Back where she should be."

Mr. Wood threw back his drink in one gulp and immediately poured another double measure into the mug. He then extracted from the drawer a small, floral-patterned paper cup, slid it toward me, and filled it nearly to the rim.

"No doubt you need one too, then," he said.

CHAPTER SIX

MR. WOOD TO THE RESCUE

After my painfully strong drink, I checked in on Mrs. Escobar. I watched her for around ten minutes, but not a single finger drummed, no toes started tapping, and her eyelids showed no signs of fluttering. Convinced she was finally resting peacefully, I gathered up Pablo's carrier and started home. Over the course of the walk, although the prickling feeling still itched at the back of my neck, my guilty thoughts pushed aside most of my usual worry over Stranger Danger.

Mr. Wood was right. He had taken a huge chance on me. He'd also kept me from being kicked out of my apartment when my previous employer suddenly closed up shop and vanished without bothering to issue my final paycheck. I'd been barely scraping by on those paychecks and, after coughing up the astronomical fee to have Louise chemically murdered, I'd come up short on rent. Again.

To say Mr. Wood saved my life might be an exaggeration, but it was sort of true.

This was right about the time I started noticing a few shady characters loitering near my building and was perpetually walking around with that creepy crawly feeling of being watched. Most people would have assumed being kicked out would be better than dealing with weirdos invading the area and putting up with a landlord who gave a whole new meaning to sourpuss. But like I said, the price of Morelli's one-room apartment was a steal. For me, having a cheap roof over my head was far more important than experiencing warm fuzzies over my neighborhood.

But back to Mr. Wood.

After discovering I wouldn't be needed for any shift at my previous job ever again, and having just been given the twenty-eight-hour rent countdown by Morelli, I came home, tossed my messenger bag into a corner, flipped open my antique laptop, and logged onto Morelli's very unsecured, but also very free Wi-Fi to troll Craigslist for anyone who was hiring immediately.

And that's how I found Mr. Wood.

The ad didn't state what the business was, only that he needed a cleaner to start as soon as possible for "a spring tidying" even though it was November. It called for someone who was self-motivated, which is job ad speak for, "You'll be working on your own and we don't want any screwing off."

The only other job requirement: Must not be squeamish.

I emailed, told him I was a college grad (well, almost) looking for a job, and used to working on my own. I barely had time to sift through two pages of lost pet postings before a reply came through.

Could you start tomorrow morning?

It couldn't be that easy, could it? I had a sneaking suspicion this was either going to be a "massage" parlor, a "modeling" agency, or a serial killer who hated the grunt work of cleaning up his messes, but my curiosity and my need to eat won out over my concerns. I replied that if he sent the address I'd be there at nine the next morning — which, as Morelli would gladly inform me, would be exactly eight hours before my rent was due.

The following morning, I woke with a bundle of nerves over

the idea of an interview that would most certainly involve making small talk with a complete stranger. In case you hadn't guessed, that's not my thing. I dropped my brush three times while trying to tame my black hair that's meant to come to my shoulders, but since haircuts weren't in my budget, had grown several inches past. Then came the dilemma of what to wear to apply for a job that could very well be a front for a prostitution ring? Not a skirt, that's for sure. Since it was supposedly a cleaning job, I opted for black leggings and a tunic-style sweater over a t-shirt. It only took me two tries to get the t-shirt on right-side out.

In an effort to make my rent, I'd been scraping together every cent I could scrounge from between my couch cushions and had no extra money for food. This meant my breakfast was a bowl of imaginary cereal. Low in sugar, guaranteed gluten-free, one hundred percent non-GMO, but not very filling. Thankfully, the address I'd been sent was only a few blocks away, which meant I wouldn't have to waste money on a bus ticket or use my hunger-starved muscles to pedal my bike up and down the many hills that make up the Portland landscape.

When I showed up to the address and saw the sign for Wood's Funeral Home, I had to laugh. Although those giggles may have been giddiness caused by low blood sugar.

This had to be some sort of cosmic joke, right? Forcing my face into a sane and somber expression, I entered through the front door and into the reception area. Mr. Wood, smiling like a jovial human beach ball, greeted me as warmly as if I'd known him all my life. For my part, I experienced a rare feeling of comfort around him.

That's not to say I was ready for heartfelt hugs and cozy conversations, but I didn't feel as tongue-tied as I normally did around other humans. Some people are like that and I'd always wished I could find more of those people.

"I know there are services for this," Mr. Wood began, "but you have to schedule them so far ahead of time. And since I live upstairs, I don't like those nighttime janitorial folks banging around below me. Plus, those services hire the oddest people. I'd prefer to have someone I can trust in here." So said the man who'd just hired someone off Craigslist. He strode over to a side table below an ornate mirror and swiped his finger over the surface. "The place gets so dusty. Where does it all come from, I wonder?"

"Skin cells mostly," I said.

"Oh, well, that's disturbing."

I shrugged, and while I didn't mind interacting with Mr. Wood, I needed to earn some money ASAP.

"So, where should I start?"

"The chapel, I suppose," he said hesitantly, then showed me the kitchenette where there were a few cleaning supplies. He also told me I was free to help myself to any of the tea and cookies I'd like. Probably not the best thing to tell someone who'd barely eaten for three days.

I dusted. I polished. I vacuumed. My belly growled throughout it all, but I thought it only fair I put in a few hours before taking a break. When I did take that break, the half box of cookies was gone in five minutes.

By noon, the chapel looked far tidier than my apartment ever had. Mr. Wood came in, gushed over how impressed he was by the sparkling shine to the glass surfaces, then said he had to go out for a bit.

"If the phone rings, just ignore it. I won't be long."

I had just started on the kitchenette when Mr. Wood returned with a bag of sandwiches.

"I wasn't sure what you'd like, so I bought one of each."

Not being used to kind gestures from my fellow humans, I stumbled over what to say or do.

"I should really just work," I mumbled and grabbed my bucket.

"Nonsense, take a break. You must be hungry," he said, his eyes darting to the empty cookie box. He took the bucket from me and pointed to a chair at the kitchenette's table. I tucked my head down and slipped into the seat as Mr. Wood presented an array of seven sandwiches. Not wanting to make a fuss, I reached for the one nearest to me and glanced at the label on the plastic wrapper. Caprese. My stomach gave a loud growl of approval as Mr. Wood went for the B.L.T.

I tried to eat as quickly as possible. Not out of some stellar work ethic, but because I'd failed Chitchat 101 long ago. Unfortunately, it was even more awkward to sit in silence with my jaw getting a workout on the chewy bread, creamy mozzarella, spicy basil, and sweet tomato. Damned if you do, damned if you don't, right?

Having finished his B.L.T., Mr. Wood looked skeptically at a tuna salad, then opted for the turkey club. Mr. Wood, I would later learn, likes his bacon. "It doesn't bother you?" he asked as he peeled back the crinkly plastic wrapper.

Thinking he meant his sandwich choice, I said, "No, help yourself."

He laughed. "No, no, I mean working here. With the dead just one room over."

I shook my head. "I went to school for it."

"Funeral services?" I nodded, then grabbed a turkey and Swiss, figuring Mr. Wood might want to keep his piggy-themed lunch going with the ham and butter baguette. "Which area were you focusing on?"

I swallowed a lump of sandwich. "Cosmetics. Embalming.

Behind the scenes stuff."

This brought a sparkle to his round eyes. Although that might have been because he'd just spotted the ham and butter was still available. "Why aren't you working in your field?"

"I—" My cheeks burned. I mean, it would have been embarrassing enough to tell him this was the biggest meal I'd had all week, but to add in the truth of why I was lacking a degree— Oh well, I figured after the day's job was done I'd never see him again, so who cared what he thought. "I couldn't afford to finish the program."

"Your parents didn't help you out?"

"No parents." My shoulders voluntarily made a half-dismissive-half-apologetic shrug. "I was fostered."

"And none of them—"

Unable to stop myself, I shot him a look that stopped his sentence. I hated the sympathy on his face. This is why I avoid opening up. I don't want other people's emotions splashing all over me.

"Let's just say only one set of fosters might have ever been described as generous, and they died long before I started college." I was done with conversing. I stood and started gathering up the wrappers and the sack. I'd get the crumbs when I came back to finish cleaning up the kitchenette.

"I could use a behind-the-scenes person."

"I didn't finish school," I repeated, in case he'd missed that point. "I'm not licensed."

"We could just say you're a receptionist. No, an office manager. That would explain why you're being paid so well."

My ears pricked up at the word *paid*, but reason prevailed.

"It's illegal."

"Only if we're caught, and who would know? I prefer doing the out front stuff, and I've never been good with the cosmetics.

I've tried, but the clients end up looking like peacefully resting clowns. That's not how people want to see their loved ones for the last time. Were you any good at the work?"

"Yes. What I did got top marks."

"Then why not? I've been doing interviews left and right trying to find the right person. Hired one of them who turned out to be a complete flake, insisted on a break every hour on the hour. But you seem like a hard worker. I have a good feeling about you, license or not."

He was kidding, right? There had to be cameras in the kitchenette recording this. A trick to trap me into accepting and then, if I did ever get my schooling done, pulling out the footage and saying, "Oh, sorry, you've broken like a billion laws pertaining to the dead already, so no degree for you."

I was tempted. Besides being handed a decent job without having to suffer though an interview, if he regularly kept sandwiches and cookies on hand…

Still, I wanted to avoid making any commitments.

"Could I finish the cleaning? I sort of need money today. For rent." I felt like an idiot. "I mean, assuming you were paying today. I didn't mean to sound greedy." Ugh, I *was* an idiot.

"No, not at all. Look, tidy up the kitchen and finish the reception area, then call it a day. I'll pay you for today's cleaning, then you can start your real work tomorrow. We'll call it an apprenticeship if anyone asks. Oh, I am glad I put that ad in. My friend at bingo said I'd only attract trouble with it. You're not bringing any trouble, are you?" he said as if I was a sleepy kitten he was trying to cajole into playing.

"No, sir. Not that I'm aware of."

If I only knew how wrong that statement would turn out to be.

Incredibly full from my unexpected midday meal, I finished the cleaning, walked home, proudly slapped my rent into

Morelli's meaty palm with fifteen minutes to spare, and even had enough left over to buy myself a bottle of IPA to celebrate.

Mr. Wood had put a pile of trust in me that day. He'd been a wonderful boss in the months since and was putting his business at risk every day he allowed me to swipe blush and eye shadow on corpses. How had I repaid him? By hiding a pretty serious secret.

After all, if I ever misplaced a body (or rather, if the body misplaced itself), Mr. Wood would be in deep, deep, like Marianas Trench deep trouble.

I owed it to him to keep the problem from happening again.

Unfortunately, it did.

CHAPTER SEVEN

MR. BUSBY TENPENNY

But first, back to me and my contraband cat. I swear Pablo had gained ten pounds in the few hours since I'd picked him up from the front step of Mrs. Escobar's to when I left Mr. Wood's for the day. By the time I made it back to my place, my shoulders and hands ached from the weight of the cargo I'd been lugging around.

Despite wanting nothing more than to set down the clunky carrier, I approached the building cautiously. The gnome was in his usual place with a bright spot of dandelions surrounding his feet. Morelli's window, which faced onto the front parking lot, was open a few inches. From the unmistakeable twangy sound of the theme song, I knew he was being distracted by the antics of Bo and Luke in a rerun of *The Dukes of Hazard*. I tapped the entry code, did a series of ninja-like moves to get the door open and the carrier inside without making a sound, then hurried up the stairs, silently apologizing to Pablo for the jostling.

Pablo didn't seem fazed one bit. He settled in straight away by claiming for his bed one of my old sweatshirts I'd left on a tattered ottoman and even discovered a fuzzy mouse toy Louise had treated with pure feline disdain.

The following day, Mr. Wood, although nervous about the

event, was in fighting form for Mrs. Escobar's funeral. Since he still suspected my presence might have something to do with waking the dead, I was excused from any meet-and-greet duties. I didn't like that I was causing him to worry, but if the waking dead were going to keep me out of having to play the welcoming hostess, I wasn't going to complain.

Still, I kept an eye on proceedings through the slats of the kitchenette's pass-through window, and I'm glad to say the funeral went off without incident. Although, if I'm being honest, I wouldn't have minded if Mrs. E had leapt up and given her cat-hating sister a good scare.

With the excuse that an essential part of the closure process was reflecting on everything their loved one had achieved, once we made it through the Escobar funeral Mr. Wood added a new line to our clients' incoming questionnaire: *Do you believe the deceased felt complete at the end?*

Of course, everyone claimed their dearly departed had lived a full life with only the slightest regrets, but I still approached every new body with a hefty dose of caution.

Despite my certainty that everyone was lying or deceiving themselves about that question, each of my clients over the next couple weeks stayed put as I smoothed my layers of heavy makeup over their faces.

Until the day Mr. Busby Tenpenny was laid out on my workroom table for his makeover.

The moment I stepped into the room and saw his still form on the table, the hairs on my neck started dancing the tango and an icy feeling that had nothing to do with my chilly work environment settled in the tips of my fingers.

With an impossibly British name like Busby Tenpenny, it was no surprise to scan his dossier and learn he was originally from

London. Cause of death: heart attack.

Although his paperwork claimed he was seventy-three, even in death, Mr. Tenpenny looked hardly a day over fifty. Statistically speaking, seventy-three was a bit young, but it's nothing to shake a stick at. He'd had plenty of time to live his life, or so I tried to convince myself.

Still, the more pessimistic side of my mind warned me that with a heart attack, there was no telling what life goals might have been left undone. Half-finished manuscripts. Unfolded laundry. Cat boxes that needed scooped. Anything.

Even without my hackles not only raised but jumping around with a life of their own, I'd have guessed there was a fifty-fifty chance of Mr. Tenpenny coming back. Adding in that curious feeling thumping through me, rocketed the odds of him waking to nine to one.

Despite these worrisome thoughts, nagging for my attention was a faint scent of Earl Grey tea and something spicy that reminded me of breakfast. I put the question of what new soaps or solutions Mr. Wood might have ordered out of my head and leaned over to take a look at who I'd be working with.

Mr. Wood, who preferred a touch of modesty, had already gotten Mr. Tenpenny into dark grey trousers and a crisp dress shirt. After all that tugging and shifting, I should have been reassured that our latest client hadn't woken, but I wasn't.

Regardless of my trepidation, I had a job to do. I clipped a bib over Mr. T's chest and started with his first layer of foundation. With every gentle sweep of the brush, I half expected him to start giggling, but he remained still as I built up his color and accented his angular features.

By the time I swept the final touches of highlighter over his brow line, my hand had stopped trembling and I chided myself for my skittishness. Maybe Mr. Wood had been right and I was getting jumpy after working alone with the dead for so many months. I packed away my compacts and creams, my brushes and sponges, and prepared to put Mr. T away for the day.

And that's when the sheet twitched.

Sometimes I hate being right. But points to me for not screaming or even flinching. Okay, maybe a little flinching, sort of like you do when you mistake a garden hose for a garter snake. But there was no banshee impersonation. I was getting good at this. Unfortunately, it was probably not a skill that was going to rank high on my performance evaluation.

Groggily shifting up to a seated position with his legs hanging over the edge of the table, Mr. Tenpenny shook his head as if to clear it, touched his chest, then looked at me with bright grey eyes beautifully set off by a hint of lightly-tinted mascara.

"What's the trouble?" I asked as I pulled out my notebook and handed it to him.

Murdered, he wrote. For a guy who was mostly dead, he had gorgeous handwriting. An elegant copperplate that just isn't taught in schools anymore. Must be that British boarding school education. I'm not stereotyping. Even dead, this guy oozed posh.

"No, you had a heart attack."

I admit it was a hard diagnosis to believe because Mr. T appeared trim and fit, with good muscle definition for an old guy. But sometimes the cardiac muscles don't like to play fair. Plus, you never know, even if he did work out, he may have been following up his morning run with a hearty English breakfast. The ticker can only handle so many bangers and fried tomatoes before it rebels.

Mr. Tenpenny shook his head, slapped his chest with both hands, then made an exploding sound as his hands spread out and away in slow motion.

"Yeah, a heart attack," I said, getting a little impatient. So far, the dead had raised no fuss about whether or how they'd died. They'd merely been eager to clear up something. Mr. Tenpenny held up a finger, indicating for me to wait a sec while he wrote.

I need to go home. I must see my grandson.

This I understood and not just for its impressive lack of Zombie Speak. He had one last message for his grandson. And, thanks to Mr. Boswick, I knew just how to handle it.

"Write out what you want to tell him and I'll deliver it."

He shook his head, then went back to the pad.

I need to see him alive. I need to make sure he's safe.

The instant I read that, not only did my neck hairs switch over from the tango to a frantic jitterbug, but I again caught the spicy scent. This time I recognized it: cinnamon, real cinnamon, not the overpowering stuff they put in candies and gum. Except for the mineral smell of makeup and the nostril-clearing fumes of cleaning solutions, my work area has no other odors.

As I told myself the scent must be some old cologne that had been on Busby's suit, clanging mental alarms warned me that I didn't want to get involved in this. But Mr. Wood's business was on the line and I couldn't let him down. Sometimes when the Zombie Apocalypse meets the mortuary trade, you gotta do what you gotta do.

"Where do you live?"

Mr. Tenpenny wrote down the name of a street and that eerie, something's-tickling-the-back-of-my-neck feeling hit me again. The street wasn't far away, less than three miles, but I didn't think that was what was so strangely familiar about it. I shook off the creepy crawlies of deja-vu. I needed the guy dead and now wasn't the time to start sifting through my address book. It was time to bring peace and tranquility to one of the undead.

"I'll help you," I told him. "Just stay put for a minute."

Although not far away, the street wasn't exactly walking distance, especially if your walking companion might not be walking on the return trip. Wheels were needed.

I pulled off my lab coat and called Mr. Wood on the phone in my workroom. I don't know why it was there. I always let any outside calls go to voice mail, and the funeral home wasn't so big that Mr. Wood and I couldn't communicate by simply walking over to where the other was. But for once I was glad the phone was there because when you've got a dead person who might wander off, it's best not to leave them alone to go hunt down your boss.

Mr. Wood answered on the first ring. He sounded amused that I was phoning him. Thinking about it now, that may have been the first time I'd ever done so. His amusement didn't last long.

"I need to borrow your car. I don't need to go far."

"Why?" he asked, suspicion taking over his bright tone.

"There's sort of someone who has something to clear up."

"Oh, good gravy." Yes, he really did say *good gravy*. He might keep a stash of booze in his desk drawer, but Mr. Wood was one of those strange people who never curse. "Cassie, this really must stop."

"I know. I know." Guilt flooded over me. I'd spent too much time since Mrs. Escobar's funeral playing with Pablo and Fuzzy Mouse. I'd done nothing to figure out why the dead were waking up. Not that I had a clue where I might start, but that was no excuse.

"You know where the keys are," he replied with a heavy sigh.

I mumbled an apologetic thanks and, propping the door open so I could keep an eye on Mr. T, I hurried out and grabbed the key ring off its hook. When I returned, Mr. Tenpenny had a disturbingly pleased look on his Creamy Ivory face.

"You don't get to go in," I told him as I unclipped his bib. "I'll help you, but you have to remain in the car. If your grandson is home, you'll scare the socks off him if he sees you. Got it?"

He nodded, brushed down his shirt, and shifted off the table, ready to go. When we slipped into the car, I almost laughed at him putting on his seat belt. Safety first, even for the dead.

A spine-creeping sensation spread into my arms as we drove the short distance to Mr. Tenpenny's Laurelhurst neighborhood. See, he was gesturing and grunting where to turn, but I was already preparing to make those turns milliseconds before he indicated them. I told myself it couldn't be. That it was some other house on the same street. But even before Mr. T raised his hand with the palm out to signal me to stop the car, my foot was already easing onto the brake pedal as we approached a royal blue, two-story Portland foursquare with deep yellow trim.

Normally, I'd be raving over immediately finding parking in such a popular neighborhood, but too many bumblebees were waggling in my gut for celebration. This couldn't be for real. I rolled forward and slipped into the parking space in front of a neighboring house. Mr. Tenpenny waited patiently as I took several deep breaths, my fingers drumming on the steering wheel.

I looked at the house, then at him.

"You're sure this is the place?"

He nodded. I groaned.

This had to be a coincidence, right? No one's life goes from relatively normal to ultra-freaking bizarre with such breakneck speed.

I knew this house. I'd come here the day before my cleaning gig at Mr. Wood's.

CHAPTER EIGHT

JERKFACE GODS

A little more background before we continue.

When I was forced to drop out of school because my rent needed paid, my belly needed filled, and the community college refused to educate me for free, I was willing to take whatever odd job I could find. As long as it was legal and didn't involve me taking off my clothes in front of strangers, of course. Since delivering smiling customer service is about as appealing to me as having my toenails ripped out, retail and waitressing were options that rarely lasted more than a four-hour shift before I was asked not to come back.

Thankfully, I fell into a job as a bike messenger for a tiny delivery service not far from my apartment.

And I do mean "fell" into. I'd been riding home from another failed job interview when I hit the Grand Canyon of potholes. Like an angry rodeo bull, my bike threw me off and left me sprawled on the ground. When I dusted myself off and checked my bike, the front tire had gone completely flat.

With curses mumbling up from my throat, I'd been walking my bike past a line of small shops when a plump, white woman in her early forties with bright red hair scrambled out of one of the doors and, I kid you not, took a sniff before saying, "You're perfect."

No one in my life has called me perfect for anything — well, except for one foster mom who said I was perfectly good DNA gone to waste — so the compliment had me more taken aback than the sniffing. I looked at the hand-lettered paper sign hanging in the shop's window. The edges had yellowed from being in the sun and one corner drooped where the tape had lost its sticky.

The sign read:

CORRIGAN'S COURIER
SIGNATURE SERVICE
FOR ALL YOUR PRECIOUS PARCELS

"Sorry, perfect?"

"I assume you can ride that thing," she said, pointing at my bike. "And that you can find an address on a map."

"Yes," I said, pessimistic caution unfurling like a new leaf.

"Exactly. You're perfect and you're hired. Wait a tick." She ducked back into the shop and came out holding a small, dusty, paper-wrapped package and a fire engine red messenger bag. "If you're not busy, this absolutely must go to the director of the Historical Society. Our last courier, well, never mind that, but I've got too much to do to make up for his absence." She stared at me, likely expecting me to jump for joy at the job offer. I could do nothing but stare back at her. She gave a resolute sigh, then said, "You do drive a hard bargain. Okay, there's a fifty-dollar bonus if you start today."

"I've got a flat. I can't possibly—"

"What flat?" Before I could ask if she was blind, I caught a whiff of citrus, not lemons or limes, but the sweet scent of a perfectly ripe orange.

My stomach growled. I'd been living on markdown yogurt and rock hard, day-old bakery items for the past week to keep enough set aside for my rent (which as of that morning was due in three days and seven hours). I cursed Portland's stupid potholes for basically robbing me of fifty dollars that could buy a lot of food.

"The front wheel." I reached down to squeeze the tire to show her how squishy and empty of air it was, but when I pinched my fingers, the tire was as solid as if it had just been pumped up.

Now, I'm no bike mechanic, but even an idiot can tell the difference between a flat tire and a filled tire just by looking. When I had gotten up from my spill, that tire had most definitely been flat. Even though I was pretty sure I hadn't hit my head, I started mentally running through a list of concussion symptoms.

"Looks fine to me. So, how about it? I could really use the help."

"Okay," I said, feeling very confused, but that may have just been the hunger.

She — Corrine Corrigan, I later learned — shoved the bag into my hands followed by the surprisingly hefty package, then babbled out the address for the Oregon Historical Society in between exclamations of thanks and how lucky she'd been to find me. I knew exactly how to get to the location, so I slipped the parcel into the bag, flung the strap over my shoulder, and hopped onto my bike with its newly inflated front tire.

Just as I was about to press my foot down on the pedal, the fiery-haired woman said, "You must give it to the person. No leaving it on the stoop. We don't have a lot of rules here, but that is one that cannot be broken. If you can't make a delivery, bring it back here and we'll try another time. Our deliveries are very special and we can't let them get into the wrong hands."

And cue the alarm bells.

That explained everything. I was carrying drugs. I was sure of it. Or stolen goods. Or illegal animal parts. Still, I was on the point of malnutrition and fifty dollars was waiting for me. If ever questioned, I would just have to say I was coerced. I pedaled away, made a right turn onto Clinton to head toward the Hawthorne Bridge.

It was as I was artfully dodging tourists walking in the bridge's bike lane that I realized the other option for what might be in the package on my back: a letter bomb. The rest of the ride, I took extra care to skirt every speed bump and gave a wide berth to any potholes.

Nothing exploded, no authorities patrolled the Historical Society's doors or waited in ambush to arrest me, and the package was delivered. When I returned, Corrine said my shift was done for the day and handed me a twenty-dollar bill for the hour of work I'd just completed, then a fifty for my sign-on bonus. After ordering an extra chewy pizza margherita to go and picking up a six-pack of IPA on my way home, I dined like a queen that night.

For the next couple months, life was good. I was the proud holder of an easy and steady job, an on-time payer of rent, and an eater of a balanced diet. Even Louise was acting less grumpy.

But, as I've come to expect, good things never last. Louise left to go chase the big catnip mouse in the sky only days before everything else went to crap.

I headed out from the office of Corrigan's Courier that final afternoon with a small, rectangular box about the size of a thick paperback tucked into my messenger bag. The service had a lot of repeat customers they delivered to, but this address was one I hadn't seen before. When Corrine handed me the box, she told me it would be the last delivery of the day and I could take the rest of the afternoon off. With pay. Doesn't get much better than that, does it? I pedaled over, taking my time and enjoying the tree-lined, low-traffic streets of the neighborhood.

Once I reached the house, I rang the bell. No answer. I rang a couple more times, then rapped my knuckles on the door.

Still no answer. I waited a few moments because you never know, someone might just be trying to put on their trousers, but after several minutes no one had come to the door. I shrugged and slipped the box into my messenger bag and rode back to Corrigan's to leave the package with Corrine until the next day.

Despite the unseasonable warmth of the November day, when I neared the office, goosebumps popped up over my forearms like zits on the chin of a stressed out teenager. I tried to tell myself it was just my sweat cooling, but I'd been enjoying the day and hadn't made enough of an effort to generate a drop of real sweat except in the pit behind my knees.

At the office, the shades over the plate-glass windows had been drawn. They were old-time roller shades with ring hooks. The type that threaten to go whirring back up if you pull them just a tad too far. These shades were never lowered, even when Corrine closed up at night. I tugged on the door handle to let myself in. The bolt clacked against the lock, but the door refused to budge.

"What the hell?"

I couldn't believe Corrine would just lock up for the day knowing I was out. On the window to the left of the door, a sign had been taped into one corner. I expected it to say something like, "Closed. Be back in fifteen minutes."

When I stepped over to read it, I caught a pungent smell that reminded me of cigars wrapped in musty clothing. But what really had me wrinkling my nose was the more powerful scent of cologne. I assumed the stench must be coming from the sewer grate and the cologne had come spewing out of the car of teenage boys that was now thumping its way down the street. I hate the smell of cologne. Too many of my more aggressive foster fathers had doused themselves in the stuff. I pinched my nose, then read the sign.

I groaned.

The sign did indeed say Corrigan's Courier was closed. Not for fifteen minutes, but for good. Below the out-of-business notice, written in Corrine's loopy handwriting but with a messy slant to it, was the message:

Thank you for the years of service.

Shit.

Not only did I still have a (possibly illegal) package in my bag, but it was a Friday and Corrine still owed me my pay for the week. And since she'd been paying under the table, it wasn't like I could go to the Bureau of Labor and Industries and demand my final check even if I was the demanding sort.

This wonderful bit of timing by the jerkface gods of life came just after I had to fork over several hundred dollars to say goodbye to Louise. Because of this unplanned expense, I desperately needed that day's wages for rent. Irritated, catless, jobless, cursing the world, and wondering what I was going to do for rent money, I rode home.

At the apartment, Morelli was waiting. It's like he had a sense for when I was having a crappy day. He not only informed me exactly how many hours I had to get my rent to him, but he also made it clear that he knew I'd violated the no-pet policy and if I didn't pay exactly on time, he'd kick me out. I introduced him to several newly-invented curse words then stomped up the stairs, hurled the messenger bag into my closet, and began desperately searching for work on Craigslist...where those jerkface gods of life cut me a break by allowing me to find Mr. Wood's want ad.

Which brings us back to where I left off — six months later with me having just nabbed a great parking spot and sitting in a borrowed Prius with a dead Brit.

CHAPTER NINE

BRINGING HOME STRAYS

"Are you sure that one is yours?" I asked, pointing to the deep blue house just ahead of us.

Mr. Tenpenny nodded his head.

"How long have you lived here?"

He held up five fingers, then pressed out, "Years."

Silly me for hoping he'd say months. Because life just can't be normal, can it?

You've probably guessed already, but let me confirm for you that, yes, the house I had pulled up to, the house that was the home of the dead guy in the passenger seat of my boss's car, the house whose door I was walking up to, the house whose doorbell I was ringing, was the same house of my final delivery, or rather, non-delivery for Corrigan's Courier.

Unlike my first trip here, this time when I rang the bell, someone answered. The guy who opened the door was about my age, slightly taller than me with Mr. Tenpenny's cutting cheekbones and hair as dark as mine.

"Yes?" he said curtly. He then eyed me curiously almost like he knew who I was, but couldn't place where he'd seen me.

Despite being completely flustered and the Queen of Social Misfits, I've always been able to keep my head. So, although I would have really liked to run from this situation, I asked, "Are you Mr. Tenpenny's grandson?"

The stern scowl quickly morphed into a look of worried surprise and he shifted back, moving to throw the door closed. Before he could slam it shut, I shouted, "I work at Wood's Funeral Home."

The door creaked back open. Tenpenny the Younger still looked wary, but he shook out his shoulders as if trying to play off his panic attack. "You work there?"

Did I not just say that? Why do the good-looking ones always have to be so dim?

"Yeah. Look, I just noticed your grandfather didn't have a tie with his suit. Would you have an extra?"

"I could've sworn there was one in there. Come in for a sec. I'll grab you one."

I stepped inside. I tried to play it cool, but my toes were tapping like jumping beans in my shoes. Who had the package been for? This grandson or Mr. Tenpenny? Did either of them ever wonder where the package had gone? Was it holding some sort of treasured object? A half kilo of cocaine perhaps? Corrigan's obviously handled some "special" packages you wouldn't trust to FedEx, but had either of the Tenpennys filed a claim for the missing treasure? And if so, with whom?

I'm not exactly a slob, but I am housekeeping challenged especially when it comes to things like tidying up closets. Which meant the messenger bag was still somewhere in mine. What if I dug out the package and dropped it off here sometime? Would that be the right thing to do? Wait, what if the grandson didn't even live here? Maybe he was just packing things up. Was it better to hold onto the package rather than risk it being delivered to the wrong person?

"Do you live here?" my mouth unexpectedly called up to him. What in the world was that? I don't ask questions of strangers. I don't shout up stairs.

"Yeah, moved in about six months ago," he called from somewhere above my head. Six months ago. Oh, you mean around the exact time a certain package didn't get delivered? I was seriously exceeding my daily recommended allowance of coincidences.

"You like your work?" he asked awkwardly as he strode down the stairs on long legs.

"It's certainly interesting."

"Will one of these do?" he asked as he spread a trio of ties out on a small table in the foyer. One was striped with pale grey and sky blue, one was plain black, and the other was deep purple with a paisley pattern. "I'm not great with color coordination."

The purple paisley was the least boring, so I picked that one. After all, as I was learning, just because you're dead doesn't mean you have to be dull.

"This one should work."

"My name's Tobey," he said, holding out his hand.

I tried not to laugh. Tobey Tenpenny?

Biting the inside of my cheek, I managed to say, "Cassie Black." I gave him the *Guinness Book of World Records'* quickest hand shake then turned to go before my mouth went rogue again and blurted, "I've got your Gramps in the car!"

But then I thought of Mr. Wood. He needed Mr. Tenpenny dead and I couldn't let my desire to speak to humans as little as possible get in the way of that. Mr. Tenpenny had wanted to know his grandson was okay. It was time for some awkward pleasantries.

"I'm sorry about your grandfather." Tobey Tenpenny replied with a quick thanks. "And you're doing okay? Staying safe?"

Staying safe? What was I? A mom who just sent her kid off to camp?

Apparently Tobey Tenpenny thought the question a bit out of place, okay maybe about five miles out of place, because he stepped back, staring at me as if I'd just pulled a machete from my back pocket. He pulled the door open, thrust a pointed finger toward the tidy front walkway, and said, "I think you should go now."

"Right, sorry, none of my business," I muttered, begging my mouth to stop making noises, but it just kept going as my feet shuffled me out to the doorstep. "He just seemed too healthy for a heart attack, so I thought something might have—"

Boom! The door slammed shut. And that, ladies and gentlemen, was Cassie Black doing her rendition of the *Socially Awkward Symphony*.

I wanted to hide my face and flee the scene, but also wanted to maintain a scrap of dignity. So instead of racing back to the Prius, I walked with deliberately paced steps. I hoped I would never see Tobey Tenpenny again and I also hoped Mr. Tenpenny would now be properly dead. His grandson was clearly well and good, with strong muscles fully capable of slamming doors, and showing no signs of all-consuming grief. What more could a grandad want? But when I got in the car, there was Busby, bright-eyed and eager for news.

I tossed the tie at him.

"Your grandson is healthy, safe, and very crabby." I stared at Mr. Tenpenny, then waved my hand in a well-go-ahead gesture. "That's your cue to go back to being dead." He shook his head, opened the notebook, and pointed to the first word he had written. "Murdered? I don't understand."

He wrote. I was dying to see what he had to say, but I couldn't risk Tobey peering out a side window and catching me lurking around. Lurking, that is, with his dead grandfather riding shotgun. I pushed the button to start the ignition and headed back the way we came.

As I drove, I considered my options. What was I supposed to do with Busby? I couldn't leave him alone in the funeral home. And I couldn't expect Mr. Wood to take a client in as a roommate. In fact, I was hoping I could get the car and keys back without encountering Mr. Wood at all. Luckily, it was bingo night at the community center just up the street, and if I had any luck in this world, my boss might have already headed off for a wild night of number hunting.

There wasn't anything for it but to take Mr. Tenpenny home with me. I parked the car in the funeral home's lot. Mr. T eyed me with a curious arch to his eyebrows. "Just wait by the car for a sec. And do not go anywhere. Got it?" He gave a sharp nod of his head to show he had.

I let myself into my workroom and returned the keys to their hook. The place was silent. Thank heavens for bingo, I thought as I made a quick scan that all the storage fridges were locked and all the cosmetics were shelved. Mr. Wood would come home with his prizes and, if he bothered to check, would think the whole matter had been cleared up.

Mr. Tenpenny and I walked to my apartment. First Pablo, now him. I couldn't make a habit of this. If my zombie problem kept cropping up, I would end up with more strays than a soft-hearted animal shelter volunteer. Thankfully, Morelli was too busy shouting out the answers to *Wheel of Fortune* to bother harassing me or to notice my guest. I mean, given his strict no-pets policy, what would his no-corpses policy be like? I signaled to Mr. T to go softly up the stairs.

When we got inside my apartment, Mr. Tenpenny scanned the place rather judgmentally I must say for someone whose next address was going to be a hole in the ground. Still, I can't blame him. The place is tiny; my furniture is all second- (and in some cases, third-) hand; and I have a habit of leaving books scattered over any horizontal surface. After coming from a huge home with magazine quality perfection, my place must have looked like a forlorn broom closet.

This gave me a moment of thought. A big house in one of the better neighborhoods of Portland?

"Who will inherit your house?"

"Grandson," he exhaled.

It's not like I could ever afford one, but I like to give myself a painful reality check by reading real estate signs whenever I'm out and about. Which means I know just how insane housing prices are in the City of Roses. Tobey Tenpenny, who probably hadn't worked a full day in his life, just nabbed himself a home worth close to a million bucks.

The question was: Would he have killed for it?

"How was your relationship with Tobey? He ever hint he might have aggressive tendencies?"

Mr. Tenpenny, still judging where it might be safest to sit, turned to look at me. His skin might have been waxy, and his heart might no longer be pumping blood, but he could still fix a lot of heat into his stare. He shook his head in a way that said, "Enough with this line of questioning."

Okay, so Busby didn't suspect his grandson, but that didn't stop my cynical thoughts. Who knew? Maybe the package contained an heirloom that, if stolen and sold, would have left him set for life. Then, when the object failed to show up, Tobey Tenpenny began his dastardly plan to become a real estate tycoon by any means possible.

Or maybe I was reading too many Hercule Poirot books.

Mr. Tenpenny pulled the notepad out of his jacket pocket and held it out to me. He then pushed it a little bit closer as if I might ignore the pad if he didn't. I took my notebook back, noting that he had not returned my pen, then plunked down on the couch, and invited him to do the same.

As Pablo sauntered into the room, Mr. Tenpenny finally opted for a well-worn wingback chair and again jutted his finger impatiently toward the notepad. I flipped it open. He had a lot to say and, as I read them over, each sentence drove a chill deeper into me.

CHAPTER TEN

WHEN IT RAINS, IT POURS

It is my belief that someone came looking for something they thought I had. They killed me for it, but I never had it in the first place. When this someone knocked on my door, I thought it might be a delivery. I'd missed an important one not terribly long ago, so I hurried to answer.

I wish I had checked first. Tobey was always telling me to inquire who was at the door before answering. I never saw his face, but he was one of my sort. He had to be tall because I remember him looking down at me, but before I got a look at his face, he made a Blinding Spark. I couldn't see a thing. I didn't even have time to panic before he stopped my heart with an Exploding Heart Charm.

As I read what Mr. Tenpenny had written, a herd of elephants wearing pink tutus danced in circles inside my head while trumpeting a chorus of disbelieving alarm.

I wasn't sure what he meant by "my sort" other than British or perhaps just old, posh guys in general. I also had no clue what he meant by a Blinding Spark or why it and Exploding Heart Charm were capitalized. Could it be some sort of Cockney rhyming slang?

What I did hone in on, however, was that someone had come looking for something Mr. T was supposed to have. Something that was supposed to have been delivered.

What if my delivery, or rather my lack of delivery got this guy killed? But that was months ago. Surely if a murderous thief would do anything to get his hands on that parcel he would have done so sooner. Why would so long have passed between the expected delivery date and the supposed murder?

Despite trying to brush off Mr. T's claim, logic in this very illogical situation kicked in. Maybe it had taken the killer that long to figure out who was supposed to receive the item. Damn Corrine for shutting down! How many other people knew her delivery schedule?

Pablo, after a good deal of stretching, sidled up and greeted Mr. Tenpenny's leg with a few chin rubs before heading to his favorite spot on an old sweatshirt inside my closet. The very closet where my red Corrigan's Courier bag still slumped in a dark, forgotten corner.

No, I was jumping way too fast to stupid and improbable conclusions. This had to just be a coincidence. How many times have I said Portland is a small town? I still see people from high school when I'm out and about — and yes, I do execute a variety of evasive moves to avoid them. So why should it be odd that the same address cropped up twice in my lifetime? Besides, if someone had accessed Corrine's delivery schedule and were willing to track down Mr. T to get the package, they'd also have to know I worked at Corrigan's and wouldn't they have come looking for me?

I thought of the creepy feeling I'd been experiencing lately. What if that hadn't been my imagination? What if they were hunting me down? My heart kicked up its already accelerated pace another couple notches and my gaze instantly darted to the front door to make sure I had flipped the deadbolt.

I tried to calm my overthinking brain by hoping that maybe Mr. Tenpenny was nuts. I mean, Exploding Heart Charm? Clearly he was living in LaLa Land, and I was even battier for believing him. Still, he was dead and they do say dead men tell no tales.

Mr. Tenpenny sat there, watching me with a look in his eyes that indicated he was waiting for a response.

"Tea?" I asked awkwardly, then wondered if the dead needed or wanted to eat and drink.

Mr. Tenpenny shook his head to decline. This was too weird. I mean, I know I said I liked hanging out with the dead, but I kind of meant hanging out with them while they stayed still on a table, not when they came around to my place for a chat to figure to the meaning of their zombie life.

My head whirled with problems, possibilities, and a string of what ifs all of which seemed equally unlikely. I handed the notepad back to Mr. Tenpenny.

"Okay," I said slowly as I tried to corral my stampeding thoughts. "So you think someone killed you for something you were supposed to have?"

He nodded. There was something that had to be asked, but you know how they say not to ask a question if you aren't prepared for all possible answers? I had a gut-plunging feeling I knew the answer to this question and I was not prepared to hear it. I bit my cheek, literally biting back the words.

Suck it up, Cassie. You need to find out. If this guy isn't dead by funeral time, Mr. Wood is going to be in trouble deeper than a diamond mine.

"When—" My voice cracked and I swallowed hard to wet my throat. "When exactly was this delivery supposed to have been made?"

The pen scratched over the notepad.

Six months ago.

Sorry, did you hear that? That was the sound of my gut dropping straight through the floor and into Morelli's living room.

"Why would this person have wanted it? I mean, is it valuable?" Holding my neck rigid to keep from glancing over at the closet, I then asked, "Is it dangerous?"

Voicing that worry put an immediate halt to my cool and calm ruse. What if I'd had a bomb in my coat closet for six months? I jumped up and shooed a disgruntled Pablo out from amongst my gloves and scarves. I nearly slammed the closet door before remembering the potential explosive lurking inside. Gripping the handle and moving slowly, I gently shut the door. The very flimsy door that was not going to shield us from anything if a bomb went off behind it.

After a very lengthy and very shaky exhale to collect myself, I backed away from the closet until I banged into the couch. I then eased my butt onto the edge of the cushion and, trying to play off the notion that anything odd had just happened, forced an innocent smile onto my face. Mr. Tenpenny narrowed his eyes and watched me like I was crazy. Can't blame him for that, really. He tapped the pen on the notepad to indicate what he'd written.

It's powerful. Very powerful. And yes, dangerous in the wrong hands.

Of course my brain immediately screamed, "You have a nuclear weapon in your closet!" The only thing that kept me from whipping out my phone and calling the bomb squad was not knowing their number. Well, that and the dead guy staring at me from the comfort of a free piece of furniture I'd found on Craigslist.

"And who might have these wrong hands?"

Before he could begin writing his reply, my phone rang. The sudden noise killed any shred of my ability to keep my cool. I didn't exactly scream at the sound of the jangling ring tone, but I did let out a sharp *yip* of terror that startled Pablo. I swear my heart nearly stopped in my chest. I then thought if it did, at least one of us in the room would be dead. I fumbled for the phone and glanced at the caller ID: Mr. Wood.

My day was just getting better and better, wasn't it?

"I have to take this," I said. Mr. Tenpenny opened one hand with his palm up, signaling me to go right ahead.

"Hello?" I said in my best everything's-just-peachy voice.

"Cassie, we have a situation here."

"I know, Mr. Wood. I'm on top of it, but it's taking a little longer than the others."

"Well, you need to do something. I don't know what to tell him."

"Just tell him our policy doesn't allow family behind the scenes," I said, thinking Tobey had shown up after my odd behavior. My biggest dread when I sprawled out in my bed at night, fully awake with my mind running in circles over all the complications that could arise from the dead waking, was a family member dropping by and wanting to check on the work we were doing. It wasn't allowed, but for whatever morbid reason, people do try.

"It's not family. It's someone from the Board."

My gut that had dropped into Morelli's living room now bounced off his shag carpet and flew straight up into my throat.

"The Board?" I asked, as if I didn't know exactly what he meant.

"The Mortuary and Cemetery Board. I don't know, maybe someone tipped them off, because one of their representatives is here now. Asking questions."

Oh goodie. Not only did we have a missing body, but if they found out I was doing anything other than filing paperwork and answering phones, Mr. Wood would have his license revoked. He'd lose his livelihood and his home. I glanced at the clock. Five-thirty. Odd. Any properly trained government worker should have scurried out of the office at least thirty-five minutes ago.

"I'll be there as quick as I can."

Before Mr. Wood could say anything, I hung up, grabbed my helmet off the couch, and gave my bike's tires a quick pinch to make sure they had enough air. Mr. Tenpenny watched me all the while, looking eager and somewhat impatient.

"You need to stay here. Promise?"

Mr. Tenpenny was examining me in an unsettling way. It wasn't exactly the expression of recognizing someone, more of trying to figure out why someone looks familiar. But it was what he did next that made my skin prickle. He sniffed, tilting his nose in my general direction. Just as Corrine Corrigan had done when we'd first met. Maybe it was time to switch deodorant brands.

"Mr. Tenpenny, please promise me you'll stay here. I should be back within an hour."

He pulled out the notepad. I did not have time for this. It was a yes or no question.

He jotted a quick sentence, then showed me what he'd written.

I think we need to talk.

"Sure thing," I said, my voice straining to sound chipper, even though my knees were feeling rather rubbery.

What if he had seen me riding away from his house that day? What if he'd come running down the stairs and called after me and I'd already gotten out of earshot? That look of almost recognition. Had he realized he might be alive — actually alive, not zombie alive — if I'd just gotten that package into his

75

manicured hands? But now was not the time. "Gotta go. There's plenty to read." I waved my hand to indicate the mess of used books scattered around. "And don't let the cat out."

I picked up my bike and carried it down the stairs, trying to be as quiet as possible, but apparently not quiet enough. Morelli's door swung open the moment my foot hit the bottom landing.

"You know I don't allow two people in that apartment."

I had no brain power left to come up with a lie.

"He's only visiting."

At least I hoped he was.

"Rent's due in—"

"Four days. Yes, I know. My whole month revolves around the day I get to cram my hard-earned money into your sweaty palms. I need to go." I reached for the door, but Morelli blocked it. "What?"

He watched me for a very long, very creepy second, then pushed the door open for me. "Be careful."

Morelli? Showing a hint of humanity? I was so shocked by this sentiment, I replied, without any hint of sarcasm, "I didn't know you cared."

Snapping out of his moment of weirdness, Morelli returned his face to the half-scowl, half-sneer it usually had when he spoke to me. "I meant be careful when you bring that thing up and down the stairs." He gestured to the bike with a hand that had only three fingers. I'd noticed this when I made my first rent payment and at first assumed he'd had some sort of wood shop accident, but both hands were the same: three fingers, one thumb. He'd either been born like that, or he was abnormally clumsy around cutting tools. "I'll add it onto your rent if I have to fix any scrapes on the walls."

I gave him a sour look and left the building, relieved that

nothing had changed in our relationship. Morelli being nice to me would be more unsettling than the dead coming back to life.

With every pedal stroke, Mr. T's words, *We need to talk,* pumped through my head. He was right. We did. This actually brightened my mood. If I came out with the truth when I got back, that would solve everything. I would open the closet, get out the bag, and say, "Here's your package/possible bomb, and I'm likely the reason you're dead." Done and done. Back to dead. Right?

I just needed to stop this board rep from nosing around the funeral home and by morning all would be settled.

I should have known life's not that simple. Neither is death, apparently.

CHAPTER ELEVEN

FACING THE BOARD

The funeral home's outdoor sign had already been turned off for the night, but the lobby lights remained on inside. Mr. Wood's red Prius was in its usual spot, but was flanked by a white sedan that was too generic and forgettable not to be a government car.

I hopped off my bike and wheeled it into the lobby. Looming inside was a tall man with cropped blonde hair and a face that reminded me of one of those square watermelons they grow in Japan. He was doused in what had to be a gallon of cologne, wore a poorly fitted suit as generic as his car, and was interrogating Mr. Wood with sniping skepticism as my boss tripped over his answers.

"I'm Mr. Wood's office manager. Is there a problem?" I asked boldly. When push comes to shove, I can improv my way into being an extrovert. I keep hoping one day it might stick.

"I should say there is."

"And you are?"

"Carl," he said, suspiciously not giving his last name. "I was told the body of Busby Tenpenny should be here for processing, but there's no sign of him. And," he paused to check his clipboard, "Mr. Wood doesn't seem to know where he is."

"No, why should he?"

The man stabbed a stubby finger on the brass plate below Mr.

THE UNDEAD MR TENPENNY

Wood's photo on the side wall of the entryway.

"He *is* the director and owner. I would assume that means he knows what's going on."

"Mr. Wood interacts with the families and performs the hands-on mortuary duties. It's my job to organize and maintain incoming work. So, if he doesn't know exactly who's here and who's not, that's why."

"And Mr. Tenpenny?"

I shrugged my shoulders. "Your guess is as good as mine. He was delivered and was nearly done with his preparations when—"

Mr. Wood, possibly thinking I had turned into a complete moron, cleared his throat in a painfully obvious way. I shot him a look to hush him up. Thankfully, since he was too busy scowling at my boss, the look was missed by our friendly local government worker.

"Yes, Mr. Wood," I said, taking on the stern voice of a woman not to be interrupted, "I know you said to let it slide, but I am going to complain." Carl's attention turned to me. He wore an I-can't-wait-to-hear-this expression on his blocky face. "I had just sent Mr. Tenpenny's funeral notice to the paper when someone from the morgue called and said the body was supposed to go somewhere else. They claimed they needed to run another analysis on him because someone said the death was suspicious. Now, couldn't that have been sorted beforehand? Think of the strain on the family."

"Who said this?"

"Do I know?" I asked irritably, fully falling into my role of easily perturbed office worker. "One minute we've got a man preparing for his final show. The next, he's being carted off and I'm being told they'll have him back as quickly as possible."

Okay, as an excuse, it was awful, but I was thinking on my feet after an already over-the-legal-limit weird day.

"And you have paperwork to show this?"

"Nope."

Mr. Wood groaned.

"What do you mean 'nope'?" Carl asked sharply.

"The guy who showed up from the morgue said the paperwork was at their end and he'd fax it over in a few days. A few days! You do realize we'll have to reschedule the funeral, which is just a nightmare in itself. Still, I would hope the body will be back sooner rather than later. Probably with the paperwork clipped to it, knowing how those people work. If you want to file complaints against someone, it should be the morgue, not us."

The guy scowled at me. "And if I go to the morgue, who should I talk to?"

"Chubby Evans," I said, grabbing onto a name from the book I was reading. I just had to hope Cologne Carl wasn't an Agatha Christie fan.

The name was memorable, but it still struck me as odd that Carl wasn't writing it down. That either meant he had a superb memory and couldn't be bothered with pea-brain things like note taking, or that he had no intention of checking up on dear old Chubby. Strange behavior, but also in my favor since Chubby only existed on the pages of a murder mystery.

"You say the body is supposed to be back in two days?"

"Two or three. With Chubby, I'd err on the side of three." I crossed my fingers that I could persuade Mr. Tenpenny to get back to the business of being dead within that time.

"I'll be back in one. If you can't produce the paperwork or the body, I will close down this business."

"Understood."

He eyed me, moving in closer, but his cologne was so overpowering, I stepped back. He shifted his shoulders. "You don't seem that concerned about a missing body, Miss—"

"Black. And no, not really. We get everything from wrong deliveries to mismatched paperwork. Few things come as a shock in this line of work."

Hell, I was barely blinking an eye over dead people returning to life at this point.

Mr. Wood mumbled, "Speak for yourself."

"I'll see you tomorrow at noon, Miss Black. And for your sake," he said in a tone that was both casual and menacing, "I sincerely hope Mr. Tenpenny is back under this roof."

"Who sent you, by the way?" I asked. This guy hadn't shown us any ID, hadn't told us his full name, and was working well beyond government employee hours. I didn't trust his cologne-drenched presence one bit.

"An anonymous tip from a concerned citizen who had worked with Mr. Tenpenny on," he paused, "unique projects, shall we say. The individual had questions about the funeral arrangements."

And so he called the Mortuary Board? It was good to see I wasn't the only one telling lies this fine evening.

"Well, you can assure this person all will be taken care of professionally once we have Mr. Tenpenny in his proper place." Which was completely true.

I showed Carl the door and locked it as soon as he was outside.

"Cassie, what are we going to do?" Mr. Wood asked in a worryingly uncertain tone. "Do you even know where Mr. Tenpenny is?"

"At my apartment," I said sheepishly. After putting on so much confident bravado to face down Cologne Carl, I felt worn out.

"Your apartment!"

"It's okay. He's a tough case, but I think I've figured out what will help him. And you."

"We really need to find out what's causing this. If one does get away..." Sweat beaded on Mr. Wood's forehead. He dropped into one of the plush, navy blue reception chairs. "The thought alone makes me feel ill."

My heart sank under the weight of my guilt. Not only was I facing the possibility that I might have caused Mr. Tenpenny's death, but a suspicion was growing in the back of my mind that Mr. Wood had been right in his earlier concern. Somehow I might be making the dead wake up. If so, I was putting Mr. Wood's business at serious risk.

Because no matter how you spin it, raising the dead and taking them on field trips was a whole lot worse than letting an unlicensed employee swipe cosmetics over the skin of the deceased. We'd done well at not attracting any notice so far, but if our blonde thug really was a legit state or county worker, the Board would keep the place under heavy scrutiny from here on out even if Mr. Tenpenny was laid to rest on schedule. Mr. Wood's business would be ruined and I'd be back to being unemployed. I may not be living the lifestyle of the rich and famous, but I had gotten used to certain luxuries in life like fresh fruit and toilet paper.

"It'll be okay, I promise. Now, go do what you need to do for the evening. I'll lock up when I go."

Mr. Wood nodded and shuffled up the stairs that led to his living quarters above the funeral home. After making a quick check of all the locks and security lights, I walked my bike home to give myself time to think.

I didn't want to do it, but the only way to help Mr. Wood was to cough up the truth to Mr. Tenpenny.

CHAPTER TWELVE
CONFESSION SESSION

With all the weird things tumbling into my life lately, and with the odd behavior of our supposed health inspector, I half expected Cologne Carl to be lurking outside my building when I got home. But when I reached the parking lot, it was empty except for a few kids from the neighborhood playing soccer, using both my building's and the adjoining long-since-shuttered business's lot for a pitch. With a *whoop* of boyish excitement, the ball went flying straight toward the garden gnome.

Knowing Morelli would blame me if that bit of yard art got broken, my legs kicked into gear. I couldn't run fast enough with the bike and I grit my teeth, waiting for the crash of broken ceramic. But the ball, the ball I swear had been heading straight for the pointy red hat, veered at the last moment and ended up hitting nothing more than the wall to the left of the gnome. I didn't want to overthink this impossibility of the laws of physics. After all, I didn't know much about sports. Maybe soccer had a kick that did something like throwing the curve ball in baseball.

The kids scrambled after the ball and I let myself in, muttering a prayer to the patron saint of renters that I wouldn't have to face Morelli. Apparently, the prayer worked. There wasn't a peep from my lovely landlord even as the door's mechanical lock snapped into place. After hauling my bike up the stairs — without ever touching the walls, thank you very much — I opened my door to see Mr. Tenpenny playing with Pablo.

He greeted me with a satiny meow. Pablo, that is, not Mr. T. Standing there with a feather-tipped wand toy in hand, Busby greeted me with a curt nod of hello and an expression of wary inquiry. Despite the disturbing welcome, he was a handsome old man with thick grey hair brushed back from his face. And, oddly enough since he should be emitting the foul smell of preservation fluid, he carried a comforting scent of bergamot and old books.

According to his paperwork, Mr. T was five foot ten, the same height as me, but he had an erect carriage that made him seem taller — sort of the opposite effect of the hunch I used to adopt in high school to make myself look shorter. He had a long face with a Roman nose set below penetrating, silvery grey eyes that were currently watching me with curious impatience.

To Pablo's disappointment, Mr. T swapped the wand for my notepad and thumped his index finger on his last message.

"I know."

I gave a heavy sigh and went to the fridge to grab a beer. After dealing with an overly-scented government goon followed up by a ride home in warm weather, the cold, hoppy liquid tasted especially refreshing. I took another long swig, then walked back over, ready to spill the truth.

"Should I go first?" Mr. T turned his palm up in a be-my-guest gesture while Pablo sat at his feet, purring and clearly eager for their game to resume. I took a deep breath, then said, "I think I might have killed you."

Now, I have to admit, while I am a professional cynic, I completely expected Ol' Busby to say (or gesture or grunt), "No, no, not at all. You're being ridiculous."

But there were no such reassurances coming from my zombie acquaintance. Instead, he staggered back and narrowly avoided tripping over Pablo, who deftly snatched Fuzzy Mouse in his jaws and leapt onto the top of the wingback chair. Busby stared at me wide-eyed as he continued to back away. Once he was at what must have seemed a safe distance, Mr. T turned his head slightly to the side and observed me from the corner of his eye.

After I endured this odd scrutiny for about fifteen seconds, the tension in his dead body eased and he shook his head. He went to the table, picked up the pad and pen, and flipped to a new page. Once he finished writing, he passed the pad back to me.

It wasn't you. It was a man slightly taller than you.

I could have left it at that. I could have pretended I was off the hook and called it good, but playing make believe wasn't going to get him back to being dead, nor would it save Mr. Wood's livelihood.

"Comforting, but that's not exactly what I meant. I know I didn't pull the trigger—" Again, he did the chest thump and the exploding hand motion. He then made a gun with his thumb and forefinger while shaking his head. "No, I know, not a literal trigger, but I still might be responsible for your death."

The wary look returned. I handed back the notepad, and he wrote: *Who do you work for?*

Okay, definitely not the question I would have asked in the same situation, but I suppose Mr. Tenpenny hadn't exactly been alert when he arrived at Mr. Wood's.

"I work for Mr. Wood," I said clearly to make sure Busby understood. "He runs the funeral home you woke up in."

Mr. Tenpenny shook his head and pressed on his gut.

"Other?" he exhaled.

"No other, but there was a previous. I think your death, and my part in it, has to do with my other boss, or rather my other job. The one before Mr. Wood."

I was getting tongue tied. After all, with Busby, Tobey, and Cologne Carl, I was well beyond my spoken-word quota for the day, and even though I found it easy to talk to the dead, this wasn't a conversation I ever expected to have. Also, I really didn't like the way Mr. Tenpenny kept scrutinizing me with that look of half-recognition, half-suspicion.

To clarify my point, I set my beer down on a battered end table and went to the closet. When I opened the door, Pablo immediately hopped off the chair and came running. I reached for the messenger bag, but jerked my hand back just before grasping the strap.

Could there be a bomb inside? Suddenly, the bright red color of the bag didn't scream, "Watch out cars, here I come," but rather, "Danger!" like the markings of a poisonous tree frog.

I told myself this was ridiculous. The bag had been in there for months. Pablo had been kneading it and purring himself to sleep next to it since I'd brought him home. Even if that cat did have nine lives, he would have used them all up long ago.

No, I told myself firmly, this thing wouldn't have remained perfectly innocuous for months and then suddenly choose today to detonate. If it was a bomb, it had to be a dud.

As all this raced around my head, Pablo kept trying to sneak past me to get to his sleeping spot while I kept nudging him away with my foot. I wanted to believe that whatever occupied my closet was nothing to fear, but let me tell you, I picked up that bag in the slowest of slow motions possible. Stop motion animation figurines would have made fun of how slowly I moved.

I'd nearly extracted the bag, holding tight to the strap with both hands when something orange flashed in my vision.

Bam!

I screamed and jumped back. My heart pounded from my chest like a male cartoon character who has just seen a hot female character. But hey, at least it *was* pounding.

I dared to open my eyes, first the right, then the left. My hands still gripped the strap, and that strap was still attached to a bag that wasn't smoking from a recent explosion. At the foot of the closet was one of my old textbooks. With a scolding look on my face, I looked up to meet Pablo's green eyes peering down at me from the upper shelf.

Damn cat.

When I turned around, the upturned lips and crinkles at the corners of his eyes told me Mr. T might have been laughing at my expense. When he came up to me, I held the bag out to him, but he didn't take it. Instead, he stooped down and, using both hands, pinched the top corners of the satchel to analyze the side of it. The bag had no writing on it, no logo, but the stitching was distinctive. It certainly hadn't been cranked out in a factory and might even have been hand-stitched with embroidered loops and starbursts as accents. Deadly contents or not, lovely needlework or not, I suddenly wanted the bag out of my hands and out of my apartment.

Mr. Tenpenny stood up straight, but still didn't take the damn bag. Apparently, he needed both hands free to press on his belly. Our Busby might write in perfect English, but verbally, he was still stuck with Zombie Speak. "Where get?" he exhaled.

Did he know about Corrigan's Courier? When I was unexpectedly left without a job six months ago, I tried to look them up online. I figured they were dealing with clients across the globe, or at least the country, so there should be some reference to them somewhere. But there wasn't a single page with the courier company's information on it. I'm no Deep Web master, but I've used it once or twice, and even there Corrine Corrigan didn't exist.

"Have you used Corrigan's service?" I asked.

He nodded, then exhaled, "You?"

"I delivered for them. Or, I did. I went out for a delivery one day, came back to the office, and no one was there."

As if he already knew this and was just confirming the information, Mr. Tenpenny nodded his head, but his expression begged for more.

"You were my last delivery," I said through clenched teeth. Mr. Tenpenny gave me an even sterner look than I'd just given Pablo. "I didn't steal it. I wasn't supposed to leave deliveries if no one was home. Then the shop was closed and I was angry, so I brought the package home and forgot about it until just recently." I held up the bag that Busby was now eyeing with worried apprehension. "Do you think that's why you died? Because of what's in here?"

Mr. T gave a careful and deliberate nod.

"Is this your unfinished business? If I give this to you, will you go back to being dead?"

He shrugged his shoulders, but made no effort to take the bag from me. In fact, keeping his gaze fixed on me, he raised his hands with palms out, wordlessly telling me to stay away as he stepped back.

Oh great, I've scared a zombie. This really was a new low point in my social skills.

Showing he had no intention of collecting his damn delivery that was so important he came back from the dead for it, Busby positioned himself behind the wingback chair.

Could Mr. Tenpenny be rethinking his options? If he didn't die again and if he escaped my apartment, how long could he roam around for? Was he considering a new lease on life, or on death as the case may be? Someone had to put an end to this stubbornness.

"Look, my boss is in trouble because of you. I could lose my job. He could lose his business. I know you died an untimely death—" *or think you did* "—but it's really important I get you back to the funeral home. You know, as you're supposed to be."

Mr. Tenpenny paused for a moment, then with a look of defeated resolve, held out his hands. I reached into the messenger bag and carefully pulled out the package. Maybe it wasn't a bomb. Maybe it was a cell phone that would trigger a bomb that was hidden in some government building halfway around the globe. I hesitated handing it over, but reminded myself, if it was a cell phone, the battery would be dead by now.

Then again, Busby Tenpenny was supposed to be dead by now.

I placed the package in Mr. T's outstretched hands.

I don't know what I expected. I suppose for him to unwrap it and see what was inside, but he merely held it, closed his eyes and seemed to be waiting for something. Death? He scrunched his face as people do when they can't figure out how to make something work. Maybe he'd been sent the wrong item. Being killed for a clerical error. Wouldn't that just be a rotten twist of fate?

"Well?" I prodded. "Are you going to open it?"

He untied the string. The outer paper crinkled as he peeled it back to uncover an ordinary looking, brown cardboard box. Lifting off the lid, he revealed another box inside. This one was made of wood with a patterned design carved into the top. It took me a moment to recognize the design of a skeleton standing within an hourglass that was contained within a ring of what looked like Celtic knots. The bony guy had his arms and legs splayed like DaVinci's Vetruvian Man drawing. My skin tingled. I took a long drink of beer without taking my eyes off the box.

Mr. Tenpenny gripped the lid with his thumb and middle finger. For no reason other than silly, horror-movie fear, I slapped my hand over his. He jolted, looked at my hand, then looked at me. For a brief moment, barely half a second, his eyes gave a flash of full recognition. I slipped my hand away. He lowered his eyes, took a seat in the wingback chair, placed the box on his lap, and reached for the notepad.

I expected something like, "Stupid girl, first you want it opened, then you don't? Make up your mind."

But he didn't write much. Only three words in all capital letters: *WHO ARE YOU?*

I thought I'd told him, but again, what with all the dead guy waking, threats from government thugs, and possible bomb scare, maybe I'd forgotten to introduce myself.

"I'm Cassie Black." I held out my hand, but he was already writing another question.

And who are your parents?

I bristled. I hated being asked about my parents. Right then, I wanted to yank open that box and get Mr. Tenpenny good and dead. I plunked down onto the arm of my tattered couch.

"I don't know. I was raised in foster homes. Really crappy foster homes for the most part."

"Orphan?" he exhaled.

"Yeah, probably. Or at least I hope so. If my parents are alive, and let me go through what I've put up with, they deserve to be dead." Mr. T flinched and his face scrunched up with distaste as if I'd just kicked Pablo for a good laugh. "Don't judge me. Most likely, they were junkies who got their kid taken away. It happens. They made no effort to find me, and I did the same. Now, can we get back to this?" I pointed at the box.

He started to write something else, but hesitated after a single word. He scribbled it out then tucked my notepad back in his jacket pocket. I reminded myself to retrieve it before he got packed away permanently.

Mr. Tenpenny again gripped the box's lid. The wood was warm brown with yellow undertones like oak or maple, but had the rich sheen of myrtlewood. He lifted the lid and I leaned forward to peer at what was inside.

CHAPTER THIRTEEN

WHAT'S IN THE BOX?

In the box, nestled into a satiny, cream-colored lining, was a pocket watch. My first thought was of *Alice in Wonderland* and the White Rabbit shouting he was late. But with this timepiece, the rabbit would have no clue whether he was about to miss his very important date or not because the watch was no longer keeping time. The only mechanical movement was one of the hands jittering back and forth between two numbers. And, unlike most old-timey watches I'd seen, there was no fob to wind to get it going again. I wondered if this was some overpriced, battery-powered watch, newly-made but designed to look antique.

Dead. The word thumped into my head like a bass line coming from the overpriced stereo systems people in my neighborhood stuck into their Honda Civics. I had assumed this watch would make Mr. Tenpenny dead. I glanced back up at him. You know, just in case I'd missed him slumping in the chair or collapsing to the floor. No such luck. He sat there with his perfect posture, completely undead, and glaring with disappointed consternation at the watch.

"Is it what you expected?"

He nodded.

"Looks like it died."

He shook his head and placed a hand on his belly.

"Never stops," he exhaled.

Perpetual motion? I took a closer peek at the item and noticed it wasn't just the lack of a fob that made this object odd. The hand that looked like it had had too much caffeine was flickering between two numbers, but not the numbers you'd expect to find on a watch. Not even the Roman version of those numbers.

Instead of one through twelve, or I through XII, the numbers ran up by fives: five, ten, fifteen, twenty, twenty-five, and on up to fifty-five. Where the twelve would be was the infinity loop. Interesting and probably unique enough that I bet the designer added an extra couple hundred dollars to the price tag for it, but that clever design still didn't make the thing work. And it still didn't get Mr. Tenpenny dead.

I caught a hint of movement and looked up. Mr. Tenpenny was pointing at me, his eyebrows arched like the punctuation marks of an unspoken question.

"Yes, I was supposed to deliver it for Corrigan's. Do you know Corrine? Do you know what the hell happened to her?" *Do you know where my last paycheck is?* I barely refrained from asking.

He nodded distractedly as he lifted the watch from the box and turned it over. Brilliant! Why didn't I think of that?

"If you can open it, I might have a battery that fits, or I could run to the quickie mart and get one. If it starts ticking then maybe—" I stopped because, despite my lack of social skills, even I knew it was rude to say things like, "And then maybe you could hurry up and get dead."

Mr. Tenpenny held the watch up so I could see the face, then pointed to himself. He put the timepiece back in the box then pointed from me to the watch. "You," he grunted without even pushing on his gut, which impressed me for some odd reason.

I didn't know why he wanted me to pick up the watch, but he was dead and I thought it best to humor him, so I did. The watch itself was a gorgeous piece of machinery. On the face was a small cutaway so you could see the cluster of internal gears. They were fascinatingly tiny with their itty-bitty teeth biting into one another. I glanced up at Mr. Tenpenny. He was grinning expectantly, but I had no idea what he expected.

"It's lovely," I said appreciatively, figuring that's what he wanted. See, I'm not so socially stupid when I make an effort.

And then the watch ticked.

Let's pause here. I have never had money. In fact, as I mentioned, I was on the brink of homelessness not all that long ago. When that bizarre timepiece snapped to life, every fast- and slow-twitch muscle in my body wanted me, screamed at me, to hurl it as fast and as far away as possible. The only thing that kept me from flinging the watch/bomb through the window was some internal knowledge that it had to be valuable, and when you've lived as cash-strapped as I have you do not purposely destroy anything you could sell for next month's rent.

That still didn't mean I wanted to have my fingers on the thing any longer than necessary. With shaking hands, I gently placed the strange timepiece back into its case. It ticked a few more times, the gears rotating in steampunk synchrony, then stopped.

And Mr. Tenpenny was still not dead.

"What the hell was that?"

Mr. Tenpenny pulled out the notepad. I took the opportunity to grab another much-needed adult beverage. On my way back, Busby held out the pad and I grabbed it, reading and guzzling at the same time.

I think you may have brought me back. Have there been others?

I told him, yes, there had been, then read on.

You are, or I think you are, an absorber. You can take in magic. I thought I sensed it when I woke, but wasn't certain.

"Magic?" I said, making light of the word. "I think your brain may be melting, Mr. Tenpenny." He stabbed at his note in response and I continued reading.

There are tests we can do to verify, but it's the only explanation I can think of. Amongst other things, the watch can take years from someone's life if it's reversed, or add years if turned forward. The watch was partially drained at one time, but as you've proven, it still has some residual power in it. You may have absorbed this and that's why you're bringing back the dead.

"Me? I'm bringing back the dead," I said flatly. I mean, I kind of suspected this, but to have someone put it into words, even crazy ass words, sent my head spinning.

He jotted down, *What did you think was causing it?*

"I don't know. Ancient laylines, Indian burial ground, GMOs. You know, the usual stuff."

He shook his head and pressed out a sigh of exasperation.

Suddenly, the implications slapped me harder than my last foster father, and it wasn't just my head that was sent reeling. My knees became far more flexible than they should be. Luckily, the couch's avocado green, velvety cushions were there to catch me. Once seated, I barely refrained from putting my head between my knees.

I hadn't actually put the idea into a concrete thought, but the normal laws of physics and biology don't allow for dead folks to get up and walk around. I wasn't about to question whether magic might be real or not, but if this were true, if it was my fault the dead were coming back, I might be the one who put Mr. Wood out of business. I couldn't chalk this up to some random oddity. This was Cassie Black screwing up to a royal degree. The realization hit me like a deer falling into a pit of spikes.

"I don't want this," I muttered a few times. "How do I get rid of it? Can I just chuck the watch into the Willamette?"

Mr. Tenpenny's eyes went wide and he shook his head emphatically. He held up the pen to show me he was going to write.

Only Magics can be absorbers. The watch doesn't work by making you magic. You make the watch work by being magic.

Okay, I bring home a lot of fantasy novels from the library, and I even manage to read at least a third of them. So part of me wanted to believe magic might exist in the world. You know, like somewhere no longer accessible to today's humans. But to believe there were actual wizards roaming around? Sorry, I had to throw my cynical hat back on.

"Magic? Like I'm supposed to be a witch? Does that make you Dumbledore?"

He gave me a withering look and managed to maintain it as he scratched a sentence into my notepad. He stabbed out the final period for emphasis.

There are so many misconceptions in those books. I refuse to discuss them any further.

I bit my lip to keep from laughing. I know J.K. Rowling has her critics, but I would never have guessed Mr. Tenpenny might be one of them.

"Sorry," I said, trying very hard to sound sincere. "You were saying something about magic people."

People with magic is a more accurate way to describe them. We call ourselves Magics, although the terms wizards, witches, and wyrds are still in use.

"Weirds? As in Keep Portland Weird?"

Mr. Tenpenny's lips tightened and his writing wasn't as tidy as before as he hurriedly jotted:

The non-magics, or Norms, stole that from us. Portland was originally a popular center for divination and the fates, also known as The Wyrd — a word that later morphed into weird *and got applied to odd things in general. In the early 1900s, The Wyrd ran a campaign to maintain their role in the city using that slogan, which later got twisted into your city's motto.*

After I read this and made disapproving noises at my hometown's plagiarism, Mr. T continued writing at a calmer and more legible pace.

You have a type of power that allows you to take in magic from others and from magical objects.

"If I'm magic why hasn't anything magical ever happened to me? I can't even do card tricks." And believe me, a deft hand at Three Card Monte would have been useful in my leaner months.

Because you haven't learned. There is training, a whole community of others like you.

Here's what I read: *Training,* meant tuition, while *Community* meant involvement with other people. Neither of these were things I was comfortable with.

"Thanks, but not interested. If you're saying I took in magic and this magic is making people come back from the dead, then all I need to do is get rid of the magic, right? Can't someone just vacuum it out so I can keep Mr. Wood out of trouble?"

You don't want magic?

Even on paper I could feel the bewilderment behind the words.

"Can I use it to make hundred-dollar bills?"

"No," he exhaled.

"Then I'm sticking with not being interested. I mean, if I've been magic all this time, it sure hasn't done me any good. Now, it's proving to be a liability. It's nothing I knew I had and it's nothing I want. So, how do I get rid of it?"

It's not so simple as that.

"Of course it isn't."

You have to learn how to use it so you can channel it away properly. If that's what you want.

This was the best academic sales pitch ever. Want to be magic? You have to go to our special school. Don't want to be magic? You have to go to our special school. I can't wait until the for-profit colleges give that ad campaign a whirl.

"If I can channel the magic back into the watch, will you die for good?"

He nodded, but with an uncertain tilt to his head.

"And no more dead will come back?"

You won't make them come back.

Yeah, best to let that bit of hair splitting slide for now.

"Then I guess I better catch the Hogwarts Express in the morning."

Mr. T scowled at me. Maybe he was more Snape than Dumbledore…is what I did not say.

Soon after this bizarre exchange, I prepared for bed, during which I may have been guilty of doing a few swish-and-flicks with my toothbrush. And in case you're wondering, the only results were some toothpaste splatters on my mirror. Being dead (still), Mr. Tenpenny didn't need to sleep, but he did stretch out on the couch. Pablo, with Fuzzy Mouse gripped in his teeth, leapt up and settled himself on Mr. T's chest. I declared Pablo a traitor and went to bed, but my head was too busy processing the impossibility of what was going on to sleep.

Magic. It seemed so ridiculous. But did I not kind of believe it? That was no ordinary watch, and if I was being honest with myself, I had toyed with the notion that something about my presence was bringing the dead back to life. My supposed magic, the watch, and the waking dead were related. Mr. Tenpenny seemed to know something about all this and he was the only one offering to help me understand whatever in the world was happening. If he could help me fix this, no matter how much I did not want to take such a big step out of my comfort zone, I had to accept his offer.

I assumed, since I hadn't had to do much to get into this problem, getting out of it shouldn't be difficult either. I assumed that everything would be cleared up the next morning and the only hard part would be refraining from Harry Potter jokes.

Well, you know what they say about assumptions.

CHAPTER FOURTEEN
THROUGH THE DOOR

In the morning, Mr. Tenpenny was already up and brushing Pablo's fur off his shirt front while I staggered around in my usual morning stupor. Once I'd gotten the crud off my teeth and some caffeine in my system, I asked, "Where do we start?"

"Home," he said. There was no pushing on his belly. He merely forced a contraction of his abs to get the word out.

"Your home?" He nodded, looking at me as if I'd just asked the most idiotic question of the year. "Your grandson won't be happy about that." I might be the one bringing back the dead, but I wasn't the one who made Mr. T dead to begin with. And Tobey still remained my Suspect Number One in Mr. T's murder.

Mr. Tenpenny merely shrugged at my comment.

"And then what?"

He pulled the notepad out of his pocket, jotted something down, and turned it toward me.

We'll take you to meet the community. They'll know what to do with you.

That didn't sound good, but I had to put this into perspective. I mean, you probably had to undergo some sort of medical exam before having liposuction. Why wouldn't preparing for what was basically magical lipo be any different? Half a millisecond later, my budget-conscious brain shouted that this would be an elective procedure. Even if I had medical insurance, I doubted my plan would cover it or know how to bill for it.

"How much is this going to cost?"

The stern set to Mr. T's jaw told me my question was inappropriate. Right, more important things to worry about, but I reminded myself to read over any paperwork before signing it.

I called Mr. Wood to assure him I was handling things, but had to do some outside work to wrap up the problem. He had a few choice words to express his annoyance over the issue not resolving itself overnight, but *choice* for Mr. Wood includes words like "fiddlesticks" and "fudge bunny".

Then, since I figured our professional relationship was already being pushed to its limit, I gave it another little nudge and asked to borrow his car. In his hesitation I could hear the beginnings of a refusal, but I reminded him the faster I could get around town, the faster I could have this over and done with.

Once he grudgingly said I could use the car, I swore to him the problem would be taken care of as quickly as possible.

"It will, won't it?" I asked Mr. T when I ended the call. He shrugged. Maybe I hadn't had enough tea yet, but the gesture frustrated me. I mean, how hard could it be to be de-magicked when you never knew you had magic to begin with?

Even though he looked quite dapper and lively for a zombie, I couldn't have Mr. Tenpenny roaming around on the streets of Portland. What if someone recognized him? What if Cologne Carl drove by in a hazy fume of manly scent? I told Busby to stay put and hurried over to Mr. Wood's to pick up the Prius. Thankfully, he was in with a client, and I was able to get in and out without being noticed.

Maybe Mr. Tenpenny was a good luck charm, or maybe the stars decided to align themselves for one day out of my life, because when I came back to fetch Busby, not a single hair of

Morelli's greasy head poked out to harass me over rent, over guests, or over the cat he suspected I had. Then again, perhaps his back hair had grown into his mattress overnight, trapping him in bed like little follicle shackles he might never escape.

One can dream, right?

Once in the car, Mr. T buckled up and I drove the few miles to his house. The place was still huge and the lawn was still immaculate and this time I was able to leave the car in the sprawling driveway.

"We're really doing this?" I asked.

Mr. Tenpenny nodded. So, with the sigh of a world-weary teenager, I got out and we strode up to the front door.

I stretched my finger toward the doorbell, but Mr. Tenpenny pushed my hand back down to my side. Then, looking both eager and apprehensive, he snapped his fingers near the lock. A moment later, something metallic clacked, the knob turned of its own accord, and the door opened slightly. So, I guess magic might be handy if you were forgetful about your keys. Mr. Tenpenny stood up even straighter (which I didn't think possible) and smiled with pride, although I detected a hint of relief in his eyes.

He stepped aside, indicating for me to go inside. I pushed the door and crossed over the threshold.

"Who's there?" called a familiar voice.

Since Mr. Tenpenny could barely speak more than one syllable at a time, he wouldn't be the one who had to explain things. I was still trying to figure out what to say when Tobey peered around from the kitchen at the end of the long hallway. His face pinched into the angry scowl of someone about to start yelling. At first I thought this was just how a murderer would react upon seeing his victim was still alive, but then I realized I had entered first and my tall frame was blocking his line of sight.

Tobey marched forward. "You can't just wander in here. I'll call—" Just then I stepped aside. "Grandad?" A procession of confusion, anger, I'm-about-to-freak-out crossed Tobey's face. "Why are you here? *How* are you here?"

Mr. T pulled out the notebook. If he didn't get dead soon, we were going to have to make a run to the Dollar Store to pick him up his own supply of writing material. After a couple quick sentences, he turned the pad toward Tobey.

"No," he said firmly. "She is *not* going to the community." Mr. Tenpenny wrote more and shoved it under Tobey's nose. Tobey pushed it down to a better level for reading. "Yes, I sensed something, but that doesn't mean she's— I mean, how could she be?" Mr. T pointed emphatically to his chest, then at me. He didn't do the exploding hand motion, so I figured I wasn't being blamed for his death, just his new life.

Since his pantomiming was getting him nowhere, Mr. T wrote again. At the sight of the words, Tobey's upper lip curled like the words smelled of sewage. "She what? No one wants rid of it."

Mr. T shrugged in a way that said, "To each their own," but Tobey glared at me with pure disgust. The look of a killer who might be exposed, perhaps? Busby wrote something else. Tobey glanced at me, his revulsion shifting to surprise, then to Mr. T who merely nodded.

"Look," I said, not really appreciating being talked/written about, "I don't know what you're saying, but can this gossip session happen a little faster?"

"Fine," Tobey grunted. "Come on, then." I followed after him, being careful not to slip in the puddle of annoyance leaking out of him. Mr. Tenpenny closed the front door and fell into step behind us.

I followed Tobey down a hallway through which I caught a glimpse of a living room bigger than my apartment. From what I could see, it was decorated in tasteful furniture that was more Sotheby's than Craigslist. The hallway ended in a kitchen with gleaming white cupboards, deep green walls, and an oak table as big as my bed.

Toward the rear of the kitchen, Tobey reached for the brass knob of a small side door. I expected we'd be crossing through a breezeway to the garage. I mused on what Tobey might drive and settled on either a junker to pretend he didn't care about wealth, or a Jaguar to prove he'd been dropped into the lap of Lady Luxury and had no intention of denying it.

Before opening the door, Tobey reached out for Mr. T's hand, which I found oddly touching, but maybe he knew he had to play nice now that Grandpa was back and could write him out of the will. Busby signaled for me to go first.

"Hold your breath," Tobey advised curtly. "It's a little weird the first time."

What? Was the garage gold-plated?

I stepped through, holding my breath and, for some reason, closing my eyes. That weird prickling danced over my skin again. I was just wondering if I might need to pick up some antihistamines when something squeezed me, not so tight that I couldn't breathe, but similar to the one time I was allowed to go to Oaks Amusement Park and the overly aggressive ride conductor of the Scrambler cinched me into my seat.

Then, as now, I felt trapped, yet secure. I dared to open my eyes. Everything had gone hazy. Was I ill? Was I having a stroke? Did I have sudden-onset glaucoma? Just as I started to self diagnose, something popped in my ears, my vision cleared, and I was in—

CHAPTER FIFTEEN
I'M A BELIEVER

Hell, I didn't know where I was. It seemed like any normal street, if that street was on a movie set. It was too orderly, too fresh, and I thought if I peeked behind one of the façades, I might see nothing but empty space where a building should be.

"Keep walking," Tobey said as he brushed past me. I stepped forward and Mr. Tenpenny came to my side, giving me a reassuring smile.

"Is this part of your house?" I asked him.

He shook his head, then did an ab contraction to say, "Portal."

Of course. A portal. A magic portal. I am proud to say I refrained from making any comment about floo powder or portkeys. But that may have just been the shock.

"Busby?" called a voice flavored with a light Jamaican accent. "Busby! I thought you were—" A woman about five feet tall with rich brown skin and fluffy, grey-streaked black hair came dashing towards us. The moment she got a good look at Mr. Tenpenny she halted. "Oh, so it's true." Tears started to wet her eyes, but she shook them off.

"Lola." There was a hint of friendly warmth in Busby's exhale.

"Where's Fiona?" Tobey asked in a gentle tone, but that gentleness turned to utter derision when he added, "There's an issue."

I didn't know what I'd done to offend him. Okay, besides accidentally bringing his grandfather back from the dead and possibly ruining his chance at inheriting an amazing and very pricey house. But I hadn't done it on purpose. Did Tobey Tenpenny just have an innate dislike of people named Cassie, or was he worried that if I got more deeply involved I might figure out he had killed Mr. T?

"She's at her place. Class should have just wrapped up," Lola responded. She then glanced between the three of us, her dark eyes looking a bit dazed. "How did Busby—?"

"I don't know any more than you," Tobey said, "but he wants her evaluated."

"Is she—?" She regarded me with a kind, almost loving, expression, and for some reason I had a strange desire to reach out and hug her. I know this is going to come as a big shock, but I'm not a hugger. Especially not with strangers. "No, of course she is. I can feel it on her."

At this comment, my hugging balloon burst. What were all these people sensing on me? Did I have magical B.O.?

We joined Lola as she escorted us down the shop-lined street. It wasn't busy out, but on our way we passed a few people. And, because I know you're wondering, no one wore cloaks or pointy hats. Although most gave a quick look of surprise at seeing Mr. T wandering around, they didn't fixate on him long. Instead, their attention turned to me with that look of not-quite recognition I'd seen on Mr. Tenpenny's face. It was like one of those anxiety-fueled nightmares where everyone knows you, but you can't remember any of their names. Or am I the only who has that dream?

Walking the opposite direction came a man dressed in well-cut, cream-colored linen slacks, and black, button-down top. His dark hair was mostly combed back, but a few bits had gone rogue as if he'd missed a spot or two with the brush. The tailored attire combined with the sticky-up hair gave him an eye-catching charm. And by "eye-catching" I mean I was full-on staring at him. Yet another example of my social stupidity that often sends other humans scurrying from me.

Possibly feeling the crushing weight of my idiotic gaping, he glanced over and met my eyes. He then did a literal double take and jerked to a full stop. In his surprise, he dropped the book he'd been carrying. It took him a few seconds to recover, but even as he bent down to pick up his book, he never broke eye contact with me until a busty woman who was smoking a long cigarette and looked like she'd just walked off a B-movie poster from the 1950s, clicked her way up to him in red high heels that matched her lipstick.

She said something with a throaty laugh and the man strolled off with her, but not before looking back at me with an uncomfortably intense stare. I tucked my chin down, my cheeks burning. I did not like this place, I did not like these people, I did not like being stared at, and I really wanted Mr. Tenpenny dead so I could be done with all this.

After several blocks of the Scrutiny Parade, we rounded a corner onto a street that instantly brought to mind pictures from *Life* magazine of Small Town America. After passing a mom-and-pop hardware store, we came to a two-story house that reminded me of a Midwest farmhouse. We climbed four wooden steps and crossed a wide, covered porch, complete with a bench swing. Then, without even knocking, Lola let herself in.

I barely had time to take in the size of the house before we reached a broad, square room with four rows of desks four deep. Such a tiny class-size was a clear indication this wasn't a public school and my frugal brain began guessing how much it must cost to send your kid here.

At the blackboard, a woman with reddish-blonde hair and a rather plump behind for her slim shoulders, was waving her hands to make a pair of erasers clear away the chalk writing on the board.

At this point I'd been bringing back the recently deceased for a little over a month. I'd learned how to communicate with them, I'd discovered my undelivered parcel had some weird quirks that got weirder when I held it, and I'd watched a dead guy open a lock with the snap of his fingers. Oh, and I'd stepped through a portal into another world.

Even so, none of that had me fully convinced the whole magic thing was real. But when I saw those erasers swishing back and forth without any human or robotic hands holding them, my mind went into full "I'm A Believer" mode with Micky Dolenz singing lead vocals as Davy Jones and I hummed a background tune of "holy crap."

And before one of the erasers whisked the chalky letters away, I most definitely caught the sentence, "Invisibility is not allowed in class." It made me wonder what sort of tricks invisible boys might get up to in the girls' magic locker room.

"Fiona," Lola said. "Busby is, well, he's back."

Fiona whirled around. The erasers dropped to the floor and sent up a puff of fine, white dust.

Busby smiled and held out his hands. Fiona recovered her composure. With a slight limp, she took a few steps over and grasped Mr. T's hands. After staring at him for a moment as if to be sure he was real, she gave a sympathetic but curt nod of greeting to Tobey before turning her attention on me.

"You've done this," she said, and I couldn't tell if it was an accusation or simply a statement of what she believed to be a fact.

"I— I didn't mean to."

Busby pulled the watch from his jacket pocket. Fiona's eyes went wide. She let go of Mr. T's hands and leaned in closer to study the odd timepiece.

"So it was sent. But you said it never—"

Busby shook his head then gave me a nudge, signaling me to tell what happened.

"I was supposed to deliver the watch, but no one was home and I was under strict instructions not to leave anything on doorsteps, that everything had to be handed over to the addressee." Fiona nodded as if approving of my ability to follow a basic rule. "When I got back to Corrigan's, that's the courier—"

"I know what Corrigan's is," Fiona said.

"Right. So, when I got back, the place was closed down. This has been in my coat closet ever since." I paused, then added while trying very hard not to look at Tobey to see his reaction, "And Mr. Tenpenny thinks he was killed for it?"

"Yes, the watch is a very valuable and very dangerous tool in the wrong hands. It was meant to be delivered to Busby because Alastair thought he'd figured out some way to destroy it."

"Where is *here*, by the way? I mean, I know we came through Mr. Tenpenny's kitchen, but this is definitely not a pantry."

Tobey charged right over my question and asked, "But who wants this? Who killed my grandfather?"

As if you don't know.

"The Mauvais," Lola said, her gentle voice barely above a whisper.

"But he's gone," Tobey replied as if Lola was lying.

"He only went into hiding. He was never caught," said Fiona, her eyes darting to Busby for the briefest of moments. Busby responded by glancing at his highly-shined shoes.

Fiona continued in the tone of a teacher giving a familiar lecture. "Headquarters has feared a renewed connection between the Mauvais and the watch. Which is why it's remained under lock and key for over twenty years. HQ had it well protected and hidden from any detection. But the Mauvais must have sensed it when it was being transferred. Or one of the people he worked with in the past informed him it was in transit." Fiona's eyes met Mr. Tenpenny's, but he shook his head as if telling her to stop that line of thought. "Regardless, it was foolish of Alastair to request it. He should have just gone to HQ himself," she said irritably. "The Mauvais or one of his followers tracked it as far as Corrigan's. He lost the trail for a time, but..." She trailed off, then added, "He probably assumed Busby had it in the house somewhere."

A sinking feeling gripped my gut. What if Corrigan's hadn't willingly closed down? What if Corrine had been forced to put up that sign and was then tortured for information? What if she'd been inside getting her fingernails ripped out while I was outside cursing my missing paycheck?

"Who was it?" Lola asked. "Someone local?"

"We don't know," replied Fiona. "Corrine got wind of what might be coming and shut up shop just in time. She made a good effort to hide any delivery information as well as the various channels the watch went through to get to her, but someone still found out it was supposed to go to Busby."

Sympathetic looks fell on Mr. Tenpenny.

"Sorry," I said, interrupting the moment, "but I don't have a lot of time for the hows and whys and whos of all this." Let me just say this statement didn't win me any points with the people in the dusty room.

"Are you always this charming?" Tobey asked. Lola punched his arm and that un-Cassie-like desire to hug her overwhelmed me again.

"Look, my boss might lose his business because supposedly

I've caught a bad case of magic from that watch. Mr. Tenpenny said if I came here you could, I don't know, de-magic me or something." My thought was if the watch was back where it belonged, these people could do whatever needed to be done with it. That way Mr. Tenpenny would get back to being dead and everything would go back to normal. I was about to learn this hopeful idea was a little off target.

"I can't believe you want to get rid of your magic." Tobey heaped his words with about fifty pounds of derision.

"It's proving a little inconvenient," I replied.

He shook his head. Busby reached out as if to calm his grandson, but Tobey jerked back. "I need to go home. This isn't my business."

"Tobey, it is—" Fiona tried to say, but Tobey was already storming off, his square shoulders rigid with irritation. Guilt, I thought. Set off by seeing all these people so happy that his grandfather was sort of alive.

"It would be nice if he accepted matters," Lola said with wistful sympathy. She then passed a questioning look to Busby. He shook his head and it was then I noticed that he looked more lively. His cheeks had a touch of pink to them even though it had been well over twenty-four hours since I'd given him a swipe of Sunshine Rose blush. Even his eyes shone brighter, almost as if he was becoming more alive than dead. Exactly what I did not need.

"You'll need to be evaluated to see just how much magic you've absorbed," Fiona said. "Then we can work on channeling it back into the watch."

"And that will get Mr. Tenpenny dead? No offense, Mr. T."

He gave a tiny none-taken shake of his head then said, actually said, "None taken," with only the barest flinch of his gut muscles.

"If your magic brought him back, then, yes, it might work. But if it was the watch, well, that complicates matters." My shoulders slumped. I did not need complications. I needed quick resolutions. I was starting to sound like an overworked businessman. "We'll go to Runa, she does the exams."

Exams. That didn't create the best connotation in my head. This was either going to involve taking some weird wizard test or getting naked and being poked and prodded. But for Mr. Wood, I would muddle through. There just better not be needles involved.

CHAPTER SIXTEEN

ON THE STREETS OF MAGICLAND

We left Fiona's place and continued along several streets that seemed too quaint to be real. Most of my foster parents were giant jerk wads, but one family, the Roberts, had actually taken the "parent" part of foster parent to heart. They were kind to me, treated me as well as their own two real kids, and even stimulated my brain with educational outings.

One weekend, we all piled into the station wagon and headed up to Victoria, British Columbia, where part of the itinerary included The Royal British Columbia Museum. I know museums aren't normally places that stick in kids' memories, but this was the first one I'd ever been to, and in my dreams I kept going back to it long after that pair of fosters died and I got shuffled back into the system.

Except for the zombie and the two witches strolling beside me, this walk reminded me of the historical street life reproductions of that Canadian museum of memory.

The first block we turned down, from what I could see, had been designed to resemble something from the Wild West with raised boardwalks for sidewalks, a saloon with batwing doors, and shopfronts with big glass display windows just waiting for a bar fight to get out of hand and one of the combatants to be thrown through them.

Not far along Western Street, we angled up a small side street straight out of a 1950s' movie with a candy shop, a butcher shop, and a clothing boutique with *Vivian's* written on a cream-colored sign in red, looping letters. The shop caught my eye because, even though I'm no fashion maven, it was nearly summer but yet the mannequins in the window display were still wearing wool coats and body-hugging turtleneck sweaters. At the end, another turn had us walking along a street straight out of Sherlock Holmes's London with booksellers, tailors, and haberdasheries.

I looked to Busby questioningly. He nudged Lola and said, "Explain," while indicating the scenery.

"Oh, we all have our favorite eras and with magic there's really no limitation on building fronts, so business owners with similar interests get together and design their districts to suit their tastes. The only trouble comes when one person closes up shop and another person moves in who likes a different time period. The community either has to accept the new business not fitting in, or the new shop owner conforms to the surrounding designs. It sounds contentious, but it can be a great bit of fun."

I was getting the feeling that Lola could find the positive side to anything.

Fiona, clearly the more practical of the pair added, "It used to be much more freeform with nearly every shop being from a different period, but it had to be reined in when someone on Main Street, which we try to keep to a generic French village look, wanted to put up a replica of a full-scale Roman market smack dab between the patisserie and the Parisian jazz club. Ah, here we are."

My jaw instantly tensed. Printed on the main window in a semi-circle of formal black letters were the words: *Dr. Runa*

Dunwiddle, M.M.D. Underneath, in smaller letters, was written: *Magical Medical Doctor, License Number HP060464.*

Doctor? No one mentioned a doctor. My legs wanted to run as fast as possible, not only from the potentially devastating medical bill, but also because this place could have doubled as a nineteenth century den of torture. The exterior and interior walls might be painted a comforting shade of Easter egg blue, but arrayed front and center in the window just below the name was a display of historical medical instruments. Very pointy, very painful looking, historical medical instruments. At least I hoped they were historical.

Perched on an easel next to the display of terror was a placard. Written on it, in the same hand lettering as had been used on the sign at Corrigan's Courier was the message:

Exams given here.
Tests of ability and tests of strength.
Flat fee.

It made it sound as if the test was some sort of carnival contest, but at least it didn't seem like any of the poking or prodding tools on display might be used.

We entered the shop. Toward the rear wall of the small, square interior was a counter behind which were rows and rows of small boxes. At first glance, I couldn't tell how long they were, but their ends were about the size of your standard business card. The two side walls had shelves filled with displays of tubes, bottles, and jars. Flanking the door stood two rotating racks: one filled with candy and packets of cookies, the other lined with greeting cards. I didn't have time to browse, but one caught my eye. In big, childish letters above a droopy-eyed, cartoon puppy, it read, "We can't all be wizards, but you're still magic to me."

At the counter, a stocky woman with her back turned to us was slipping a stack of long, slender boxes into the few empty slots on the rear shelves. Her dark brown hair had a slight curl to it, but was clipped short and had a few patches of grey speckled through. She wore a lab coat, which might have struck me as pointless, sort of like those cosmetics counter workers who wear lab coats as they try to sell you overpriced moisturizer. But with her sturdy air, the coat seemed to lend an authority to what the woman was doing.

She turned when the bell above the door chimed our entry. A very large and very round pair of black-rimmed glasses floated in the air just behind and over her shoulder — the exact spot where her face had just been. She pulled an exasperated face, clicked her tongue, and the glasses zipped around to hover in front of her scrutinizing eyes.

As with everyone else, she gave a double take when she saw me. "Is it—?" she mumbled, then shook her head, the glasses jumping around, trying to keep up. She waved them away and they settled onto the counter. "No, right, couldn't be."

"Runa," Fiona said. "Miss Black needs an exam."

"Well, I can tell you right now she's one of the Magics." She stepped around the counter. "It's just oozing from her, isn't it?"

I looked down at myself. Obviously, I knew I wasn't oozing anything, but all these comments were eroding my already-miniscule amount of self-esteem. When Runa approached me, I felt that skin prickling sensation all over again and the air around me filled with the scent of mint and honey.

At the same time I caught this scent, Runa Dunwiddle halted and stepped back. She waved her hand in a counter-clockwise circle in front of her face, and the scent went away. "And quite an absorber. Who did you say you were?"

"Cassie Black. And I just want to put this," I mimicked her

hand circle, "away so I can get on with my life."

"Put it away?" she said with Tobey-like indignation. "Do you—?"

Mr. Tenpenny cleared his throat in that way that has nothing to do with phlegm and everything to do with shutting someone up. These people were definitely weirdos, they were definitely hiding something, and I was definitely convinced that the sooner I was done with them, the better.

"Yes," I said. "Away. I guess back into here since that's where it came from." I pointed to the pocket of Mr. Tenpenny's jacket where he'd stashed the watch, noticing for the first time his jacket pockets revealed no boxy bulge. I was just thinking we were going to have to go back to Fiona's place to get the watch when he reached his hand deeply into an inner breast pocket, pulled out the decorative watch case, and flipped open the inlaid lid. Dr. Dunwiddle leaned forward to look at it, took a deep breath of surprise, then passed Fiona questioning look. Fiona merely tilted her pointed chin to give a single nod.

"Even a child would know your magic did not come from there. But we'll get nowhere until we see how much you have. Step through," she said, pointing at a door in the back wall.

"How much is this going to cost? I don't have health insurance, you know." I wondered if Mr. Wood might reimburse me if the fee wasn't too bad. I mean, it was a work-related expense, wasn't it? Still, with doctors, it's always good to get an upfront estimate before letting them dig around.

"A basic test normally runs—"

"Busby says he'll pay the fee," said Fiona, holding up the notebook. I bristled. I do not like people paying my way. I might be broke, but I've got my pride. However, since this was kind of his fault, I didn't argue.

"Fine. Shall we?" She pointed to the door again. I pushed it open, half expecting to enter yet another new city as when I'd passed from Mr. T's kitchen into MagicLand, the name I'd given this place since no one had clarified exactly where we were. But the door opened onto nothing more exciting than a small, well lit, warm white room with trim painted the same Easter egg blue as the front shop.

Inside was an exam table, a couple wooden chairs, and a cabinet perched above a counter and sink. It looked pretty much like any doctor's exam room, but this one had several objects hovering in midair like a baby's mobile. If that mobile happened to work without any strings, that is. I stood gaping at them and was tempted to bat one to see what would happen.

Runa's whistle startled me back to attention. I turned to see her glasses flying through the door to catch up. While the glasses would be joining us, it appeared the others would not. I had a sudden, unexpected wish that Lola might come in and hold my hand. I shook off such uncharacteristic neediness.

Still, since he was the instigator of all this, I had thought Busby would insist on coming in with me, but he was deep in conversation with Fiona. He may only be able to get out one or two words at a time, but he was definitely conversing. I sighed. The more alive he got, the harder it was going to be to kill him off.

The door closed.

I was not invited to sit.

CHAPTER SEVENTEEN

THE EXAM

Runa had brought in a long, slender box just like the ones she'd been adding to her shelves. I know, you're thinking "wand." You're thinking "Ollivander." Or, at least I was. But no such magical luck. She opened the box and, I kid you not, extracted a file that was at least twice as long as the slim container. With the glasses balancing in front of her eyes, she jotted down a few things, gestured for her glasses to move aside, then stuck the pencil behind her ear and turned her attention to me.

"Okay, for the first test, something basic. Make one of these objects come to you." She pointed at the things floating above our heads.

I looked at the objects: a feather, a teacup, a purple pen, a pair of sunglasses, a key. It was like a levitating lost and found.

"How?"

"That's the test," she said in a way that made it clear she expected me to fail, which only made me want to prove her wrong.

Now, even though Busby wasn't in earshot and even though I really wanted to, I did not say, "*Accio*, pen."

In truth, I didn't know what to say or do. I felt like an idiot. How long was I supposed to stand here waiting for one of these things to bob over to me? My cheeks flared with embarrassment.

I figured the only thing for it was to do something, anything. Then when nothing happened, it would prove my lack of talent and we could move on to sucking the magic out of me.

I took a deep breath and tried what always worked on Pablo.

"Come here, ink pen. Come on," I said in a high, sing-song voice while patting my hands on my thighs.

Dr. Dunwiddle, the woman who I might point out had just whistled a pair of well-trained eyeglasses into the room, cocked an eyebrow at me. However, as she was reaching for her pencil, the pen floated over almost shyly. I held out my hand and the pen dropped into my palm.

"What the hell?" I said, not sure if I should laugh or fling the possessed writing implement as far from me as possible.

Runa made a note in the file, then looked at me quizzically. "You've never trained before?"

"I tried the Duolingo app for Spanish a few weeks ago, does that count?" I'd thought perhaps Pablo might like it if I spoke to him in Spanish, but it turns out the only international language for felines is the sound of a can opener.

Runa didn't answer, so I took that as a "No."

"Put the pen back and then line the objects up in a row."

I asked how, but she merely shrugged her square shoulders and waited for me to make a fool of myself. Dr. Dunwiddle wasn't exactly winning points for being helpful.

I didn't know any cat-tested commands that might organize random objects, so I said, "Shoo," to the pen and, let me say, I never thought a pen could scurry, but it did. Once again, I was left without a clue of what I was meant to do. After a minute of thinking over how silly it would look, I mimicked Fiona's hand movements with her erasers while imagining I was holding one object at a time and lining it up on a shelf.

The first object, the pen, continued to prove its obedience by pointing upright as if standing at attention. The next two, the teacup and the sunglasses, shifted reluctantly into position, while the key looked like it was moving through molasses. I was glad I saved the feather for the last, because by the time I got to it, I was exhausted. My arms ached and I'd developed a throbbing headache.

With the feather in place, I dropped into one of the chairs. Runa jotted more in the file, then opened a drawer and turned to me.

"This will help," she said, handing me a bright green sucker the size of a quarter.

"A lollipop?" I asked critically.

"You don't want it?" She pulled the treat back, but I jerked out my hand. Cassie Black does not turn down food and right then I was famished.

The moment the paper stick was in my grasp, I tore off the plastic wrapper and started crunching away at the sugary, vaguely apple-flavored sucker. In little time, I was chewing nothing but sticky remnants and the headache had dialed itself back a few notches.

"I'll need a blood sample."

I pulled the empty stick from my mouth.

"No way, no needles."

"No, of course not," Dr. D said, clearly offended. "What kind of barbarians do you think we are?"

Runa rummaged in a drawer and I hoped she might be digging out another lollipop. Instead, she pulled out a tiny vial, showed it to me, then placed it on my arm. I tensed, expecting it to sting, expecting it to bite into me like a leech and begin sucking the life out of me. But it didn't.

I did feel a warm sensation where the vial was attached to my arm, but no poke, no prick, and no pain as the glass bulb filled with blood. When Runa took it back, a small reddened area showed on my forearm but no cut, no gaping wound, not even a scratch. I swore if I ever needed to see a doctor for blood work, I would rush back to MagicLand no matter how crabby this particular doctor was. Then I reminded myself I was only here to get Mr. Tenpenny dead so I could return to the zombie-free life we all crave. I doubt I'd be welcomed back after that.

"How does that work?" I asked, pointing at the vial with my sucker stick.

Runa's glasses dutifully zipped back into position as she wrote out a label for the vial. She glanced up over them and replied, "Magic." I rolled my eyes at her sarcasm. "It's a vampire spell. A type of Absorption Spell. I enchant a dozen at a time to have on hand."

"Absorption. Busby said I'm an absorber. Is it the same?"

"Similar, but no. The spell only allows absorption of a specified substance — blood, urine, etc. An absorber only absorbs magic." She paused. "It's very rare."

"So is Parkinson's, but I don't want that either."

"Let's go speak with Fiona and Busby. If you're feeling up to it."

I got up to show I was ready. I still felt a little lightheaded, like when you stand up too fast, but as soon as I took in a whiff of the mint and honey perfume Runa was wearing, the dizziness faded. I'd prefer caffeine, but if this was some sort of energizing aromatherapy scent, I might have to order some.

In the front area of the clinic, Lola was browsing some lotions while Fiona and Busby were at the card rack sifting through the greetings. Mr. T chuckled at the one he'd pulled out. When he noticed us emerging from the exam room, he slipped it back into its slot and all three turned expectantly to Runa and me.

"Well?" Mr. Tenpenny asked as Lola pressed a packet of two

sugar cookies into my hand. My body suddenly craved cookies more than it ever had before. There was no finessing that package open. I ripped the waxed paper wrapper down the side, then crammed one of the cookies into my mouth.

"She's just passed the two hardest tests for someone who supposedly hasn't been trained," Runa told them.

"You said they were the easiest," I complained through a mouthful of cookie crumbs.

"If I said they were the hardest you wouldn't have even tried. Now, she's a little clumsy with it and has no endurance, but she's definitely not taking all this from the watch, no matter how powerful it was."

"Is," Busby said, and some of Runa's confident certitude fell away.

"That's another matter, but if I was in any doubt before, the skills exam cleared it up. She's also unwittingly pulling magic from us, so I'm doing a blood test to verify where she is on the spectrum. If she is who I—"

Once again, Mr. T cleared his throat to cut her off. The room went silent.

"So, can I be de-magicked now?" I asked, finishing off the second cookie, then crumpling the empty wrapper and cramming it into my back pocket since I didn't see a garbage can handy.

The three looked at each other as if holding a telepathic conference call.

"She has an obligation," Busby said. Said! It took effort and he had to really push to get out the last two syllables, but he spoke the words in a clear, upper-crust British accent.

"Busby, are you sure?" Fiona protested.

"I've died once," he said. He paused, perhaps refilling his lungs, then pushed out, "It'll be okay."

"I don't agree with it one bit," Runa said, crossing her arms over her hefty chest. "She may have been unaware she had it before now, but you know her magic has potential. If she bothered to learn to control it, that is."

"Runa," Busby said, filling the word with stern warning.

"No, I know," she said, putting her hands up in an I'm-not-arguing way. "I'm not the Council on Magic Morality. If she wants to get rid of the talent she was born with, then I have to do it."

Born with it? I wanted to ask more questions — many, *many* more questions — but when I saw the time was already a quarter to eleven, I pictured Mr. Wood wringing his chubby hands and fretting over whether I'd make good on my promise to be there before Cologne Carl showed up at noon.

"Let's do it then. No offense, Mr. Tenpenny, but I hope this works."

"Think nothing of it," he said with pure British gentility as Fiona placed a comforting hand on his shoulder. Lola meanwhile, reached out to pass me another packet of cookies.

"Lola, put those back right now," Runa ordered. "This procedure is going to be hard enough."

Zero points for helpfulness. Zero points for reassurance. As she ordered me back into the exam room, I wondered how low Dr. Dunwiddle's Yelp! rating must be.

CHAPTER EIGHTEEN
REVERSE HAIRBALLS

This time, we all crowded into the exam room where the objects still remained tidily arranged. I'll admit, I was tempted to point at the lineup and say, "Look what I did!" But I held back.

Busby sat on the chair, which I thought was a smart idea since, hopefully, he'd be keeling over dead at any minute. I hadn't sorted out how I'd get him back to Mr. Wood's, but that was not the biggest problem of the day. Perhaps these Magics might be able to levitate him back to the funeral home, or at least to Mr. Wood's car.

"Is it going to hurt?" I asked as Runa, her glasses peering out from the top of her lab coat's breast pocket, cleared up my floating homework. My palms had gone clammy at the realization that I didn't know what this might entail. What if all the magic in my body was located in a molar or my big toenail and they had to yank it out by the roots? My toes scrunched involuntarily.

"Only me," Runa said in a snarky tone. She was either staunchly against people getting rid of their magic, or my very existence irritated her. Either way, she was a doctor and probably knew clever ways to cause discomfort to people she didn't like. To be on the safe side, I kept my mouth shut while she arranged a collection of objects in a circle on the floor. One looked disturbingly like a clump of cat fur pulled from a brush, one was a box of wooden matches, one was a bottle of water, and the last was a small pot of basil. "Now for the watch."

Since I was between him and the doctor, Busby handed me the timepiece. As I passed it to Dr. Dunwiddle, I noticed the gears were now moving smoothly with a gentle ticking sound. Runa took it gingerly. If she didn't seem like the stalwart sort of woman who never gets frightened, I would have said she was afraid of the watch as she placed it in the center of the circle.

"This might be fairly easy since you were never trained," Lola said reassuringly. "After all, you never learned how to hold onto your magic in the first place."

"Or it could make it a hundred times more difficult," said Runa under her breath.

"So what are these?" I asked, ignoring her comment and pointing at the objects.

"Earth, fire, water, and air," Runa said, indicating the basil, the matches, the bottle, and the cat fur. "The basic elements of magic. But since you've gone and woken up things that should have been left quiet," she indicated the watch, "time is an additional element in this case."

"Sorry, what but what does cat hair have to do with air?" I asked. "Was this from a particularly flatulent cat?"

Somehow, my attempt at humor proved not to be the miraculous method to win over Dr. Dunwiddle. Her lips pursed and she exhaled slowly yet forcefully through her nostrils before saying, "If you must know, it's from a flying cat. The fur is hollow for loft and to retain heat. Hence, air. Now, shall we?"

I shifted my gaze to Mr. Tenpenny. This test might be miserable for me, but it could kill him. But, with perfect stiff-upper-lip Britishness, he merely nodded and smiled encouragingly. I gave a resolute nod in return, then stepped into the circle, standing next to the watch where Dr. Dunwiddle had pointed.

"Concentrate on pushing your magic into the first four items," Runa told me. "This will be your basic magic, your elemental magic."

I did what she said. Okay, I tried to do what she said. How was I supposed to know how to get rid of something I never knew I had? I thought of Mr. Wood and told myself to do my best.

I've picked up my fair share of yoga videos from the library over the years, and although awful at the meditation, I always did feel something warm besides coffee moving within me on the relaxation poses. I figured this couldn't be much different.

I closed my eyes, picturing that inner warmth going into the water bottle, the plant, the matches, and the cat fur. I imagined tapping each one with the warmth, like tapping your hand on a kid's head in a game of Duck Duck Goose. This visualization didn't help. I bit my lip, trying not to laugh as I pictured myself blurting, "Goose!" then running in a circle with the water bottle chasing after me.

I had just managed to push this image out of my head when I heard the hiss of a match lighting and caught the wicked scent of sulfur. Behind me, Fiona gasped. A harsh stench of burnt hair bit into my nostrils. I opened my eyes. The cat fur glowed red as matches jumped one by one onto the crackling pile. I reached down for the water bottle to put out the flames when the bottle did the work for me by tipping over to flood the tiny bonfire.

I expected to see the basil withered and crusty from whatever malevolent evil had seeped out of me, but it was fine. Very fine. In fact, it had grown half a foot and was bushy with new leaves. Pesto must be easy to come by in MagicLand.

"You said she had no training," Dr. Dunwiddle said accusingly to Busby. He shook his head and emphatically shrugged his shoulders in denial.

"Try to understand," said Lola. "She doesn't even know herself."

"What?" I asked, dying to find out how I'd managed to do something wrong without even trying. Not that screwing up would be unusual for me, but I could typically pinpoint my errors once I'd made them. "Is my magic out?" Surely I had to have gotten rid of some it. I mean, just look at that basil.

"Not in the slightest. That," Runa jabbed her index finger at the mess on the floor, "is the reaction of trying to rid a trained person of their power. The only thing you managed to get out was a small amount of your Earth power and even that result is not normal. She's got a lot of magic coursing through her. With that level of strength, I wonder if she can be drained at all."

"You don't mean to suggest an extraction," Fiona asked, a tinge of horror in her voice.

"Of course not, but — and this isn't my personal opinion speaking, but my professional one — she cannot be drained. Not yet. Not like this."

"No, no, no, no!" I may have stomped my foot to drive home my point. "I need this out today. Do what you have to. Needles, scalpels, Shop Vac, whatever it takes."

"Perhaps it was too much at once," Lola said as the others ignored my tirade.

Fiona nodded in agreement. "Maybe she should start by returning any power she's taken from the watch. That's the most important, isn't it? Once we have that, we can keep it safe from the Mauvais until it can be destroyed as was meant to happen. That wouldn't require draining all her power."

"Will that stop the dead from coming back to life around me?"

"It should," Runa said.

"And get Mr. Tenpenny dead?" I asked. Fiona grimaced. I suppose my tact could use a little polish, but now was not the time.

"We can try. I would have preferred to get it all out so we could put the unwanted magic to good use. Maybe even try a transfusion." She looked over to Mr. T when she said this. He gave a terse shake of his head.

I didn't know what any of this meant and didn't care. I was on a deadline. As the watch was reminding me, time was ticking. Cologne Carl would be arriving at Mr. Wood's soon. Things needed to get a move on.

"Should I just do the same with the watch, then?" I asked, hoping to hurry things along.

"No!" Runa snapped. "With your absorbing, if you try it that way, you're likely to take even more power from the damned thing, and Merlin only knows the trouble you'd be in if that happened. We'll try a different method. Pick it up." I did as she said. "Now think of anything going in reverse, like someone walking backwards, a river flowing in the wrong direction, an avalanche going uphill."

I tried to think of these things, I really did, but the only image that would stick in my head was Pablo yakking up a hairball, in reverse. Hey, don't judge. I was trapped in a tiny room with four people giving me a serious case of performance anxiety. Imaginary Pablo had to reverse vomit six hairballs before I heard the ticking slow. There was a collective gasp.

"Keep it up," Dr. Dunwiddle ordered, but it wasn't as easy as that. The watch had become incredibly heavy. My arms shook as if the thing weighed fifty pounds instead of a few ounces. My body resisted like someone was putting up a stone wall to the energy I imagined flowing from me. I forced poor Pablo to keep reverse puking, but the damn watch insisted on ticking. On what felt like the hundredth hairball — I swore to give Pablo a good brushing when I got home — the ticking ground to a halt.

My knees changed from solid bone to wet noodles. I staggered and knocked over my lovely basil plant. Someone, I smelled chalk so it had to be Fiona, caught me and eased me onto the exam table.

"Set it down," Dr. Dunwiddle said.

I handed her the watch, but she refused to touch it and instead pointed to the countertop. I stretched forward and placed the offending object on the edge. She then glanced toward the chairs by the door.

"I think it's worked," she whispered. Behind me came the sound of muffled sobs.

CHAPTER NINETEEN

EXTRACT ME NOW!

I turned toward the sniffling. Lola had her pudgy arm draped over Fiona's slim shoulder while Fiona held Mr. Tenpenny's limp hand. He had slumped forward in his seat.

"I'll need help getting him back," I said. I tried to speak gently, but my voice was as groggy as if I just woken up after a night of drinking a bottle of bargain basement merlot. I was also famished. I hoped Mr. Wood wouldn't mind me dashing off for lunch after I saved his business.

I was pondering whether to have olives or sun-dried tomatoes on my pizza — I settled for both, it wasn't every day you get de-magicked — when the thick blanket of silence of the room crept over me.

Runa had inched away from the counter, keeping her eyes on the watch as if it might turn into a rabid coyote. I don't know if her worrying was rubbing off on me or if I was keyed up over the need to get moving, but I felt keenly more alert than just a few seconds ago.

Then the silence was broken by a tick. It was only the gentle tick of a watch, but it snapped through my ears like the crack of a whip. Then came another. And another.

"It's going again," Fiona whispered, as if confirming it wasn't just her hearing the sound coming from the counter.

I'd shifted off the table to examine the watch, but out of the corner of my eye, in the very spot where Mr. T should have been resting in peace, something moved. You'd think I'd be used to this sort of thing by now, but I startled so badly I staggered backward, bashed into the exam table, then tripped and went straight down on my butt. With an apologetic look on his face, Mr. Tenpenny extended a hand to help me up. A hand that was warm and very much alive.

Well, hell.

"I need you dead." I was frustrated, confused, and hungry. Let's just say I was not having my best moment, so the complaint came out far ruder and far whinier than I intended. Fiona clucked a scolding sound at me.

"I'm not doing it again," Runa insisted. "She's trained whether she admits it or not. She could be a criminal. You know some of them get temporarily drained by charlatans before a trial so the magic can't be traced. I don't know what she did or why she's covering it up, but I'm not going to have anything to do with draining her."

"I am not trained," I said, emphasizing each word. "I don't even know what *trained* is. Time is ticking on my boss's business and I'm still sitting next to a dead guy who stubbornly insists on remaining alive."

And that's a sentence you can't imagine yourself ever saying, even after it comes out of your mouth.

"She's really not done anything, Runa," Lola said. "You can feel her magic is just sort of scattered. It's like the magic of a five-year-old."

I took a little offense at this, but appreciated that I had someone in my corner.

Fiona then explained, "Magics need a basic level of training by age sixteen, otherwise their magic is scattered, as we say.

Unfocussed. That lack of focus makes it harder for them to learn. Sort of like the difference between teaching a child a foreign language versus teaching an adult."

"She's well beyond the proper age, but the only way for her to get rid of her magic is to get it under control and that means putting her in training," Runa said. "There's no other way, unless you want me to do a full draining on her and accept the consequences."

"No," Lola said and reached for my hand to give it a comforting squeeze. The squeeze only lasted a second before she snapped her hand back. "Not an extraction. That'd be too much like, well, you know."

This was followed by the other three exchanging sheepish looks.

"So this training," I said, breaking the awkward silence and getting back to what seemed like the original point. I was tired of these nonsensical conversations they kept having around me. "How long will that take?" I'll be honest, I was hoping there was a quick-study program.

"Training, basic training, is at least eight weeks." Dr. Dunwiddle evaluated me, then said resignedly. "But you have inborn talent. It could be shortened to six weeks. Four at the very least, but you'd be exhausted."

"I don't even have four hours, let alone four weeks. This is too much. Let's just do this extraction thing. How bad can it be?"

I thought I was making things easy for everyone, but this was clearly the wrong thing to say because all four stared at me with horrified expressions on their faces. Imagine I just said, "Hey guys, let's go drown puppies." Yeah, that's how they looked.

"That," said Runa, her jaw trembling with tension, "is a punishment reserved only for the most wicked of wizards or witches. It is cruel and the only person who did it on noncriminal Magics was the Mauvais."

"But it would get the job done, right? I've no interest in magic, training, or being in this community. I just want to go to work and do my job and not have my clients waking up while I'm trying to apply their mascara."

Again, another sentence that doesn't come out of the mouths of people living normal lives.

Mr. T's fingers instantly went to his eyelashes. Fiona pulled his hand down as I watched Dr. Dunwiddle turn a very frightening shade of red. Think of a beet that had a baby with a slice of red velvet cake and you'd be close to the color, but probably still a shade or two too pale.

"You are the daugh—"

Busby cut Dr. Dunwiddle off with a hissing sound. She took a deep, shaking breath, then continued tersely, "The procedure would also suck away your essence. You would not be you any longer. Although from what I've seen, that might not be a bad thing. You've heard of the unfortunate results of the lobotomy procedures from the nineteenth century?" I nodded, picturing the vacant faces of people whose brains had been permanently scrambled in the name of mental health. "Those patients were veritable Einsteins compared to what's left after a full extraction."

"So, no extraction," I said, feeling the sting of frustrated tears in the corners of my eyes. I blinked them away. This was it then. I'd failed Mr. Wood. He was going to be out of a business, probably even out of a home because of me and this stupid magic. I had to be rid of it even if it meant putting up with these judgmental people for a while. "But something needs to be done for Mr. Wood. Today."

"I have an idea," Mr. Tenpenny said, then perhaps reassessing his speech capabilities, pulled out my notepad and wrote. He then turned the pad to me.

If I pretend to be dead, promise me you'll do the training.

"Training will help me get rid of my magic without turning me into an imbecile?"

His gaze flicked up to Dr. Dunwiddle. I don't know what expression she was passing him, but I swear I could feel the electricity of her bristling.

If that's what you wish.

"Since magic doesn't seem to be doing me much good other than dumping me in the middle of some very odd situations, yes, I want rid of it. But I don't have four weeks. Can we do it in two? A crash course, maybe?"

"We most certainly cannot," Dr. Dunwiddle said, and I decided my education timeline was an argument to bring up later. I needed a corpse and I didn't have time to bargain.

"Fine, if you play dead, I'll do the training, but we need to hurry back. One of your doors doesn't happen to open near Mr. Wood's, does it?" I asked, both hoping to save time and avoid Tobey.

"Mr. Tenpenny's home is the only portal," Fiona said too quickly to be the whole truth.

"I'll leave it to you to explain this to Tobey," I said to Busby. "I don't think he likes me."

Dr. Dunwiddle snorted. "No, I can't imagine he does." As you can see, my charm, cleverness, and pleasant attitude had fully won her over. She then pointed at the watch on the counter and told Mr. Tenpenny, "If you don't mind taking care of that for me. Until I can build up my protective spells, I'd rather not touch it. You, however, well, there's no need to worry about much in your state. Come along, I'll show you where it can go."

Runa led us back out to the front of the shop, then selected one of the long, slim boxes from the shelves behind her counter.

Even though I'd just seen her pull an entire file folder out of one, my first thought was there was no way the square, bulky case the watch was housed in was going to fit in the narrow container she'd pulled out. But when she lifted the lid, Mr. T angled the watch's case to get one edge started. The box bulged out as he pushed the object in. Once the case was fully inside, Mr. T removed his hand and the box snapped back to its tidy, compact size.

Okay, maybe magic was a little bit cool.

As Dr. D placed the box back into its slot on the shelf, my mind raced with possibilities of how handy such a box could be for storing books and perhaps hiding cats from landlords.

"Lola, can you stay behind and help me organize a few things?" Runa asked, and Lola agreed with cheery enthusiasm. She then, while the others were saying their goodbyes, slipped another packet of cookies into my hand and bid me good luck.

After leaving the clinic, Mr. Tenpenny and I, with Fiona volunteering to come along and smooth things over, headed back over to Magic Main Street. This time I kept my head down to avoid acknowledging any odd looks from the citizens of MagicLand until we reached Mr. T's house and slipped down the side alley where the portal to his kitchen waited.

CHAPTER TWENTY

AN INSPECTION

As I stepped through the portal I prepared for the strange squeezing sensation, but this time it felt like nothing more than a firm tug. Maybe the doorway worked differently when going back to the real world. Once through to Mr. Tenpenny's kitchen, I checked the clock and realized with dismay that MagicLand was in the same time zone as Portland, which meant I only had twenty-five minutes to get my zombie companion to Mr. Wood's.

Thankfully, Fiona offered to stay behind and asked Tobey to wait with her. Ditching Temperamental Tobey didn't do much to change what was turning into a really bad day, but it was enough to put me in a slightly better mood. With wishes of luck from Fiona, Mr. Tenpenny buckled himself into Mr. Wood's car and I rushed us to the funeral home's rear door just in case Cologne Carl chose that moment to show up out front. It wouldn't help our case one bit if he saw Mr. T wandering around.

In my workroom — aka "the morbid beauty parlor" — I gestured Mr. Tenpenny to the table. "Up you go. And if you could be as dead as possible, I'd appreciate it."

"Of course, my dear," he said and slipped up onto the stainless steel surface. To complete the ruse that we'd already started in on his final make over, I pinned a plastic bib over Mr.

T's chest to protect his shirt and set out a tray of cosmetics, sponges, and brushes.

From the reception area, just as the grandfather clock rang in the noon hour, the entry bell chimed its ding-a-ling welcome. My heart jumped into my throat. Mr. Wood didn't know I was here and would likely be in a state of near panic. I gave a quick look at Mr. Tenpenny. He gave a reassuring nod, then closed his eyes. His chest remained disturbingly still. I dashed out from the workroom and ran face first into Carl's barrel chest. My head ached as I was enveloped in a soupy fog of his cheap cologne.

"Going somewhere?" he sneered. I really was winning the hearts and minds of everyone lately.

"I heard the bell. Didn't want to keep you waiting." Just then, a very pale Mr. Wood came through from his office. And by pale, I mean the dead British guy in the next room currently had more color to his cheeks than my living and breathing boss. I should have phoned. I cursed myself for making him worry. I gave Mr. Wood a small yet confident smile and, dare I say, like magic the tension eased from his shoulders.

The thought of magic made me wonder exactly what powers I possessed. Could I ignite Carl's hair? Make his paperwork disappear? Make his nose hair sprout as vigorously as the basil?

"Is something funny?" Carl asked. I bit back my grin.

"Just thinking how silly this all is. Mr. Tenpenny is back here, if we're still going through with this."

"We are," he drawled. I ushered him in with Mr. Wood trailing close behind. They hovered over Mr. Tenpenny and I wanted to gag from the miasma of Carl's cologne in the confined space. Then paranoia struck. What if Mr. T was sensitive to cologne? What if he sneezed? Could he sneeze? I only hoped that if he did, it would be enough of a shock to scare Carl to death. Then again, with my luck, Carl would probably just come back to fragrant life and resume shutting us down.

Cologne Carl opened a manila file folder, examined the picture, looked Mr. Tenpenny over again, then snapped the file shut. "He seems very lifelike."

Mr. Wood's eyes went wide and his mouth started twitching as if he was trying to come up with a response.

"Mr. Wood does very good work," I said. Carl nodded and Mr. Wood relaxed again.

"And I assume you now have the paperwork showing the transfer?"

Crap.

This was problematic since the only place Mr. Tenpenny had actually gone was his home and MagicLand, and neither of those places issued signed documents. That I knew of. Still, I'd just learned magic existed. I'd visited a magic community. I'd been tested and had proven I could do magic. Surely, I could handle such a minor matter as paperwork.

"No," I said with a tone of knowledgeable innocence. "For all I know, it's probably been sent to Stevens Funeral Home across town."

"I don't understand why there's all this fuss," Mr. Wood said politely. "We can all see Mr. Tenpenny is here. My job is not only to conduct funerals, but to ensure the deceased maintain their dignity. After what his remains have been through, this inspection, or whatever it is, is a very disrespectful intrusion."

Nice one, Mr. Wood!

"Be that as it may," Carl said with pure disdain. "We will need the paperwork as proof of the transfers."

"This is the most nonsensical use of government time I've ever seen and I fail to understand its purpose. Is the word 'harassment' in your vocabulary?" Even I was startled by Mr. Wood's tone. My boss normally spoke in the calm manner you'd expect from a funeral home director, but Carl's bullish demeanor had clearly rankled him. His words came out with as much heated vehemence as the time when he returned from bingo night and was convinced Myrtle Norton had cheated her way into winning that night's grand prize. "In all my years—"

Carl cut Mr. Wood off. "I understand that there have been complaints of strange people, people who match the description of some of your deceased clients, being seen in the area. And on one occasion of walking with a tall, dark-haired young woman carrying," he paused and gave me a knowing look, "a baseball bat."

"This is Portland," I said. Mr. Wood had gone pale and silent again. "People see weird things all the time. It's like a citywide pastime. If you're trying to imply something, just come out and say it."

"I'm not implying anything. I'm saying that I think this establishment is either performing unsanctioned, and unethical I might add, experiments or you are deceiving loved ones with some ruse. Now I have evidence of this Mr. Tenpenny disappearing and reappearing in an industry that thrives on paperwork, but yet you have no paperwork. If you can't prove where Mr. Tenpenny was from the time he died to the time of his funeral, I'm afraid you will face fraud charges at the very least, and your license to operate will be taken away. So let me ask you, how long until you can get that paperwork?"

I thought of the training. I had no idea how I was going to forge the paperwork, but in my mind I was convinced that once the magic was out of me, somehow things would go back to normal. But getting rid of that magic required this stupid training. Four weeks of stupid training. This guy wasn't going to wait four weeks. I didn't care how hard it was or how much effort it might take, I had to resolve this in—

"Two weeks," I blurted. From the table I heard a groan. Mr. Tenpenny obviously didn't approve of what I was thinking.

Thankfully, due to the various metallic and tiled surfaces, sounds in my workspace bounce in unusual ways. Carl's gaze shifted suspiciously around the room. Mr. Wood dramatically cleared his throat before saying, "Is that the fastest, Cassie? Can we not get this taken care of sooner?"

"Believe me, I'd love to, but like so many things in life, these things can't be rushed."

"Then I must insist on the delay of this man's interment until it can be verified he hasn't been tampered with." Carl made Mr. Tenpenny sound like a bottle of aspirin. "And I will insist on seeing him again before the funeral."

"Fine," I said. "The family, the very distraught family, is not going to take this well. They need closure and I'll be sure to let them know who is keeping them from that closure."

"That's really no concern of mine." He jotted something on the cover of his folder. Despite his casual air, goosebumps jumped over my arms at Carl's next words. "I was told the body might have come in with a rather valuable object. Any idea if it's still with the deceased?"

Without any hesitancy, Carl strode forward and, while keeping his eyes firmly fixed on me, began patting down the pockets of Mr. Tenpenny's jacket.

All my false bravado dissolved. I swallowed hard, trying to bring moisture back into my Death-Valley-dry throat.

"You'd probably want to ask the county morgue," I managed to say, even though I felt like a baby grand piano had been dropped onto my chest. "Those government people can't be trusted."

Carl tucked his pencil behind his ear. Then, with a sly grin on his face, he pointed at me with his thumb and forefinger held to mimic a gun as if we were playing a game of cops-and-robbers. "See you in exactly two weeks. In the meantime," he lowered his hand and tapped his thick index finger on the folder, "I'll start the formalities of Mr. Wood's license revocation."

"You have no cause," I protested. I swear if I knew how to use whatever magic was in me, I would have made boils, really painful and really gross boils, sprout up all over his body.

"Don't I?" he said, then nodded toward the baseball bat in the corner.

CHAPTER TWENTY-ONE
MOVING ON

Mr. Wood ushered Cologne Carl out. The minute they were out of earshot, I cursed until I ran out of creative expletives. Mr. Tenpenny sat up and was removing his bib when Mr. Wood walked in. "Oh good heavens, he's still, he's still—"

"Mobile?" I offered. Mr. Wood nodded. "Afraid so."

"Miss Black, you can't possibly—" While Mr. Tenpenny paused to refill, Mr. Wood blanched to a shade lighter than my Ivory Cloud foundation.

"It speaks?" he squeaked.

"When he's not interrupted," I told him gently. I turned to Mr. T. "Can't possibly what?"

"Be trained in two weeks." Pause. "If that's what you're thinking."

"Trained?" Mr. Wood asked, color blooming back into his cheeks. "Cassie, are you quitting? I thought you liked this job. Then again, I should fire you. But on the other hand, I can't blame you for leaving since there might not be a job soon."

"I do like it here. I'm not quitting. And there will be a job to come back to if I take a couple weeks off to do something about this. I don't think we'll have much business anyway," I said, indicating the Closed Until Further Notice paper in Mr. Wood's hand. "I'm going to take care of this, okay?" I started to reach out

143

to pat his arm, then pulled back from such an un-Cassie-like gesture.

After making sure Mr. Wood was settled, I said my goodbyes to him and reassured him — even if I wasn't so sure myself — that everything would work out. This of course made him even more suspicious since I don't have a lot of practice with false optimism.

While I ate the packet of cookies Lola had slipped me, Mr. Tenpenny used the workroom's wall phone to call Tobey and ask, although haltingly, if he could come pick us up.

"Us?" I asked after he hung up. "It's already been a really long and really weird day. I'm more than ready to go home."

"We have matters that need settled." Pause for breath. "Wouldn't you agree?"

I agreed with a heavy sigh to show I didn't really agree. Before I shut the door behind us, I gave a final glance back at my stainless steel and ceramic-tiled workspace, wondering if I'd ever see it again.

When Tobey showed up a few minutes later (who would have guessed he drove a Nissan Leaf?), Busby got in the front and I climbed in the back for a silent ride back to Mr. T's house.

In the Tenpenny kitchen, Fiona had prepared a snack of apples, almonds, carrots, cheese and crackers, and (thank Merlin) bottles of microbrew. Tobey popped one open, then leaned against the counter with his arms crossed over his chest. While I nibbled (okay, devoured) the snacks and sipped (okay, guzzled) a beer, Fiona and Mr. Tenpenny stood off to one side speaking in undertones. I heard the words *cologne* and *looking for the watch*. When I caught the phrase *two weeks*, I knew they probably weren't discussing when their library books were due. Finally, they came over to the massive, wooden table and sat across from me. Mr. T opened a beer for himself. Fiona and I both stared as he took a drink.

"What?" he asked.

"I just didn't think…" Fiona couldn't come up with the words.

"What she means to say is, you give Dead Guy Ale a whole new meaning," I told him. "Are you really able to drink that?"

He took another sip. Paused as if waiting for something, then nodded. "It seems to be doing the trick."

"Anyway," said Fiona, "I don't think training can be completed in two weeks. Even four would be pushing it."

I hadn't just been stuffing my face and sucking down beer while they'd been whispering. I'd been pondering this very topic and was prepared to make my case.

"But I don't really need full training, do I? It's not like I'm going to need to refine my skills or pass my O.W.L.S." Mr. T glowered at me. "Sorry, but you know what I mean. I'm not doing this to become part of your community. I just need to learn enough to channel this magic back into wherever it needs to go."

"Why are you so set on giving up your magic?" Tobey grumbled.

"What's it to you?"

"You don't realize how lucky you are, do you? You're so magic the others can smell it on you like bloodhounds. Why do you think Corrine hired you without question? And yet you want to just give it up." I had no idea how he knew about my employment history, but throughout this tirade, Mr. Tenpenny was hissing Tobey's name, trying to get him to shut up. "I don't want to hear you standing up for her. You're supposed to be dead, but here you are catering to someone with no appreciation for what she's got. You used to hate people like her." Apparently having reached the top volume on his lungs, Tobey jerked away from us and stormed out of the room.

While part of my brain was thinking Tobey was acting very

murderer-esque with his aggressive behavior, I felt very small at what he had said. Indignant yes, but very small and very confused. And maybe that's what he had intended.

Please understand. He's not normally like this, Mr. T jotted onto one of the last empty pages of my notepad.

I nodded. I understood Tobey Tenpenny was a Grade-A piece of jerkmeat, but his reaction and what he said had me thinking again of how much he might want Mr. Tenpenny dead. He certainly didn't seem pleased his grandfather was alive. There'd been no joyful reunion, no delighted cheer. Hell, he barely even smiled to see his grandpa up and walking around. And why was he so abnormally angry about what I wanted to do with my magic? Magic sure seemed to be a pain in the ass, that's all I had to say.

"We should get matters underway," Mr. Tenpenny said. He still needed the notepad, but his syllables-per-speech rate was increasing greatly and the pauses were getting shorter. A Shakespeare soliloquy wouldn't be long in the coming.

"I'll need to make a call," said Fiona. "I doubt Runa will allow you to push your training to two weeks, but we'll do what we can since it seems important to you. Regardless, two weeks or four, you're going to be exhausted and will need a convenient place to stay. You're welcome to stay with me during your coursework."

My skin tensed. I wasn't super comfortable staying in other people's homes. Too much togetherness, too little privacy. Luckily, I had the Pablo excuse.

"I need to take care of my cat."

"You could bring him along. Cats adore magic. You've probably noticed." That would explain why Pablo and any other cat I'd owned had turned from aloof nomads into lovable monsters when I took them in. Finally! An upside to magic. Still,

I probably could've accomplished as much with a bag of treats and a catnip toy.

"I'd really rather commute," I told her. "Besides, there's been some creeps hanging around my building and I wouldn't feel safe leaving my apartment vacant for that long."

"Oh, don't worry, I believe that will be sorted," Fiona said with annoying vagueness. She then gave a quick, determined nod and went over to the phone on the far wall. She clearly knew her way around this place and I noticed, not for the first time, Mr. Tenpenny watching her with fondness. I couldn't hear what she was saying, but I assumed she was calling Dr. Dunwiddle to break the bad news that Cassie Black was coming back.

"All settled," she said once she was done. "Now, back to your place, Cassie."

"For what?"

"To collect whatever you'll need for school. Training begins this afternoon."

CHAPTER TWENTY-TWO

QUESTIONS & MORE QUESTIONS

Since no one wanted to risk asking Tobey the Terrible to drive, and since it was a nice day, we opted to walk back to my place. I don't know if it was the better neighborhood or because I had other people with me (even if one of them was dead), but not a single hair on my neck sent up a warning signal during our stroll. Still, the cloudless skies and chirping birds did nothing to calm the questions that were churning in me faster than a blender on Margarita Monday. It got to the point that even my introvert instincts couldn't contain them.

"All this, the dead waking, you being killed, is because of some watch?"

"It's likely," Mr. Tenpenny replied.

"What's so special about it?"

Fiona touched Mr. T's arm, as if indicating she'd take this question.

"It's an object that should never have been made. I still can't believe it was invented by a teenager trying to show off," she said with a critical shake of her head. "It started out as a practical joke, a way to steal magic from others, and that goes against all rules of etiquette and at least a dozen regulations from the Council on Magic Morality. But the real problem came when someone figured out it could steal much more. I suppose the best way to explain it is that under the power of a strong enough witch or wizard, the watch can control time, magic, and life. Busby told you about turning it forward and back?"

"One way adds years, the other takes them away."

"Sort of. By moving it forward you add years to someone's life. That is, you age them. Add enough years and you'll kill the person, or several people if you have the strength. Moving it in reverse, you subtract years from your age, meaning you can extend your own life, or those of others, if you choose."

"So it can make you immortal?" I asked as we skirted a broad roundabout, the center of which was planted with dozens of rose bushes. The whole block was filled with their floral perfume.

"If you have the power to turn it that far. It's a rare Magic who does. Not even the person who made it has that much power. But the aging aspect, although worrisome, is one of the less troubling properties of the watch. As I said, it was built to pull power from others. But that power doesn't just stay in the watch. It flows between the watch and its handler, enhancing the strength of both. With the watch, a witch or wizard can boost their magic. This renders the watch even more powerful. And more troubling."

This only added questions on top of my already heaping mound of questions, but I let Fiona continue. "It's a snowball effect of strength. Building up enough magic eventually gives the possessor the power of life over death, the power of unlimited power. And unfortunately, both in the magic and non-magic world, certain people with too much power will abuse it. You can imagine what would happen if the watch ended up in the wrong hands. Even the right hands might find it too tempting to resist."

Despite the sun warming the late spring air, chills ran along my arms. Tobey. He seemed just like the kind of wizard who would want more magic, no matter how much he'd been born with. Otherwise, why would he react so bitterly to me wanting to get rid of mine? If he thought Mr. Tenpenny had the watch, that would've been the perfect motivation for murder. Well, that and instant wealth through Portland real estate.

"So why was it sent to Mr. Tenpenny?"

"For years we've been trying to figure out a way to destroy the watch. See, about twenty-five years ago, it ended up in the hands of a terrible wizard who operated under the name of the Mauvais. It's a long story, but three of our agents lost their lives seeing him to his end." I caught Mr. Tenpenny giving Fiona an elbow nudge. She elbowed him right back, then continued. "Just before that, though, they managed to get the watch. Unfortunately, their deaths, along with the confusion and distrust the Mauvais had stoked within the magical world, led to the watch being misplaced when it should have been immediately put into headquarters's safest vault."

I wondered if goblins oversaw this vault and if there were dragons in the deepest part of it, but I was learning to tame my Potter references, at least around Mr. Tenpenny.

"Finally, maybe five years later, we tracked it down to the archives of the British Museum. It was an object of curiosity to the museum's employees, but thankfully no one could find information about it, so it was never put on display. One of our people works there — often reporting on magical objects they come across that MCs—"

"MCs?" I interrupted.

"Magically challenged. Non-magics. Norms."

"Got it."

"Anyway, MCs often donate objects they find in the attic, unaware that great granny was a witch and that the donated objects are filled with magic. Our insider at the museum spends his days roaming the archives, sensing for magic objects. When he detected the watch, he knew exactly what it was and sent it in immediately to be safeguarded.

"After being away from magic for so long, we thought the watch had been deactivated. Then, about nine or ten months ago, the watch that had remained relatively silent for nearly two decades, started showing signs of activity." I recalled the jittering minute hands. "Because any activation could be an indication of the Mauvais's presence, or of his followers starting up again, word was immediately sent to us about what was happening."

"Through some magical communication system?" And okay, yes, I was thinking of snowy owls carrying little envelopes in their beaks, or at least some Westeros-style ravens with missives attached to their legs. I really need to get out more.

"No, through a text," Fiona said as if this shouldn't be completely obvious. "Anyway, Alastair had a theory of how he might be able to deactivate the watch for good. To destroy it. After lengthy debates of the risks involved, it was decided the watch should be sent here to let him test his theory. Since Busby is the main contact between HQ and Portland, they transferred it through the proper channels so it could be delivered to him via Corrigan's. When it went missing again, rumors started up that the Mauvais had taken the watch and was on the rise once more. We woke up each day fully expecting an attack at any moment. But the attack never came. Then, after we'd fallen into a sense of security, Busby was killed."

"But he didn't have it," I said as we turned a corner that instantly took us out of Mr. T's tree-lined residential neighborhood and into a grungy business district.

"No, he didn't, and I imagine the Mauvais, or whoever was acting for him, must have sensed the watch. They could have been tracking it." I thought of the creepy crawly feelings of being watched I'd been having for the past several months. "Whoever it was had to have known Busby didn't have it. Killing him seems more an act of frustration than anything else."

And who do we know that seems quick to overreact when he's annoyed? Tobey Tenpenny, that's who.

"Anyway," Fiona went on, "whoever killed him had also been able to pull information from somewhere else in the chain of transfer or from Corrigan's system. We don't suspect Corrine, but we think it had to be traced to Corrigan's since the watch was the last object they received and Busby's was the last address they were scheduled to deliver to."

We turned onto my busy street and when we passed a boarded-up business, something ticked in my head.

"What did Tobey mean about Corrine hiring me?"

Fiona smiled. "I was wondering if you picked that up. I do remember Corrine having said she hired a new messenger she'd just come across. I asked if it was wise to hire an MC, but she said she wasn't hiring a Norm. It is true, you have a great deal of magic and we can sense that."

"Sorry," I muttered, thinking again of magical B.O.

"No, don't be. If a Magic knows how to reduce their power loss from your absorbing, your strength can be quite calming."

"It certainly doesn't calm Tobey," I said, hoping to steer the conversation to his being my prime suspect, but we had arrived at my building. The second I pulled open the main door, Morelli stomped out of his apartment. "Or him," I said under my breath.

"No parties, Black."

I glanced at the prim Fiona and the dapper Mr. Tenpenny. Did he think I was going to throw a roof-raising game of bridge?

"There's no partying planned."

He scowled at Mr. Tenpenny, then Fiona. Then something in

his face changed. I might almost say he looked friendly if I knew Morelli couldn't even spell the word *friendly,* let alone comprehend its meaning.

Fiona arched an eyebrow at Morelli and I was hoping more than I had ever hoped before that she was going to cast some sort of Duct Tape Spell on him that would seal his mouth shut for at least a year. But no such luck. Seriously, what's the point of having a witch at your back if she's not going to rustle up some sort of useful mayhem against your ill-tempered landlord?

Morelli's mouth didn't get sealed shut with tape, nor did he turn into a toad, but he did do something as equally unlikely: He smiled warmly. Seriously, the only time I'd seen him smile was when I'd paid my rent early one month, and even that had been more of a greedy grin than a true smile.

He nodded to Fiona, let us through, then reminded me rent was due in four days as I passed by. It was good to see the whole world hadn't completely turned on its head.

Once in my apartment, Pablo greeted me with a burst of enthusiasm, then proceeded to make it next to impossible for Fiona and Busby to walk as he twined between their legs, rubbing his chin and purring as loudly as a leaf blower. I dug out a couple more notepads for Mr. Tenpenny, although I wasn't sure he was going to need them much longer. Then, not knowing how much note taking I'd be doing myself, I stuffed a new notebook into my satchel along with a couple pens.

"Ready?" Fiona asked.

"Unfortunately, I just ran out of eye of newt last night. Do you have a student store or anything?" I thought it was funny, but neither of my magic companions showed any hint of amusement. Tough crowd. "Do you think Tobey might be over his mood yet? Or should we just hop the bus back over to your place?" I asked Mr. Tenpenny.

"That won't be necessary," Fiona said and pointed to my coat closet.

I should have understood straight away, but my immediate thought was that this had all been a setup, that these two were the Bonnie and Clyde of MagicLand and would lock me in the closet, then steal all my belongings. Boy, would they be disappointed.

When I didn't jump right in, Busby pulled open the door and walked in himself. Without a single complaint about my untidy shelves, he closed the door behind him. I expected grunting curses, tumbling boxes, but all was quiet. After several moments of unsettling silence, I peeked inside to see coats, shoes, mittens, and a fur-covered sweatshirt, but no sharply-dressed British guy.

Because my week needed to get weirder.

"What the...?" I muttered. Then my heart jacked up its pace. Busby had escaped! This was exactly what I didn't need. I could not lose him. After all, Cologne Carl was on the case and there was a high likelihood that if Mr. Tenpenny wasn't back on that stainless steel table or in a coffin in a couple weeks, I was going to be buried under a deep pile of elephant dung.

When I turned to her to ask where he'd gone, Fiona was grinning at my unease. "I had a portal installed in your apartment so you could come and go more easily. Unless you want to make the trek to and from Busby's before and after each lesson."

That I definitely did not want to do. The farther I stayed from Tobey Tenpenny, the happier I'd be.

"A portal," I said with utter disbelief as I checked inside the closet again. Now that I looked more closely, there was indeed a door in the back where there had only been solid wall before. "Seriously? How?"

"The phone call. I had Runa put it in before we got here. Shall we test it out?"

I stepped into my closet and promptly tripped over a pair of old running shoes. When I opened the new door, I expected to see a street scene from MagicLand, but saw nothing but a grey haze. I glanced back and Fiona gave me an encouraging nod. I stepped in, bracing myself for the squeeze, but Tobey had been right, the first time really was the worst. I still felt a pinch, but it was more like a firm handshake than a death grip.

Once through, the grey haze vanished. I was standing in front of a small outbuilding on a quiet portion of Fiona's Small Town America Street.

"What took so long?" Mr. Tenpenny asked.

I couldn't answer. I could only laugh. I, Cassie Black, had a portal into a magic world. In my closet. If Morelli ever found out, I'd definitely lose my deposit for the unsanctioned remodel.

CHAPTER TWENTY-THREE

FIRST LESSON

By the time Fiona stepped through, my giggling fit had kicked up another pile of questions about the Mauvais, about portals, about the weird looks I'd gotten earlier from the Magics, about what my training might entail. But just as Fiona shut the door, someone was squealing my name and running toward me. I'd recognize the hair anywhere: flaming red in stark contrast to Fiona's subtle, strawberry blonde. It was Corrine Corrigan. And she was pulling me into a vice-like hug.

"You really are here," she exclaimed, holding me out at arm's length. "I wanted so many times to tell you, but it was decided it would be better if I didn't. But now you know. Welcome!"

"Thank you," I said hesitantly, uncomfortable with having been discussed by strangers. Maybe that explained the bizarre looks everyone had been giving me.

"We'll catch up later. I hear you're going to train. I'm so excited for you." Another squeeze and then I was freed from the Corrigan Crush. "You be nice to her, Fiona."

After Corrine bustled away, Mr. Tenpenny said, "I've a few matters to see to." Pause for air. "Will you be all right?" I didn't like the idea of Mr. Tenpenny wandering off on his own. He must have seen the apprehension on my face. "I won't get lost."

"If you feel death coming for you again, be sure to find me

straight away."

"I'll do my best," he said and gave a little salute. As he sauntered off, I could have sworn I heard him humming a tune.

"Shall we?" Fiona said, pointing to the schoolhouse. I followed after her, but instead of going to one of the lower rooms, she headed up a steep wooden staircase. "My home is located above. You'll have your lessons with me up here."

The room we entered was filled with books from floor to ceiling. Any empty wall space was clustered with photos showing groups of students standing on risers four deep. Just like the teachers in my grade-school class photos, Fiona knelt at the center of each one with a smile of pride warming her small face. "My students. I'd like to tell you I remember all their names, but I don't. Some stand out, but not all."

"Do all these people live here?"

"Some, but certainly not all. After all, MCs don't necessarily keep living near the school they went to, do they? Students who attend my training come from near and far. Some choose to stay, others go back to their own local communities. I'll go get us some tea. Make yourself at home."

For lack of anything better to do and not feeling comfortable enough to simply flop onto the couch and start reading, I scanned the photos some more. They were mostly chronological and I noticed, as they went back in time, Fiona switched from being the teacher to being one of the pupils standing on the risers. I looked over the faces of the students and thought I recognized Lola and Dr. Dunwiddle. Mr. Tenpenny, I was certain, must have gone to wizard school across the pond. Probably Hogwarts, even if he would never admit it.

"Here we go," Fiona said, setting down a tray of tea things on a circular table by the window. She poured me a cup, put a cookie on the saucer, and slid it to me.

"Thanks. So, what's first?"

"Since you've already had a good workout from the exam, I suppose we should stick with learning some basic principles today. You're going to have plenty to cram in if you really expect to learn enough in two weeks to make a difference."

"I have to be rid of this."

Fiona gave a skeptical twitch of her eyebrows, but stifled any argument by taking a sip of her tea. "Then let's get started. Now, some Magics start out without any ability to even scoot a feather across a table, but as it seems you can manage a few things already, we won't bother with teaching you to tune into your powers. Still, you need to realize that magic is all around us. It's like energy. Did you take any science classes?"

Despite not completing my degree, I'd crammed both a year's worth of biology and physics into one summer and pulled straight As throughout. Being a bit of a science nerd had helped. Quantum physics for light reading? Sure, why not? But I didn't say any of this, I just nodded and let Fiona go on. "Like energy, magic can neither be created nor destroyed, but it can shift from one form to another and can be transferred from one vessel to another, much like putting the sun's energy into a battery for later use."

"Like Dr. Dunwiddle saying she could recycle my power when I give it up?"

"Exactly." Another sip of tea followed this taut word.

"So if magic is all around us, why isn't everyone magic?"

"Could a piece of wood be turned into wiring for your house?" I shook my head. "That's because just like any material, wood can conduct electricity, but its physical properties make it inefficient at doing so. However, copper has the physical structure to channel that very same electricity with amazing speed and efficiency.

"It's similar with people. In everyone's molecular structure resides magic, but not everyone can access it to use it efficiently. Some have the inner structure to use magic, whereas others don't. Some things, like lightning bolts, run wild with power, other things like a battery contain power and dole it out at precise intervals. We want to turn you from a lightning bolt to something more in control of your power so you can direct it out of yourself. Does that make sense?"

I said it did, then waited eagerly for her to tell me more. Even though I didn't want my magic, all this science-y stuff had me intrigued by it.

"I suggest you read something." She stepped over to a bookshelf and ran her finger along the spines looking for the title she was after. "Ah, here we go." She pulled a black, leather-bound book from the shelf and handed it to me. On the front, printed in silver, block lettering, was the title *The Principles of Physics and Magic*. "It will dispel some notions of what you think magic can do and clarify what it can't."

"I don't really need to learn all that, do I? Isn't there some core curriculum module that focuses on channeling magic?"

Fiona pulled off a rather good impersonation of Dr. Dunwiddle by scolding me with her eyes.

"Draining is dangerous business, even when you have been trained from a young age. For someone with no training, or limited training, it is incredibly risky. You're already rushing the process without ever having any prior exposure to this, so you need to know as much as possible to ensure you understand why you're learning what we're teaching you. Reading this will give you a head start on what we'll eventually be doing with your magic. If you know where you're heading, the road will be easier to follow." She paused to bite into her cookie. A mischievous grin came over her. "I should put that on one of Runa's greeting cards.

Anyway, the basic magic we'll be going over will teach you how to move things, guide you in how to change objects' shapes, and school you in other principles regarding the magical manipulation of matter. These 'tricks', as one might call them, are nothing more than using energy to affect an object. Just as you used the energy of your arm muscles to lift that book, we will use your magic muscles to move whatever we wish."

She gave a little twist of her hand and drummed her fingers in the air as if playing scales on a piano keyboard. The book floated out of my hand and hovered for a moment before she lowered her hand with the palm down. The book eased back into my grasp.

"Levitation," she said proudly. "Basic, but requires finesse, control of movement, and control of your power. You've already shown you can do this, but we want you to be able to do it without exhausting yourself, and with precision."

"So, magic is going to teach me an easier way to take out the trash?"

Without missing a beat, Fiona said, "And from my brief glimpse of your apartment, it's a skill you could use. You might want to reconsider giving it up."

Nice try, lady.

"I don't want magic," I said flatly.

"Then you'd be smart to cut the wisecracks and pay attention. We have a lot of work to do, but for now, read your book. We'll start again first thing in the morning."

"One thing," I said, feeling a little bad for being so rude. "Busby said something about an Exploding Heart Charm having killed him. Do you think that's true?"

"Unfortunately, I do and it's not an easy spell to pull off since the heart, although it's brimming with magic itself, has to be strong enough to resist the magical effects around it. Same with all the major organs in your body. I would give you *The Magic's Guide to Medical Anatomy* to look over, but you'd only scoff at the extra work.

"Nevertheless, because of the heart's inherent strength, any spells against it require strong magical ability and getting close to the person. Using magic to influence another person's body — from making them move against their will to making their organs fail — isn't exactly outlawed, but it is strictly against the Magical Moral Code."

"Wait. So, murder isn't outlawed here?"

"Of course murder is illegal, but it's very hard to prove. Magic leaves a trace, but most Magics who would commit murder would also know to disguise their magic, or they would use someone else's magic to do the deed."

"Use someone else's magic? Is our magic just floating around for anyone to grab, or are you talking about holding someone hostage and making them commit magic against their will?"

"You're more on the mark with the hostage idea, but you're not too far off with the floating magic. It's not much different from what we'll be doing with you, although you'll be doing it willingly. Magic can be channeled out of a person. If done by someone whose scruples aren't top notch, that magic can be stored and used later against another. When the magic is traced, it won't show any hint of the true perpetrator."

Okay, did I say I was intrigued? Strike that. I was fascinated. Still, that didn't mean I wanted anything to do with magic, especially if it could get me framed for murder.

"Then how do you prove anything? A Magic could kill someone, then say, 'Wasn't me, I must have been magically robbed.'"

"You would have made a great addition to the Magic Legal Defense Team," Fiona said wryly. "That's why conviction is so tough. Obviously, if someone is witnessed deliberately harming another Magic or non-magic, that person is punished, but without a confession or an eyewitness, convicting someone can be a tangled mess. Besides, even magic in the most highly trained hands can get away from you if you're not careful. There is a theory that the push for Prohibition was started because Magics were getting drunk too often and losing control of their powers."

"So someone gets sloppy with their magic and someone else ends up dead? That's more than a little scary."

"And that's why we train Magics from a very early age. Typically."

"And it's another reason why I want rid of it."

"Read your book, Cassie," she said with a tone of disappointed exasperation.

CHAPTER TWENTY-FOUR
SORCERER'S APPRENTICE

The thing with taking in strays is you worry about them when they stop coming around. This is especially true when your "stray" is a dead guy you need to keep track of. Which was why I balked when, after we left Fiona's and returned to my portal, Mr. Tenpenny (haltingly) told me he planned to stay the night in his own home.

"I can't just let you wander around. What if you get lost? Or what if someone killed you again? Wait. Can you be killed twice?" I shook my head. "No, never mind. I can't risk it. Mr. Wood's business depends on you."

While I was ranting, Mr. T had been writing. He turned the pad around for me to see.

There's no risk. There will be protections put around my house. And I have lived here for a couple decades. I have never gotten lost. I doubt I will start doing so now.

I wanted to ask if those protections would guard him from his grandson, but held back my accusation.

"You promise you won't go wandering off on some *Weekend at Bernie's* escapade?"

I don't know what that means, but yes, I promise not to wander off, get lost, or get murdered a second time. You'll be better able to study without me in your apartment. Besides, your couch is terribly uncomfortable.

With a *Titanic* amount of misgivings, I relented. Mr. Tenpenny wished me farewell and told me what time my lessons would start the next morning.

A hollow pit of worry formed in my gut as I watched Mr. T. head off toward Magical Main Street. Once he was out of sight, I opened the door to my portal and stepped through my messy closet and into my apartment.

Don't tell the Magics this, but despite the background hum of worry over Mr. T, a love of magic thrilled through me at being able to come and go from my place without dealing with Morelli. I would also hate them to know that once I'd gotten Pablo fed, I whiled away the rest of the afternoon devouring the entirety of the book Fiona had given me. I didn't even stop to eat, and instead spent my usual dinner time attempting to use the principles covered in the book.

I'll admit my attempts were clumsy. After Fiona's comment, I decided my apartment could use a tidying up. Since my books were the biggest source of the mess, it was time for those puppies to get themselves on the shelves where they belonged.

I'd like to say this went as smoothly as arranging those objects in Dunwiddle's exam room, but I hadn't even earned my magical learner's permit, so the slightest twist of my hands or flick of my fingers sent several tomes slamming into the wall. This prompted Morelli to shout up at me to "cut out that racket," so I merely tidied up the books the old-fashioned way before moving on to something softer.

I probably should have practiced on towels before jumping right into my already limited wardrobe, but hindsight is twenty-twenty and I ripped more than a couple t-shirts in half while trying to magically fold them. Again, feeling frustrated, I cursed my supposed super powers as I ended up using nothing but elbow grease to hang and fold my scattered clothes. By the time I got to dusting, I was starving and had to take a break, during which I instantly made a box of donuts disappear. Voila!

I must say, once I'd consumed that completely unbalanced meal, I felt more energized and managed to polish, sweep, and tidy my way into the midnight hour, after which I fell into my freshly-sheeted bed exhausted and craving more donuts.

In the morning, my breakfast was interrupted by a knock coming from my closet. This gave me only a slight start, but it scared the furballs out of Pablo, who had been curled up on the couch with Fuzzy Mouse. I checked the clock. Exactly the time Mr. Tenpenny had told me to be ready. You certainly couldn't fault the Magics on their punctuality.

I couldn't hold back my wry grin when I opened the door and Fiona scanned the front room with an approving arch to her eyebrows. We then headed to her place for Day Two of Magic 101.

I thought I'd be training solely with Fiona, but that wasn't the case. We passed the better part of an hour discussing what I'd read. This had essentially been a more detailed explanation of what Fiona had told me the previous day about energy being magic, and how every living thing was magic to a degree. Like energy, magic can shift but it can't be created. Essentially, there's a finite amount of magic in the world and certain people can tap into it to boost their own magic. Taking magic from an object doesn't destroy it, but sapping all magic from a living being can kill it.

"So I'll never be truly rid of magic?" I asked her.

"No one is. Even MCs have magic within their cells, but only Magics can access their power to influence matter," she said, going over a bit of what she had told me the day before. "It's like we've all been given a door, but only some of us have the key to it. That's not to say some non-magics might not figure out how to get that door open, but it won't be as easy for them. So, yes, you will be left with the rudimentary vestiges of magic, but we'll be taking away your key to it."

"And this vestigial magic won't influence my work?"

"No," she said, but her tone didn't sound entirely convinced. I wanted to ask what she was hiding, but before I could, her doorbell rang and she announced it was time for my next lesson.

I followed Fiona down the stairs. Waiting on the ground floor was Lola, who looked especially glad to see me. She gave off the warm aroma of spicy cumin. It overtook the scent of Fiona's chalk and textbooks, and I wondered what amazing meals she'd been cooking. On the way to her place, which was a couple blocks over on a street that resembled and sounded like a street market on some Caribbean island, I asked her what she'd be teaching me.

"Let's just say you'll be learning how to tap into your magic to move objects in a controlled manner," she said with a suspicious amount of delight. "At its essence, everything I'll be having you do is a variation of the Shoving Charm."

"Shoving Charm?"

"Shoving, yes," she said as if she was concerned about my intelligence levels if I didn't know what the word *shoving* meant. "You push things away." Hell, this was going to be a cinch. I'd been keeping other humans at a distance my entire life. How hard could doing the same with inanimate objects be? "By varying the strength and dexterity you use, you can move whatever you need."

"I think I did that last night. I didn't know the name of the spell, but it did the trick to get my apartment cleaned up a bit."

"Oh, you really shouldn't be doing magic on your own like that."

"Why?"

"Well, I—" she said, clearly hunting for the right words. "Let's just say you need guidance. After all, if you learn a spell wrong, you might develop bad habits that can take months to correct. Best to learn it right the first time. And with me, you will learn it right."

She was covering something up and I wanted to point out that I wouldn't be sticking around for months, but with Lola I couldn't find any motivation to argue. I just felt so content with her and even a little excited about my upcoming lesson.

Unfortunately, that excitement faded as I soon realized my lesson was going to be very hands on. Not that I minded the practical work, but after showing me what she wanted done and giving some vague instructions on how to perform the Shoving Charm with precision and control, Lola went to the kitchen to work on a crossword while I spent my time doing a good deal of magical broom sweeping, charming a cloth to swipe itself over dusty surfaces, and conjuring dishes into the dishwasher, which she claimed was meant to teach me how to manage delicate objects. I'd basically been roped into an hour of free housekeeping.

The only thing that kept me motivated were the coconut-and-almond butter cookies Lola kept insisting I eat. Regardless of the treats, I was beginning to feel like Mickey Mouse chasing after brooms in *The Sorcerer's Apprentice*.

"Couldn't you just magic the food off the plates?" I asked.

"You could, but the dishwasher is much less time-consuming."

"So is having someone else do it," I muttered, but Lola's ears were keen.

"Oh, but you are a natural, Sweetie. You excel at the Shoving

Charm." See, told you I would be good at it. "I have to say, this level of work normally isn't even attempted until second-year midterms are over." Despite myself, a warm burst of pride zipped through me. "But that should be no surprise." Before I could ask what that meant, she was rambling on without pause. "Are you tired? It's always exhausting using your power the first few times."

I hadn't noticed until she mentioned it, but even though my domestic skills were long out of practice, for just doing a light bit of housekeeping, my muscles felt heavy with fatigue and the only thing that kept me from flopping onto the couch was the fact that I had just spent five minutes concentrating on magically fluffing the cushions without ripping them to shreds.

"I am. A little."

"Well, it's a lucky thing you're off to Alastair next. Alastair," she said the name wistfully, her eyes sparkling with a nostalgic smile, "he always doted on you."

Doted? Always? I didn't even know who this guy was. I wondered if Lola was confusing me with someone else.

"Anyway," she said, snapping back to her usual bubbly tone, "he'll be doing more background work with you."

I soon came to learn that *background work* meant lectures, while *practical work* meant actually using magic instead of simply being told about it. I honestly couldn't fathom why I needed so much background work. I mean, wouldn't it be a better use of everyone's time to concentrate on the steps needed to cram my magic genie back into the bottle it came from?

Just as Lola started eyeing the mop and bucket, a timer went off. With a disappointed twist to her lips, Lola gave me directions to my next class. It didn't sound too far, so I figured there was little risk of getting lost. I headed straight down her boisterous and colorful street until I reached Main Street where I turned left. About a block later, came the temptingly sweet, rich scent of chocolate. Like a cartoon character lured by a cloud of fragrance, I followed the chocolate vapors until I came to a cake shop with the name Spellbound Patisserie written in scrolling silver letters on a lavender sign. In the main window a display of artfully decorated desserts tempted passersby, while outside stood five bistro-style wrought-iron tables with two chairs each.

My stomach let out a loud grumble. Magic did take a great deal of effort and I was famished. I checked my pocket and felt several bills. If I skipped class, what would it matter? I could just say I got lost. I mean, I'd only be missing background work. A boring lecture versus a colossal cupcake? Not a tough competition. I veered off course and approached the patisserie's door.

CHAPTER TWENTY-FIVE

SPELLBOUND WITH ALASTAIR

I had my hand on the ornate door pull, when the shop's door whisked opened and I came face-to-face with the dark-haired, book-dropping man from the day before. At the sight of him, my heart jumped into my throat. I told myself it was just the shock, but I found myself staring dumbly into bright blue eyes.

Darting my gaze away from this social blunder, I saw he was holding a lavender box with a tidy white ribbon looped around it. Would he drop it like he did the book? I was so hungry, if he did, dignity be damned, I might just fall to my hands and knees and nibble the crumbs off the ground. Luckily, he kept tight hold of the box and I didn't have to embarrass myself.

"Cassie! Oh good I thought I was late. I'm Alastair," he said, shifting the box to his left hand to shake with the right. His hair still looked like it refused to be fully tamed by a brush, but his eyes shone when he took my hand, which he withdrew more quickly than is considered polite. "So, it is true about you. I was going to have our lesson at my workshop, but since we're here, have a seat."

He indicated one of the outdoor tables. We sat down and he began undoing the ribbon of the box. A plump woman with rosy cheeks and grey hair bustled out with two plates and two forks.

"Coffee, tea?" she asked as Alastair fidgeted in his pocket for something. I agreed to a tea, feeling annoyed by my lack of control over my own schedule. I mean, what's the point of being an adult if you can't skip class now and then?

"And I'll have coffee," Alastair said to the woman who passed him a knowing smile as she deftly whisked the ribbon off the box and extracted a square cake on a silver cardboard platter from the container. After setting the treat in the center of the table, she waddled off to fill our order.

In a record amount of time, she returned with our drinks. As I dunked my tea bag just to have something to do with my hands, Alastair rooted around in the pocket of his perfectly fitted jacket, pulling out bolts, some pieces of copper wire, and finally a silver metal sphere slightly smaller than a ping pong ball. He then placed the ball on the table. As he stuffed his other trinkets back into the jacket pocket, the ball unfurled and sprouted legs, making it look like some type of beetle. It then began pacing back and forth across the table top.

"Timer. My own invention," he said with a touch of shy pride before we both fell into an awkward silence as we tried our best to avoid eye contact, which wasn't a challenge for me as my eyes kept drifting back to the platter of deliciousness before me. My stomach broke the silence by letting out a circus-lion level growl.

"Stupid me," Alastair said, clearly flustered with himself. He reached for the cake server, got a clumsy hold on it, then fumbled and dropped the utensil. In a flash, he snapped his fingers and the silvery utensil paused in midair about two inches from the ground. After an audible sigh of relief, he glanced up through thick eyelashes and gave a self-deprecating shrug. "I assumed you'd be famished after Lola's and I've been dying for an excuse to buy this. I hope you're not sugar-free or gluten-free or any of that. If you are, that'll quickly change once you delve deeper into your magic."

"No, not in the least." I stared at the cake. It was coated in a layer of ganache so shiny it reflected the bakery's awning. Decorating the center of each pre-sliced square was a fine sprinkling of gold leaf. It looked like golden stars over a decadent chocolate sky. That sounds poetic, but really I just wanted to drop my face into the thing and munch my way to the bottom.

Luckily, my manners were stronger than my hunger and I waited as Alastair used the server to lift one piece onto my plate before serving himself. "Sacher Torte. Enough chocolate richness to kill an elephant." He caught himself and I was glad to see I wasn't the only socially awkward human at the table. "Don't worry, I'm not going to be teaching you animal murder. Actually, maybe we should just start with any questions you might have."

No one had given me a class schedule or syllabus, so I had no clue what Alastair was supposed to be teaching me. I'm sure I was meant to ask something about how magic works or why being magic should require me to give up a sugar-free lifestyle if I'd ever been mad enough to adopt one, but I had a more pressing question.

"You were startled when you saw me yesterday. So much so, you dropped your book. Why?"

Alastair's cheeks flared with warmth. Then, along with the smell of chocolate and, oddly enough, raspberries even though there were none on the cake, I caught an aroma of nutmeg, or perhaps cinnamon, and assumed the barista must have added it to Alastair's coffee.

"I thought you were someone else," he said softly. "And then to see Busby with you after what I'd heard. Well, it was just a surprise." He finished his answer by filling his mouth with a forkful of cake.

His answer was clearly not the whole truth, but if he wasn't going to be honest about it straight away, I wouldn't press it. Not yet anyway. After all, there was food to eat.

I took a bite of the torte and swore I would never be able to eat a Hostess cupcake again with any satisfaction. My whole body tingled as if my very cells were vibrating with the deliciousness of what I had put in my mouth. So what if Alastair had been evasive, so what if he was acting weird. Who cared? Cake as good as this suddenly made me feel very non-confrontational.

"What is true about me?" I asked, then took a sip of the rich, fragrant tea whose bergamot scent reminded me of Mr. Tenpenny.

"Sorry?" Alastair said after taking a drink of coffee that smelled like the version of coffee all other coffees aspire to be.

"When you shook my hand you said it was true what they say about me. What do they say about me?"

"Well, since you're on the crash course, I might as well be out with it. You're an absorber."

"So I've heard. What's the big deal with that?"

"To put it simply, you pull magic from others. You haven't learned to control yours, so just being near you is draining." He'd been lifting another forkful of cake to his mouth when he said this, but the action halted almost as if someone had tapped the pause button. "Sorry, I didn't mean— You're not—"

I put up a hand to stop the apology. I swallowed the cake that no longer tasted so sweet. "I've heard that from more than one person," I told him, thinking of a couple terrible first dates, a few foster parents, and Morelli.

"They were idiots," Alastair said quietly. The mechanical

beetle paused in its duties, then turned to Alastair as if watching him. Alastair made a shooing motion with his fingers and the creature resumed its pacing while I shifted uncomfortably. Did I say the cake lost its sweetness? This seemed like the perfect time to double check, so I ran a very scientific taste test with another couple bites. I'd been wrong, the cake was just as tasty as before and I would have been more than willing to shove the rest of it into my face.

The discomfort was eased by the grey-haired serving woman dropping by to bring us a second round of coffee and tea. Once she bustled away, Alastair continued the lesson, if that's what this was.

"Anyway, absorbing is very rare — have Runa explain the genetics of it better when you get to her. It's one reason why it's vital to get you trained. Normally, we start officially training Magics when they're eleven or twelve, although they do get some education at home before then. But the few children born with absorbing skills start training at five or six to make sure they control their ability. Did you never notice some people feel tired or cranky after time with you?"

Tired I wasn't sure about, but cranky would be a nice way to describe the various foster parents I'd been passed between. And Tobey Tenpenny. It was like my very presence annoyed him.

"I don't spend time with many people. Not living ones anyway. But I don't understand, Fiona said my magic could be soothing."

"To some Magics, yes. Your magic is very strong and you give off a, I don't know, a *hum* I suppose is the best word. That hum can relax a well-trained Magic who's confident in his or her abilities. But that's also a problem since that relaxation can be used to lull a Magic and make him or her a little dopey. Combine that with your absorbing, a dark motivation, and you can see how it could be a problem. It's one reason," he pointed to the beetle, "why we're only spending an hour with you at a time. Your ability to absorb is so strong you pull magic from others."

"I'm sorry?" I wasn't sure why, but it did seem like something to apologize for. "So, I'm like a magical vampire?"

"But unwillingly so. And yours is different. Most absorbers have a condition which limits the amount of their natural power, the power they're born with. That's why they need to absorb to maintain any functional level of magic."

"That seems a bit leech-y."

Alastair gave an off-handed shrug with one shoulder. "We allow it to a degree. It used to be a requirement, like giving alms to the poor. But in the past century we've perfected the ability to give transfusions. Well, I say perfected, but transfusions are still only reliable between blood relatives, and even that's not one hundred percent. Still, it's a much safer, more controlled way to share magic.

"But you, you don't need donations or transfusions. You don't need to absorb magic since you're already naturally endowed with so much. Once you can tap into your skills, you'll be able to block the channels that unwittingly cause you to absorb power and we'll all be able to spend more time with you."

At that comment, Alastair tried to hide the bloom in his cheeks by taking a long sip of his coffee. I'll admit, his fumbling mannerisms, attractive face, and great taste in desserts gave him a definite appeal. But I had no desire to get involved in this community, and that meant keeping my distance from any flirtations. Not that I had any talent at flirting, mind you, but if I did, this would be a good time to crush that talent under the heel of my off-brand Keds.

"Is that why everyone reacts so strongly toward me? Magics, anyway."

"No, not exactly." He paused to take a bite of cake, but I think he was biding time to decide how to answer. When he had finished his morsel, he continued, "Part of it is your age. You're what, late twenties?" I nodded, somewhat surprised. Despite my height, most people assume I'm still in my teens. "By your age most people have completed training and are in full control of their magic. Think of it like how little kids run around naked without any thought about their nudity because they're innocent. You're sort of still at that magically-innocent, running-around-nude stage, and it's a little surprising to people."

I tucked my head down to concentrate on my cake crumbs. It was like being told you had a chronic case of bad breath when you'd never noticed it on yourself.

"Sorry, I'm an idiot. I didn't mean to embarrass you."

He reached out and gave my arm a consoling pat.

"It's fine, really."

Because I was busy telling the fluttering butterflies in my stomach to knock it off or I would dose them with pesticide, the words came out more curtly than I intended. Alastair jerked his hand away at the rebuking tone. But even the brief touch left my bicep tingling where his fingers had been and I wondered if I'd been sucking power from my teacher. Was that grounds for detention?

"It's nothing to worry about and if you were going through the full training to stay with us, you'd have it whipped into shape in little time. I'm sure of it."

"And the other part?" I asked, taking a forkful of cake to hide my grin. I liked Alastair. Not as in *like* like. I was firmly resolved to not add any more factors to this already complicated equation, but as in liking him as an ally. After all, so far, he had been the person most open to telling me things straight and I planned to take full advantage of his chocolate-

and-caffeine-fueled rambling.

"That's exactly what I hoped we could talk about. I was wondering if maybe we could get—"

Was he going to ask me out? I think he was going to ask me out. My mind was screaming that I had to say no, there could be no romantic or platonic attachments to this place. I mean, I wanted to talk to him more, but that had to be strictly confined to a classroom setting. Or a patisserie setting, as the case may be. But the little lovelorn devil on my shoulder whispered at me to say yes. After all, there might be dessert.

Just as the devil was about to take over my tongue and blurt "yes" before Alastair could even finish his question, someone was calling my name. Holy Merlin, I groaned inwardly, not sure if I was disappointed or relieved. I heard my name again.

The voice was familiar and easily recognizable. It couldn't already be time for another lesson, could it? The timer beetle was still strolling and there was still cake to eat. I turned toward the sound and there was Corrine Corrigan, red hair flopping as she hurried toward us. Was I learning delivery management systems in my next class?

"I heard you were here and I just had to catch up to you. Here," she reached into the pocket of her flamboyant muumuu and pulled out a wad of cash. "Your back pay. I felt just awful about closing up like that since I knew you needed the money, but I had to. I thought if I closed up tight enough I could stop him, but it all went tits up in the end anyway. Oh my." Her eyes bulged from her head like a cartoon wolf who's just caught sight of a sexy she-wolf. "Is that Sacher Torte?"

"It is," Alastair said warily, then offered, "Have a piece?"

"Should you be feeding her that?"

I slowly put down my fork. Alastair caught my reaction and gave an apologetic grin. I couldn't tell if the apology was over

Corrine's intrusion, over missing out on asking what he'd been about to ask, or over whatever it was he shouldn't be doing with me and the cake.

Corrine, between devouring mouthfuls of the sinful dessert and gushing over missing her shop in Portland, didn't leave much dead space for conversation.

After we'd polished off another round of drinks and two slices of the cake, the mechanical beetle emitted a tinkling chime then curled itself into a tight ball that rolled into Alastair's waiting palm.

"Runa should just be back from her lunch."

"It must be twelve-thirty," Corrine said, amusement filling her words.

"She's more reliable than most clocks," said Alastair.

Corrine turned her attention to me to explain. "She really is, you know. Very punctual. Always in the shop at eight on the dot, lunch exactly at eleven-thirty, and never more or less than sixty minutes for that lunch. And, dear Gandalf, don't ever be late for an appointment." Corrine shook her head gravely as if she'd experienced the wrath of Runa on more than one occasion.

Inwardly, I groaned. If Alastair was proving himself my favorite teacher so far, Runa already ranked as my least preferred resident of MagicLand. But that was okay. I had a feeling I wasn't top on her list of new acquaintances either.

"Which means you best be off," Alastair said. "You're cutting it close, but if you hurry, you'll still be on time."

I thanked Alastair for the cake, much of which was quickly disappearing into Corrine's mouth. He stood and shook my hand.

Instinctively avoiding eye contact, I glanced down and noticed that despite the perfect cut of his suit, he'd put on two different shoes that morning — one black oxford and one red Converse sneaker. The sight amused me so much I forgot myself and looked up. When I met his eyes, they held a strange mix of apology and admiration. The introvert in me balked at the look. It felt too much like something I could get used to. I pulled my hand back — the tingling sensation more intense this time — and, without saying another word to him, I dashed off to Runa's clinic.

CHAPTER TWENTY-SIX

FEATHERS AND FILMS

The overhead bell jingled when I stepped into the cheery blue interior of Runa's shop/clinic/pharmacy. She was at the counter, a smile brightening her broad face as she chatted with a couple of customers. Her glasses hovered near her shoulder, giving the impression they were eavesdropping. The moment I entered, Runa's eyes locked on me. Her gaze shifted to the clock on the wall and her smile dropped faster than a boulder on a cartoon coyote.

The two people turned to see what had changed her mood so suddenly. They looked at me, then looked back to Runa. She pulled a see-what-I-have-to-put-up-with face. They nodded sympathetically then collected their purchases and headed for the door, giving me strange, sidelong looks the whole way out.

Um, could I just go back to the chocolate torte now?

"In there, Black," Runa said as she jutted a finger toward the exam room. Part of me wanted to turn around and walk out. I didn't have to put up with her attitude. But another part knew I had to do this for Mr. Wood, and an even bigger part swarmed with a mix of curiosity and of wanting to prove myself to her.

Dr. Dunwiddle had me do the same tests she'd put me through the day before. Not the channeling thing, perhaps her fire insurance wasn't paid up, but the arranging of objects. I found I could do it more easily this time, and the task didn't wipe me out. Once I'd arranged everything in alphabetical order, then reverse alphabetical order, then in order by weight, she eyed me in that skeptical way like she was just dying to find something that could throw me off so she could claim I wasn't worth her time. When the corner of her lips lifted into a knowing smile, I have to say I was a little nervous.

"Try to make the feather disappear."

"Can I do that?"

I didn't mean did I have the skills to make it disappear. I'd read *The Principles of Physics and Magic,* and nothing in there had indicated that invisibility was physically possible. Of course, I was no expert — as Dr. Dunwiddle would be the first to proclaim — but it seemed if, like energy, magic couldn't be destroyed, it shouldn't be possible to make something vanish.

"You don't actually make it disappear," she said with annoyance, as if I should have been learning this stuff since I was twelve. Oh wait, I guess I should have been, but the foster parents I had when I was that age probably ate my Hogwarts' owl. "You displace the molecules so the feather isn't visible. You're using your magic energy to stretch apart the bonds of the object." She abruptly stopped talking and her eyes widened as if she just remembered something. "As part of the Magic Morality Code, I have to remind you this is something you should only use on non-living objects. It can get messy with living things. Fiona will teach you more of the principles behind it, but I just want to see if you can do it."

I bet you do.

"So, if I'm just putting some distance between the molecules, I can't make it disappear in one place and reappear in another?"

She eyed me as if I shouldn't be asking such a thing.

"With the amount of magic you have, you probably could, but

you're getting rid of your magic," she said with tart dismissiveness, "so you won't need to advance that far, will you?"

"Nope," I said curtly, trying to give the impression that I wasn't one bit curious. Which I totally was. I started to concentrate on the feather, then a thought struck me. "How do I get it back together in the right order?"

"That's where the real lesson begins. But I'll give you credit, most trainees don't think that far ahead. They just want to—" She waved her hands in the air in a magician's flourish.

I focused on the feather. As before, I was given no instruction. For all their emphasis on the whole training thing, "training" seemed mostly about making me figure things out on my own. I probably could've done an online self-study course for all the instruction I was being given. The only thing I could think of was the feather becoming a bunch of tiny feathers and those tiny feathers becoming microscopic feathers. Sort of like zooming in on a fractal in which each component is a smaller version of the larger design.

To create and hold this image in my mind, I kept my eyes closed. I'd just zoomed in on the fourth level of my feather fractal when Dr. Dunwiddle gasped. My eyes flew open, expecting to see a real screwup, like maybe having coated Runa in feathers and making the whole room disappear. Instead, I saw nothing. Well, not nothing. The room was still there, Dr. Dunwiddle was unfortunately still there, but the feather was visibly gone.

I smiled with a sense of pride I wasn't used to.

"No training?" she asked again, as if I had somehow secretly acquired a PhD in Magic. I shook my head and started to say something smart when she snapped her fingers. The feather reappeared, then settled itself back on the shelf. "Time for genetics," she said abruptly.

The moment she said this, the lights dimmed and an image appeared, not exactly on the wall opposite me, but sort of hovering just in front of the wall. A short movie went on to explain that magic was a genetic trait just like eye color. There were recessive genes that could be masked by dominant genes, which explained why some people had more power or different skills than others.

I started to drift off at this point. I had too much sugar in my system for sleep, but the narrator had a droning, monotonous voice that sent my attention wandering. Where was my Transfiguration class? Potions, perhaps? Wasn't Madame Hooch expecting me for my first broom-riding lesson?

However, when the narrator said something about absorbers, I perked up. Absorbing was apparently recessive, as was giving, which was the ability to put magic into others. Reverse vampire magic, as I thought of it. If two absorbers or two givers had a child, the power of the offspring's absorption would be exponentially more than either of the parents. This was followed up by an old, severe-looking white man giving a public service announcement that basically said, if left uncontrolled, a strong absorber child could take power unwittingly. And in some cases, could even drain other Magics.

"Parents," he said with stern gravity, "for the safety of yourselves and for the community, get your children tested and trained at an early age. They could be absorbers."

Dr. Dunwiddle stopped the film with a snap of her fingers and scowled at me. "Now do you understand things better?"

That guy's final words had dug a pit in my stomach and the digging had not been done by a recently sharpened spade, but by a vinegar-coated, raspy-edged tablespoon. No one had ever told me exactly why I'd been raised in foster care. Now I knew the reason for all the surreptitious half sentences and the truth to the questions no one wanted to answer. No wonder all my foster parents despised me. They must've known.

"I need to go," I said and pushed past Dr. Dunwiddle. When I charged out of her clinic and into the street, the spoon's painful digging finally hit bottom and my legs felt like the muscles had turned to Jell-o.

CHAPTER TWENTY-SEVEN
KITCHEN CONFESSIONS

Knowing what was about to happen and trying to avoid another round of strange looks from the stupid Magics, I staggered into an alley, then bent over and hurled out an unfortunate amount of Sacher Torte. When my stomach stopped heaving, someone's hand gripped my shoulder. I swatted it away.

"Time for a break," said a posh voice. I glanced over my shoulder. There was Mr. Tenpenny in a well-cut, navy blue suit. To keep it casual, he wore no tie and had left the top button of his crisp, white shirt undone. "I worried this would be too much."

"Eight. Eight syllables," I said and started laughing. I hadn't gotten very far down the side street and people passing by stared as I cackled, but what the hell, I was a witch, damn it! I had every right to cackle. I must've really been enjoying my own humor because my cheeks were dripping wet from my tears of sheer amusement. The worried stares turned sympathetic. I hated all of them. I hated all of this. I slumped into Mr. Tenpenny's cold embrace.

"Time for a rest. My kitchen's not far."

"Tobey won't like that," I said, or rather, gurgled through the phlegm my tears had worked up. Let's just say, I'm not the prettiest of criers.

"Never mind him. He's not home."

Mr. Tenpenny guided me down a couple zigzagging side streets. A small bookshop caught my attention. And it wasn't the books that drew my eye. Inside, just past a broad display window, were Tobey and Fiona. They were arguing and he had Fiona by the arm in a bruise-leaving grip. My foul mood roiled in me. Fiona's lessons may not include cake, but she had been kind to me. I thought of lightning, of any wild, dangerous thing, and Tobey's hand jerked away. Just like he'd been shocked.

Fiona stared at him, backing away as he spun to look out the window. I whipped my gaze forward, pretending I'd seen nothing, and kept pace with Mr. Tenpenny. I did wonder if I should say something to Mr. T, but surely Magics could take care of themselves if an untrained idiot like me could do what I think I had just done.

Once inside Mr. Tenpenny's kitchen, I dropped into one of the wooden chairs at the solid oak table. Mr. T put a beer in front of me. I do appreciate someone who understands my needs.

"Tobey usually keeps a good supply."

It almost made me feel better knowing I was drinking Tobey's stash. Tobey. What had he been doing with Fiona?

I guzzled it, barely coming up for air, while Busby remained politely silent as if he had all the time in the world to wait for me to be ready. Then again, he was dead. It's not like he was in a hurry to get anywhere.

Having just emptied my stomach, the potent microbrew hit me and my head buzzed pleasantly from the alcohol. I set down the bottle and looked up to Mr. Tenpenny, the heat of more tears just behind my eyes.

"I absorbed their power and everything else right out of them, didn't I? It's why I'm so strong. I've got the power of three Magics in me." The more I spoke, the more it made sense. *Oozing magic,* isn't that what everyone kept saying? No wonder. After sucking dry two adults, I must be like an overfilled water balloon, jiggling and about to burst at the lightest touch. "I need rid of this. Take it. I deserve to be extracted." I held out my arms like I was ready to give blood. "That's why everyone looks at me like I'm such a freak, isn't it?"

Mr. Tenpenny wore an expression of consternation mixed with pity. Great. A guy who had likely been murdered by his own grandson was taking pity on me. Not exactly a mood booster.

"What are you on about?" he asked.

"I killed my parents, didn't I? I just—" I made a sucking sound "—the magic and life right out of them."

"Don't be ridiculous." Pause. "Of course you didn't." Pause. "You were far too young."

"Then who?"

"The Mauvais."

Mr. Tenpenny paused and grabbed one of the new notepads I'd given him, but he didn't write. It was like he wanted it nearby just in case. Interspersed by many pauses to catch his breath, he told me, "The Mauvais had been plotting a coup. In fact, he had already been implementing many of the vicious and cruel measures he hoped to expand upon. He believed the Magical Moral Code should be abolished.

"He claimed to want the best for everyone, but what he truly desired was unlimited power over all Magics, with non-magics relegated to the status of little more than servants, slaves, pack animals. He never put out a full manifesto..." By the time he got to this pause, his face was drawn, and his upright posture had sagged. He was worn out.

"Maybe you should use smaller words," I suggested as I mentally tallied all the syllables he was managing in between pauses. Mr. Tenpenny smiled. Although his sharp features made his face stern at times, his smile was warm and kind. The sort of smile I hadn't seen much of in my life. He held up a finger in a give-me-a-moment signal, pulled in a few deep breaths, appeared revived, and went on.

"He used fear and lies to stir up a revolt against MCs who he claimed were keeping Magics from our true potential. Hogwash! We were doing quite well for ourselves, but some Magics, those who thought they were entitled to more from the world and who believed his lies would help them achieve that, fell into line behind him. He thrived on their hatred and greed. He craved the power he took from them even though, like you, he was naturally powerful."

Like me? A big pile of poo bricks came tumbling down.

"Was this Mauvais my father?"

Mr. Tenpenny shook his head, his upper lip curling in disgust.

"Certainly not. Never say such a disgraceful thing. Amongst other things, he took givers, some of the very givers who were backing him, and drained them to the point of near death." He paused, too briefly to fully catch his breath. "Very strong he became." Possibly realizing that swapping Zombie Speak for Yoda Speak was no way to keep the Grammar Police happy, this time he gave himself more of a break before continuing, "But he couldn't retain it. It leaked." Probably a common ailment of the older wizard. Did they wear Magical Depends? I bit back my smirk.

"The watch was the key. Your parents were investigators, the best ones we had. They succeeded in getting the watch, but—" He paused again for air, leaving me dangling on his cliff of information. "They didn't get him. Some wanted to call securing the watch a job done, but your parents saw it as a job unfinished." Pause. "They weren't supposed to continue on the case, but they received approval to go after the Mauvais." Pause. "On their last mission they, well—" At this pause, Mr. Tenpenny had to blink away the moisture in his eyes.

188

"He killed them?"

"Not your fault, okay?"

"What's not my fault?"

"They had a bad feeling. If they got caught—" Pause.

"He'd use them to boost his powers."

Mr. Tenpenny nodded. "Before they left for the mission to London — this is where the Mauvais had fled, we assume he had contacts there — they put a good amount of their power into you. They meant to only give some. They didn't know about you being an absorber." Pause. "Only the strongest Magics are in our police. You both inherited, as well as took in their strength."

"I drained them?"

"No, that would have been impossible. You were barely four years old." Pause. "But they might have given more than they intended."

My head suddenly felt like someone had poured bubbling lava into it.

"So I didn't kill them," I said, my words tainted with self-loathing. "I just made them too magically weak to fend him off."

"No, absolutely not." Mr. Tenpenny shook his head. "Listen to me. They were told they'd done enough, but they weren't ones to quit." Pause. "You have some of that stubbornness, I believe. I'd grown close to them in the time they were in London." Pause. "I was convinced they could do it. I made the call. I approved them to return to the building we suspected was the Mauvais's bolthole. I should have thought more of their safety."

"You?"

"I was their commanding officer. I oversaw the London side of the mission, I reviewed the case, I wrote up the reports." Mr. Tenpenny's fingers tapped on the notepad, but he refused to use his papery crutch. He pulled in a deep breath, then continued. "The decision was mine." The next pause seemed to have nothing to with gathering his breath and more to do with gathering his nerve. "They seemed in fighting form and one of my former top agents of security, Devin Kilbride, offered to go with them for added protection. We had just gotten the watch, we were riding a wave of confidence, and we believed any delay would waste all our efforts. In my rush, I may have been mistaken about their fitness. None of them returned. My haste meant the loss of three brave Magics."

The utter distress in his voice and in his face as he fought through this lengthy statement lessened my own self-pity.

"So, the Mauvais was able to kill them because they gave too much?" Busby nodded. "But maybe it wasn't your fault. What if my parents tricked you into thinking they were stronger than they actually were?"

"I don't know. None of the bodies were recovered. Without that evidence we can't say exactly what happened on that mission."

Mr. Tenpenny got up. This time, he pulled two beers from the fridge.

His hands shook as he levered the caps off with an opener attached to the side of the refrigerator. He handed me mine, then took a deep drink of his before sitting down. I sipped mine. The crisp, bitter taste hit my tongue as an idea popped into my head.

"Could they still be alive? Drained— No, extracted, like Runa said, and turned into magical imbeciles?"

Mr. Tenpenny shrugged. There wasn't even a milligram of hope in the movement.

See, this is why I'm a pessimist. Every time I try to look on the bright side, that little pixie of optimism gets crushed under the steel-toed boot of reality. I decided to change the subject.

"I've been thinking, I gave you back your watch and all that's settled, but you're still not dead. You claim you were killed.

Maybe you need someone to find your killer and bring him to justice?" Notice I said *him*. I wasn't being politically incorrect, I had my prime suspect and *he* was clearly a *him*. Mr. T nodded very slowly, as if not sure how to proceed. "If that happens, then you'll have settled your unfinished business, you'll go back to being dead, and Mr. Wood can stay in business."

Busby tilted his head in a way that said, *I haven't given it much thought.* I kicked myself for the blunt statement. Here he was playing the good host while I was plotting his death. Well, his second death. We sat in silence while we finished our beers. I don't know what Busby was getting from his, but I was hoping enough beer might cause the thoughts dancing around in my head to tumble over and stay down.

But I had no such luck as a vague image of my parents waltzed in with their heads lolling about dumbly and saliva drooling from their moronic lips. The dancing duo stopped in their tracks when the kitchen clock chimed.

"Not another lesson," I groaned.

This whole day had seen too many ups and downs. Why couldn't they just find another absorber to take my power from me and be done with it? Oh that's right, because I was one of the few absorbers in the magic world. Lucky me!

I started to get up, but Mr. T signaled me to remain seated. He opened the notebook and wrote:

I know you're in a rush to get trained and drained, but I think you've had more than enough for one day. I'll make arrangements so you can begin tomorrow's lessons with the class you were meant to finish today with. You'll have to start an hour earlier than you did this morning, but Gwendolyn's an early riser.

"Another class?" How many damn subjects did I need to study?

"Just one," he said.

"Great. What now? The Zoology of Magical Creatures?"

"No, that's a specialty course of study only offered after basic training."

Damn, I was kind of hoping to see a unicorn.

"What then?"

Mr. T grinned. I did not like that grin.

"You'll see. It's most students' favorite subject. Your parents excelled at it."

My parents also excelled at getting themselves killed and leaving me an orphan, but I didn't remind him of this.

CHAPTER TWENTY-EIGHT
A DEFLATING DEMONSTRATION

The following morning, I woke up just as the sun was beginning to lighten the sky. And in late May in Portland, that means early. This change in schedule didn't seem to trouble Pablo who was up and in the kitchen yowling for food as I did my best to get dressed, plop some breakfast into his dish, and gulp down a cup of tea before heading through my magic door.

The instructions Mr. Tenpenny had given me said to be at Spellbound Patisserie by five. There was a betraying skip in my chest when I saw the chairs upside down on the bistro tables and no one waiting for me with chocolate cake. I reminded myself that Alastair was a Magic and, therefore, off limits. I would be turning my back on this place in two weeks. No attachments. No commitments. The way I liked to live my life.

With the closed sign facing out, I expected the door to the shop to be locked, but when I pulled the handle, the latch clicked and the door swung open without any alarms being sounded. I would later learn that the majority of Magics don't bother much with locks because, as Mr. T had demonstrated at his own home, it wasn't difficult to magic them open.

The front of the shop was empty, but from the back came the

sound of someone humming. Feeling a bit like one of the Pied Piper's rats, I followed the tune behind the counter, through a swinging door, and into an open-plan kitchen with several workstations. At a sink, her back turned to me, was a tall woman. Keep in mind that I'm five-foot-ten, so me calling another woman tall means she's got to be Tall with a capital T.

"Hello?" I said hesitantly. "I'm here for..." I didn't really know what I was here for. Cake making? KP duty? Had Lola told this woman about my magical cleaning skills?

The woman whirled around. Her eyes were enthusiastically bright, and I couldn't fathom how anyone could have a face so filled with delight at such an early hour of the morning.

"Potions," she exclaimed.

My latest instructor had a long, oval face and a crown of brown curls. I surprised myself by instantly liking this woman, something incredibly rare in the World of Cassie. I usually start off hating people and assuming they detest me in equal measure. Except, of course, Mr. Wood, Lola, and Alastair, but liking him was mainly due to his cake-sharing ways.

The woman, who introduced herself as Gwendolyn after her boisterous greeting, handed me an apron. Thankfully, I didn't have to don a chef's hat, although she was wearing one. After our introductions, she told me to stand beside her at a wooden kitchen island on which were arranged small, unlabeled dishes of ingredients. I felt as if we were preparing to film a cooking show.

"Do you know why I love potions?" she asked. Her voice carried an accent that blended upper crust East Coast with a touch of random European flair. She gave me no time to answer. "Because even the least talented Magic can read a recipe. You only need the barest smidge of accessible magic to make a potion work."

194

Accessible magic, I was to learn during Fiona's lesson that day, was the magic that made Magics magical. As Fiona and Lola had informed me, all living creatures have magic in their cells, but that magic remains dormant for most. Unlike Norms, Magics have a way of nudging their cellular-level magic to raise it from dormancy. Dolphins, elephants, whales, even octopi also have this ability, but they seem to mostly use it for communication, social hierarchy, problem solving, and what we humans think is their instinctive navigation.

Gwendolyn continued, "That's not to say there aren't more complicated potions that require advanced skills, but even an Untrained can sometimes manage a simple spell."

"Sorry, Untrained?"

"Oh, I don't like the word either." Her hat slipped to one side as she shook her head in distaste. "It's not even accurate. All children are untrained until they're pre-teens, except for absorbers who start early. I'm working to get the term *Untrained* changed. It should really be *Untrainable* since it refers to a person who should be Magic but simply can't tap into their power. They can't be trained. So, really, they're untrainable. But I suppose it's easier to say untrained."

"Why *should* someone be Magic?"

"If someone has Magic parents, the child should be Magic, but there are rare instances when that doesn't happen. Oh, enough of this, we're delving into Runa's territory. Let's get cooking, shall we?" She readjusted the hat on her head. "We'll begin with a simple recipe for color change."

Okay, while I did like Gwendolyn and admired her ability to be so enthusiastic at this hour of the day, it wasn't long before I wanted to beat my head on the wooden surface in front of me. As Gwendolyn instructed me on how to read a recipe and the purpose of each ingredient, I couldn't stop wondering what in all of MagicLand this had to do with getting my magic out. Still, if this class was meant to be easy, it might be a nice break in the routine of energy-draining practical work and brain-draining background work.

After her lecture was over, Gwendolyn and I each placed a bowl in front of us. And sorry to disappoint, but these were just regular glass mixing bowls, not cauldrons. Together, we measured out the ingredients and stirred them together at the same rate and in the same direction, which apparently was very important. I was tempted to give one backward stir to see what might happen, but I decided to behave on my first day.

Once she declared the concoction had been thoroughly mixed, Gwendolyn pulled out a pair of white mice from her apron pocket. I slapped down my mixing spoon.

"We can't give them this," I protested. "One of those plants we used is poisonous."

"Excellent identification skills, Cassie. But don't worry. The dash of chameleon skin we added not only serves as a color reagent, but also reverses the effects of most poisons. Now, watch."

From a drawer she took out a pair of droppers. She handed me one, then used hers to suck up some of the clear potion from her bowl. Gwendolyn gave the bulb a squeeze until a bead of liquid dangled off the end of the dropper. She then held the tip out to one of the mice. Its whiskers twitching, it sniffed the offering for a few seconds, then lapped up the droplet.

I waited for the mouse to collapse, convulse, or cry out. It didn't. Instead, its fur turned pink. And not just any old pink. The bubble gum tone shimmered, then bands of white and hot pink faded into each other and seemed to cascade over the mouse like a neon sign.

"Just a little of my own touch," Gwendolyn said cheekily. "I'm such a showoff. Now you. Yours will just turn pink. Normally, trainees can only manage a weak blush, but I bet with your power, your mouse is going to end up a very brilliant magenta."

Using my own dropper, I gave my mouse a taste. As easy as everything else had been — except, of course, getting rid of my magic — I fully expected my mouse to put on a Vegas light show like Gwendolyn's.

I waited. Nothing happened.

"That guy is a little chubby," said Gwendolyn as her hat drooped a few inches forward. "Maybe he needs another drop to get the right dosage. Go on, try again."

The mouse licked up two more drops and still nothing. Gwendolyn made a noise of confusion and levitated the mouse so it was level with her face. She pushed her hat back and examined the creature, who didn't seem to mind being airborne and kept twitching its whiskers with interest. "No, he's definitely swallowed it." Her pink-strobing mouse watched as his friend was lowered back onto the table. "Maybe another taste."

I gave him another drop. He did really seem to enjoy it and even sat up to beg for more, but after drinking the full contents of the dropper, he remained stubbornly white.

"I was never much of a cook," I said to Gwendolyn's look of utter despair. Her hat had fallen in on itself like an unsuccessful soufflé. I couldn't help but want to find excuses for my failing. "It is really early for me and I did skip breakfast."

"Yes, maybe that's it," she said, her tone full of doubt. "I do hope it's not my teaching. I don't normally have a problem with this potion. Although, this is a third-week recipe. I just thought you'd be able to handle it. More basic then," she added with a decisive nod that flopped her limp hat forward then back. Running her index finger straight up from her head to a point about a foot above, the hat rose back into its proper upright place. "Now, how about something more natural? A hair growth potion, perhaps."

I'll just save you the agony and tell you that my naked mole rat remained very naked while Gwendolyn's ended up looking like something that could rival the fluffiest of dust mops.

By the time I left the Spellbound kitchen, I hadn't succeeded at a single recipe and Gwendolyn's hat had fully deflated.

CHAPTER TWENTY-NINE

LESSONS CONTINUE

Other than utterly disappointing Gwendolyn, the rest of that first week went well. I still didn't understand why I was a magic absorber, but I had come to accept that I was a total nerd for absorbing magical knowledge.

Fiona's job before she started her regular classes each day was to teach me the laws of magical physics, a topic I excelled at. She also sometimes drifted off into the social aspects of the magic community, which I was glad to let roll over me without ever sticking.

Runa taught me the biology of magic with a heaping dose of surliness. She held a grudge against me and it would have been tempting to skip her classes, but the information was simply too intriguing. Plus, I enjoyed throwing her complex questions. She acted irritated by them, but I like to think she was secretly impressed by my curiosity. Still, her usual demeanor toward me would have made Oscar the Grouch seem like a charmer, and there were a few times when I had to work very hard at controlling my magic to keep boxes of pills from flying at her head.

With her unending list of chores, I thought of Lola's class as my physical education time. Unlike high school gym class, her workouts always included at least half a plate of her homemade coconut cookies.

"I have to tell you, I've never had so many sweets since starting this training."

"It's important you keep your strength up."

"Yeah," I said with a laugh, "but I don't think this is the healthiest energy booster."

"Oh, but it is. Sugar is just what Magics need. It helps replenish your power and perks you up after a series of tough spells. The stuff goes straight into the magic bit of your cells and," she shimmied her shoulders like she was buzzing with excitement, "energizes them."

Before I could ask for more details about this amazing aspect of magic health, Lola indicated some streaks on the windows that needed taken care of before the lesson wrapped up. I don't know how she did it, but every time I showed up she managed to find something new that needed cleaning. By the end of my two weeks of training, her house would be gleaming from top to bottom.

Then there was Alastair. Although I found him attractive, my innate stubbornness to form any attachment to this community prevailed. Sure, we both stumbled over a few moments of awkwardness, and yes, I experienced some intense blushing when our eyes met for too long or our hands brushed against each other, but for the most part my determination to maintain an emotional distance and cool demeanor was winning out. We would be professional and practical, and I would not, definitely *not*, be charmed by the fact that he seemed incapable of leaving his house with matching his shoes, his socks, or both.

While they could have been the most awkward, Alastair's lessons were the ones I looked most forward to. And the presence of desserts at each one had only a small amount to do with it. Mainly it was that, once we settled into a lesson, he was easy to talk to, he didn't mind my endless questions, and in my second week of training, he came to my defense when Tenpenny the Younger strode by Spellbound Patisserie one afternoon and gave me a contemptuous sneer.

"Careful, Tobey," Alastair had said. "A Magic in a bad mood might set a Glacier Charm on your face." Tobey instantly looked away and seemed to be fighting against his own facial muscles in order to relax his snarl.

"What's a Glacier Charm?" I asked once Tobey had marched off.

"It freezes someone's face, arms, or whatever body part you're aiming for. It's not permanent, but it takes quite a long time to wear off. So, how are the lessons going?"

"I think I've fully destroyed Gwendolyn's confidence."

"Yes, she's making all her younger students work twice as hard to prove she really can teach." Alastair's eyes glinted with amusement. I chided myself for how much I liked that glint. "Now, Runa's schedule has changed, which means we only have fifteen minutes. So, questions?"

This was how every lesson started. Once cake, donuts, strudel, or tart had been served, I could ask whatever was on my mind regarding magical matters. Sometimes we never got to any of the cultural, legal, or historical stuff Alastair was supposed to be teaching me, but then again, when was I ever going to use that?

Actually, I wasn't sure what Alastair was meant to be teaching me. His timers — for this class he had pulled out a tiny metal turtle — showed he had mechanical skills, and Lola had mentioned once that he was well-trained in defensive spells. But was he teaching me anything fun like building an automaton that could defeat Morelli or a slick hand motion that could erase Cologne Carl's memory? No. Instead, I could ask questions. And, despite telling myself I had no interest in the world of MagicLand, I somehow always had more questions than could be answered in the time we were allotted.

Alastair snapped his fingers. The turtle began trundling between us as I launched into my first question of the day.

"Why are givers more common than absorbers? I mean, if two givers can make an absorber, and there's lots of givers, it seems that absorbers should be everywhere and the numbers would eventually even out."

"Givers aren't common. Most people have a fair balance of giving and absorbing in them, but there's just a slight favor toward the giving side."

"Okay, but relative to absorbers, givers are supposed to be common."

"We need chocolate if we're going to tackle this." Only moments after he said this, the grey-haired serving woman brought out two of the biggest brownies I'd ever seen. Alastair pulled off a piece with his long fingers and popped it in his mouth, savoring the taste before answering.

"Absorbers were treated with suspicion in the past. No matter who it was or how much good they did, they were assumed to be bad wizards. Evil. The leeches of magic. We can go over the cultural history of all this if it interests you." I shook my head to decline. I only had to get through the next week and didn't want to add to my workload.

Alastair shrugged, then continued, "It was only discovered relatively recently that absorbing was merely an uncommon recessive trait — sort of like albinism. It wasn't something that could determine a Magic's goodness or badness. My theory of why absorbing is so uncommon is that absorbers were shunned for so long. The gene simply didn't have the time or chance to spread much. Givers, on the other hand, were seen as too good.

People were afraid that by marrying a giver, other Magics would think they were taking advantage of the giver. That's why givers often paired up together, and it's why Busby never wed Fiona. He's still of the old mindset and worries what others will think."

"Mr. Tenpenny is... *was* a giver?"

"No, Fiona is."

About a dozen gears went clicking and clacking and whirring in my head. Tobey. What had he been doing to Fiona that day at the bookstore?

"So, could a giver be forced to share their magic, say if threatened?"

"A long time ago givers used to have to do just that. It was called Contribution and they were forced to give magic to people who wanted more power. The Mauvais took this to an extreme level."

"Like magical rape?" Alastair nodded and broke off another piece of brownie. "Does it still happen?"

"Where are you going with this?" he asked, still holding the morsel.

"Look, I think we're agreed that Mr. Tenpenny died because someone thought he had a watch that could boost power. So let's assume that someone close to Mr. T wants more magic. I saw Tobey with Fiona. He was angry and grabbing her arm. If Fiona's a giver, Tobey could be working with the Mauvais. Fiona said there had been rumors of the Mauvais trying to come back to power. He'd need support from someone in the community for that. Tobey seems disgruntled with so many things. He'd make an excellent helper monkey for an evil wizard. Or," I blurted with sudden insight, "what if Tobey wanted to become the new Mauvais. He might—"

"He's not," Alastair said, sharply cutting me off. Then he said nothing. No clarification, no apology, nothing. Did he not realize that only made me more curious?

"It should be looked into, though, shouldn't it?" I persisted. "I mean, he's too young to be the Mauvais, but if he's working to help—"

"Enough, Cassie. Tobey—"

Just then, Alastair's turtle timer stopped walking and tucked its legs into its shell. "Lesson's over. Promise me you'll drop the Tobey matter. He's got attitude, but he's not a bad guy."

"Until you surprise him by bringing home his dead grandfather."

"Promise me, or I'll start making you pay for all these pastries."

I made a vague promise, but underneath the table, I had my fingers crossed.

I then spent a very distracted hour with Dr. Dunwiddle. I had read plenty of Agatha Christie. I knew my Sherlock Holmes from Baskervilles to Belgravia. I was bursting with my brilliant deduction and I was itching to reveal the truth about Tobey Tenpenny with a Hercule Poirot-style flourish.

CHAPTER THIRTY

THE WANDERING WIZARD

After what seemed like eternity, Runa's lesson finally wrapped up. My toe tapping, finger drumming, and general fidgeting made her snap at me a few times, but other than that, I was too wrapped up in my own thoughts and plans to purposely irritate her.

Why should I do this? Why not just keep my head down and remain my usual Cassie self? The Cassie who didn't get involved. The Cassie who didn't stick her neck out. The Cassie who most definitely did not make public spectacles of herself.

Because of my parents. I had no idea who they were. I didn't even know their names. If one ever existed, no heartwarming photo of Mom and Dad cuddling their infant girl had made it with me beyond Foster Home Number One. But all my life I'd blamed them for my lot. I'd cursed them for ditching me and leaving me to be raised by a string of horrible people. Okay, there was one nice family, but my time with them was cut abruptly and painfully short.

But after learning my parents had been killed. Killed while trying to protect an entire community, including me, made me see them in a whole new light. I wanted whoever hurt them, whoever stole them from me to be punished. Because that person, or persons, had caused much of my childhood to be spent in pain and fear and had turned me into the socially moronic, introvert-to-the-extreme you see today.

And if Tobey was now part of the group who did that to me, I wanted him to face the consequences. Like I told Alastair, Tobey was too young to be the original Mauvais, which meant I couldn't lay my parents' deaths on him. But if he was working for the Mauvais, he deserved a very big wrench thrown into his attitude-filled gears.

After that first lesson, my classes with Gwendolyn had been held after the patisserie closed. But this evening's class had been cancelled so Gwendolyn could give the Spellbound kitchens a deep cleaning. And no, this had nothing to do with my disastrous potion making. It had been planned long before I'd ever stepped foot into the Spellbound kitchens.

This meant once the bell above Runa's door ting-a-linged my exit, I was done with classes for the day. I'd never loitered around MagicLand after lessons. One, I had no interest in this place or these people. Two, Pablo was very demanding in his feeding times. But tonight I had an interest, which meant Pablo's greedy belly would just have to wait.

I stood outside Runa's clinic pondering which direction to head. It was Friday. Where would most people be right now? Where would a beer-loving guy like Tobey go? I turned on my heels, passed Vivian's shop — which still showed a display of winter wear — and headed toward the pub.

The Wandering Wizard Pub was in the Victorian England section of town. There was also the Burning Wand Saloon over on Western Street, but I had learned that was more of a day drinker's place. Even though its clientele were pretty subdued during the daylight hours, Alastair had advised me it was best to avoid the Burning Wood at night.

But with its broad, glass windows, baskets of flowers hanging from hooks along the exterior, and a carved wooden sign featuring a hooded wizard with a staff, the Wandering Wizard dripped with charm. When I entered, the dark wood and gleaming brass interior was packed. A couple fiddles hovered in one corner playing a rollicking ditty. Taking in the tempting scent of hoppy beer and grilled burgers, I scanned the room for my prey.

I didn't take long to spot him standing at the bar and sharing a laugh with a few people.

I marched over to him.

Despite being full of people and despite the fiddles, the pub wasn't overly noisy. There was no television blaring, no jukebox, no muzak. And while there was plenty of chatter, it would be a couple hours before it reached that boisterous drunk stage. I then wondered what did happen when Magics got drunk? Fiona had told me about the Magics' connection to Prohibition, but were there rules about casting spells while under the influence? I'd have to ask Alastair.

Speaking of the devil, as I strode determinedly forward, out of the corner of my eye, I caught Alastair trying to flag me down to join him. Besides my determination that there'd be no extracurricular outings with him, I was a woman on a mission and I would not be distracted from that mission.

Over the course of the week, my rambling lessons with Alastair drifted now and then into magic law, and I'd learned a smattering of magical legal procedure. While I did appreciate the strawberry shortcake, the blueberry crumble, and the apple turnovers that had accompanied the information, I had thought it yet another pointless bit of background work when I needed to be doing more practical stuff. But now I was ready to make use of that pointless information.

Or was I? My gut already had the sloshy feeling it used to get in school when a teacher called on me to speak in front of the class. I stopped in my tracks.

This was madness. This was not something I did. This was getting way too involved in a world I had no interest in. It should be up to the Magics to sort Tobey Tenpenny out.

My feet shifted, ready to turn around and leave. Then someone broke a glass. The sound of it shattering churned up a peal of laughter from several people, but it only made me cringe.

How many times had Foster Dad Number Four threatened me with a broken beer bottle? He'd only ever used it on me once for the dastardly crime of getting my socks wet on a rainy walk home from school. The gashes on my upper arm had long since scarred over, but sometimes, especially when I was keyed up, my body still tensed in terror at the sound of breaking glass. The memory of that guy, of the bleeding wounds on my biceps, stirred a new determination in me.

I continued forward. My hands clenched into fists, I stopped dead center in front of Tobey's group. Sticking with the predictable relationship we had established, he sneered with annoyance when he saw me, but his friends gave him little nudges as if I were here to ask him to dance.

Not quite, guys.

CHAPTER THIRTY-ONE
J'ACCUSE!

"Tobey Tenpenny," I said very clearly. The bar went mostly silent except for the twin fiddles that now sounded as if they were challenging each other with faster- and faster-paced tunes. A chortling group of men at a booth in the back egged them on. "I accuse you of using the Exploding Heart Charm on Busby Tenpenny, of intent to steal a magical object, and of trying to use a giver to enhance your own power."

Personally, I thought that sounded good and wondered if my parents would have been proud. I'd spoken with a confident voice. I'd not wavered. I'd clearly impressed everyone in the bar because now it had gone fully silent. Even the fiddles were quiet and all eyes were on me.

Tobey switched from scowling at me to regarding me with disbelief. As if I'd finally gotten a color-changing potion to work, his face switched from a healthy tan to tomato red. His buddies were shifting uncomfortably and whispering to one another while stealing snide glimpses of me.

Finally, the silence of the crowd was broken by a single, "Boo." And just to be clear, this was not a playful, Casper-the-Friendly-Ghost *boo!*, but a shaming, insulting, should-be-followed-by-hiss *boo.*

Tobey's friends stopped fidgeting with their beer coasters and joined in. Soon, most of the pub was expressing their dissatisfaction.

That's right. *Boo, Tobey!* I smiled. I'd done it. Mr. Tenpenny's killer had been identified. Mr. Wood's business was safe. Yay, Cassie!

So why was no one arresting Tobey? And why were they staring at me? Damn. I should have looked into the protocol of this before doing it. Maybe the accuser was meant to do the takedown. I'd gained a fair amount of muscle working with the dead, but I was still far leaner than the muscular Tobey. To bring in this devil, I'd need help.

I glanced around, looking for some backup, but the faces behind me showed not a single ounce of support. Some were shaking their heads, others were glaring at me, a few looked like they might spit on me. The place had gone from convivial, to ready-to-brawl in under sixty seconds.

"Boo, Cassie!" This single call of named derision was picked up by Tobey's friends, then the rest of the pub joined in.

No, you mean, "Yay Cassie," I thought, my stubborn brain refusing to see the truth.

But it was hard to miss that truth when Tobey's friends set down their beers and started toward me.

"How dare you say that about him?" said the biggest one, a red-haired brute whose face was spattered with freckles.

Tobey, standing taller now that his henchmen were coming to his aid, looked about to say something. Before he could get the words out, someone yanked my arm and jerked me back just as the goon nearest to me lunged forward.

"Ain't his fault," he growled as I staggered backward and fingers dug into my upper arm.

"Best mate we have," I heard. I didn't see which one it was because I was being forcefully dragged through an angry mob. I whirled around, ready to fight off my attacker, but the crushing grip on my arm deftly slid down to clench my hand, squeezing so tightly I could feel my knuckles cracking. I swung my other arm, making a fist and aiming it toward my assailant's nose. It was only then I caught the scent of chocolate and my brain registered the familiar face.

Paying no attention to the fact I was tripping over my own feet, Alastair pulled me out of the pub through a barrage of insults. Once outside, he kept a tight hold of my hand and marched me down the block to a side street where he finally stopped. He let go of my hand. A tingling sensation danced across my palm as I flexed my fingers.

"What the hell, Cassie?" For once, he was looking at me with something other than shy admiration. In fact, the furrowed brow and narrowed eyes showed quite the opposite of admiration.

My first instinct was to tuck my head down and murmur an apology. But I fought it and kept my eyes defiantly locked on Alastair's. I was right all along. These Magics were a bunch of loons, and they were all covering up Tobey's crime. What kind of world was this? No wonder Alastair had told me to drop it.

Alastair, I thought with dismay. Of all the Magics, why him? I chastised myself. I should have been used to betrayal by this point in my life, but my blood still churned at my stupidity.

"All the signs point to him," I said. "He was the one who—" My body pulsing with too much anger to speak, I did Busby's exploding heart motion with my hand.

"Tobey didn't do it," Alastair said, his jaw so tense it barely moved.

"You sure about that? Because I also saw him threatening Fiona."

"I don't know what that might have been about, but he can't have done the Exploding Heart Charm."

"Oh, and why's that? Because you all think he's such a great guy?"

"No, because he doesn't have any magic."

The words hit me like a chickadee flying headfirst into a picture window.

"What?" I asked. All my anger morphed into curiosity.

The change in my tone gave Alastair pause. His shoulders relaxed and a hint of the warmth and mischief that made him so attractive returned to his face. Still, when he spoke, a terse, scolding tone lingered behind his words.

"Tobey's an Untrained. Despite a long line of strong Magics in his family on both sides, he came up lacking. Theoretically, he shouldn't even be allowed here, but Busby has a certain amount of pull in the magic community. We look past it. Most of us don't even think about it, but it's considered viciously rude to throw any lack of power in an Untrained's face."

He paused, took a deep breath, then after clenching and unclenching his hands, he pointed to my arm. "Did I hurt you?" I shook my head. That arm had endured far worse than someone trying to save my butt. "I didn't mean to grab so hard, but fear for you took over. If I hadn't gotten you out of there, well, best not to think about it. That's not to say I'm thrilled with what you did," he said, but took some of the sting out of the words with a shy smile.

"Well, how was I to know? It's not like anyone handed me a how-to book on day one."

"*Eloise's Guide to Magical Etiquette* would have been issued in your first week if you were doing the normal course of study. This is where rushing through gets you."

Just then, Tobey and his goons swarmed us like angry cartoon hornets. Alastair shielded me, but that didn't stop Tobey's tirade.

"You think you're so great just because you were born to it? Oh, the clever Cassie, she's just dripping with magic and talent," he said with wicked sarcasm. "You're nothing but a freak, you know that? No wonder your parents—"

"Tobey, stand down now," Alastair growled. "She didn't know better and you know that."

What was I? A puppy who's just chewed up the designer couch?

Tobey threw me a final, very unimaginative insult, but it didn't pack as much punch as his earlier rant. As his friends tugged him back, encouraging him to go back to the pub, I could have sworn there was a hangdog look in his eyes, the look of someone who's embarrassed. But since I knew damn well that Tobey Tenpenny was an emotionless jerkface, I figured it was probably just gas.

"You better go home for the night," Alastair said once they'd gone. His voice had lost some, but not all, of its impatient irritability. "I'll walk you back in case anyone decides to try anything."

As we walked, Alastair's hand brushed against mine more than once. I kept expecting him to take it, but he never did. I told myself I didn't want him to take it, that I needed to be the one to maintain the distance between us, but I wasn't good at lying to myself after such a long, messed up day.

"What did he mean, I was born to it?" I asked after the silence between us got to me. "Or am I supposed to already know that too?"

Alastair gave me a scolding look at my smart tone, then answered the question.

"Tobey has always wanted magic. It makes him envious of people who do have it, especially those Magics who have a natural talent for it like you. Your parents were both very strong

Magics. We refer to their kind as Kissed by Merlin Himself. You," he gave a little chuckle and nudged my arm with his elbow, "haven't just been kissed by Merlin, but fully and properly shagged by him."

"Well, it's not like I had any say in that. More like molested by Merlin."

"Just as Tobey had no say in being an Untrained."

This was too complicated. Remember a couple months ago when my life was simple? Dead people stayed dead. Morelli shouted insults and timelines at me. I was blissfully ignorant of my parents' demise. I wanted that back and was grateful that by the end of the week I would never have to see these people again.

When we got to my portal, Alastair stopped in front of me. His hand slipped into his trouser pocket. When he pulled it out, something golden glinted in the light of the streetlamp.

"I've been trying to figure out a good time to give you this. I meant to at our first lesson, but then Corrine showed up. Then I was thinking of waiting until your training was complete, but you'd probably see that as some type of bribery to get you to not go through with the draining. Anyway, here."

He held out his hand and opened his palm. From his fingers dangled a chain. Weighting it down was a locket, heart-shaped with crystal sides and a gold wire frame. I put my hand, palm up, directly under the charm. Alastair let go of the chain and it pooled into my hand. In the low light, it was hard to see exactly what the wispy stuff inside the charm was.

"It's your baby hair. The charm was your mother's."

I had something along the lines of a billion questions, but the sight of this object left me dumbstruck. I muttered a thanks, stopped staring stupidly at the necklace, and glanced up. My heart, already overwhelmed by what was in my hand, jumped at the look in Alastair's eyes. It had changed back from annoyance to admiration and, despite myself, I was relieved to see its return.

He leaned toward me in slow, hesitant increments. I knew what was coming and that I needed to step back to avoid it. I liked Alastair more than I should, but I could not have any involvement, any entanglements in this world. Plus, as an absorber, I wasn't even sure if I should be swapping spit with another Magic. If I sucked out some of his power, would they arrest me for magical thievery?

But despite my mind telling me to duck, to turn, to slap him, my body remained still as Alastair placed a warm, gentle kiss on my right cheek just beside my ear. The tingling in my palm was nothing compared to the charge of electricity that thrummed across my face. I breathed in, taking in his chocolatey scent that carried a layer of raspberries with just the faintest hint of cinnamon underneath.

A wonderful sensation of delight coursed through me, but before it could get all the way to my toes, Alastair stepped back.

"I better go now." When he spoke, he was a little breathless. Unfortunately, it wasn't a lusty kind of breathless, but a fatigued one, as if he'd just sprinted full out for a bus. "Good night, Cassie," he said and turned away, leaving me at my door.

I watched him go. Pablo would be dying for dinner, but I didn't step inside. Before Alastair got very far down the block, the bombshell Vivian slipped up beside him. She pulled a sultry drag on a long cigarette, letting the exhaled smoke waft around them rather than blowing up and away as would be polite. Her non-cigarette-holding hand then instantly snaked along Alastair's arm and she leaned her head on his shoulder as she let out a flirty laugh that filled the evening air.

My upper lip tensed so hard I thought I might damage my

incisors. This was stupid. I didn't like Alastair. I didn't want anything from Alastair except for some pointless lessons. Okay, and pastries. But that still didn't keep me from yanking open my door and slamming it behind me in jealous frustration.

From below, Morelli's front door *whooshed* open and he shouted, "Cut out that racket, Black!" To which my very mature side took over. I opened the closet door and slammed it again.

"I'm warning you, Black. One more sound and you're out of here."

Do I need to clarify that I was in a really bad mood? I stomped across the apartment, yanked open the front door, and yelled, "Go suck a toad."

Looking up at me from the ground floor, Morelli's face scrunched in such disgust that I wondered if the juvenile order had actually been a curse. Personally, I would have thought he'd be the kind of guy who'd enjoy sucking toads. Both Morelli and I scowled at each other a moment longer. Then without another word, we backed into our apartments and slammed our doors shut.

Pablo stared at me with a curious look on his face as if he worried I'd gone crazy. It probably didn't help my case when, thinking of Morelli's reaction, I began giggling despite my horrible evening.

CHAPTER THIRTY-TWO

NEW DAY, NEW DISAPPOINTMENT

The next morning, five minutes before the alarm went off, Pablo began meowing for his breakfast. I pulled the blankets over my head and let the reality of last night sink in. I'd just spewed one of the worst insults that existed in MagicLand to the grandson of a guy whose death might be my fault. This is why I don't have friends. This is why I stay holed up in my apartment alone. Not because I wouldn't like to go out and have a social life, but because my social I.Q. is somewhere deep in the negative digits.

How was I supposed to face going back to MagicLand? What were people going to say? Would they throw rotten fruit at me? Probably, and the rotten fruit would likely be charmed with some spell to make sure the muck couldn't be washed off for at least a month. But more to the point, why did I care?

Pablo pawed at my head. The alarm blared and there was a soft *thunk* beyond my down-filled cave as Pablo, knowing I'd soon be heading to the kitchen, jumped off the bed. I slapped the noisy appliance to turn it off and threw aside my blankets. There was no avoiding it. I needed this magic out of me, the only place that could be done was MagicLand, and the sooner I got out of bed, the sooner I'd learn how to make that happen.

As I dressed, my mind wandered until it found itself back on the familiar path of pondering who had killed Mr. Tenpenny. Now that Tobey was off my list, I had no other suspects to accuse. Which was probably a good thing. Everyone I'd seen seemed genuinely glad to see Mr. Tenpenny up and walking around. No one bore him ill will and it appeared that only Corrine Corrigan and perhaps the sender knew about the watch's destination. Well, and me, but I was pretty sure I hadn't killed Mr. T, not directly anyway. And I doubted that Corrine, with her flaming hair, her raucous personality, and her animated voice could ever get the drop on Mr. Tenpenny who was pretty spry even as a corpse.

Pablo gobbled down his kitty kibble, then leapt up on the table and made every attempt to share my yogurt with me while my mind drifted to Alastair. What had that been about last night? It was just a peck on the cheek, but he was my teacher, shouldn't one of us maintain a professional distance? But what if—

The two thoughts that popped into my head were such a revelation, I dropped my yogurt spoon. Pablo was on the splattered mess of dairy products like a flash.

Thought Number One was more of a question. My hand went to the center of my chest where my mother's locket dangled. My mother didn't die in Portland. She died in London. So how had Alastair gotten it? Thought Number Two was more of a foggy memory of my first day with Busby. Hadn't he or Fiona said something about the watch being sent to Mr. T so Alastair could destroy it? Which would mean Alastair likely knew Mr. T was supposed to have received a special delivery.

Alastair was slightly taller than me. Alastair had hair that was nearly black. Tall and dark-haired. The only two identifying features of his assailant Mr. T had been able to pinpoint.

Sparks of suspicion bounced around my head, igniting all kinds of connections. What had Alastair done when he first saw Busby and me? He had dropped that book like a man who was so surprised he lost control of his muscles momentarily. And not a good kind of surprise. In fact, he'd been the only Magic who had a less-than-enthusiastic reaction to Mr. T's return. He claimed he'd dropped his book when he saw me, but what if it had been fear over seeing his murder victim wandering around?

And what if Alastair's shy flirtation was just his calculated way of getting close to me? Say he worked for the Mauvais. What better way to please your evil overlord than to deliver to him the daughter of the people who stole the object that gave you the power over life and death, the power over strength and weakness?

I thought of the cake, all that cake. Hadn't Corrine said: *Should you be feeding her that?*

What had Lola told me? That sugar boosted magic. It helped Magics recover from exertion by feeding right into our cells' magical properties and energizing them.

What if Alastair didn't just have a sweet tooth? What if he was boosting my already strong magic for his own, or his master's, gain?

Pablo, having cleaned the spoon better than my struggling dishwasher ever could, was back on the table. I pushed the rest of the yogurt over to him and wrapped my hands around my tea mug with a sense of irritation with myself.

This line of thought was utterly ridiculous. I was just grasping at straws to make up for the Tobey incident. Some things in my overactive mind needed to change.

First, I needed to stop reading so much into Alastair's behavior. He probably pulled that bumbling charm act with every woman he came across. Second, I was making too much of a fuss over free cake and a fumbled book.

My accusatory thoughts were likely a defense mechanism that had kicked in after finding out he and Vivian were a thing. I mean, I should have known. Hadn't I seen Alastair with Vivian on that first day? With these suspicions I was trying to find excuses to distance myself from him, to convince myself he wasn't worth my time. Besides, what gain could he get from me? I absorbed. If I was a giver, then maybe all this sugary indulgence would be worth his effort, but the only thing slices of Sacher Torte could do to me, other than give me diabetes, is to make me absorb more strongly.

I also needed to tame my motive-seeking mind. I'd clearly been reading too many mysteries and swore my next library check out would be something firmly rooted in science.

After lingering longer than necessary over my tea, it was time to face the music. Or was it? I looked at the front door to my apartment. Maybe I could skip classes today and go see Mr. Wood. I did miss him and I was sure — or at least I hoped — he would be worried about me. Hell, he probably thought I'd hightailed it. It would only be right that I go over and reassure him, and perhaps reassure myself that one person in the world didn't despise me.

No, I told myself with a Runa-level of firmness, I had to put on my big girl pants and get this magical mess over with. But I swore I would visit Mr. Wood when classes were done for the day. After all, after last night, I doubted anyone would be inviting me to linger around MagicLand.

I scratched Pablo — who had yogurt on his nose — behind the ears, cleaned up my dishes, and stepped into my closet. Then, my gut fluttering like the wings of a hummingbird on crack, I crossed the threshold of my portal. After passing through the light squeeze, I glanced around. Relief washed over me at the sight of the empty street. At least I could get to Fiona's without anyone coming at me with a pitchfork.

As I shuffled over to Fiona's porch I promised myself to buckle down and stop questioning why I had to learn such and such. I needed out of this world where it had only taken a week for me to wear out my welcome. A new record for me.

When I entered Fiona's house I halted at the top of the stairs. Mr. Tenpenny was standing in Fiona's living room, examining the class photos on her wall.

If I didn't already feel like burying myself in a pit, the look he gave me when he turned around made me wish I was skilled enough to conjure a shovel and charm it to start digging. The problem was that his lips weren't pinched white with disgust, his face wasn't scowling in anger. I could at least react to anger. Instead, he didn't appear mad at all. His shoulders slumped and he stared at me while giving a little shake of his head. I'd disappointed him. Rather than say anything, he turned his back on me and went back to looking at the class pictures on the wall.

I'd disappointed a corpse. I had no idea where to go from there.

Fiona came in and broke some of the tension by pretending there was nothing wrong. There was some strain in her voice as she made every effort to sound chipper, but she rambled out a greeting and told me what we'd be going over that day. Mr. Tenpenny shook his head at the photos then went over to a bookshelf, scanning it for something as if Fiona's living room was the local library.

When Fiona started explaining the physics of shifting ink, Busby made a disapproving grunting noise. I glanced up at him. Had my screw up sent him back on his verbal progress? He spun away from the bookshelf, his face hard with what looked like annoyance. "I don't know what I'm looking for." Oh good, apparently I hadn't broken him. "I'm going to go join the others."

He gave Fiona a brief peck on the cheek, didn't once bother to look at me, and let himself out.

"I've really made him hate me, haven't I?"

"He shouldn't behave like that. I mean, you couldn't have known. Just, you know, try to think before you speak in the future, and if you have concerns about others, address them to one of us first."

"Okay, I have a concern." She showed her palm in a gesture that told me to continue. "I saw Tobey threatening you the other day. What was that about?"

Fiona shifted and a wobbly expression on her face made her look strikingly uncomfortable.

"I know I said to ask, but that is a personal matter. It's nothing bad, I promise. He just got a little frustrated about what I had to tell him. Trust me, if he'd been hurting me, I'm more than capable of defending myself." She waggled a couple fingers, and a heavy lamp rose from one of the end tables to demonstrate exactly how she could have fended off Tobey.

"Anything else?" she asked once the lamp was back in place.

"What was Mr. Tenpenny looking for in the photos?" I pointed toward the far wall.

"He was trying to see if he could recognize the Mauvais in any of them."

"Wait. He doesn't know what the Mauvais looks like?"

"No one really does. I believe it's a topic Runa is planning to cover."

With that, I knew question time was at an end. Fiona then delved into the physics of changing words on a document by rearranging the ink molecules of each letter. I immediately saw the logic of how it worked. The same amount of ink was still there, but by delving into the ink's molecular structure you could shift it. She demonstrated with a copy of *The Oregonian,* showing me how, with a simple spell, she could change the words of a few headlines from doom and gloom to happy tidings.

"How does this affect contract law, or any legal document for that matter, if you can just change things to terms you find more favorable?"

"We have people who can detect the change. Plus, everyone gets a copy of all paperwork. If there's a dispute, experts are called in to determine which has been exposed to magic most recently."

"So, magic is really nothing more than being able to tap into the underlying physics of everything."

"Very good, Cassie. It normally takes months for students to grasp that. I think your work is going to go much easier from now on. So long as you stop resisting it so much."

"Is it that obvious?"

"There's a certain sneer to your face when we're doing background work. It's not to say most students don't prefer the practical side, but they accept getting a rounded education, and many eventually come to enjoy learning where magic came from and how it all works."

"That's because they'll be living in this world. I won't."

Fiona gave me a disapproving look. Me and my big mouth. So much for my attempt to go cold turkey with not annoying anyone.

Thankfully, the rest of the lesson went smoothly, and after an hour, the timer went off. My stomach lurched with excitement and apprehension. As soon as Lola had me dust every square inch of shelf space in her house, it would be time for Alastair's lesson. Would it be awkward? What would I do if he tried to kiss me again? Was he working for the Mauvais? Was he the

Mauvais? Should I ask about the locket? What kind of cake would we have?

"You're to head straight to Runa's today," Fiona said, derailing my roller coaster ride of worry.

"No lesson with Alastair?"

"Nor Lola," she said, and I swear I sensed a knowing scold in her words.

"That's what I meant. Why the reduced schedule?" I tried to sound casual.

"I'm not sure what Lola's got herself up to, but I believe Alastair got roped into helping Vivian with something and told me to tell you he can't make it. But I believe Dr. Dunwiddle has some practical work for you today, so you should like that better than another Alastair lecture."

Despite my firm resolve back at my kitchen table, I had to admit my disappointment was a close match to that I'd seen on Mr. T's face. But I had to be done with this. Even if Alastair wasn't serving an evil master, he did have someone. And of course that someone would be the vivacious Vivian, not Cassie the MagicLand miscreant.

I would no longer let myself be lured in by pastry and a pleasing face. Actually, I was glad for Vivian. She was like a buxom road block to my foolish emotions — both the silly crush I'd been developing and the suspicions that had tried to take hold. From here on out, I would chop the head off this very pointless Alastair flirtation.

I told myself all this, told myself quite sternly in fact, but I couldn't douse my flare of jealousy at the idea of Alastair with Vivian, the woman who looked like she walked off the cover of a noir detective novel. Full red lips, hefty bosom, itty-bitty waist, and impossibly long calves that ended in four-inch stilettos — shoes she could wear because she was a normal height for a woman, not a tall gangling thing like me.

The lingering jealousy, a tinge of self-loathing, the disappointment that Alastair had ditched my lesson, and the irritable fact that he couldn't bother to tell me himself, had me in a foul mood when the bell jingled as I stepped into Dr. Dunwiddle's place.

Well, fouler than usual, that is.

CHAPTER THIRTY-THREE

THE SCENT OF A MAGIC

"Oh look, it's the Untrained Sensitivity Chairwoman," she said, wearing an amused expression. Thankfully, no one was picking up their prescription for eye of newt, wing of bat, or whatever it was people collected from the good doctor. "Tobey as the Mauvais," she chuckled. Her hovering glasses bounced with delight. "Ridiculous."

"Yeah, yeah, Cassie bad. If you're done being entertained at my expense, can we get on to what I'm learning today?"

Dr. Dunwiddle made no further comment about what I'd done the night before, but she did put me through my paces. This involved an object obstacle course in which she would randomly shout, "disappear," "change shape," or "push aside." I managed to keep up, but it was the first time in days that I felt exhausted by the magic.

"Tired?" she asked bitingly. "You should be building up your endurance. Doing a draining without scrambling your brain takes a lot of concentration and stamina."

"I can manage. Let's do it again."

This time Dr. D threw in new spells I hadn't done before. Some of them I'd only heard of from Fiona's lectures, including making an object glow as if it had a light bulb inside. Full of the knowledge of magical physics I'd gained, I reacted without hesitation. After rearranging some photons, I coaxed them into the visible light spectrum. Then, feeling cocky at Dr. Dunwiddle's surprised expression, I reshaped a piece of glass into a prism and made a rainbow.

Runa stopped barking commands and smiled, truly smiled. "That was well done." Coming from her, it was the equivalent of winning the *Jeopardy!* Championship, getting the Pulitzer Prize, and coming in first in the Boston Marathon all rolled into one. Speaking of marathons, I was sweating as hard and my legs felt as shaky as if I'd just completed one.

"Take a break. You've earned it. Come on."

I followed Runa out to the front of the clinic, then plopped down into one of the chairs in the waiting area. She handed me a lollipop from a giant jar of candy like I was a little kid who'd just survived getting a shot. It wasn't cake, but I was too hungry to care. For the first time ever, Runa encouraged me to ask questions. I bit my tongue against asking anything about Alastair, about the watch, or about the locket. I mean, I couldn't go around spouting conspiracy theories two days in a row. Instead, I stuck with safer topics.

"Why do I feel so content when I'm with Lola? I mean, the woman is a slave driver, but there's something cozy about being around her."

"Don't you know?"

"Would I ask if I did?"

"She was your nanny when you were a baby. Your parents worked a lot, often late at night, and she was always there to watch over you. She has a type of giving magic that's especially calming. Very handy when dealing with temperamental babies," she said, then eyed me as if I didn't know exactly who she meant. "She was very upset when you went missing."

"Missing? I thought I was put up for adoption."

"You went missing. We never knew what happened to you. Well, someone might. It's not a subject I'm comfortable getting into, but it's thought the Mauvais had something to do with it, otherwise, why could we not detect you?"

She shook her head as if annoyed at not having all the answers to something.

"Okay, then what about the Mauvais? Why can Tobey not be him?" I asked as I sucked on the grape-flavored candy. "I mean, besides not being Magic. Who is the Mauvais? And why can't anyone find him?"

"As for who, we never knew, which made tracking him all but impossible."

"How could you not know?" I pictured video clips of Hitler shouting his proclamations of superiority to the masses. How could you attempt a coup without ever showing your face?

"For one thing, whoever the Mauvais is, he's one of the Magics who excel at altering their appearance."

"Alter how? Like a mask?"

"With a Morphing Spell. And yes, some will just do a face mask since that's relatively easy, but very talented Magics can do a full body change — fat man, emaciated man, teenage girl, old hag. It's a hard spell and very exhausting. Most highly-trained Magics can do it for a short period, but even for the strongest Magic, it's a challenging spell that can only be maintained for short periods of time. The Mauvais was able to maintain it. What the cost was to him, we don't know. Long periods of morphing are terribly exhausting. A little like long periods of time with you," she added with a sardonic grin.

"Wait. Then how would I know I wasn't sitting in this very room with the Mauvais?"

"The MMCE prohibits mimicking any living Magic or Norm. If you can do the spell, which some learn for parties or the theater, you must come up with an individual of your own imagination or someone who is long gone. But, you're right, when you don't care about the law, anything is possible and we suspect he had another trick up his dark sleeve."

"Which was what?" I asked.

She handed me another sucker, cherry this time, before continuing.

"Mind control using the BrainSweeping Charm."

"You're joking with me now."

"I wish I was. As I said, Morphing is allowed by the MMCE, but BrainSweeping is strictly forbidden. It doesn't work on Magics, the power in our cells rejects any attempt, but it can be done on MCs. It allows you to use their body and their voice, but it's your mind in the driver's seat."

This was the stuff of nightmares and *Twilight Zone* episodes, and I really wanted to linger on the topic, but since Dr. Dunwiddle was abnormally chatty this morning, I thought I better get as much out of her as possible. I pushed on with a question that had been nagging at me.

"So what happened to the Mauvais?"

"We had hoped he was dead, that maybe your parents somehow cursed him before they lost their lives, but as you know, rumors have started that he may be rallying again. I say rumors, but these are actually pretty concrete reports from trusted sources."

"Do you know where he might be? I mean, where was he last seen?" I asked as cold fingers crept up my spine. What had that feeling of being watched been about over the past couple months?

"We have ideas. He was likely in the Portland area, but some people think since he didn't find what he wanted here, he might have gone elsewhere to look for it."

"But not you?"

"Not at all. I'd bet this very clinic that since the watch wasn't destroyed as it was supposed to be, he's still in Portland waiting for one of us to make a mistake."

"Creepy."

"Yes, and a topic I'd rather leave for today."

"But you have the watch now." Runa's eyes darted to the rows of boxes behind the counter. Gandalf's gonads! Was the watch still here in this unsecured shop where people came in and out all day long? These Magics had something to learn about security measures, that's for sure. "Why didn't you destroy it?"

"Alastair had worked out how it could be destroyed. That's the only reason it was sent here. Busby was supposed to oversee its handling, but then a complication arose."

"Complication?"

"You woke up the watch. It changed its magic composition. Alastair could no longer take care of it. He's been working on some other ideas, though."

So, Cassie Black screws up again. I shifted in my seat. Runa had never been so open with me and I knew she wasn't going to mince words to spare my feelings. I had to ask.

"What are people saying about me after yesterday? Do they hate me?"

"You'd be surprised how forgiving the community can be toward idiots. What you said, what you accused Tobey of, wasn't exactly done with full knowledge. They were mad, shocked at first, but they've had time to think it over. Now, if you went in today and taunted Tobey with having enough power to kill someone, then I'd suggest you go away for a long, long time."

"I plan to anyway."

Runa gave a heavy, dramatic sigh.

"Be that as it may. We still have a little time left. Maybe I can get a few things through your thick skull. Now, tell me what have people said about your magic."

I thought for a moment. I thought of Alastair's reaction after kissing me goodnight, but I didn't want to bring up anything about him. I couldn't bear Runa laughing at me for falling for Alastair's untrustworthy charms, nor did I have any desire to discuss Magical Sex Ed with her. I recalled what others had said most often.

"They say they sense it on me. Or smell it."

"Exactly. Every Magic has a signature odor that can be detected by other Magics. We're not mongrels going around sniffing each other out, but our magic does leave a scent for a brief amount of time. When we perform a spell, some of our signature odor lingers behind. If our detectives can get to the scene quickly enough, the culprit can be caught. The stronger the magic within you, the stronger your scent and the longer it would linger behind. Of course, we know one another's scent, but we also acclimate to the scent of those around us, otherwise we'd be overwhelmed with it. Tell me, what do I smell like to you? No smart answers," she said, just as the image of Pablo's cat box came to mind. I inhaled. There was the cherry scent of my lollipop, but then I picked it up as I had the first time I met her.

"Mint and honey."

"Interesting. Most people tell me it's some sort of citrus. Be that as it may, what one Magic smells like to you may not be how that Magic smells to another."

I thought of Mr. T smelling of Earl Grey, of Fiona's chalk and textbook smell, of the chocolate-raspberry scent of Alastair. What else did Alastair smell like? Cinnamon. Hadn't I smelled cinnamon on Mr. Tenpenny? No, Cassie, you are not Sherlock Holmes and the game is most definitely not afoot. My self-scolding halted when I recalled that Tobey carried no scent.

"Will I still smell when I am drained?"

"Only faintly, and it would take a bloodhound to detect it. As I've mentioned, your magic is in your cells. It's been woken, so to speak, so you'll always have a faint scent, but if a Magic smells you after a draining, he or she will likely either pity you for your loss or shun you for doing something they see as morally reprehensible."

I could tell where she was going with this and since I didn't want a Magic Morality Code lecture, I moved the center of conversation away from myself.

"So, the Mauvais, he has a scent?"

"Yes, and even if he changes his appearance, he can't change his scent."

"But how would anyone know what his scent is if a Magic's scent comes across differently to other Magics?"

"A Magic he was close to could identify him, but we would have to fully trust that person. That's why scent identification is a matter our police are looking into. I'm part of the project to help them see if there's a test we can come up with that can be done in the field to assess the underlying molecular signature of the scent. The signature would be unique, much like fingerprints in the MC world."

Runa's glasses jumped from her jacket pocket, flew over to the clock, and tapped the face. It was 11:27.

"Right," Runa said abruptly. "It's time for my lunch. Gwendolyn has a break in her schedule today, so you'll head to Spellbound next. And, since we've wasted so much time chatting today, you can look forward to a rigorous session tomorrow."

With this cheery thought in my head, I left Dr. Dunwiddle's and was making my way to Gwendolyn's for another round of lackluster potion making. Just as I turned the corner to head down the zigzagging route to Main Street, I saw Tobey marching toward me. I looked to my left, thinking I could duck into the nearest shop, but I found myself staring at the winter clothing display of Vivian's boutique. It might have done in a pinch, but the place was closed. She was probably still with Alastair. I tried to bite back my dismay.

So, no easy escape and no one rushing to my rescue. I continued on my way, taking those quick steps that are meant to signify you've got absolutely no time to stop. Trying to avoid full eye contact but wanting to assess my enemy, I darted a furtive glance at Tobey. I couldn't read his face. The stern countenance hovered somewhere between resolve and irritation, but nowhere near warm and welcoming. Maybe he would just brush past me and we could fully cement our animosity-filled relationship here and now.

No such luck. Tobey Tenpenny seemed to be all about confrontation.

He stopped right in front of me, blocking my way with all seventy-four inches of his athletic frame and staring at me with a pair of fiercely scowling eyes that were a mix of Mr. T's grey and a hazel that was a close match to my own. If I didn't hate him so much, and if I could look past his vile attitude, I might actually admit he was good looking.

I stared up at him, waiting for the yelling, waiting for the verbal scolding, but he just stood there making angry exhalations through his nostrils.

"Go on. Out with it, then," I said. "I've got places to go."

"What you said yesterday," he said irritably, his jaw tensing as if he was chewing on disgust. But then he stopped, rolled his eyes up to the sky, took a deep breath, and said in a very un-Tobey-like way, "You couldn't have known." The tone shocked me like a splash of icy water in the face. It was calm, forgiving, bordering on tolerance.

I took a single step back. Who was this and what had he done with the real Tobey? I was too stunned to actually say this, to say anything really, so he continued.

"It wasn't right for me to react like I did, or for anyone to get mad at you. It would make as much sense as getting mad at a toddler for saying *shit* when he doesn't even know what it means. I should've explained what I was early on."

"Why would you?" Tobey flinched. My blood was still coursing with defensive wariness, so my question came out a bit harsher than it should have. I forced myself to adopt a gentler tone. "I mean, why explain yourself? You act like you hate me because I've got magic."

"No," he said, then shrugged as if to play off the half-lie. "I hate that you don't appreciate your magic. I hate that you just want to throw it away. And I am a little jealous that you have so much of it you don't know what to do with it. I hate that you don't want to be part of this world, but I don't hate you."

Although I bet Tobey would make a fair Mr. Darcy, this was all getting a bit Jane Austen-y for my taste.

"Look, I just want my life to go back to normal and for Mr. Wood's business to be safe. That means getting rid of this magic. Since it's never done me any good, I don't have any reason to keep it."

"I understand. I just wish—"

Tobey's wish was cut off when a cloud of cigarette stink and a laughing couple rounded the same corner I'd just turned.

I may not be a bloodhound and I may have been new to all this magic stuff, but I knew from the hint of chocolate I picked up underneath the cigarette smell, that one of the pair was Alastair. From behind me, a woman with a breathy voice cooed, "Oh, Allie." Her accompanying giggle made me want to gag.

I glanced over my shoulder. Vivian. Of course she would have a film noir voice to go with her film noir body. She was reaching to pat Alastair's arm in a perfect move from Flirting 101, but Alastair smoothly avoided her touch. He had a grin on his face, but it was tight and didn't reach his eyes as it normally did. Was he uncomfortable at seeing me, or was the discomfort caused by being unable to shake off the clingy Vivian? Okay, I know I was supposed to be enacting Project Keep Distant, but I was kind of hoping for the latter.

I turned back to Tobey. His attention was — to no surprise — riveted on Vivian. A stony look crossed his face, and in it I detected the familiar seed of jealousy. Did Tobey have a crush on Vivian? Was Alastair a rival? For once I sympathized with Tobey. The couple stopped next to us and I cocked an eyebrow at Alastair.

"Cassie," he said warmly.

"Allie," I mocked.

"I was just walking Vivian back to her shop. I'd been trying to find you, but I came across Vivian and—" He cut off the sentence as if he knew exactly how terrible it would sound to say Vivian had distracted him from looking for me. "Anyway, sorry I missed our class." He gave a quick nod to Tobey. "Everything okay here?"

"Perfectly fine. And no problem with the lesson. I can see you were busy," I said pointedly and flicked my eyes toward Vivian, who now had her back to us. She was wriggling her shapely behind as she finagled some keys out of her red, patent leather purse.

I had no reason to feel put off. Alastair had done nothing more than save my ass from being pummeled by Tobey's thugs. Okay, and possibly steal a locket from my mother's dead body. No, I had to stop playing detective. These people all had lives before I came here, lives I had no part of and wanted no part of except to get rid of my magic, get Mr. Tenpenny dead, and prevent any further problems for Mr. Wood. This was it, I decided. No more involvement, no more cheek pecks, no more jealousy. It would be Business Cassie from here on out.

"I'm late for Gwendolyn's lesson," I said and gave Tobey a brief smile of thanks for his apology, or whatever it was, and dashed off to the comfort of recipes I would never master.

CHAPTER THIRTY-FOUR

A SPOONFUL OF SUGAR

Gwendolyn's head jerked up the moment I stepped into Spellbound Patisserie. Her hand gripped the serving tongs she was using to pick up a scone. The ends snapped together with a sharp clack and the scone crumbled apart.

"Oh, it's you," she said fretfully, worry filling her eyes as she clumsily brushed away the mess.

"Sorry, did my time change? Runa didn't tell me."

"No, I just don't know how much more my kitchen can take." Did I fail to mention my last recipe exploded? Gwendolyn had made short work of cleaning up the debris, but the scent of smoke still lingered in the air. "Maybe we should just have a demonstration. As you keep saying, you won't be using this again. That's assuming your other lessons are going better than mine," she said, her voice trailing off with dismay.

After her failures with me, Gwendolyn had grown insecure in her teaching skills. On the good side, though, Fiona had told me Gwendolyn's younger students would likely end up as masters of potion making with the intense coursework she was giving them.

"A demonstration would be perfect," I said. Some of the fear fell from her eyes and she eased her death grip on the tongs.

She led me through the rear door and into the main kitchen area. I did not appreciate the smirks on the faces of her assistant bakers. One of them even pulled out a fire extinguisher and set it beside the loaves she'd been forming. Gwendolyn handed me my apron, and we sidled up to her workstation.

I took in the ingredients on the countertop: flour, sugar, eggs, oil, and some spices. Since I'd missed my mid-morning snacks with Alastair, I wouldn't complain if this demonstration ended with a cake sampling.

"Let's talk about sweets," Gwendolyn said as she settled her slumping chef's hat over her thick curls. "I believe Lola touched on this briefly with you, but now would be a good time to go into more detail. Sugar is a Magic's friend and we must do our best not to avoid it or our magic will weaken."

Did I say I wanted rid of magic? Never! Magic is amazing! Where else but in this community would you hear, "No, no, eat more sugar, it's good for you"? I was about to announce my newfound love for magic, but Gwendolyn continued to lecture as she moved all the ingredients out of my reach and started cracking the eggs into two different bowls.

"Honey was used for the longest time, but when they started growing and harvesting sugar cane, magic truly took a turn. And not always for the best."

"How do you mean?"

"Sugar enhances a Magic's skills. Boosts them, so to say." She started whisking the eggs and slowly incorporating the other ingredients. "Deny a witch or wizard sugar for too long and they feel depleted, like magical wimps. Almost like an Untrained," she added tartly, her confidence returning as she went through the familiar motions of baking. Even the hat had gone from a teenage slouch to a military rigidness. I ignored the comment as she switched to the other bowl and repeated what she'd just done in the first.

"It was this depletion that allowed sugar growers to enslave people to do the hard work. The sugar increased the Magics' power, gave them control over the non-magics, as well as control over any enslaved Magics who were kept from ever allowing sugar to touch their lips so they wouldn't get too strong."

"So sugar's role in the slave trade was actually a plot to enhance the power of some Magics?" Never mind. I was right all along. Magic is terrible.

"At first. Magics started the slave trade, but later, non-magics saw the sugar-slave routes as a way to also shift cotton, build empires, and gain wealth. By then, MCs had also developed a taste for sugar. They're the ones who truly turned the slave trade on its head and made it into a system of widespread cruelty."

"Could the Mauvais withhold sugar to enslave people again?" I asked as Gwendolyn patted the dough she'd made into two long, flat loaves.

"He could. His overall goal was to subjugate MCs. It's a strategy that might have worked if we were dealing with him a century ago, but sugar is so prevalent in everything these days it would be impossible to fully deny it to people. However, he could still use it in another way. If he captured a giver, he could boost their power with sugar. This would allow him to take several times more power from a single giver."

Despite the warmth that wafted over me when Gwendolyn put the loaves into the pre-heated oven, chills ran along my skin. Considering how much cake I'd been eating lately, it was a lucky thing I was an absorber.

Gwendolyn went on to share a few tales of the extremes Magics will go to to get sugar. Did you know the practice of handing out candy at Halloween actually started when Magics coerced their neighbors as part of an All Hallows Eve prank? It worked through a Voice Modulation Spell.

Lola — while I was being made to magically clean her gutters a couple days ago — had explained Voice Modulation to me. Apparently, a Magic who has enough strength and control over his power can use his words to convince non-magics to do things against their will. It can work on Magics too, but you have to be really strong to pull it off. Lola had told me that for Voice Modulation to work, it takes a heavy dose of confidence in your abilities and being very clear in your request. But of course, its use was strictly regulated by the Council on Magic Morality because you can imagine the slippery slope it could send the world tumbling down.

Anyway, according to Gwendolyn, the phrase "trick or treat" was actually derived from a Gaelic or Old English (she wasn't sure which) term for, "Hand over the sweets, you lowly Norms." I'm not sure if I quite believe that, but it made for a good story while the kitchen filled with the tempting scent of baked goods.

An expert on all things sugar, Gwendolyn continued telling me sweet-based facts while she pulled the loaves from the oven, cut them into perfectly angled slices, then popped them back in the oven. Once the timer went off, she performed a Cooling Charm and placed one of the biscotti in front of me from the first loaf, and one from the second loaf.

"We'll see how good you are and you'll get a practical demonstration of what we've been discussing. One of these," she waggled her long finger between the two cookies, "was made with sugar substitute. The other with pure sugar."

I tasted the first one she'd placed before me. Orange, almond, the rich taste of freshly laid eggs, and sweetness. Then a sense of melancholy, of boredom. Thinking I was probably just imagining this, I crunched into the second one. It had the same flavors, but the sweetness was different. It made me feel warm, energized, ready for anything. I glanced up at Gwendolyn. "That's the real thing," I said, pointing to the second biscotti.

"Amazing," she said, and we both seemed surprised by her response. For the first time in the Kitchen of Failure, I hadn't screwed up, embarrassed myself, or made anything explode. Gwendolyn's eyes shone with success.

"Yeah, they're both really good."

"No. Both have sugar in them." I knew I'd been imagining it. Why did no one warn me this was Prove Cassie's an Idiot Week? "But the first one had half a teaspoon replaced with the sugar substitute. You're a super taster. You may have no skill for potion making, but you've got some sensitive magic in your tastebuds."

Any pride over my sugary instincts crumbled away. Everyone kept gushing over how much magic I had in me like it was some great thing, but I was beginning to picture it as a cancer that had not only invaded my lungs, but also my liver, my kidneys, and my pancreas. Hell, I felt like I might even have magic cancer of the hair.

Thankfully, there was a treatment for my disease and that appointment was only days away. I nibbled on another biscotti and tallied the hours until I'd finally get my magic chemo session.

CHAPTER THIRTY-FIVE

PAYING A VISIT

Magical melancholy aside, I was glad to leave Gwendolyn with renewed confidence in her teaching skills. But when I stepped out of the shop with my packet of biscotti, I had an overwhelming sense of being out of place. Not that this was an unusual feeling for me, here or in the real world, but it had never hit me so keenly. I needed something familiar. I needed a place where I felt like I fit in. And I needed it sooner rather than later.

I recalled my earlier resolve to check in on Mr. Wood and let him know I was close to fixing everything. It struck me harder than I expected that Wood's Funeral Home was exactly where I needed to be. Yes, I realize that may sound odd. Most people can't stand being anywhere near funeral homes, but it was the one place that gave me a sense of belonging. After all, the dead don't judge you.

Well, they didn't used to.

Not wanting to run into anyone else who might feel the need to remind me my cells were bursting with unwanted magical abilities, I stuck to side streets to return to my portal. When I got to my door, a note written on paper torn from a prescription notepad from Dr. Dunwiddle's office had been tacked to it. Again, I wondered what kind of prescriptions witches and wizards needed. I mean, couldn't they just magic away a headache or high blood pressure?

I shook off the quandary, snatched the note off the door, then went inside. After pushing my way through the mess of my closet, Pablo rubbed up against my legs and started drooling with happiness. Trying not to trip and fall on my face, I stepped over him and flicked open the note.

Come see me as soon as possible. Do not use any magic until then.

Great, she probably had another test for me.

I wasn't in the mood, so I crammed the note into my skirt's pocket.

The biscotti had done nothing to quell my hunger, so I stacked together a pile of ten pieces of cheddar sandwiched between wheat crackers. With Pablo successfully snagging the cheese for himself, I barely managed to eat half of my snack. Somewhat refueled, I grabbed my bag and headed for the door that opened not onto MagicLand, but onto the real world.

My hand trembled as I reached for the knob. Suddenly, this didn't feel like going into my world, but a foreign one. A world I didn't know anymore. Then I told myself I was being ridiculous. I'd only been in MagicLand a little over a week. During that time, I had managed to anger an entire pub full of people, churn up a monster-sized conspiracy theory against my teacher, get my crush dashed by a hotter woman, and blow up a commercial kitchen. MagicLand was not my world. I gripped the knob, turned it, and stepped out.

I don't know why, I guess I'd gotten spoiled by my portal, but I expected to pop out right in front of Mr. Wood's. Instead, I opened the door to my building's dingy interior landing. I trudged down the stairs, staying to the edge to avoid any creaking risers that would alert Morelli to my presence. Not that

I didn't have my rent, but I was in no mood to deal with his stench of musty clothes and stale, generic beer right now.

I only had one stair to go when Morelli's door whipped open. Apparently the world needed to solidify the fact that if I didn't have bad luck, I'd have no luck at all. The sound of a game show's pinging and buzzing came from the television inside. My charming landlord narrowed his eyes, and I was already sifting through a mental inventory of my various comebacks, when he nodded his head and simply said, "Black." Not like he was damning me to the bowels of hell, but like he was greeting me. Like he was a semi-normal human capable of the niceties of society.

Not that the scowl ever left his face, mind you.

Shocked all the way down to my secondhand Doc Martin's, I returned the nod and said, "Morelli," although with more questioning bewilderment than salutation in my voice. Before anything weirder could happen, I scurried down the final step and out the door as a studio audience roared their approval.

I strode to Mr. Wood's, enjoying the feel of real world air on my cheeks and real world sun on my face. And in my eyes. I thought about using magic to see if I could conjure a pair of sunglasses, but figured it would be a bit hypocritical to resort to using something I only wanted rid of.

With guilty dismay, I saw Mr. Wood's sign was still turned to the closed side, but he'd tacked a note to the bottom saying it was only for a small renovation and that, "Wood's will be back to tending to your grieving needs as soon as possible."

I smiled at his clever resolve, even though I knew it was my fault the sign was there. No matter what embarrassment, shaming, or social discomfort I had to endure, I had to get Mr. Tenpenny back to being dead. I had no idea exactly how I was going to do that, but I refused to let Mr. Wood down.

I used my key to let myself in. At the sound of the chime, Mr. Wood came bustling out to see who was there. When he saw me, he hurried forward and pulled me into a hug. The embrace was so surprising after all the scorn of MagicLand that my throat tightened and my eyes stung with the tears I was fighting back.

"You're back!" he said, stepping back, his round face beaming with true happiness — something I hadn't realized I'd missed in my time with the sour pusses of MagicLand. "Have you fixed the problem?" He looked behind me as if I might be hiding Mr. Tenpenny's body in my satchel.

"Not entirely." Mr. Wood's beaming face drooped as he let out a sigh of disappointment. "But I am working on it. And getting really close," I added, but it tasted like a lie on my tongue.

Was I getting any nearer to fixing this? I'd gained plenty of knowledge and random trivia about the magic world and could move objects around like a natural, but was I really any closer to shoving this magic out of my system? So far, I'd had no lesson that even hinted at how to get my magic out. I'd only received grumpy grumblings over wanting to do so. I wondered if maybe the community didn't want me to give up my magic. Okay, I knew most of them thought I was crazy for wanting to, but could these lessons (and cake) and demonstrations of all the cool stuff I'd be missing out on simply be a delaying tactic while they tried to lure me into their magic world?

Sorry, magic folks, not gonna work. Cassie Black is highly immune to cults.

"That's good to hear, but that Carl called and is asking to see the Tenpenny paperwork tomorrow."

"Tomorrow? You were supposed to have until Friday."

"Oh, he still is. He just wants the paperwork ahead of time. I guess to verify matters. He wasn't very forthcoming with explanations."

Inwardly, I groaned. I knew there was no way I was going to convince the very stubborn community to drain me ahead of schedule. I also suspected that while it was a key part of the equation, just getting rid of my power wasn't going to kill off Mr. Tenpenny. In order to put his mind and body at eternal ease, I needed to find his killer. Or someone did.

Speaking of which, had the community been doing anything to look into Busby's death? Although I'd learned a few things, I didn't fully understand how their legal or investigative system worked, but it didn't seem like anyone was following up on a pretty obvious magical murder. But that was a problem for another day.

"I'm going to get this settled, Mr. Wood. Don't worry about Cologne Carl coming tomorrow."

I considered my options and I considered the warning in Runa's note. I didn't want to rely on magic, but I thought this might be a good time for it. One last hurrah to make use of this stupid "gift" before tossing it in the bin. As for Runa's warning, I'd just eat a box of donuts to replenish myself before subjecting myself to whatever test she had planned for me.

"Oh good, because that paperwork still hasn't come," Mr. Wood said, as if he actually expected it would.

Paperwork. Gears started whirring in my head. I could fiddle with the documents we had in the filing cabinet, but I needed more than that. If I could get my hands on a few specific pieces of paperwork, my magic training might finally come in handy.

It was time for a trip to the county office that housed the Mortuary Board's records.

CHAPTER THIRTY-SIX

THE RECORDS ROOM

I left Mr. Wood's and hopped the bus that would take me downtown. Portland isn't exactly a city filled with architectural marvels, but the county building is an edifice that haunts architects' nightmares. It's square with no external enhancement and painted a shade of deep blue-grey even a prison warden would hesitate to use. The exterior of the building should have been banned by the city for being an eyesore, and let's just say, the fluorescent-lit interior wasn't much better.

At the front desk sat a woman with an enviably rich skin tone and straight, black hair. "Can I help you?" she asked with a cheery Indian accent.

I'd thought hard on the ride over about the Voice Modulation Spell. It was a form of mind control, but unless you had dark intentions, was no more evil than a song lyric making you want to dance or a line from a movie making you want to cry. You simply had to state things clearly and confidently.

"The records room wants to see me," I said. It came out haughty, not confident, and the woman raised a perfectly arched eyebrow at me.

"No, I don't think they do. They're in a meeting."

I was supposed to be Cassie the Great, more magic than Houdini himself. I should certainly be able to bend a mere mortal to my will. I focussed my attention. I had tried to be clear with about I wanted, but maybe something got lost in translation.

"No, not the staff. I need to see the records room," I said, drawing out the last word.

For a moment, she evaluated me. Her hand reached under the desk and I assumed she was tripping a silent alarm. I backed away, ready to hightail it before security tackled me and dragged me out. Her hand reappeared. In it she held a little plastic clip-on badge that read *Visitor*. "Just through there." She pointed to a doorway to the left of the entryway.

Okay, don't tell any of the Magics I ever had this thought, but at that moment it felt damn good to be a witch. Magic was cool. Creepy, but cool. Once I stepped through the door, a few people at their desks glanced up as I passed by, but most just went back to clacking away on their keyboards, probably searching for cat videos or some other useful government work.

I slipped into the records room. The receptionist had said the staff were at a meeting, but I doubted she kept tabs on everyone, so I checked around before I started rifling through things. Apparently, she was better at her job than I gave her credit for because the records room was a total ghost town. Taking up most of one wall was a whiteboard with boxes made from thin, black tape. On one side ran times. Across the top, someone had written the days of the week. A meeting had been scheduled that day from two to three. The clock above the white board read 2:27.

Needless to say, I had to hustle, but other people's filing cabinets are uncharted territory that newcomers must navigate purely by guesswork. The confidence I'd faked at the reception desk was quickly being replaced by nerves. Luckily, the adrenaline that had my heart pounding with as much ferocity as a giant stomping through a fairy tale village was also honing my focus. After scanning the labels on half a dozen cabinets, I landed on the death records.

I grabbed a handful of files. Trying to remember what I'd told Carl about the supposed adventures of Mr. Tenpenny's corpse, I flipped through the stack of paperwork, scanning the sheets for a morgue transfer, the letterhead of Stevens Funeral Home, and an autopsy report. I knew what I was looking for, but that didn't make the damn documents pop into view. After sifting through the first two-inch thick file, I had come across dozens of pieces of letterhead from every funeral home in Portland except the one I needed. I cursed myself as my hands started shaking. Why had I specifically said Stevens?

Starting on the second file, I nabbed a morgue transfer straight away, then an autopsy report about halfway through. But still no Stevens letterhead. Did they email everything? Stupid digital age.

My gaze darted to the wall clock. I'd already been in the room too long. Assuming they kept their meeting to schedule, I only had about ten minutes to get what I needed, work my magic on it, get it copied, get the originals back in order, and get my butt out of here.

I couldn't bother with the letterhead from Stevens, the funeral home I'd told Carl the remains of Mr. Tenpenny might have been taken to. I'd have to improvise. I could grab another funeral home's papers and call it good. I was about to slap the manila folder shut when, as if the fates were cutting me a rare break, on the final page I caught sight of the somber scrolls of the Stevens logo.

I bit back a whoop of joy and set to work.

I needed a transfer request from the morgue insisting on the return of Busby's body for more analysis, an autopsy report with chemical analysis declaring foul play had been ruled out, a transfer report sending his undead remains to Stevens Funeral Home, their denial of acceptance, in fact, their denial that any body had accompanied the paperwork, and a note stating the paperwork had been sent to the wrong place and was now on its way to Wood's Funeral Home.

The clock said I had six minutes to manage all that bureaucratic runaround.

I laid the sheets out and focused on rearranging the words, hoping I was getting the dates I'd told Cologne Carl correct. Hovering my hand over the forms (Fiona could do it without any hand flourishes, but I wasn't quite up on my forgery skills yet), I concentrated on moving the molecules and rearranging them into the letters and numbers I needed. When the ink began shifting, I almost cried out with delight. With my lips tightly pinched to keep quiet, the dates changed, the locations changed, and finally, the name of the deceased changed. Never mind the fact that that particular person was showing great resistance to being deceased.

I sound all cool about this, but my hands were shaking like fir branches in a wind storm. I'd also developed a headache from concentrating so hard on the spell. Once I had the final Y of Tenpenny in place, my gut was roiling worse than the time I'd eaten week-old tacos, and my legs had an unstoppable tremble to them as I hurried over to the photocopier to make two copies of my handiwork. I slipped one copy of the paperwork into one of the folders as I crammed the files back into the cabinet. Worried someone might inspect my satchel on the way out, I slipped my copy under my shirt.

I stepped out of the records room just as three of the staff were coming back from their meeting. There were a few questioning looks, but no one tried to stop me or ask what I'd been doing in their little kingdom.

Press my luck? Why not?

I raised my finger and eyebrows to signal to the last person that I had a question. I also added an apologetic smile that would make her think she was the only person in the world who could help me. "Do you know where—" Oh hell. I had no idea what Carl's last name was. "Ugh, I'm so bad with names. Carl, I think, wears too much cologne. Do you know where he is?"

The woman, her hair tied up in a bun and wearing a turquoise shirt decorated with cat paw prints around the collar said, "Oh me too, it's embarrassing how many times I can meet a person and still forget their name. But I don't know any Carl. What department?" I told her. "No, I know everyone who works there and there's no Carl. You sure you have the name right?"

The roiling in my gut made a sudden halt as my innards turned to ice. Who exactly was Carl? I thought of his pat down of Mr. T and his asking about any objects Busby had been brought in with.

"Um, maybe not," I stammered, then put my hand to my belly, gently so the hidden papers didn't crinkle. "Sorry, I need to go."

"I have some Pepto in my desk—"

"Thanks, I'm good."

I hurried toward the main lobby. I said a quick thanks to the receptionist, who didn't seem to recognize me. I hoped the Voice Modulation Spell hadn't caused any permanent brain damage as I handed in my visitor's badge.

I caught the bus back over the bridge and got off at the stop nearest Mr. Wood's, the same stop where Mr. Boswick had waited after his waking. I thought wistfully back to the days when dead people's problems were so much easier to solve.

When I entered, I could hear Mr. Wood in his office. He was on the phone and if the bright voice and chortling laughter were any indication, it was a welcome conversation. I waited, biding my time by raiding the kitchenette cabinet for a packet of cookies, but Mr. Wood was chatting up a storm that showed no signs of dwindling anytime soon. So, I put the paperwork into an envelope then jotted *For Carl* on the front.

I left a separate note for Mr. Wood, telling him to hand the envelope to Carl and to play innocent about its contents and to most definitely not let Carl into the funeral home beyond the lobby. Hopefully, I added, the paperwork would buy us time until Carl returned Friday to see that we did indeed have the remains of Busby Tenpenny sorted and ready for burial.

But would we? Within the next two days, I had to complete my training and draining, I had to figure out who killed Mr. T, and I had to get him dead, truly dead, none of this wishy washy dead-ish nonsense. With new resolve, I left Mr. Wood's to walk home.

The day was still bright with late spring sunshine, but when I stepped outside, my skin instantly tingled and my senses went on high alert as if I were roaming the streets alone at midnight with a big "Easy Victim" sign taped to my back. I looked around, half-expecting, half-hoping Mr. Tenpenny or one of the other Magics to be somewhere nearby, but I forgot that most of them weren't speaking to me. The feeling didn't go away as I picked up the pace to pass by the park's looming shrubbery where any sort of madman or evil wizard might be lurking. I kept telling myself I most definitely did not hear footsteps behind me.

I don't like feeling scared. I know, you'll say no one does, but is that really true? People bungee jump to relish the thrill from a brush with death. Horror movies keep getting released because people like shelling out their hard-earned cash for a couple hours of terror.

Not me.

I spent enough of my childhood cringing while someone

screamed at me, of having food withheld as punishment to the point I feared I might starve to death, and of thinking someone cared for me only to find out they just needed a new pint-sized punching bag. So to purposely go around seeking out fear? Not for this girl. I try to live a quiet life — well, I used to — and I like things to be predictable because predictable things aren't scary.

I could have walked home. It was only five blocks, but my nerves felt like they'd been run through a cross-cut paper shredder. I needed something predictable, something familiar, something nearby. I turned on my heel and went back to Mr. Wood's, telling myself I was only popping back in to make sure he got the paperwork. And okay, to perhaps see if he'd want to order anything to eat.

Mr. Wood didn't let me down. He was so relieved to see Mr. Tenpenny's paperwork that he picked up the phone and ordered an army's worth of Thai food. The delivery driver arrived, we worked our way through a variety of curries and noodle dishes, and Mr. Wood politely skirted the topic of what I'd been up to the past week. Since I wanted to have a MagicLand-free evening, I was content to let him prattle on about what had been happening on his favorite TV program, the great bargain he got on a hunk of ham, and gossip about Myrtle Norton being kicked out of the bingo hall and asked to never come back. Turns out she really was cheating. Why she would cheat at bingo of all things is a matter I'll never understand.

A full belly and plenty of light conversation did the trick. Most of my MagicLand woes had fallen away and a comforting, easy warmth filled me.

Until I thought of walking home.

The sun was setting by now, but with Portland's longitude, light lingers long into the evening in late spring. Even though it was well past eight, it was still twilight out. It didn't matter. It could be as bright as noon in August, and it wouldn't have stopped something itching at back of my neck that had nothing to do with the cheap detergent I'd picked up at the Dollar Store.

I felt like a paranoid idiot. I was a witch. I could just send a tree branch flying at someone's head if they attacked me, right? I didn't know. I had heard there was a Magical Self-Defense course, but that wasn't part of my curriculum. Finally, I sucked up my pride and asked if Mr. Wood could drive me home. He didn't ask questions, he didn't hesitate to drive me the five blocks, nor did he mock my laziness. Seriously, where had Mr. Wood been when I needed a foster parent?

When we reached my building, I got out, told Mr. Wood thanks for the ride and for dinner, and as he pulled out of the parking lot, he tooted his horn to say goodbye. I waved, but the fear gremlin kept gnawing away at my gut.

At the main door, I tapped in the entry code and gripped the handle. Out of habit, I glanced down at the gnome. It was gone. For the first time since I'd moved in, it was gone. Sure, it moved now and then. I assumed Morelli did it when he weed whacked the sad patch of greenery. But it was never gone.

The skin prickling sensation crawled over me again, but this time it was more intense than ever. It had me utterly creeped out, but even that was pushed aside by the stench near the door. Imagine someone took restaurant refuse and doused it in essence of skunk. It was so strong I released the handle and put my hand to my nose. The electronic lock clicked back into place.

I told myself that I really was being ridiculous. Morelli was all about security. He didn't even give me the entry code for the first two weeks after I moved in — which had been a fun fourteen days of speaking to him on a daily basis since I had to call him every time I came home. As part of his safety measures, my apartment door was adorned with a high-quality lock and deadbolt. Surely once I got in, I'd be safe and everything would be fine.

I entered the code again. When the lock released, I whisked open the door, scurried over the threshold, and gagged on the stink wafting from Morelli's apartment as I tugged the door closed behind me.

This time on the stairs I made no effort to be quiet. I was hoping Morelli might want to follow me up to make sure I wasn't performing any satanic rituals in my front room or whatever it was he suspected me of. But he must have been lost in the task of braiding his back hair because there was no sound of the TV coming from his apartment and he didn't even bother to crack open his door to scowl at me. What's a lady have to do to get some attention, right?

When I got to my door I breathed a sigh of relief to see it was still closed. It hadn't been barged in with the door hanging off its hinges, the deadbolt hadn't been blasted out with an explosive, and the knob remained as securely locked as I'd left it.

None of this stopped the sensation that someone wearing needle-soled shoes was using the skin on my neck and arms as a dance floor. My hands shook so badly my key missed its slot a couple times. Once I finally managed to unlock the door, I stepped warily into the darkness.

I flicked on the light. And my gut dropped into my boots, crashed through the landing, then splattered onto the ground floor.

CHAPTER THIRTY-SEVEN

THE SACRIFICE

My home, never tidy to begin with, had been ransacked. I'm sure Fiona would have made some comment about not being able to tell the difference, but as I scanned the disaster area something bubbled up inside me. I didn't care about the slashed sofa. I didn't care about the books I'd recently shelved being tossed back onto the floor. I didn't care about my dishes broken all over the linoleum.

My concern honed in on one thing. You can ruin my couch, you can make a mess of my reading material, but you do not mess with my cat. Or, well, Mrs. Escobar's cat.

"Pablo?" I called.

I heard a soft meow, and my heart jolted. I didn't know yet if Pablo might be hurt, but if he was meowing, at least he was alive. I wanted to run to him, but I held my ground, caution telling me not to step beyond my welcome mat. I kept the door open. I needed an easy escape route if someone came after me.

Still standing on the landing, I pulled out my phone to call the police. I'd just dialed the first two numbers of police dispatch when a boulder bashed into the side of my head. Okay, it probably wasn't a real boulder, otherwise my brains would have ended up all over my shag carpeting, but it was a heavy punch that would have made my second foster father envious.

I staggered a couple steps. Then, fearing I'd go tumbling down the stairs, I forced my legs to stop moving. My eyes blurred. Not good when someone's trying to bash your skull in. I don't know what instincts or inner sense churned through me, but without even seeing my attacker, something told me to duck. A *whoosh* of air sounded just above me as I narrowly avoided another blow to the head.

If I'd learned one thing from all the beatings I'd endured as a kid, it was how to move quickly. And how to fight back. At eight years old my defensive punches weren't terribly effective, but once I realized that having the crap beat out of me by my caretakers wasn't the norm, I never once just took a beating.

From my crouch, I sprang toward my attacker's legs. The brain does the oddest things in times of stress. Mine, for instance, bothered to notice that the man was wearing linen slacks and that, from the smooth feel of them, they weren't cheap. Good. I hoped I was bleeding all over them.

Two quick punches pounded into my back. They made me want to throw up, but I managed to stagger backward, aiming my body toward my apartment where I hoped to slam the door and get to MagicLand where someone might help me. Instead of tripping through the wide open doorway, I ended up butting into the doorjamb. My attacker grabbed my upper arm. I looked up to see who it was, but I still couldn't see properly and the pain was making me dizzy. All I could make out was a masculine face topped with dark hair.

Cinnamon.

Cologne.

The words popped into my head then were promptly obliterated as a fist plowed into my cheekbone. Any lower and I'd have been knocked out and at his mercy. I remained upright, but the pain was so bad I didn't think I'd be able to stay that way much longer.

Of all the times for Morelli to mind his own damn business.

I drove my knee up, aiming for my assailant's groin but hitting only his thigh. Beyond possibly giving him a good charley horse, my attack did nothing but piss him off. Through the haze, I saw his fist coming toward me. It was going to connect with my eye and it was going to hurt.

A noise midway between a growl and a howl filled the air around me. I thought it was coming from me. I was so disconnected from any sense other than pain, I wouldn't be surprised if I started spouting Shakespeare in my injury-induced delirium.

I braced for it, but the punch never came. Had I ducked aside? Had the guy suddenly become a pacifist?

The howling cry came again. I opened my eyes. My vision had cleared enough to see a big ball of orange fluff in the place where the man's face should be. He, the man that is, was screaming. Pablo, rampaging with teeth and claws, yowled, hissed, screeched.

My attacker raised his hands, placing them near Pablo's body. Near, but not touching. My legs twitched, ready to lunge, ready to tackle the villain while he was blinded.

Before I could move, Pablo went flying backwards like someone had just yanked an invisible cord tied around his chest. When he crashed into the far wall, I heard a crunch and then a rush of air forced from his lungs. The man, clutching at his face, staggered back and stumbled down a few stairs. I hoped he would fall and break his neck, but he caught himself, ran down the steps two at a time, and threw himself out the front door.

I didn't go after him. I suppose that's what a hero in a movie would have done, but I freaking hurt. My face felt like a pulsating mass of bruises and I wasn't sure if my kidneys would ever be the same again. I couldn't stand, so I reached up, fumbling to shut and lock the door. I then crawled over to Pablo. The angle of his body told me all I needed to know. Unless he'd somehow evolved a rubber spine, he couldn't survive a twist in his back like that. I knelt down by him, stroking his body. He had saved me.

There was a knocking at my door. My magic door, that is. I startled and hovered protectively over Pablo's body as if that would help him. Despite the fear of what might be behind that door, it was all I could think to do. It was all my body could manage. I'd used up all my adrenaline reserves for probably the next six weeks. Then I realized if another attacker was coming for me, he certainly wouldn't bother with niceties like knocking.

The light rap came again. I turned my back to it and didn't answer, but the latch clicked open anyway. So much for privacy. I glanced over my shoulder. Through the blur of tears, I saw Tobey shutting the door. Tall, with dark hair. Could he—?

No. Even in the blur of things, I knew my attacker's hands had never touched Pablo. Pablo hadn't been physically thrown; he'd been magically sent flying with a Shoving Charm. Tobey couldn't even shift a feather, let alone an entire cat. At least I'd learned to think before throwing accusations around.

"I was leaving Fiona's and I heard noises," he said. I couldn't speak. My throat was closing up with emotion over Pablo's sacrifice and my face throbbed so hard I was afraid my jaw muscles might explode if I moved them. Tobey rushed over. "Is he—?" Then he caught sight of my face. "What the hell happened?"

"He saved me," I mumbled, then burst into tears as snot threatened to bubble out my nose. I may not be a pretty crier, but sometimes you can't help it.

Tobey gripped my arm. I winced, but he pulled me to my feet and scooped up Pablo, being amazingly careful with the poor thing as he cradled the cat corpse in his arm. "Let's get you both to Runa."

"Pablo's dead," I blubbered.

"He died helping a human, and he's a cat." I staggered after Tobey, who maintained a tight hold on my hand. My back screamed with every step. "There's special circumstances. Cats are natural absorbers. There might be a chance."

CHAPTER THIRTY-EIGHT
MORE TEST RESULTS

When we barged through the door of Dr. Dunwiddle's, she was stocking a shelf with more of those long slim boxes. Her back was to us as she said, "Be right with you."

"It's an emergency," Tobey said. Emergency? Pablo wasn't breathing, his eyes weren't fluttering, and his sleek body was withering with every second that passed. We'd gone well past the triage stage.

Tobey placed Pablo on the counter next to the register as if he were buying eight pounds of dead feline. Dr. Dunwiddle turned, her glasses lagging slightly behind. When the glasses caught up and Runa got a good look at me, she winced sympathetically then looked down to examine the cat. I probably needed more immediate attention, but she ignored me and hovered her hands over Pablo for a few moments. Her lips tightened as she shook her head.

"He can't be helped," she said as her glasses came to rest beside Pablo's head. "The spell needs to be instantaneous with a spinal fracture."

"He fought for her. Doesn't that give him special privileges?" asked Tobey. "There has to be something you can do."

"It does, but with these injuries, it's too late. I'm sorry," she said, more to him than me. Tobey slumped his shoulders.

"Someone attacked her. Just as they attacked my grandfather."

"You think it was for the watch?" My words slurred drunkenly through my swollen cheek. "How would they know I had it?"

"They wouldn't have unless they'd been tipped off," said Runa. "You didn't do any magic when you went home, did you?" I didn't think I was capable of moving any of my facial muscles, but something in my expression must have given me away. "Girl, you are not worth our trouble. Because of what you are, until you learn control over your magic, when you use it away from MagicLand where we know how to conceal it, you're sending up blinking arrows that point to a glowing neon sign that says, 'Magic being used here.' Do you think I left you that note specifically telling you not to use magic just for my own amusement?"

Actually, before dismissing it altogether, I thought her warning had been out of worry that I might blow up my entire block.

"A little explanation of why might have deterred me," I said. Or rather, grunted since moving my mouth sent hot agony thrumming from my chin to my forehead.

"I doubt it," she muttered.

As Runa worked some Soothing Spells on my face and back, I stared at Pablo. Every tiny bit of emotion I'd experienced over the past week and a half seemed to be piling onto his limp body.

"I hate this," I said flatly. Runa stopped her ministrations and the throbbing instantly started up again. "This is what happens when you care. This is what happens when you make an effort."

"Cassie, you couldn't have known you'd be attacked," Tobey said and placed his hand consolingly on my shoulder. I flicked it away, regretting the action as it sent a new jolt of pain through my back.

"I don't mean that," I yelled. "I mean all of it. Pablo is dead because of me, because I helped your grandfather. I should never have helped any of them in the first place. If I'd just kept to my own business, I wouldn't have helped Mrs Escobar and I wouldn't have ended up with her stupid cat. Her sister was going to kill him. I only delayed the inevitable. You can't change fate, no matter how much magic oozes from your pores." I held my arms out and jiggled them as if shaking off droplets of magic.

I pushed past Tobey and out of the shop. I was through with this day. I just wanted to go home and stick my throbbing face in the freezer for a few hours. But apparently even that small wish wasn't to be because Dr. Dunwiddle came running out calling my name and telling me to stop. Tobey jogged in front of me to block my way.

"What is this? Magical intervention? Just give me some magic aspirin and let me go home."

"Cassie, I need to speak with you," Dr. Dunwiddle said so sternly her face twitched with tension.

"About what?"

"In my office, not here on the street."

"Oh good, a private magic consultation."

"I'll wait for you," Tobey offered.

"Don't bother," I said.

His eyes flared with indignation, then disappointment. He muttered something about ingrates, then pointed in the direction of Runa's clinic.

Grudgingly, I went back inside Dr. Dunwiddle's. Pablo was still lifeless on the counter, and I thought bitterly that she hadn't even tried. Probably because it was my cat. If it had been Fiona's cat, it would be rolling in catnip right now. I mean, how hard could it be to rework the bone molecules back into their proper place, give him a little Frankenstein-style jolt, and wake him up?

"What now?" I snapped once we'd gone into her consulting room, leaving Tobey out in the shop.

"You're the one always wanting explanations. Well, I'm giving you one." She paused as if waiting for one of my snide retorts. "I told you not to do magic away from here because your blood test results came back."

"It took that long? You know they can do that in less than twenty-four hours in the non-magic world."

"Yes, well, the sample had to be run a few times to verify something."

"Well, that certainly sounds like good news."

"Look, I'm sorry your cat died. I'm sorry you were attacked, but we are working as hard as we can to get you trained so you can be done with us, you ungrateful brat."

"You have no right to judge me."

"Don't I?" she asked sharply as she grabbed a small towel and wafted her hand over it. Ice crystals formed on the terrycloth surface. "We have, with short notice, made time in our schedules specifically for you, while you've done nothing but be bitter, irritable, and rude ever since you came here." She didn't realize they had nothing to do with it; that's how I always was. Still, maybe I had ratcheted up the attitude a few notches since stepping through the door to MagicLand. I broke my harsh stare and glanced away. I suppose I'd been a jerk. Runa handed me the icy towel. I pressed it to my eye and felt an instant sensation of relief as she continued more calmly. "We will get your magic out, but you need to work with us. This isn't exactly something we do every day and I've just found out it's going to be a lot harder."

"Please don't tell me this involves extra potions work."

"No, but you have a condition that is very rare." That didn't sound good. Was I going to die? Maybe I really did have magic cancer. "It's not deadly," she said as if reading my mind. Wait, could she read my mind? "You are an absorber."

"So I've been told."

"But you're also a giver. Now, giving isn't your dominant trait, but you actually have both sides of an uncommon magical coin."

"I'm a magical hermaphrodite?" This actually got a smile out of Dr. Dunwiddle. She pressed a hand to my back and my kidney suddenly felt like it wasn't about to burst out of my body.

"In a manner of speaking. It's incredibly rare and it really complicates things. Like I said, the giving side isn't your strongest aspect. No surprise there. The absorbing side is much more prominent, but what this basically means is you can both take and give power."

I'm a god!

"Is that a good thing?" What I meant was, *Worship me, you puny mortal!*

"It's good as long as you aren't ever in the hands of the Mauvais, or at least as long as he doesn't realize what you are. You're— Fiona could explain it better."

As I mentioned, I'd read my *Principles of Physics and Magic.* From cover to cover, in fact. In it had been diagrams to illustrate the concept of givers versus absorbers. Each had positive and negative poles, and the way their magic worked depended on the directional flow of energy between those poles. If I had both in me, the energy would be flowing both ways.

"I'm like a rechargeable battery?"

Dr. Dunwiddle arched an impressed eyebrow. "Exactly. And what is the benefit of a rechargeable battery?"

"You don't have to throw it out?"

She looked at me in that way that told me I hadn't quite made the connection I was supposed to. After telling me to lower the towel, she worked her hands over my cheekbone. As the tightness in my skin eased, I racked my brain for what else it could be. Why had she mentioned the Mauvais getting hold of me? The answer hit like another kidney punch.

"The Mauvais could use me as his own personal battery."

"You may be unpleasant," Runa said, lowering her hands, "but you are smart. Yes, he could. And while sugar will enhance your magic and your absorbing side, it also boosts the giving side, and that means your magic could be taken. All this also makes you far easier to track when you successfully do magic, which is why I told you not to do any."

I tried really hard not to think about all the cakes Alastair had fed me. I tried really hard not to wonder what he might have taken from me during that peck on the very cheek that had been punched. I tried really hard not to picture the linen slacks he'd worn when I first saw him. Did those slacks now have blood on the leg? Could he be—?

No, Cassie, you will not start accusing people again. Keep your mouth shut and focus.

"It seems a little more urgent to get this out of me, then."

"Yes, but unfortunately, it's not going to be as simple as I hoped it might be." Because that's what I wanted to hear. "Not that it was going to be simple to begin with considering your strength, but it's going to require extra skill to drain you. One benefit, though, is that if we can tap into your giving trait, we can drain your absorbing through it and that should clear you of most of your magic."

"What do I need to do?"

"We've only got a few days. Just please train harder and be patient." That I could do. With effort. "And we need to keep the Mauvais from finding you." Leave it to Runa Dunwiddle to add a storm cloud to one of my rare moments of optimism. "You could stay at Fiona's, but I imagine you'd prefer to remain at your apartment."

Apprehension filled me over going home, but it was home. I told her I would.

"We can add some protection over it. Someone was supposed to have done so earlier, but I'll sort that out with him later. I can't think of how anyone got past..." Jumping right over this mysterious half-sentence, Runa continued with uncharacteristic brightness, "Well, never mind. Did you pick up any scent on the person who attacked you?"

Cinnamon. A scent that reminded me of Alastair. It wasn't his dominant scent, but it was nearly always there, lingering under the aroma of chocolate and raspberries.

But there'd also been another odor.

"Cologne."

"Coward." Runa practically spat the word and pulled a disgusted sneer. She stepped back and scrutinized my face. "I think I've done all I can do. Nature will have to do the rest. Now, come on, let's find something for your cat."

I followed Dr. D out to the front shop where Tobey stood looking over the greeting cards. While she searched under the cash register counter, I ignored Tobey and gave Pablo a final pet goodbye, secretly hoping he would wake, but the damn cat remained stubbornly inert. Eventually, Dr. Dunwiddle pulled out a shoebox. I slipped Pablo in, glad he was still limp and rigor mortis hadn't set in yet.

Dr. Dunwiddle snapped her fingers over the lid. "That will keep him from decomposing until you can pick a burial spot for him." I perked up at this bit of witchery. How handy might that be in my trade? I detested the stench of embalming fluids and formaldehyde. If I could just—

No, I needed rid of this. The negatives far outweighed the positives in my book.

Runa and Tobey walked me back to my portal, and oddly

enough, both came through with me. Runa stepped in and worked a few spells. I assume these were for protection. They certainly weren't cleaning spells, and she left without even performing a Stitching Spell to fix my sofa. And for the record, I don't really know if there is a Stitching Spell, but there must be, right?

Without a word to one another, Tobey and I began tidying up the mess my unwanted guest had made.

Eventually, even I began to be weirded out by the silence, so of course I broke it as clumsily as possible with a question that had been irritating me ever since Fiona refused to answer it.

"So, if you're not a wicked wizard," I asked as I swept up a pile of what used to be dinner plates, "why were you threatening Fiona? I saw you, you know, grabbing her, yelling at her."

"I was mad," he muttered, then palmed five books and placed them on a nearby shelf, arranging them with far more attention than necessary.

"Clearly. I may be awkward with other humans, but I'm not clueless about reading their emotions. Why were you mad?"

Tobey gave a dramatic sigh during which his shoulders lifted and slumped. He turned around and looked about to argue with me until I fixed a stern gaze on him that told him I would keep pestering until he answered. Surprisingly, it worked.

"I asked her about your being drained. I wanted to know if I could try for a transfusion." Before I could joke that he'd be chock-full of Cassie Magic, he continued, "But she said I was low on the list since previous efforts to transfuse me had failed. I felt stupid and disappointed, and I lashed out."

"You really want to be Magic?"

"Yeah," he said, returning to his book shelving chore. "You don't know what it's like to be on the sidelines of a community that your family and friends are full members of."

"Trust me, I think I know a thing or two about feeling out of place, about feeling unwanted."

"Right. Sorry."

The silence resumed and this time I let it fester. When things were back in order — except for Pablo's spine — Tobey paused at my real world door. "I'm sorry about your cat."

"I'm sorry about accusing you of being a homicidal maniac."

He smiled at that and closed the door behind him.

If I hadn't been so exhausted, I might have been kept awake by thoughts of Tobey's strange change in his attitude toward me and what it might mean. But I was exhausted, and the instant my head hit the pillow, I ventured into the land of sleep.

THIRTY-NINE

A STRANGE DAY

When I checked the mirror the next morning, my face was as bruised as I'd feared, but whatever Runa had done had deflated the swelling and closed up the wounds. I smeared a little makeup over the bruises, but the foundation only turned them a sickly shade of crusty purple, so I gingerly washed it off. I would just have to wear my injuries with pride.

I was in my closet and about to step into MagicLand when my phone pinged. I batted a coat out of my way to check the message. It was from Mr. Wood:

Carl said can't come this AM. I think we're off hook, but thx for getting paperwork. BTW, I never asked, where'd U find it? Everything else going OK?

This was followed up by Mr. Wood's usual signature of three happy face emojis.

I replied back that all was well and on track. Still, something bugged me about Carl's schedule change.

I slipped the phone back into my pocket and was barely out my MagicLand door when I saw the silhouette of a man moving toward me. My body tensed. My heart churned, sending extra blood to my muscles and readying them to fight since I no longer had a tabby to defend me.

Once he stepped into better lighting and I recognized who was heading for me, my tension only increased. I might not be able to pick out my attacker from a police lineup, but there were features that stood out. Dark hair. Cream-colored linen slacks. A faint hint of cinnamon. Features all found on the man striding determinedly toward me.

As he got closer, Alastair's face showed no menace and revealed nothing but fretful concern. Despite telling myself to believe the expression in his eyes was genuine, despite begging my suspicious mind to shut up, I glanced down at his pant leg. No blood. But wouldn't magic be just the thing for getting out stubborn stains?

"I'd heard you were attacked. Are you all right?" He reached up to touch my cheek. My feet instinctively stepped back, my hands clenched into fists, and the locket under my shirt felt cold against my skin. Alastair, taking the hint, pulled his hand away without touching me.

"Does it hurt?" he asked. Everything, his voice, his eyes, his demeanor, showed sympathy, concern, worry. Why couldn't I believe they were real?

I examined his cheeks. I'd seen Pablo's claws digging into my attacker's face. Alastair's skin showed no scratches, but he could have closed the wounds as easily as Runa had done mine.

"No, I just—"

Alastair reached for my hand. I was just thinking it might be comforting to let him do so, and that now might be a good time to ask him about the locket, when an overly perfumed Vivian swayed her hips up to us and latched onto Alastair's extended arm.

"Shall we?" she said, giving a very clear indication they had a prior engagement, one that didn't include letting him moon over someone's mangled face. She passed me a vicious smile and I wondered how her layers of makeup didn't crack. "You look awful," she said sweetly.

"Thanks for the update."

Alastair bit back a smirk, then extended his free arm as if he wanted to squeeze my hand. When I stiffened at the offer, he quickly drew back and hurt disappointment filled his eyes. Missing all of this, Vivian clutched tighter to the arm she'd latched onto, giving it an insistent tug.

"We should really go, Allie. I've just got to tell you the latest." As they strolled away, she tried to lean into him, but Alastair kept his own stance rigid, then jerked his arm out of her grasp. I did the mature thing and flipped them off behind their backs.

"Vivian not to your taste?" asked the voice of Mr. Tenpenny, scaring me half to death. He's a stealthy one, I'll give him that.

"She's got something I don't, that's for sure." I turned to him and he flinched at the sight of my colorful face. "Does this mean you're speaking to me again?"

"I heard you and Tobey have settled your differences. He appears to have been a bigger man than I was. I should have understood your lack of knowledge."

"Well, you are a corpse. One has to make allowances for your kind." This drew a smile from his stiff upper lip.

"I thought I should go with you to your lessons today. I feel if we both attend, maybe I can steer things in the right direction."

"Did Dr. Dunwiddle send you to watch over me?"

"I fear we've made our own mistakes in this process. We haven't exactly done this sort of thing before and we all feel you deserve a little more attention."

My cheeks were already a bizarre shade of eggplant from my attack and I hoped it hid the blush that flared over them at this gesture of kind protectiveness. I don't know what it was about that morning. I should have been miserable over Pablo, and deep down I was, but somehow I felt I'd gotten to the low point and I'd now be on my way back up.

After all, what could be worse than making a huge magic faux pas, getting beaten half to death, being told you're so magical you almost can't be de-magicked, and having your cat killed? Oh, and don't forget the possibility of being tracked by the Wicked Wizard of Oz who might want to turn you into a magic battery.

I thought of my assailant. He was Magic, that was revealed in the way he'd sent Pablo flying. But how strong was he? Not very, it would seem, otherwise why wouldn't he have been able to just magic me into submission? That wasn't the most comforting thought, but it was better than imagining I'd been face-to-fist with the Mauvais or one of his minions. Then the question crawled in of why I had smelled cinnamon, one of Alastair's underlying scents? No, I swore to myself I wasn't going to go around suspecting people. I'm sure there's a perfectly reasonable explanation for why my cat killer had been wearing Alastair-esque linen slacks, had Alastair's dark hair, and carried the same scent I'd detected on my once-favorite teacher.

But what if the person wasn't Magic? I had just come out of a vision blur. Maybe I hadn't seen correctly. Maybe whoever it was had grabbed Pablo and thrown him across the room the old-fashioned way. Maybe I'd simply had a run-in with your average thug.

Or maybe I was deluding myself, I thought as Mr. T and I strolled over to Fiona's where my first lesson of the day was waiting.

"Ready?" Mr. T asked. I nodded and we stepped inside. Fiona flinched when she saw me.

"Don't worry, I don't think it's contagious," I said and smiled. Or tried to, anyway. Kind of hard to manage a welcoming expression when only half of your face feels like it's behaving.

The lesson went well. Despite my grumbling resistance to most things in MagicLand, I did love this class. I'd always liked science and looked forward to Fiona's explanations of how physics and magic intersected. Mr. Tenpenny spent a fair amount of time scanning the photos, but he also kept sneaking admiring glimpses of Fiona, so I didn't really believe he was too put out to be here. When the lesson was over, he stepped over to the bookshelf and pulled out a large book, at least four inches thick with a black cover. I really hoped this wasn't the magical etiquette book Alastair had mentioned.

"I think this might be good for you to read. You don't have time to cover it in your lessons or to finish it before you, well, you know. But if you wanted to look it over during the next couple evenings, you might find a few things of interest."

I opened the cover. Inside, the title page read: *An Enchanted History of the Portland Community*.

I looked up, unsure if the are-you-kidding-me expression was coming through the facial bruising.

"More history?"

"You don't have to read the whole thing. But I think it might give you some insight into where you come from. Promise me you'll at least thumb through it."

"We all keep one, each community," explained Fiona. "It's updated every few months to include local events, births, deaths, marriages, photos of daily life."

I wanted to tell them I had little interest in learning anything more about the community than I had to, but I'd done my fair share of pissing people off over the past week, so I merely mumbled a thanks and slid the monstrosity into my bag.

CHAPTER FORTY
A STRANGER EVENING

Even though she'd been eyeing her ancient floor buffer after I'd already magically cleaned her chimney, I had no urge to escape Lola's to go to my next lesson with Alastair. With my suspicious mind refusing to take a break, a layer of apprehension thicker than Lola's creosote was building in me.

Still, with Mr. Tenpenny chaperoning me, I couldn't exactly skip class. Besides, now that I suspected Alastair of being a cat-killing menace, I wanted to observe him with a more critical eye. But regardless of how much I tried, as we settled into a discussion of a Magic's rights and responsibilities in regards to interfering in Norm politics, I got no murderous or coup-plotting vibes from him. The presence of Mr. Tenpenny made my time with Alastair less awkward than it could've been, and the cake did wonders for my mood, even if it was frosted with Dr. Dunwiddle's warnings about the risks of boosting my magic.

I did a lot of sniffing during that lesson. It didn't look as strange as it sounds since the face pummeling had left my nose a little runny. But the only cinnamon I picked up on was the dash Mr. T added to his coffee.

When the lesson and the cake were finished, Alastair shook Mr. T's hand. He then shook mine, holding it a bit longer than necessary. I wanted to enjoy this, but the suspicions raging through my head and the uncertainty of how deeply Vivian had her claws in him were like pesticides being sprayed on any romantic butterflies that might have wanted to take flight.

At Gwendolyn's, Mr. Tenpenny got plenty of amusement from my lack of magical culinary skills. After another attempt at the color-changing potion and witnessing my mouse go bald rather than pink, Gwendolyn's hat had slumped so low I worried it might never puff up again. Then Mr. T had a suggestion: What if I measured and Gwendolyn did the mixing?

So I measured, Gwendolyn stirred, and her hat inflated bit by bit as we worked through a recipe that was meant to produce a wound-healing poultice. With the combination of lemon and lavender, it did smell soothing. Still, I was involved in the making of this witch's brew, so when Mr. T said, "Give it a try," I kept my hands pinned firmly to my sides. "Go on. Have a little faith in yourself."

Reluctantly, I scooped some of the cool gelatinous goo onto my fingers, then hesitated. Mr. T raised his eyebrows and I'm not sure if it was an expression of encouragement or a goading dare. I accepted the dare and smoothed the concoction over my face. I half-expected horns to sprout from my cheeks, or my scabbed-over wounds to burst open and my skin to fall right off my face and onto the floor. But the more I worked the stuff in, the more I delighted in an unbelievably soothing tingle.

"Your bruise is definitely more periwinkle than eggplant now," Mr. Tenpenny said, then rubbed some of the mixture between his fingers. Had I just served as his guinea pig?

"Well, if nothing else you are a decent magical prep cook," Gwendolyn said, but I could tell she wanted to add, "Just don't ever apply for a job in my kitchen."

At the end of the day, Mr. Tenpenny walked me to my door, then said his goodbyes and that he'd see me in the morning. I stepped inside, realizing that, one, the apartment felt weird without Pablo, and two, Tobey and I had finished off the beer while we'd been cleaning.

I thought of the past twenty-four hours. Mr. Tenpenny had given his borrowed time to be my bodyguard, and Tobey had voluntarily helped me clean this place up. Maybe I still had the creepy crawlies over being in my apartment alone, but I decided I'd show I could be a thoughtful human being and go see if they'd like to pop over for a drink at the Wandering Wizard.

Who could say, maybe when all this was said and done, Tobey and I could be friends. After all, we'd both be non-magics with a knowledge of the magical world at large. Cassie Black with friends. That would turn the universe on its head, wouldn't it?

Before venturing out, I picked up the book Mr. Tenpenny had loaned me. I figured it might be a good conversation point. Using my closet portal shortened the distance between Mr. T's and my place from a few miles to a few blocks. While this did save me bus fare, it also meant I had little time to practice what I might say once I got to my destination.

"Hey, want to go grab a brewski?"

"I just happened to be in the magic neighborhood and thought you two might be as thirsty as me."

"Me, you, beer now."

Ugh.

Just to be clear, in case you haven't guessed, I'm not a reach-out-and-risk-emotional-embarrassment person. For anyone else, this would just be a normal evening after class or work. For Cassie Black, this was a scary step. I'd rather confront my attacker again while getting a root canal. That's how far beyond my comfort level I was reaching.

But I'd had a good day, I wanted a beer and, weirdly for me, I wanted company. My fingers squeezed against the book's binding as I headed toward Mr. Tenpenny's, practicing my lines the whole way.

The door to the Tenpenny kitchen was on a small alley not far off Magical Main Street. Just after I rounded the corner from Main Street, I caught the heady scent of cheap perfume. I immediately ducked into Mr. T's alley, not wanting to run into Alastair and Vivian.

I peered around the neighboring building and saw no one on the street. When I turned back to the alley, I froze. Tobey. My heart leapt and not for joy. He was leaning forward, holding himself up with his right palm against the wall, his arm slightly crooked at the elbow. Between him and the wall was Vivian. It was the first time I'd seen her without a cigarette, but that small detail wasn't what grabbed my attention and slapped it around a bit.

With her back against the wall, she gazed up at Tobey, whose other hand rested on Vivian's impossibly tiny waist. Her head tilted as if eager for a kiss. The surprise of it made all the muscles in my arm turn to jelly and I dropped my book. As if guided on the same puppet strings, both their heads whipped toward me. I stood there, too confused to move. I couldn't even work up the motivation to be annoyed.

Vivian smiled that same wicked smile she'd given me earlier as her eyes locked on mine. Tobey at least had the decency to back away and look sheepish, shaking his head as if clearing it from Vivian's god awful scent of stale cigarettes and cheap perfume. Finally, after my brain took a few seconds of vacation time, the muscles of my body decided to function. I stooped down, hefted the book back into my arm, and turned on my heel to march back to Main Street.

"Cassie!" Tobey called. I halted but didn't turn.

"Never mind her," Vivian said. "Let's go upstairs."

I stormed off. Screw this. Screw magic. Screw making friends. Screw Tobey. No, let Vivian screw Tobey. It must be Alastair's night off.

Tobey ran up, grabbed me by the arm. The old me would've whacked him with the book. The new me had training. I jutted my free hand toward him. The gesture sent him staggering backward thanks to my super duper Shoving Charm that had been honed by all of the cleaning I'd done at Lola's.

"Magic," I sneered, and stormed my way back to my portal.

Mr. Tenpenny was waiting by my door. Could I not get rid of these people? He smiled, holding up three square, white boxes that looked like Chinese takeaway. His grin fell flat at the sight of me. I did the Shoving Charm again and sent the food splattering against the wall.

Mr. T started to say something, but I yanked open my door and slammed it in his face. Once out of my closet, I hurled the stupid book into the corner where Pablo's bed still rested. The massive book hit the wall hard enough to leave a dent — Morelli would no doubt make me pay for that. With a muffled thud, the book landed sprawled open on Pablo's bed.

I ripped open the fridge door and screamed in frustration.

Thanks to Tobey drinking more than his fair share, I still had no beer.

Wanting nothing to do with MagicLand, I left out my front door and hurried down the stairs. If Morelli saw me, he was going to regret it. But maybe he was engrossed in a YouTube video on *How to Tame Your Back Hair* because he didn't even bother to yell at me for stomping on the stairway.

I marched three blocks over to the nearest quickie mart. On the way, I experienced none of that neck-tingling eeriness, or maybe I was just too annoyed to feel it. Besides, if anyone even thought of messing with me, they would get a good dose of misdirected anger. I grabbed a six-pack of Terminal Gravity. As the pock-faced cashier mindlessly dragged the carton over the scanner, several police cars went zooming by with their lights flashing. Then a fire truck whizzed along and an ambulance wailed close behind as the clerk and I watched.

With the minimal amount of words being exchanged, I completed the transaction and stepped outside into the crisp night. Why was I so angry over this? I didn't even like Tobey. Had I really thought of reaching out and trying to be friendly? What kind of idiot was I? And not that I cared what Tobey got up to between the sheets, but why was Vivian latching onto men who spent time with me? I knew Tobey had no interest in me. He was only being nice the night before because I'd gotten my face bashed in. I still wanted to scream with the confusion of it all because that's what happens when you have a social I.Q. smaller than the average shoe size.

Just as I was entering the code to get in my building, just as I felt a hint of amusement at seeing the gnome had returned to his usual spot, my phone squawked out its ring tone.

I set down the beer, pulled the phone out of my pocket, and checked the number. I didn't recognize it, but something about it looked familiar. I answered.

And my world fell apart.

CHAPTER FORTY-ONE
THINGS GET WORSE

The number had been police dispatch. The same number I'd started to dial the night before. All my frustration over Vivian, all desire to lose myself in hoppy goodness, all focus on any other woes fell away. I abandoned the six-pack at the front door and ran the five blocks to Mr. Wood's.

Lights flashed and throbbed with such intensity someone could have thrown on thumping electronica tunes, sold some ecstasy, and held a block party rave. As I charged toward the funeral home, a burly policewoman, who could have passed for Gwendolyn's grouchy sister, blocked my way by physically placing herself in my path and holding out her arms as if to corral me. I was sorely tempted to use the Shoving Charm, but just managed to resist. The officer scrutinized my face as she held me back. "Can you tell me where you were this evening?"

Another cop raced up to us. He was slim, had Hispanic coloring, and was probably in his mid-fifties. "What's going on here?" he asked in a patient, yet concerned tone.

"Suspect. Clearly she's been involved in something," she responded, pointing to my cheek.

"I was attacked recently. You can see very well the wounds aren't fresh." Thank you, magic.

"So why are you here?" Bad Cop accused.

"I'm Cassie Black. I work for Mr. Wood." I held up my phone. "You called me." Before either of them could respond, two paramedics wheeled someone out of the building on a stretcher. Someone very round. Someone who wasn't moving. I shouted his name.

"Let her through," Good Cop said and escorted me to the stretcher, probably to keep me from running and trampling over any evidence.

When I got to the stretcher, I almost wished Bad Cop had done a better job at keeping me away. They had Mr. Wood in one of those neck stabilizer thingies and there were so many wounds he looked like he'd been attacked with a weed whacker. These were jagged cuts like those from hard punches, not smooth cuts like those from blades — believe me, I know my cuts. He had been in his pajamas. The top had been torn open, I assumed by the paramedics, but who knew. His pale chest wasn't moving as they rattled him into the ambulance.

In a daze, I asked what happened.

"Looks like the office has been broken into and ransacked. Probably just someone looking for drugs," the officer said reassuringly, because, you know, the idea of a larcenous junkie trying to get a fix is so much more comforting than the idea of some random person breaking in just to beat up your boss.

I didn't set them straight. This wasn't for drugs. This was for the watch. Just as my place had been broken into. The only reason I was still mobile was because I had Pablo the Attack Cat, quick reflexes, and a little magic on my side.

"Was your attack related, do you think?" Good Cop asked, his dark eyes showing genuine concern.

Oh, if you only knew.

"No, my boyfriend drinks too much," I lied. "Gets a little punchy."

"You should leave him. Or at least report him. We can't do anything if you don't press charges, you know."

"I'll take it under advisement, but I think we're through."

Luckily, "drug-related crime" fit the statistics of the neighborhood, and the police seemed happy to stick to their assessment. The ambulance's siren whooped to life and the vehicle sped off.

"And Mr. Wood? He's going to be okay?"

"He's going to emergency. There were back injuries. They'll do all they can."

And in case you didn't know, that's a euphemism for "Don't get your hopes up."

"He's being taken to Providence Emergency on Glisan," Good Cop continued. "I could have them call you unless you're planning to go there tonight."

"That's all right. I'll head over in a bit."

It was a lie. I wouldn't go. If Mr. Wood woke up, I'd have to look at his mangled face and his broken and possibly paralyzed body knowing I'd been the reason for his injuries. If he died, I'd be just as responsible. Call me a coward, but I couldn't really see the point of sticking around waiting for the death of another creature I cared for.

"Do you want a ride?" Good Cop asked.

"No. Thanks, though."

I left the scene and headed back to my apartment. Someone who really wanted that watch was roaming the streets of Portland. And if it was who I thought it was, he also wanted me. Oh wait, a man wants me? Better alert Vivian. Never mind that this man wanted nothing more than to turn me into a human battery.

Who cares? Let him. Once the petulant thoughts started rolling in, they continued tumbling like boulders in a landslide.

It's not like anyone would care if I disappeared. And so what if the Mauvais renewed his evil plan? I didn't care about the stupid magic community, and if Mr. Wood died, there wouldn't be any Norms I cared about either. If the Mauvais wanted to rule the world, let him.

I don't remember walking the five blocks home, but somehow, like an old draft horse, my feet knew the way. Surprisingly, my beer was still on the front step. I gave a morose grin at this tiny sign that goodness still existed in the world.

Assuming the bottles to be full of bubbly hop juice, I lifted the carton by its handle, using enough force to hoist seventy-two ounces of beer plus the glass to contain that beer. Silly me for making assumptions.

As the six-pack went jerking up way too fast, the sound of small pieces of metal pinged on the concrete at my feet. A scream of frustration balled up in my throat as one of the bottle caps rolled into the grassy strip and stopped at the gnome's feet.

In the time I'd been gone, someone had managed to drink all of my beers, put the bottles back in the holder, and settle the caps on top as a clever cosmic joke. Good to know the world wasn't being inconsistent. It was all horrible. And just to add a cherry on top of my Horrible Evening sundae, Morelli emerged from his apartment the second I stepped through the main door. The same garbage stench that had been lingering before smacked me once again.

"What?" I snapped, putting my hand to nose.

"Someone left this for you. Dark-haired guy. You better not be trying to sneak in a roommate," he said, flinging a small, square envelope at me. I had to uncover my nose to catch it. This not only meant I got walloped with another hit of Eau de Morelli, but when my fingers clenched onto the message, I caught the scent of perfume that smelled unbearably like the brand Vivian wore. Great. She's probably writing to tell me all about her and Alastair. Or her and Tobey.

"Thanks," I grumbled. I crammed the note I had no interest in reading into my back pocket and started for the stairs.

I'd barely gotten my boots up the first riser when Morelli said, "Also, you ought to know I'm raising the rent. Goes up three hundred bucks next week."

"Fine. I'm moving out anyway," I said without hesitation. I hadn't thought about moving out in months, but the moment the words came out of my mouth, it seemed like the best notion since the invention of the ballpoint pen. Why not leave? Mr. Wood was dying, if not already dead. I hated the Magics, and they didn't like me very much. And this place certainly wasn't worth a three hundred dollar rent increase. I needed a change and the sooner the better. I didn't have much. I didn't even have a cat. I could literally pack up tonight and go.

"And I'm keeping your cleaning deposit. I know you have a cat in there and that costs extra money you never paid."

"Fine. Keep it. Maybe you can use it to hire someone to shave your back."

I stomped up the stairs making as much noise as possible, slammed the door on Morelli's shouts to treat the place with respect, and gathered up any box or bag I could find.

I crammed my clothes into my suitcase and filled two cardboard boxes with books. From the main closet I grabbed my backpack and the stupid messenger bag that had started all this. Most of my dishes were broken, but I did have a bowl, plate, cup, and a set of silverware. I shoved them into the Corrigan's satchel.

Pablo still rested in peace in his box. I'd have to give him a sendoff wherever I ended up, but where was Fuzzy Mouse? Pablo would want Fuzzy Mouse in the kitty afterlife. I can't explain why, perhaps it was the stress chemicals overdosing my exhausted brain, but the need to ensure Pablo was reunited with Fuzzy Mouse for eternity became incredibly important. The damn cat had sacrificed himself for me, the least I could do for him was to let him silently decompose alongside his favorite toy.

I dropped to the floor to peer under the couch — the place Fuzzy Mouse normally ended up after Pablo batted it around. Nothing was lurking under there except some dust. I surveyed the room.

My eyes landed on Pablo's bed, which was smashed under my unwanted copy of *An Enchanted History of the Portland Community*. When it had fallen, it had landed open with the cover side down. I reached for the massive tome, stupidly cursing it for possibly squashing Fuzzy Mouse. Just as my hand closed in on the mouse-murdering manuscript, my eyes caught sight of the page the book had randomly opened to on its descent.

I froze in place. The room went still, and everything — Mr. Wood, Alastair, Morelli, Tobey, the beer, even Fuzzy Mouse — faded to insignificance.

CHAPTER FORTY-TWO
MOVIE POSTER

The page the book had opened to was mostly taken up with a photo. In the picture was a couple — the woman had my dark hair and pale features, but the man had my height and face shape. They both wore crisp, white dress shirts and navy blue blazers with a small badge-like insignia embroidered into the lapel.

Between them, his arms around my parents' shoulders was a white man with a deep tan and a roguish glint to his eyes. He wore a similar blazer, but had paired it with an equally dark blue top. My parents both held a medal in one of those flip-open boxes, but the guy in the middle, grinning as broadly as a model in a dental ad, had his medal around his neck.

The faces of my parents caught my attention, but what held it was the movie poster behind them. It had been pinned on a notice board. On the poster, posed with bum and breasts thrust out and lips pursed into a kiss like a stereotypical pin-up girl was Vivian. Or someone who looked very much like Vivian, right down to the mole on her upper right cheek.

I dropped the messenger bag. I placed Pablo gently on the floor and picked up the book. The caption read:

Simon and Chloe Starling and Devin Kilbride receiving honors for their unparalleled police work.

Taken in London, this is the last photo of the three who volunteered to travel there to follow their investigation into the Mauvais. Chloe Starling, it should be remembered, was the one who recovered the watch that if used by the Mauvais could have sent both the magic and non-magic world in a very dangerous direction. After missing for a time, the watch has now been transported to a safe location until it can be destroyed according to the prophecy.

Some claim there is no need to wait, that Alastair Zeller should have the talent to destroy the watch, but others have expressed concern about his past. Zeller insists he can't destroy the watch at this point — a statement that some sources have deemed as dubious. Therefore, after hearing the arguments, Headquarters insists on keeping the watch under guard. Still, a method of fully destroying the watch, not just deactivating it must be discovered. When it is, the watch will be transferred, handled, and supervised by a trusted member of HQ, Detective Inspector Busby Tenpenny. Until such time it will be kept safe, but some state there is no place that's safe from the Mauvais.

Someone had added a note in the margin in ink so red it practically glowed against the white page. Recognizing Mr. Tenpenny's formal handwriting, I traced my fingers over the words.

This photo was taken the day before Kilbride and the Starlings vanished. They are all presumed dead. The Starlings' daughter, four-year-old Cassandra Starling, who had been placed in the care of Lola Lemieux, went missing not long after her parents disappeared. She has not been found and is also presumed dead. Witness statements were taken by Lola Lemieux, an unnamed witness, and Alastair Zeller. Some still express concern over his previous interactions with the Mauvais although that had ended long before the day in question.

A confusing array of emotions pounded through me as I looked more closely at the photo. My hand went to the charm dangling from my neck.

How had Alastair gotten my mother's necklace? What in the world was this vague interaction he'd had with the Mauvais? If the Mauvais killed my mother and Alastair had her necklace, who did he get it from?

Rage boiled in me and I wouldn't have been a bit surprised to hear steam whistling from my ears. Someone killed these people who should have raised me. Someone made it so I lived a childhood of terror. That same someone attacked and possibly killed Mr. Wood, one of the few people who had ever treated me like a worthy human being. That someone had taken me from Lola who might have raised me on coconut cookies, kindness, and Caribbean cuisine.

This person, the Mauvais or someone trying to carry on his legacy (because how could he still be young enough to ignite another coup?), was hunting down the watch. In his search, he was going to each place the watch had last been.

I stared at my bags. The sight of them drove home how cowardly I was being. After Mr. Tenpenny's murder, after my apartment had been ransacked, after Mr. Wood's attack, it didn't take a genius to trace the next logical step: MagicLand.

The community had put their lives on hold to help me. Lola,

who I wanted to hug every time I was near despite my card-carrying status as a non-hugger. Fiona, who had shown a great deal of patience with me. Gwendolyn, who sacrificed her kitchen in her attempts to make a magic chef out of me. Dr. Dunwiddle, who was no friend of mine, but who had devoted more hours to my training than anyone else and who was willing to go against her beliefs to let me have what I wanted. Alastair. I couldn't untangle him and I didn't know if I wanted to. But as for the rest, I couldn't leave them to be attacked. Well, okay, except for Vivian.

Vivian.

I examined the poster again. It was definitely her. Did Magics age differently than normal people? No one had brought it up, but it was definitely the first question I'd be posing the next time I saw Dr. Dunwiddle. Something about Vivian had put me off right from the start. I mean, there's a fair number of people I don't like, but Vivian had instantly raised my hackles, and not just because she kept appearing when I least wanted her to. That shop. Why was it still displaying winter wear?

When I set the book aside, I caught sight of something on Pablo's squashed bed. A tattered and battered Fuzzy Mouse. I picked up the mutilated thing and slipped it into Pablo's cardboard casket.

"We'll get out of here soon, dude. But not just yet."

I replaced the lid and went through the closet door.

CHAPTER FORTY-THREE

FINAL NIGHT, PART ONE

It was full dark in MagicLand. A few people roamed down Main Street, enjoying the night. A couple giggled into each other's shoulders. If the pair got any closer, they might merge into a single, two-headed creature. I turned off Main Street and zigzagged my way along side streets to the quaintness of 1950s Street.

Two shops down from the corner stood Vivian's boutique. Closed as always. She was probably off getting busy with Tobey. Or Alastair. Or, who knows, maybe Alastair and Tobey. The two MagicLand men, besides Mr. Tenpenny, I'd spent the most time with. I didn't think that was a coincidence.

I looked around to see if anyone was approaching. The street was empty, so I tried the handle. Most people around here didn't bother with locking doors since locks don't pose much of a problem for Magics, but Vivan's was locked tight.

I glanced down at the keyhole. Alastair may have been assigned to be what was basically my Social Studies teacher, but his mechanical timers proved he was a fair hand when it came to tinkering. So, during one lesson last week, I'd pestered him to teach me a bit about magical mechanics, and that included a quick primer in locks. Thanks to that pestering, I now knew breaking and entering took little more than a quick charm. I reached again for the handle to cast the spell when I caught a faint whiff of cheap perfume.

I paused.

Vivian wears perfume.

I stepped back from my act of larceny. Something prickled just under my skin about that damn perfume. I knew it was something more than my own distaste for fragrances, but I couldn't pinpoint exactly what bothered me so much about it. I took in the window display.

A man in wool trousers and a navy blue turtleneck sweater posed next to a woman in a dove grey, cowl-necked sweater dress and fuzzy boots. In front of them stood a fake snowman, and in the air dangled glittering snowflake ornaments. A façade of winter. A season six months gone.

"Cassie?"

Alastair's voice startled me so hard had I actually been able to consume any of my beer, I would have peed it all out. "I thought I saw you turn down here. I wanted to talk to you."

As my heart tried to resume a normal pace, cynical questions and suspicions pounded through my mind. Was he looking for Vivian? Had he followed me? Was I in danger? *He always doted on you,* came Lola's words. Did he still dote on me, or was his interest in me more sinister?

But the book had said: *Some still express concern over his previous interactions with the Mauvais.*

Interactions? In some way, Alastair was, or had been, associated with the Mauvais. Alastair had my mother's locket. Alastair had been shocked to see Mr. Tenpenny up and roaming around. Alastair regularly fed me large doses of power-boosting sugar. Was he working with someone who wanted to turn me into a human battery?

It was time for confrontation.

"Where did you get this locket?" I demanded, pulling the charm up from under my shirt. His face dropped its warm greeting.

"Your mother gave it to me."

"Why would she give it to you?"

He swallowed hard and looked to his shoes. I didn't exactly think Alastair was Mauvais 2.0, but he had a connection to the original Mauvais. What was his tie to the Mauvais now?

"Well?" I insisted.

"I was younger than your parents, but I looked up to them. I had a crush on your mother. She knew it, so did Simon, your dad. I think he admired your mom for her kindness to me. A school boy crush wasn't anything to ruin what they had, and I don't know, I became something of a confidante to her."

His voice faded. After clearing his throat, he continued, "She and your father volunteered to chase after the Mauvais. I told her it was a terrible idea, that it should be left to Headquarters. The truth was that I wanted to go. I wanted to prove myself. But HQ said I was too young. That I had to stay behind. I wanted her to stay behind too, to stay safe, but she was so determined. Stubborn. Maybe it runs in the family," he added with a grin.

"I don't know what got to her. She didn't want to tell your dad because he'd have called it off immediately, but she told me the night before she left that she feared it might be her last mission. She worried something might go wrong, so she gave me the locket to give to you. I refused. I got a bit dramatic and told her she could damn well return to Portland and do it herself." Even in the low light, I could see Alastair's cheeks darken with embarrassment. "But I ended up with the locket and that was the last time we spoke."

"Why did she give you a locket and not ask you to watch over me?"

Alastair laughed and I hated how the light in his eyes gave my stomach a little flip.

"I was thirteen at the time. I mean, I was advanced for my age, but I couldn't even adopt a cat without permission. Many people would have willingly given you a home and raised you as their own, but you vanished before they could." His voice changed slightly when he said this. More clipped. More careful. Almost as if he were choosing his words carefully. It made the hairs on my neck itch. "The community tried to find you. They had their best trackers looking for your scent, but you were just gone. After a while they had to assume that whoever had—" he swallowed hard, struggling with the next words, "—killed your parents and Kilbride had done the same to you."

"But I wasn't dead. I was in Portland for over twenty years. It's not like I was far from MagicLand."

"MagicLand?" he asked with a gentle chuckle.

"It's what I call this," I said, gesturing vaguely at the world around me. Alastair laughed.

"It's official name is Rosaria, but these days we just think of it as a neighborhood of Portland. Anyway, why are you outside Vivian's shop?"

This seemed too much like he was changing the subject. The book that was making my satchel dig into my shoulder stated that people once had concerns about something in his past. The question of what that something might be left me unwilling to divulge everything to Alastair. He was chummy, if not intimate, with Vivian who had somehow walked off a movie poster looking the same as she had over twenty years ago. He had been close to my parents who had ended up dead. He was known to have "interacted" with the Mauvais. And he had immediately latched onto me, someone the Mauvais would be very keen to get his hands on.

"Just distracting myself with some window shopping." I indicated the sweater dress. "That's not my style, but maybe I could use a little change."

I desperately needed to talk to someone about all the ideas that were making a bouncy house of my head, but this time that someone was not Alastair.

Who then? Mr. Tenpenny? I'd been a jerk to him, but he already knew I wanted him dead. Could he really take offense to a little temper tantrum? "I think I'll go visit Mr. Tenpenny now. Did you want to walk with me?" I asked, secretly hoping to see how he would react if Vivian was still swapping spit with Tobey.

"No, I think I'll call it a night." He reached out and gave my hand a squeeze. Despite all my worries about his true motives, a heavy thump pounded in my chest at his touch. When he let go, my hand felt emptier than ever. As Alastair's arm lowered, he sniffed. His shoulders tensed and his voice was sharp when he asked, "Has Vivian been here?"

I said she hadn't, not that I'd seen.

Alastair eyed me and his jaw twitched like his own tongue was fighting over what to say. There was a wary look on his face, but also a worried one. Finally, after what seemed like the longest of awkward silences, he said, "Be safe, Cassie."

And with that, he turned on his heel and strode off.

CHAPTER FORTY-FOUR
FINAL NIGHT, PART TWO

While my mind buzzed like a colony of confused bees over Alastair's motives, behavior, and relationship to Vivian, I made my way over to Mr. Tenpenny's. Before I entered the alley, I peered around the corner to make sure Tobey wasn't still latched on to Vivian. The light was on inside the house, but the alley was empty. I climbed the stoop's three steps and peeked into the kitchen. Mr. Tenpenny sat at the table picking at a sandwich. He looked lonely, dejected.

Why did I have to be such a jerk? He'd done nothing but be in the wrong place when I was angry. I'd been embarrassed, and I took my frustration out on him. Bad Cassie. I tapped on the window. When he glanced up to see who it was, he gave me a very dirty, very non-British look.

"I'm sorry," I mouthed, and he resignedly got up to let me in. "Sorry sorry sorry." I kept repeating the word until he cut me off.

"Why are you here?"

"I was just thinking about a few things Dr. Dunwiddle told me. They kind of go with something I've been wondering about."

"So go speak with Dr. Dunwiddle."

"I don't think she likes me much."

"I don't think I like you much either right now." The guy may not be able to draw breath, but in the brutal honesty department, Mr. Tenpenny wasn't lacking one bit.

"Good, then you'll tell me if I'm being an idiot who's jumping to conclusions."

"True. What are these conclusions?"

"All Magics have a scent that can be recognized by people who've been around them, right?" Mr. Tenpenny nodded. "I'm guessing perfume and cologne covers up that scent."

"Yes, that's why it's a terrible breach of etiquette in some communities to wear perfume."

"Because you'd be hiding something, right?" He nodded again, but more cautiously, as if he didn't like where I might be heading. "The only person I've come across here who wears perfume is Vivian. Do you know much of her background?"

"No, she only opened up the shop—" He shut his mouth and began paying extra attention to his sandwich.

"What, maybe about six months ago?"

"Yes," he said, pushing the plate away, "but that's surely just a coincidence. She's been very involved in the community. She can't be the Mauvais, if that's where you're going with this."

Just like a man to defend the hot bimbo in town.

"That's not what I'm saying. I don't think she's the Mauvais."

"Good, because she is well-liked."

So I've seen.

"But I do think she's covering up something about herself, like maybe her true identity," I said. "If the Mauvais really is kicking up things again, she could be one of his agents, one of the people helping him."

"Dear Merlin," Mr. T said under his breath as he slumped back in his chair and gave an exasperated shake of his head. "It's not as bad as accusing Tobey of killing me, but now you think Vivian did it?"

"No, I think Alastair killed you."

"Oh good heavens, Cassie. Should I go get the phone book so you can add every resident of Rosaria to your list of suspects?"

I did briefly wonder if there was a MagicLand phone book, but I quickly focused back on my argument.

"I'm not out of line here. He had some connection to the Mauvais in the past. What if that connection was never broken?" Mr. T tried to cut me off, but I spoke over him. "Think about it. Alastair knew the watch was coming, he knew who it would be delivered to, and he's taller than you with dark hair, which matches the only two things you remember about your attacker." Mr. T tried to cut me off, but I wan't quite done. "Plus, you have to see that Vivian is hiding something. She's covering something up about who she really is. She and Alastair seem to be close. What if they're both serving the Mauvais right under your noses?"

"Cassie, Alastair has a past, but it's not—"

As he was speaking, I pulled out the book and opened it to the page with my parents' photo, which was pretty easy since the spine had broken when it landed. His words cut off when I pointed to the poster in the background.

"If Vivian isn't suspect, then how do you explain that? Alastair aside for now, Vivian is using the Morphing Spell and using gallons of perfume to mask who she really is."

"You are aware that people like to emulate famous people. Even Portland has its own resident Elvis impersonator."

"So Vivian's just playing dress up?" I said, annoyance filling my words over him not taking me seriously. Mr. Tenpenny must have picked up on the tone.

"Look, I agree with you in one respect. People who encountered the Mauvais always reported that they never got a good look at his face. It could be because when he was at his most powerful, he was performing the Morphing Spell. I've been studying the photos at Fiona's, trying to find a face that resembles that of my attacker. Morphing would explain why none of the students in those photos rings a bell."

I was about to give a cheer of triumph when Mr. T raised his index finger, signaling me to hold back my gloating. He then continued, "But what you're talking about, for a Magic to morph their entire body and maintain it for long periods of time as you're implying Vivian is doing, would be next to impossible. The spell is simply too exhausting." It was my turn to slump back in my chair. "Look, I'm well aware of the rumors about the Mauvais's return. They come from credible sources. I don't doubt that the Mauvais is active again. Where he's been all this time, I don't know. I also don't doubt that he has agents, as you call them, but I sincerely believe that those agents are neither Alastair, nor Vivian.

"What I do believe, what I know, is that the Mauvais is weak. In an effort to boost his strength as much as possible, he placed most of his magic in the watch. Once we got the watch in our hands, we quite literally took a great deal of his power. And if there's one thing the Mauvais doesn't like, it's being powerless. To regain his magic he has to get that watch."

"But maybe he wouldn't need the watch if he had me," I said. I desperately wanted to bring up all the sugar Alastair had been feeding me. I also wanted to point out that Vivian's shop was rarely open and still displaying six-month old fashions — perhaps because morphing left her too tired to manage her wares. But now that I had Mr. Tenpenny listening to me, I didn't want to start lobbing more evidence at him. I needed to ease him into my way of thinking.

"Which is why it's vital we put whatever power you've pulled from it back into the watch," he said. "It's the only way to keep you safe."

"And what then? If the watch's power is returned, he'll keep coming for it. Eventually he'll find it." I told him about what had happened to Mr. Wood.

"Cassie, you have to realize the same is true if you don't put the power back into the watch. He will find you."

I was pretty sure he already had.

"He killed my parents. He killed you. He killed Pablo. And he tried to kill Mr. Wood. It's my fault the watch woke up. I should be the one to stop this. I mean, isn't there some way for me to magically call him out and get it over with?"

"No, Cassie. Even if we could locate the Mauvais, you can't face him on your own. You haven't been trained for any type of magical combat."

"Trained? I've apparently got power on top of power. You people can't even be near me too long because I might suck up your power—"

I paused. The flickering lightbulb of an idea hovered over my head.

"Get whatever thought you've just come up with out of your skull this instant or I'll tell Gwendolyn to give you a knockout potion. You cannot face the Mauvais."

"What's your suggestion, then?" I asked.

"What you have wanted all along. Your draining is scheduled for tomorrow. I will drag you there myself if I have to. You absolutely must get your power into the watch to be safe."

Be safe. Was that the MagicLand mantra tonight? But apparently I hadn't been safe since I was born. Parents hunted down, me kidnapped and left to fend off abusive foster fathers, then just as I'm settling into a nice career of illegally dressing up the dead, I'm thrown into a world with my own version of Voldemort. Be safe. Yeah right.

"You can't outsmart him, Cassie. He will figure out whatever is ticking around in that head of yours. Put your power into the watch, go back to your world, and let us handle this. We will take care of ourselves as we always have."

"Then I should go get my rest," I said. I didn't think I'd get a wink of sleep, but it was getting late and I had little hope of winning this argument.

"I think that's the wisest idea you've had all night. Should I walk you to your door?" The offer was presented not as a gentlemanly gesture, but as a I-don't-trust-what-you-might-get-up-to one.

"I won't get lost," I said, then stood and put my hand on Mr. Tenpenny's shoulder. He patted my hand and my throat tightened at the sincere warmth of the action.

Just as I headed out the door, Mr. T warned, "And promise me you'll stay away from Vivian's."

I gave him a thumbs up and headed home to spend some quality time with my dead cat. As I walked the few blocks to my own door, thoughts rolled over me faster than a Maserati proving its worth on the Bonneville Salt Flats. And, despite Mr. T's certainty, those thoughts started with Vivian and Alastair.

I mean, "flirty bimbo" could simply be part of her disguise, but she had sidled up to Alastair nearly every time he'd had any physical contact with me. Was there more to that than just flirting?

Did Alastair know exactly what he was doing as he'd ordered all those cakes and pastries? He'd always made sure I had an equal share and never once asked me to foot the bill. He'd been feeding me sugar since my very first day of lessons, and he was the only living Magic who wasn't afraid to touch me. Could he have taken power from me with those touches? Vivian then comes along, he passes the Cassie Power Baton to her, and she transfuses my magic to the Mauvais to boost his strength. Had all

Alastair's shy flirting simply been his way of gaining my trust, of working his way toward delivering my magic to his evil overlord?

Eventually, this path of possibilities merged onto the Tobey Turnpike. Two weeks ago, he couldn't stand the sight of me. Then, out of nowhere, he shows up and spends several hours with me to help me tidy up my apartment. How did he know about the attack? And who did I see him with next? Vivian. Spinning her busty web wherever she could.

I don't know, maybe I simply didn't want to believe Alastair had used me, but Tobey did have a motive. He wanted magic and couldn't get it through the proper channels. Could he have made a deal with the Mauvais? A little trade of Cassie Juice in exchange for a transfusion of supernatural power?

I suppose it was good I left Mr. Tenpenny's without running into Tobey. After all, with this new possibility jumping around in my head, I might have accused him again and you can only cry wolf so many times before the magic villagers chase you out of town with flaming pitchforks.

CHAPTER FORTY-FIVE

TEST PREP

Big surprise I know, but I didn't get much sleep that night. My head ached from the circular onslaught of suspicious scenarios, and by morning, it was woozy from exhaustion. On the up side, no one had broken in and tried to suck any magic from my veins.

Since sprawling in bed was proving pointless, as the sky began to lighten, I got up and dug my tea mug out of the Corrigan's satchel. As I had done all through the night, after making my tea, I thought about what I was going to do.

Be safe, both Alastair and Mr. T had told me.

Why start now?

I had two choices. The first: Give up my pathetic existence and accept the Mauvais, now that he was on my trail, would eventually capture me. The MagicLand community would suffer, non-magics would suffer, and I would suffer as I was turned into a Human Duracell.

My other choice: Channel my power into the watch, walk away from all this, and let the community sort it out for themselves. Mr. Wood, if he recovered, would be safe from me ever raising the dead again, and I could stick to my status quo of not getting involved because, as should be obvious by now, getting involved really messes up your life. I got involved with the dead, and now I was possibly being hunted by an evil wizard. My parents got involved, and now they were corpses.

But was there another option?

My bumbling brain failed to remember Pablo was also a corpse. Out of habit, I dropped some kibble in his bowl, then went to my room to get dressed. Since my other clothes were crammed into a bag, I pulled on the pair of jeans I'd worn the day before. As I tugged them over my hips, I heard the sound of crinkling paper and caught the distasteful scent of Vivian's perfume.

The note.

I pulled it from my pocket. It was one of those small, square envelopes that often come with gift-wrapping. As I held it, I could feel the folded note inside, but that wasn't all I felt. A shocking tingle went up my fingers, kind of like the shock you get when you put your tongue to a nine-volt battery.

Just as I slipped the note from the envelope, the doorbell rang. Cursing and cramming the note back into my pocket, I marched over to my front door. He's more of a pounding-with-fist kind of guy, but I expected to see Morelli glowering at me, demanding the deposit for Pablo, and huffing and puffing his stink on me after climbing the stairs, but when I opened the door, no one was there.

The bell rang again. This time I realized the sound was coming from my left. No one had told me my magic door had a bell. I stepped over to the closet. Just as I touched the knob, I hesitated. I was a hunted woman. Should I really open the door so readily? Then I chided myself. I mean, would the Mauvais really bother to ring the bell like an eager Avon lady?

I thought maybe it was Mr. Tenpenny come to chaperone me to my appointment. But when I opened the door, there was Alastair, dressed as ever in mismatched loafers and a perfectly tailored shirt that emphasized his lithe but trim physique. He held out a square, pink box. Only one thing came in boxes of that size and color. Donuts. My mouth watered. I swear, if I didn't think he was feeding me these things to help out the Mauvais, I'd be melting for this guy.

"Thought you could use a treat."

I thanked him and pointed him toward the kitchen.

Now, before you start shouting at me about letting the enemy in, I'm no moron. I still worried about whose side he was truly on and kept an eye on his every step. If he made even the tiniest of wrong moves, I would shove him with full magical force and make a break for it. But the only odd thing he did when he stepped from my closet was pause and sniff. I can't explain the look on his face. There was concern and worry, but also fear and guilt. Was it distress for me or for himself? Had his wizard boss issued some sort of ultimatum? He glanced at the box. This seemed to reassure him. His face relaxed, although some worry lingered in his eyes.

Merlin's balls, I was so tired of trying to figure out Magics.

As Alastair started dishing up his first donut, my guard was up, but I was also completely distracted by what was in my pocket. Don't get me wrong. I am a self-proclaimed donut addict, but at that moment, I wanted nothing more than to rip open the note and find out what was inside.

"I figured the sugar will give you a boost for what you need to do today," Alastair said, moving and speaking hesitantly. His attitude wasn't the awkward shyness I'd gotten used to, but more like he was unsure of himself. Or perhaps, unsure of what he was doing.

"No lecture on the immorality of channeling away my power?" I asked, taking the donut he offered, eating it in only a couple bites then grabbing another.

"MagicLand, as you call it, will be closed to you afterward. I would have liked more time with you, but I can understand the difficulty of coming to this world so late in life."

"You make me sound like I'm a hundred," I said as I pulled apart an apple fritter and slipped a piece into my mouth. I swear I could hear cheers coming from my cells' magical mitochondria.

"Some of the magic you've inherited, the magic deep in your cells, is well over a thousand years old."

"Then I better apply for Medicare the minute I'm done with this," I said, then a thought came to mind. "Not to be rude, but how old are you? I mean, if you were friends with my parents, shouldn't you be in your forties?"

"I turned thirty-seven this year."

Last night, he'd mentioned how old he was when my parents died. I was four then. I was twenty-eight now. I could have done the math, but my mind had been more preoccupied with plans for today than with number crunching. As I finished the apple fritter, I scanned his unlined face, his perfectly black hair, the smooth skin on the backs of his hands. I'd have guessed him to be no more than two or three years older than me, not nine. This guy was either doing some crazy beauty regimen or—

"Do Magics age differently?" I asked, curiosity pushing my suspicion to the side for a moment.

"Smart as ever. The magic in our cells is old, but it keeps the rest of us young. No one has ever sorted out how. We age like MCs up until the age of sixteen, then we just, I don't know, switch over to aging only a few months for every Norm year." Despite my height, ever since I'd turned eighteen, everyone had underestimated my age by quite a number of years. And here I thought it had been my youthfully buoyant demeanor. "Go on, try to guess someone's age. How about Busby?"

"He's like eighty, eighty-five," I said, thinking this sounded high. His paperwork said he was only in his early seventies, but even Magics might be guilty of lying about their ages.

Shaking his head, Alastair broke into an amused grin and I hated the little flip my stomach performed at the sight of it.

"He adjusts his documents every decade to avoid drawing suspicion."

"So how old is he?"

"Busby's a hundred and eleven."

"Shut up, he is not."

"Well, not anymore. It'll be curious to see how he ages, if..."

"If what?"

"If he stays alive, or as alive as he is. There's no guarantee Busby will die once the watch has its power returned."

Ah, hell. I hadn't even considered that. If it was the watch's magic mixing with my magic that kept him alive, then putting the magic back into the watch would mean both magics were still viable. They'd just be stored in a different vessel. Which meant there was no certainty my draining would be Mr. T's death sentence. His second death sentence, that is.

As I munched my way through a cinnamon twist, the letter was burning a hole through my pocket. Given that he didn't just drop the donuts off and hightail it, I had to assume Alastair was planning to stick with me from now until I got to Runa's. Luckily, morning tea and a small bladder gave me the perfect escape.

I excused myself and exerted an impressive amount of self-control to keep from breaking into a run to get to the privacy of the bathroom.

You don't need the details, but suffice it to say there was enough liquid that had worked its way through me to make it seem like I'd made a legit trip to the loo while my eyes devoured the message.

Let's make a deal, Black. You don't care about the community and I have a good sense you would choose your own gain over their harm. So here's the offer...

I have information about your parents' whereabouts. If you agree to help me I will give you that information and leave you to find them. Don't believe everything the others have told you about their demise. In exchange for this information and my assurance I won't pursue you, you will bring me the watch. Simple as that.

If you agree, meet me at Vivian's Boutique at noon. Come alone and don't come empty-handed.

My heart pounded with thrumming vigor. My parents. Were they still alive? If I went along with this, I could find out. Maybe I could find them. A fuzzy plan that had been doing the backstroke in my head all night suddenly emerged from the pool with perfect clarity.

The watch. A hand over. It wouldn't be difficult.

But could I do this? Could I betray people I'd grudgingly come to like just to get a scrap of information I might or might not be able to use? I washed and dried my shaking hands, my mind calculating the steps I'd need to take to carry this out.

If I did it, that is.

I caught my reflection in the mirror. My features a blend of my mom's and my dad's. What would it be like to see those features on the faces of the people who gave them to me? What would it be like to speak to them? I could almost picture myself hugging them, and believe me, coming from a firm non-hugger, that's saying a lot about how much I craved finding them.

I glanced at the note once more. Was there any magic way to discern subterfuge behind the words? It had been typed, so the sender was clearly trying to disguise their handwriting. It smelled of Vivian, but she hadn't delivered it. Morelli had said it had been left by a dark-haired man. I stared at the door as if I could see Alastair through it. Again I wondered whose side he was on. Whose side had he been on all along? I crammed the note back into my pocket.

"I should probably head out," I said when I emerged from the bathroom. Alastair watched me for a moment. Did he know what I'd just read? Did he sense what was clicking through my mind? Did I have toilet paper stuck to my shoe?

"So you're really going through with it?" he finally asked with a tinge of disappointment, almost as if he wanted to talk me out of it, but knowing he'd get nowhere for his efforts.

This really was driving me bonkers. Was he a wicked warlock or a concerned friend? I didn't have the people skills to sort it out. I wanted to tell him everything. I wanted to ask him to help me make this insanely momentous decision, to help me come up with a way to see it through without hurting anyone else. But I couldn't trust Alastair. I couldn't trust anyone, it seemed, until this was done. I needed to play my cards close to my chest, so I replied with what he likely expected to hear.

"I don't think yours is my world. As you say, maybe if I was younger, if I had come at the age when I should have started training, it would have been different, but I'm an outsider. And I'm not good at fitting in."

"I think you've done well so far."

"Except for accusing Tobey of magical murder, blowing up Gwendolyn's kitchen, and," I added pointedly, "finding out I was treading on Vivian's interests." His face tightened, but not with anger, more like he didn't want me to continue that line of thought. Before he could butt in, I added, "And I want Mr. Wood to get better and return to business so I can go back to my work."

With that, I grabbed a maple bar. I'd need plenty of fuel for my plan to work. I then hefted my satchel over my shoulder and we headed through my closet door. When we stepped into MagicLand, Alastair paused. He brushed his fingers along the back of my hand and a tingle of magic pulsed between us. Or maybe it was just the sugar high from gobbling down four donuts in less than fifteen minutes.

"I will miss you," he said.

My throat tightened up a bit. Damn it. Despite my theories about him and the Mauvais, despite my trying to keep my heart neutral toward him, some warm feelings for Alastair had seeped through the cracks of the emotional wall I'd built from bricks of suspicion and doubt. Stupid Cassie.

But it wasn't just Alastair. I would miss my magic acquaintances. At that moment, I thought of my options. What if I kept my magic? What if I stayed a part of MagicLand?

Just as I pictured the shocked look on Runa's face if I walked in and said I'd changed my mind and didn't want to be drained, the image of Mr. Wood on his stretcher and of Pablo in his box flashed into my mind.

No, there was nothing for Alastair and me. Evil minion or not, Alastair wasn't in my future. Even if he wasn't boosting my magic and planning to deliver me to an evil wizard, even if he and Vivian weren't in league together, if I stayed he would no doubt come to harm just as everyone else who cared about me had. And even though they tolerated Tobey, I knew once I was drained, I would be shunned from the community. After all, most of them would probably be glad to never see me again.

I slapped some mental mortar to shore up my emotional wall as we strode toward Magic Main Street.

CHAPTER FORTY-SIX
THE DRAINING

Alastair did indeed stick with me all the way to Dr. Dunwiddle's. Once we got there, he leaned in close. I waited for another of his cheek pecks, but he only stuck out his hand like I'd just completed a job interview. I shook it, the action feeling strangely formal.

"It was good seeing you again, Cassie," Alastair said, eyeing me as if trying to read something in my face, his jaw tensing as if wanting to say something. He then broke eye contact, dropped my hand, and strode away without another word. I pictured myself running after him, telling him I'd stay, asking him to swear he wasn't one of the bad guys. But my legs stayed rooted on Dr. D's stoop until he was out of sight.

When I entered Runa's, the main shop was empty. I scanned the back wall. The shelves were tightly packed with tidy rows of slim boxes except for one vacant space. I rang the bell on the counter and browsed the card rack while I waited. I wondered if there was a Goodbye Magic or Good Luck on Your Draining card, but decided that would be like finding a Happy Abortion Day card at the Republican National Convention headquarters.

Dr. D emerged from the exam room and greeted me. Well, *greeted* might be an overstatement. She acknowledged my presence and gestured me back to where she'd just come from.

311

Lola, Fiona, and Mr. Tenpenny waited inside. A pot of basil, a clump of fur, a new matchbook, and a bottle of water had been arranged on the floor with the watch in the center just as before.

I stared at the watch. Could it really be so powerful? I sensed something from it, but I wouldn't describe it as magic. It was that same feeling as when stepping into a low-lit, artifact-filled room of an archaeological museum. It was that feeling of being near something ancient and mysterious and a little creepy.

At some point, it had given a kick start to my magic, but I hadn't felt any different. To be honest, eating sweets woke more of my magic than this thing had. Which begged the question: Was the watch itself evil, or did it merely enhance the evil nature already present in the person who possessed it? After all, I certainly hadn't experienced any urges to stage a magical coup over the few months it had been in my closet.

My point was, would the Mauvais having the watch make that much of a difference? He was evil. He was corrupt. If he truly wanted to get back into business and seize control and he didn't have the watch, wouldn't he find another way to increase his powers? I mean, I assumed he was a resourceful go-getter if he had hopes of taking over the world.

"Are you ready?" Dr. Dunwiddle asked. I nodded, but doubt nibbled into me. Was I? Was I truly prepared for the deception I was about to attempt?

"Is she?" Mr. Tenpenny asked, looking between Fiona, Lola, and Dr. Dunwiddle. I noticed he was back in his funeral suit, complete with the paisley tie I'd selected from Tobey. He looked dapper and composed, but there was a strained appearance to his eyes that hadn't been there before. I was sorry I had given him trouble on his last days of being undead.

"She has learned to tame some of her power and she understands the basic principles," Dr. Dunwiddle said grudgingly.

"My house has never been cleaner, and that's saying something," Lola replied.

"Gwendolyn may have another opinion, but she does agree that Cassie made her best effort in the potions kitchen. And I'll admit she's done quite well, surprisingly well, at the studies I've given her," Fiona said with a proud smile. Shame filled me. The note felt like a brick in my pocket and I couldn't meet her eye. Could I really go through with what I was thinking? Could I risk their suffering? Hell, would it even work?

"Then let's begin," Mr. Tenpenny said. Fiona squeezed his hand. Her eyes were misty. At least they'd been able to say their goodbyes this time.

"You know where to stand. Try not to burn down my office this time." Once I moved so I was in the center of the circle and straddling the watch, Dr. Dunwiddle began guiding me through what I needed to do. "Concentrate on your power and think of it as a shirt needing to be packed into a suitcase. Fold it up, ball it up, however you can make it fit."

I concentrated. For some reason I couldn't picture my magic as a shirt. Instead, maybe because I'd been eating so much sugar lately, I ended up with an image of cramming ice cream into a cone. I kept my eyes on the watch and ignored the other objects. I knew those were to hold my elemental energy which would find its way there without much effort on my part. The watch, on the other hand, was made to hold intrinsic power, but only if that power was willingly put (or forced) into it. Once filled, the community would have to safeguard it.

Or I could betray them all and learn the truth about my parents.

"Concentrate."

In little time, the watch glowed red, a sign I was packing in too much magic too quickly. I was agitating the molecules to heating and if I didn't control it, the watch — and all of MagicLand — might explode and I'd never truly be rid of my power. To slow the flow I imagined a spigot being turned to decrease the flow of water. Or in my case, ice cream.

This slow down gave me more time to think about what I was doing. What I was potentially giving up. Everyone kept going on about how strong my magic powers were. I mean, just because I hadn't done much with my life didn't mean I didn't have ambitions. Who's to say I couldn't be the Mauvais? Cassie Black, Evil Ruler of the Universe. Just as I bit back my laughter, something akin to a lightning bolt cracked through my head.

"It's done," Dr. Dunwiddle said from what sounded very far away. My legs went wobbly, but Lola, sniffling away her emotion, caught me and eased me down to the floor. In front of me, the watch ticked out a steady rhythm.

I glanced behind me. Mr. Tenpenny had slumped over. Fiona's arms draped across his back. He was dead. Again. I only needed to get him back by this afternoon to prove to Cologne Carl that nothing was up. How soon would my magic door lock and never open again? The idea of not being able to visit here struck me harder than I expected. Then again, my emotions might have been slightly off kilter from having just been magically wiped out. Regardless, I needed an excuse to remain here until lunchtime.

"Could I stay a while today? Just to say goodbye to a few people."

"I don't think it's a good idea—" Dr. Dunwiddle started to say.

"She's too exhausted to do any harm," Lola said. "It's her last chance."

"So be it," said Dr. Dunwiddle, who used tongs to carefully put the watch into its ornate box before tidying up the other objects that I knew would be taken to give a boost to a couple ailing Magics under her care.

"I'll need to get Mr. Tenpenny to Mr. Wood's."

"We'll see it's arranged," Fiona said.

Lola squished me with a bear hug. A hollow spot formed in my gut when I inhaled. Without my magic, her spicy scent had vanished. Once she let go, I left the exam room, placed a dollar by the cash register, grabbed a card off the rack, then stepped outside.

I didn't really want to see anyone. Of course, I am an introvert, so that should be no surprise, but this time it wasn't me being anti-social. I just needed a moment to think. I also needed Runa to leave the clinic.

There was a choice to be made. I could think of myself or I could think of the community.

Be safe.

I ran through my options once again, but the truth of it was the only way to be safe was to betray everyone in MagicLand.

CHAPTER FORTY-SEVEN

BARGAINING CHIP

I bided my time by loitering in an alleyway across from the clinic until I saw Fiona and Lola leave, both patting their eyes with tissues. I wasn't sure what they'd done with Mr. Tenpenny and I felt a little pang in my heart that he wasn't walking alongside them. I checked my phone for the time. 11:24. Just a few more minutes until the predictable Dr. Dunwiddle would head off for lunch. Which she did right on cue.

Once she'd turned the corner toward Main Street, I walked as casually as possible across to the shop and pretended to examine the window display. I then slipped the greeting card up the doorjamb to lift the latch. Proving you didn't need magic for a little breaking and entering.

I went over to the shelves. The open space was now filled in. I had a vague idea where the empty slot had been, but amongst the thousands of boxes, I couldn't be certain exactly which was mine, nor did I have time to sift through the dozen or so boxes it might be. Instead, I closed my eyes and angled my head so my left ear faced the general area.

Thanks to my foster parents never allowing me to go to rock concerts or have any sort of music player that required headphones, my hearing was in amazing shape. As such, it took only a few seconds before I detected a faint ticking coming from one of the containers. I teased the box out of its spot, then slid it off the shelf.

The slim box appeared no larger than a pencil case, but the interior was as deep as a file drawer. And at the bottom rested a familiar, intricately designed wooden case. I tipped it out, removed the watch, then put the empty case back into the depths of the box before returning it to its place on the shelf. A warm tingle danced across my palm as I tucked the watch into my satchel.

The side streets near Runa's place that had always been nearly empty now seemed to bustle with activity as I headed to my destination. Every person I passed gave me a pitying look or a scornful scowl. Honestly, their facial expressions didn't bother me. I was too amazed that they couldn't see the watch-shaped bulge as big as a bowling ball (or so it seemed to me) in my bag, or hear my pounding heart that I swear was as loud as a diesel-powered jackhammer to my ears.

After turning a few corners, I stopped in front Vivian's out-of-season window display. I reached for the door handle, then hesitated. Was this what I wanted to do? I lowered my hand. My legs itched to turn around. It wasn't too late to hurry back to Runa's and replace the watch.

For the first time in my life I wondered what my parents would think of what I was about to do. Whoever was inside had information on them. This was my only chance of getting that information. It would be worth it. It had to be.

Indecision banished, I tugged the door open and ducked into Vivian's shop. When I entered, Vivian stood near a rack of sweater dresses like the one in the window. She did nothing to hide her surprise at seeing me. My skin prickled and my nose wrinkled at the power of her perfume. I glanced around, wondering if Alastair would be here too, both of them working together to please the Mauvais.

But there was no sign of Alastair. A strange sense of relief swirled around me and I wasn't sure if it was relief over not having to fend off two conniving Magics on my own, or relief that maybe, just maybe, Alastair wasn't one of the Mauvais's agents.

But I'd been right on one count: Vivian was working for the Mauvais.

She stepped toward me, her heels clacking on the shop's wooden floor. Behind me, the door's lock snapped into place. "You have it?"

"If I give it to you, you can't let him use it against the community. Or at least not this one."

She sniffed and her upper lip curled from a sneer to a smirk.

"You've just been drained. I don't think you're in a position to make deals, so you're going to listen to my proposal."

"My coming here means we already have a deal. I provide the watch, you leave me out of whatever you're planning to do with it. And you tell me about my parents."

"But I have a new proposal."

Proving even Magics weren't above a bit of bait-and-switchery.

"I'm listening."

"You and me."

"Sorry, I'm into guys."

Vivian laughed in the way you do when someone doesn't get an inside joke. Snidely. Derisively.

"Not what I meant. If we worked together, we could be great. I'd even take you to see your parents."

This halted me from telling her to screw herself. So the note hadn't been a ruse. My parents really were out there somewhere. I couldn't stand Vivian. I trusted her about as far as I'd be able to walk if I donned those stilettos of hers, but she was offering me not just information on my parents, but to actually take me to them. Sure, I would be in league with a wicked witch, but hey, what's a little evil damnation among friends?

"Just give me the watch," Vivian said hypnotically. She still held out her hand. I pulled the watch from my satchel and wrapped my fingers over the strange timepiece. Although the metal housing should have been cold, it radiated warmth and I could feel the faint thump of its gears ticking through my palm. I handed the odd timepiece over to Vivian as if the thing meant nothing to me.

She took the watch and snaked her long fingers around to get a tight grip on it. She then hauled back and whacked me in the face with the fist she'd made.

I should have seen it coming. I mean, how many years of my life had I spent dodging blows? But I was so full of my own plan, I hadn't anticipated the speedy jab. I staggered back. Vivian laughed. A nice, villainous cackle that would have stirred up envy in any Disney witch.

"You fool," she said. "You've been drained. Do you really think I'd want anything to do with you? Just the thought of willingly giving up power goes against everything I stand for."

She'd been closing in on me as she said this and brought down a hard punch to my eye on the final word. My mind reeled and my nostrils burned with the stench of her perfume. She drove a fist into my back. This all seemed far too familiar. I hadn't seen Vivian in anything but a dress before, but there's no reason she couldn't own a pair of linen slacks. She was tall, nearly the same height as my attacker. What if she'd tied a dark scarf over her blonde bouffant hair?

"It was you who attacked me," I grunted. "You covered up your scent with cologne."

"I wasn't expecting you to come home, but I like to be prepared. I also made sure to shut up that pig landlord of yours. Hated to do it. His sort let out the worst stench when you curse them."

"Did you attack Mr. Wood?" I asked, practically growling with the fury of realization.

"Guilty," she answered brightly.

I charged forward and rammed into her gut with my head. She latched on and sent a series of punches to my side and to some newly sensitive regions in my back. My skin prickled again. I reached around to grab the hand that held the watch and twisted as hard as I could. She screamed at the unexpected pain. She didn't let go of the watch, but she did stop hitting me. For a second.

Fists working like a cartoon boxer, the bimbo battered me countless times. Okay, not countless, but I lost track after the eighth hit.

Defend yourself, you idiot, I told myself, but I couldn't get my arms up to punch.

Be safe.

As those two words came to my head, I felt a surge of something in me and suddenly Vivian was thrown back. Her face, which looked swollen and misshapen even though I hadn't landed a single blow on it, was a blaring neon sign of shock. And under the heady scent of perfume, a faint whiff of cinnamon wafted over the air.

"You were drained." Her slinky kitten voice still dominated, but there was another layer that sounded deeper, rougher. Had I hit her throat? I kept my good eye, the one that wasn't swelling shut, on Vivian and wondered if I'd taken one too many hits to the head over the past week.

The human before me was Vivian, but at the same time

wasn't Vivian. There were traces of Vivian, the blonde hair was still long and lush, but it was morphing to black from the roots out. The body remained pin-up curvy, but was growing slightly taller, the chest becoming more square than rounded, the waist losing its itty-bittiness, and the hips slimming.

Although the change was only partial, recognition crept through me. The dark hair, the shape of the face, the glinting eyes. It was a face burned into my memory because of the context in which I'd first seen it. A flash of his arms around my parents' shoulders blazed through my mind.

CHAPTER FORTY-EIGHT
TRUE MOTIVES

"Devin Kilbride," I whispered. My mouth had gone salt-pan dry — whether from fear or from gaping open, I can't say.

"I prefer Mauvais."

Kilbride's lips curled, cracking Vivian's crimson lipstick.

Oh hell.

This was not what I signed up for. Sure, I suspected something about Vivian wasn't on the up and up. But this was way more than I had bargained for. The reality of how stupid I'd been to come here alone, to think I could take on any Magic with years of hexing and cursing experience, struck me a bit too late as complete and utter idiocy.

I stood there unable to move, my fists still poised to punch as shock settled over me and froze me in place.

The Attacker Formally Known as Vivian wasn't being quite so passive. She/he lunged at me. Instinctively, I jutted my hands out, palms facing forward. Once again, without me ever touching her, Vivian went hurtling back, this time into a rack of ironically hideous Christmas sweaters.

Someone pounded on the boutique's front door. My head whipped toward the noise. Alastair jerked at the handle. He waved his hand in front of the lock, but the door remained barred to entry. He shouted for me to let him in, but my attention turned back to Vivian. Her wonky face glowered at him as she got to her feet and clumsily untangled herself from a sweater that featured a blinking tree on the front.

I tried to remember what Dr. Dunwiddle had told me about morphing. It's exhausting, especially a full body transformation. That exhaustion was probably the only thing keeping me alive. That and the extra boost I'd gotten from a breakfast of donuts. It hadn't just been gluttony inspiring me to wolf down so many of those sugar bombs. I'd had a plan. A plan that had really gone tits up.

I rushed toward the door. Just as I started to release the lock, I halted. Vivian and Alastair had been chummy. Alastair had to know all that sugar he gave me this morning would raise my power to its peak. But had he given me that boost to help me, or to make me more valuable to the Mauvais?

Alastair shouted my name. His eyes were frantically wide as he yanked on the door handle, rattling the glass in its frame. He'd also eaten his fair share of donuts that morning. He wasn't worn out from morphing. He would be at his full power. Would that power be used for or against me? I couldn't say.

I withdrew my hand from the lock. Not yet, I thought, then turned my back on Alastair to keep an eye on the person changing before my eyes.

While the donuts were helping me rapidly recharge my magic for this encounter, the only way to fool Runa into thinking I was de-magicked for good had been to allow her to drain me as much as possible. Which meant I wasn't as strong as I had been.

But neither was the person before me, and that was a lucky thing. This was the freaking Mauvais, after all. Had Vivian/ Kilbride not been exhausted by the amount of time she/he had spent morphing over the past months, she/he could have sent an Exploding Heart Charm my way with the waggle of his lacquered fingers. But he had pushed himself too far and Devin Kilbride looked like he knew it.

We both startled into action when a wall clock went off with a tinkling little chime to signal the noon hour.

Like two rams about to butt heads in a nature video, we surged toward the watch that rested on the floor between us. With the advantage of long limbs, I slapped my hand over the watch first.

I clutched it with fierce intensity, but Kilbride slammed his hand over mine and held tight. His hand had become broad and meaty with masculinity, but was still tipped in long, blood-red nails. If I wasn't fearing he'd recover enough power to kill me, I'd have laughed at the odd combination.

Had I been more giver than absorber, Kilbride would have had an easy time of it. He could have simply sucked the power out of me to boost his own depleted power stores. But even for an evil wizard, magic isn't the only way to win a fight and take home the prize.

Vivian/Kilbride tightened his grip on my hand and squeezed. And I'm not talking about a firm-handshake amount of pressure here. I once saw a David Attenborough clip about the insane amount of force an alligator's jaw can deliver. At the time, I couldn't fathom how that might feel.

Now I knew.

"Let it go," Kilbride growled.

My hand released its hold on the watch. Not because of the threat, not because he was using magic to control me, but because I heard and then felt the bones in my hand snapping.

I screamed at the bolt of pain shooting up my arm. Kilbride grinned at my agony, and I'm not ashamed to say the expression on his face filled me with more fear than I'd felt in a long time. The only thing that kept me from panicking was the sight of the sweating exhaustion in his pale, grey face.

Even though I had released the watch, Kilbride maintained his hold on me. I had one trick up my sleeve. It was my only chance to save myself from anything worse than a broken hand. I grit my teeth and absorbed as much of his remaining power as possible. Power he couldn't afford to lose.

If I had more training, if Alastair had bothered to teach me any defensive spells, if I actually knew how to fight with magic, I could've easily inflicted some damage. But all I had in my arsenal was shoving and absorbing. Well, and cleaning, but I didn't think that was what the situation called for.

Possibly sensing what was happening to him, Kilbride flung my mangled hand out of his grasp. I screeched when it slammed against the wood flooring. As I whimpered, he snatched up the watch and you wouldn't believe the smile on his face.

I was in one foster home where they had two of their own real kids, twins. They were the ones I'd gone to Victoria with. The ones who could have given me a true home if my time with them hadn't been cut short.

Anyway, I was there during Christmas and they were the sort of family who stuck to tradition and didn't put up the tree until Christmas Eve after the kiddies had gone to bed. Because you know, Santa, in addition to delivering toys around the globe, has time for a bit of holiday decorating when he drops by.

I was eight and already a cynical non-believer in Santa, but those six-year-old twins were still die-hard upholders of the faith. When they rushed down the stairs on Christmas morning and saw that tree and all their presents, I swear their grins would've put both the Joker and the Cheshire Cat to shame. Even I couldn't help but smile at their happiness and surprise.

As his long-nailed fingers closed around the watch, Kilbride-Vivian-Mauvais had that same glee on his face, but his glee was accented with malevolence. After all, he was an evil wizard, not a delighted six-year-old. When he stood up on legs that were still entirely feminine except for dark hair sprouting along the calves, he staggered back and caught hold of the cashier's counter to support himself.

"This isn't over, Black," he said in his gravelly yet slightly feminine voice.

As far as threats go, it did have a bit of Snidely Whiplash lameness to it. I'd expected better from an evil, murderous wizard, but I let it slide. After all, he wasn't at peak performance right now. I'm sure if he was in top form he'd have come up with something much more threatening that would've sent chills through me.

Don't get me wrong, chills were running through me, but they were mainly from the overdose of adrenaline and agony flooding my system. Still, there was one thing I had to know.

"Are my parents really alive, or was that just a lie to get me here?" I demanded in a raspy, shaky voice.

My attention was laser focused on him. My whole body trembled from pain, from the fight, from anticipation of the answer.

Already on edge, I screamed when, just as the Mauvais opened his lipstick-stained mouth to answer, the glass of the main door shattered then rained down onto the floor. Alastair knocked the rest of the glass away, then stepped through the opening and marched over to me. I still didn't know if he was here to help me or to help the Mauvais. Why had he been near the shop last night? Why had he brought me donuts?

I tried to scramble away from Alastair. In the confined space of the boutique, I don't know where I thought I might go. Under a clothing rack like a little kid hiding from his mom? But scrambling isn't easy to do with a broken hand and hot pain surging from your fingers to your toes. Trust me on that one.

My head swayed, but I forced myself to stay alert. The Mauvais might have been weak, but I knew exactly what he was capable of. Mr. Tenpenny. Pablo. My parents. All dead because of him.

Yes, my parents too, because I knew I'd been tricked. My unexpected and overwhelming desire to find them had led me to this boutique. I thought I was being clever, I thought I could pull a fast one, but I'd been played a fool. Vivian had teased me with the possibility of their being alive to lure me to the shop.

Alastair rushed to my side, helped me to my feet, then faced the Mauvais straight on. Was this when he handed me over? Was this when he abducted me to turn me into a power source for evil? Alastair shifted, blocking me from Kilbride/Vivian. Over Alastair's shoulder, I watched the Mauvais's pale, clammy face twitch in disgusted amusement.

"She betrayed the rest of them. I guess you two make a great pair," he said, and the words made my gut jump. "You can have her. She doesn't matter to me now. Thanks to her, I have this back." He held the watch up so Alastair could see it.

Alastair's shoulders flinched and he whipped up his hands, sending out a blast of, well, I don't know exactly what. Because at the same instant, the Mauvais snapped the trembling fingers of his empty hand. This sent up a ripple like when you see heat shimmering the air from a hot road surface. It deflected Alastair's attack, sending racks of clothing to both sides slamming back into the walls.

The deflection lasted just long enough for the Mauvais to run toward a changing room door. When he opened it, I caught a glimpse of the Portland skyline. I wondered what people would think of a man running down the street in a tattered red dress and nylons.

In Portland, probably not much.

CHAPTER FORTY-NINE

A LACK OF SKELEGRO

The shop's floor suddenly became mushy, like trying to stand on a half-filled waterbed. I didn't pass out, but I did drop to the ground, too weak to hold myself up any longer.

"What are you doing here?" I asked Alastair, who had crouched down beside me.

"Making sure you did exactly what I thought you were going to do."

I backed away.

"You knew about Vivian's note? Her offer? His offer. Whatever."

"When I smelled Vivian's perfume on you last night, I had a feeling something like this was coming."

My head might have still been swimming, but I didn't think that had anything to do with his answer coming across as purposefully vague. He stood up and held out a hand to help me get to my feet. I took the offer, cradling my broken hand that was already starting to swell.

"What exactly are you saying?"

"Do you think I brought those donuts just because I was hungry? Sweets are the last thing you give to a Magic who's about to be drained. The sugar keeps your cells too energized, making it nearly impossible to get all the magic out."

Exactly what I'd been thinking when I gobbled down those bits of deep-fried goodness. It had only been a theory, and thinking back on it, I can't believe I risked so much on concepts I'd gleaned from Fiona's textbooks.

With the donuts, I had planned to hold onto a small amount of my magic during the draining. The sugar would help with that. I had also planned to absorb any magic from the watch just before handing it over. Another part of the plan the sugar would help with. What I had not planned on was facing down Evil Wizard Number One, and if not for the sugar, I wouldn't have survived.

So, my sugar plot had scored a solid two out of three, but what had been Alastair's motive for bringing me those donuts? Again, I wondered if those breakfast treats had been a power boost to make me more of a prize for the Mauvais, or had he truly been trying to give me the strength to keep myself safe?

Alastair seemed about ready to explain further when Dr. Dunwiddle stormed through the boutique's broken door. She was fuming. Her cheeks raged red and her eyes narrowed into a hard scowl like a bull ready to take down a pesky toreador. I half-expected her to kick me. I wasn't too far off the mark.

Runa launched toward me, grabbed my shoulders, and shook me. I tried to protect my hand, but the jostling was too much and shocks of pain bolted from my floppy fingertips up into my jaw.

"You stole the watch." She cocked her arm back. "You thieving, backstabbing bitch!"

When you've been hit as many times in your life as I have, you usually know when a blow is coming. I would not defend myself this time. First, my mangled hand couldn't even form a fist, let alone strike someone. Second, I was too tired to muster a Shoving Charm. Third, my fight wasn't with Dr. Dunwiddle.

I cringed, waiting for the impact.

Thankfully, someone else didn't mind fending off the good doctor. Alastair magically shoved her back, not with full force, just enough to get her away from me. She came charging right back. This time Alastair didn't conjure his spell quickly enough and Runa laid into me.

Lola and Fiona, who must have been chasing after Runa, rushed in. I kept trying to shield my head with my good hand as shouts erupted in the small boutique. Soon, someone pulled Dr. Dunwiddle off me and twisted her arm up behind her back. All this happened without any hands being laid on her.

With Lola standing behind Runa and keeping the doctor's arms magically restrained, Fiona and Alastair blocked me from anything Runa — who must have conveniently forgotten her Hippocratic oath and was proving herself more than willing to do harm — might throw at me.

"She's injured, Runa. You can't attack an injured person."

"Like hell I can't. She gave Vivian the watch. She broke in, stole it, and gave it to Vivian. They've probably been plotting this the whole time." Runa's venomous glare turned from me to Alastair. "I warned you about letting her take lessons from him."

"Enough now, Runa," Fiona said. "Cassie, is this true?"

"No."

"See."

"I gave the watch to the Mauvais."

Wrong thing to say. I'm not sure what language it was, elvish perhaps, but it was clear from the tone and the vehemence with which they were delivered that the words coming out of Runa's mouth were curses of pure hatred.

Once Fiona slapped a temporary Silencing Spell on Dr. Dunwiddle, I tried to tell them about Vivian being Kilbride, but I don't think my jumbled explanation got through Runa's wall of anger. Even Fiona looked about ready to hit me. I needed to get to the crux of the issue before I got a double-dose of witchy whacking. Luckily, Alastair, who hadn't just been beaten half to death, was able to relate what he'd seen with more clarity.

"But you were drained. You have no power," Dr. Dunwiddle snarled. No, really, she snarled, like a pissed off dog. Then a spark of realization burned across her face. "Sugar. You had sugar, didn't you?"

I nodded. Unsure of his true motives, I decided not to implicate Alastair and his sugar-supplying role that morning.

"I thought I could handle it," I said. "I honestly thought I'd just be giving the watch over to Vivian. I suspected her of morphing, but seeing who she turned into was an unexpected surprise."

"I imagine so," said Fiona.

"Vivian. Who you assumed worked for the Mauvais," Runa said, the words cracking like a whip.

"You actually planned to betray us?" Lola asked.

"No, I actually planned to protect you. I figured that if I gave Vivian the watch, she'd pass it on to the Mauvais. He'd have what he wanted and leave you alone. I was trying to be helpful."

"Helpful?" Runa barked. "Thanks to your help, he now has the very thing we've spent over two decades keeping out of his hands. You gave the Mauvais the most powerful gift he could have wanted. Your parents gave their lives to keep that watch from him."

The last sentence hurt as much as I'm sure she had intended. It compounded with the strain of what I'd just gone through and the throbbing ache in my hand. I couldn't stop the stinging behind my eyes.

"I may have given him the watch, but it won't do him any good," I said, biting back my tears. "It's useless."

Even Alastair showed surprise at this. "Useless how?" he asked.

"I absorbed its power before Vivian, Kilbride, whoever, got it out of my grasp." I showed them my broken hand that had now swollen to a frightening size. "It's what I'd planned all along. Vivian promised me information to find my parents. As soon as he/she told me about my parents, I was going to take the watch's power. The watch would be useless, but Vivian would be none the wiser when I handed it over. That's why I didn't want to be fully drained. That's why I had sugar this morning."

Fiona scolded Dr. Dunwiddle with a glance. Runa's face finally dropped the scowl. She wasn't smiling, but there was a tiny hint of appreciation in those cheeks.

"You stupid girl," she said. "You won't be safe at all now. You only got away this time by dumb luck."

"How do you mean?"

"He's going to figure out what you did. He's going to want the watch's power back. Once he regains his strength, he's going to come after you."

The pain and the stress were too much. The room started spinning. Lola threw an arm around my waist and her spicy, familiar scent steadied me.

Dr. Dunwiddle performed a Numbing Spell that temporarily blocked my pain receptors until we could get back to her exam room to properly take care of my injuries. This was great at first, but let me tell you, there's a reason your body has pain. It's to remind you that the injured area should be treated with the utmost care. Without pain telling me not to, I kept reaching out with my broken hand and bashing it against things with my innate clumsiness. By the time we got to the clinic, I'd broken another three bones that had only been cracked before.

Once she'd assessed the damage, Runa applied a poultice to my hand then set it into what I hoped would be a magical splint that would heal me in less than an hour. But nope, it was just a regular splint. Apparently, even the great Dr. Dunwiddle couldn't instantly heal bones regardless of how many times I asked about Skelegro.

With my hand bandaged and treated, Dr. Dunwiddle slowly let my pain trickle in. I may have been a little whiny at this point, but eventually she found a suitable pain level that would keep me from misery while still reminding me not to use my hand.

"You know," she said quietly, almost as if she wasn't sure she should be speaking, "Vivian wasn't lying. There are reports that your parents didn't die."

"But everyone says they did."

"It's what we'd rather believe."

"But," I prodded.

"They could have been extracted. They could be out there somewhere." She suddenly seemed very keen on dabbing away blood from my face. "I just thought you ought to know."

I honestly didn't know what to say to this. I'd always assumed my parents abandoned me. Then I learned they died heroically. And now to learn my parents might be lolling around somewhere as de-magicked morons? What the hell was I meant to do with that information?

Of course, she delivered this news right before swabbing a healing poultice over my face and telling not to move or speak for ten minutes so the mixture could work its magic.

Once the poultice was cleaned from my skin and a soothing lotion had been smeared over my cheeks, Dr. Dunwiddle stepped back. There was a grudging look on her face, like a child being put before a plate of broccoli. The child knows he has to eat the green stuff, but is dead set against enjoying a single second of it.

"You did well, girl," she finally said.

The wallop of this slim compliment nearly knocked me off the exam table.

CHAPTER FIFTY

BACK TO MR WOOD'S

Fiona and Alastair offered to help me with Mr. Tenpenny. We had only an hour to get him through my portal and settled at Mr. Wood's before Cologne Carl was due to arrive. While Fiona and Alastair arranged Mr. T into a rather undignified IKEA box Lola had found in her garage (the one spot I hadn't cleaned), I scooped up Pablo's cardboard coffin in my good hand. The two Magics gave me a questioning look but remained silent.

Using a Lighten the Load Spell to make the box easier to carry, Fiona and Alastair worked Mr. Tenpenny down the stairs from my apartment. We'd almost made it to the door when Morelli took a break from what sounded like *I Dream of Jeannie* reruns to harass me. He stared at Fiona a moment too long, then focused his attention on me.

"You were supposed to move out yesterday."

I shrugged. "Changed my mind. I'll have your rent when I get back."

"If you're moving back in, you owe me another deposit."

I was about to argue with the logic of this, but when you're carting around a dead body, it's not the time to complain.

"Add it to my tab," I said as I held the door open for Fiona and Alastair to ease Mr. Tenpenny through. We got a few stares on the way to the funeral home, but again, few things surprise weird-loving Portlanders. At my instruction, they slid Mr. Tenpenny onto my work table and pulled away the cardboard box. I placed Pablo on the rack under the table and gave Mr. Tenpenny's hair a quick smoothing down before straightening his suit.

"Who's there?" called a voice from the chapel. My heart leapt.

"It's Cassie." I jogged through the kitchen and into the chapel, every step sending an aching throb into my hand. At the chapel door, I halted.

Mr. Wood was in a wheelchair. One leg stuck out in a cast and his chest was wrapped in a mummy's worth of bandages. His swollen face sported an array of jagged cuts, around which the skin had turned a gross shade of grey, yellow, and purple. Someone had brought his television, reading lamp, and end table down from his upstairs apartment and arranged them on the daïs of the chapel. Mr. Wood had the television on with the volume turned low. A book rested on his lap.

"You're home so soon?" I asked, truly bewildered. This guy looked dead the last time I saw him. And here he was, propped up and looking cozy.

"They said the injuries weren't as bad as they looked at first. The leg's been set, but the damage the paramedics reported mostly resolved itself a few hours after being admitted. The doctors said they've never seen anything like it and saw no reason to keep me in."

I wondered which of the Magics I had to thank for coming to Mr. Wood's aid when I'd utterly failed him.

"Are you here alone?" I asked.

"Only for a bit. My nurse went out to get some sandwiches." Unlike his usual warm manner, he spoke curtly, distantly.

"I'm sorry I didn't come to visit, I—" I broke off. There was so much to explain. Of course, Mr. Wood knew about the living dead thing, but I didn't know if I was allowed to tell him about a whole community of magic, of witches and watches, or of my own personal Voldemort. I also knew I hadn't come to visit because I'd been afraid of losing him. I couldn't admit to him that I'd been a coward. "I just couldn't."

"It's fine. I didn't expect you would. Hoped, though." That stung worse than my hand. "Is everything settled, ready?"

"Yes. I'll handle things. I promise."

I patted Mr. Wood on his arm, reaching with my bad hand at first, then using my good hand, but he noticed the bandages. "Have you been in trouble?"

"Nothing I couldn't handle."

Carl, blissfully free of cologne and any other scent for that matter, showed up on time to scrutinize the paperwork like an eleven-year-old boy examining every inch of the Victoria's Secret catalog. He checked Mr. Tenpenny against the photos they had.

"He seems remarkably lifelike for being gone so long."

My gut clenched. Carl had said nearly the same thing when he'd first come around. Was this simply his usual line? A way to win over funeral home workers? I didn't think so. Runa had told me a Norm's mind could be taken over by the BrainSweeping Charm. Had the Mauvais been controlling Carl? A shiver shot along my arms.

"Sorry," I said, curiosity getting the better of me, "this seems like a silly question, but have you been here before?"

"No, this place seems kind of familiar, but I just got assigned to this case. Everything seems in order, though. I can't imagine what the fuss was. Paperwork gets mislaid all the time. Still, your client does look really, um, fresh, if you don't mind the expression."

Although several blocks were falling into place about Carl's behavior, I'd observed exactly the same thing. I may have tidied his hair only moments ago, but Mr. T's cheeks hadn't been touched up since the day we met. Yet they still showed a slight blush. Of course, he'd only been dead again for a few hours, so maybe that explained his skin's lingering hint of warmth.

"Mr. Wood does good work," I replied. Again.

"I suppose it all looks in order, but I have to put this establishment on probation. It's standard procedure," he added apologetically. This was definitely not the original Cologne Carl. "Still, if we hear of any strange dealings going on, we can't be lenient."

"Things will be quiet from now on," I said as I walked with him to the door. "Thanks for everything, Carl,"

"No problem. And it's Colin, not Carl."

So that would explain why Ms. Kitten Sweater at the county building hadn't heard of him.

"Right. Colin. It's been a long couple weeks."

I peeked in on Mr. Wood to tell him we were back in business, but he was sleeping. The television was still on, the news showing some fluff piece about a man racing down the streets of Portland in a tattered dress but who had disappeared before police could locate him. I closed the door and went back to Alastair and Fiona. I lifted Pablo's box and peeked in on him. Thanks to Runa's spell, he too was remarkably well preserved.

"He really liked Busby," I said, and placed Pablo on Mr. Tenpenny's chest. Together again.

"Once your hand heals, we can schedule the draining again," Fiona said. "You'll heal faster with a little magic in you, so we'll wait until then."

A *little* magic?

I'd unwittingly sapped a good deal of magic from the Mauvais and had sucked the watch dry of its power. I now recognized the sensation and, even with my draining having been done only a few hours ago, I sensed a heaping helping of magic pulsing through me.

I looked up at Fiona's kind face, then to Alastair. There was an evil wizard on the loose who, once he figured out he'd been tricked by a barely-trained witch, would do everything he could to capture me and use me for his own gain. I should want to get this magic out to save myself.

But according to Runa, my parents might be out there somewhere, and had been for over two decades. If I was excluded from MagicLand, who would search for them?

"I want to be trained," I said, stroking Pablo with my good hand.

I caught the warm glint in Alastair's eye, but I refused to be captivated by it. He was hiding something; I felt it as keenly as Pablo's soft fur under my palm. I turned my attention back to the bodies on the table.

"Yes," said Fiona, a tinge of annoyance in her voice, "I just said we'll schedule the draining with Runa once you're healed."

I moved my fingers from Pablo's velvety ears to Mr. T's cold digits. He'd been close to my parents just before they died. I might need his help.

"No, not drained. *Trained.*"

I squeezed Busby's hand.

Fiona gasped, not at my news but at the annoyed curse Mr. Tenpenny grunted as Pablo stretched his body to an extraordinary length with claws out and digging in as cats will do after a long nap.

AUTHOR'S NOTE:
ON FUNERAL HOMES

The premise for this book started with the idea of a woman working in a funeral home and somehow bringing her clients back from the dead.

Let me be very clear, the operation of Wood's Funeral Home is NOT how funeral homes function. The working conditions, the handling of the dead, and Cassie's ability to work without a license are nothing but pure fiction to make the story work without being too cumbersome.

As part of the effort that went into this book, I did try to contact local funeral homes to get a feel for their day-to-day business practices, what might happen in a legal sense if a body went missing, and what their working conditions were like.

But apparently the mortuary business is a tight-lipped one, because although a few offered to answer my questions, they never responded to any of my follow-up inquiries.

And so, Wood's Funeral Home and Cassie's "work room" had to be based on my imagination (and a few things gleaned from the Internet). I'm sure there's errors, but as this is a fabrication of my imagination, I hope my readers can accept those errors.

If any offense has been caused, I apologize...it wouldn't be the first time my imagination has upset someone.

—Tammie Painter
January 2021

BOOK TWO PREVIEW

THE UNCANNY RAVEN WINSTON

What havoc will an over-magicked Cassie wreak? Are the rumors about her parents true? Who will take care of Mr. Wood? And what in the world is up with that garden gnome?

Find out in The Uncanny Raven Winston, Book Two of the Cassie Black Trilogy.

***

PROLOGUE

THE REPORT

"Report in from the Yanks, sir."

The grey-haired woman glanced up at the stout, somewhat hairy man who'd just stepped into her office.

No, she thought upon noticing his hands had only four digits. Not a man. A troll. Judging by his lack of a bulbous nose, and with ears that didn't stick straight out from the side of his head, he was only half troll, but he still possessed that frustrating troll trait of being difficult to train out of a habit. Once a troll got an idea stuck in his or her head, it was near impossible to get it back out.

It's what made them excellent guards. You simply made them promise to keep whoever they were meant to guard alive, and that became their primary focus, even if some of them went about it in unconventional ways. However, this sticky-idea quirk was also why you always had to be careful when working with them.

"I've told you before, I'm not a sir. Ma'am, mum, even just Olivia would be fine."

"Yes sir, mum," he said, mumbling the two titles together.

Olivia Waylon rolled her eyes, and even though she made a great effort to hold it in, let out an exasperated sigh. It was too early in the day for this, and someone — probably one of the pixies they hired as cleaners — had hidden the cords for all the electric kettles, which meant Olivia was not only having to deal with a pile of troubling information that had surfaced about the Starlings, but also with a dim-brained half-troll without the benefit of caffeine from the tea department of Fortnum & Mason.

No witch should have to endure so much before ten a.m.

Olivia pushed back from her desk. The chair's wheels stuttered over the stone slab floor.

"What is it?"

Before the troll — she thought his name might be Chester, but she wasn't certain — could begin, a man entered her office. He was in his mid-thirties and slim with cheek bones so sharp they could slice cold butter.

"Ah, you've heard the report, then?" Rafi said, taking a seat in one of the chairs before Olivia's desk.

"Not yet."

"Chester, why haven't you told her?" he asked, speaking in a tone of mock reproach as he twisted his lithe frame around to grin at the troll. "Never mind. Tell her now."

"The Mauvais is back," Chester said as flatly as if delivering a weather report.

"Damn, Chester, you could've eased into it," Rafi chided. Olivia caught a hint of Rafi's sandalwood scent as he turned back to face her.

"Sorry," said Chester. "That was the report, though."

Olivia's dark cheeks had paled to an odd shade reminiscent of a paper sack left in the sun too long. Did this have anything to do with the information she'd just received on the Starlings? The single sentence from Chester — and the lack of any tea — left her head pounding. She rolled forward, put her elbows on the desk and began rubbing her temples.

"Never mind, then," Rafi told Chester. "Go to the next person on your list and relay the news."

"Yes sir. Goodbye, sirs." Chester gave a little bow and touched his three fingers to his forehead in a salute.

"You do know we're only supposed to use them as guards," Olivia criticized as soon as Chester's heavy footsteps could be heard thumping down the hall.

"I know, but I keep thinking there's more to them. I mean, with their level of dedication to a job, it just seems with the right training..." Rafi's words trailed off under Olivia's it's-not-going-to-happen stare.

"So, what's this about?" Olivia asked. She couldn't shake the idea that whatever Rafi had to say had something to do with the file humming under her fingers. Her throat went dry and she swallowed hard to relieve it.

"Turns out some American girl—" Olivia scolded Rafi with her eyes. "Sorry, a young American *woman* woke up the watch, brought some dead people back to life, and this alerted the Mauvais's senses as to the watch's location. He'd already been on the hunt for the watch, but we assumed he lost the trail when Corrine Corrigan shut down her messenger portal."

"That was an inconvenient fiasco." Olivia watched Rafi's face. He met her scrutiny with a patient, level gaze. "There's more, isn't there?"

"The Mauvais got the watch." The words rushed from his lips

in a tumble of syllables as if, like ripping off a bandage, he could make delivering the news less painful if he did it as quickly as possible.

Olivia burst up from her desk. "What the hell, Rafi?"

In rapid, angry strides, she paced the office from one tapestry-lined wall to another. With each step she mentally listed everything that needed to be put into place immediately. When she realized her head was going in circles with tasks, she stopped at the desk, hovering over Rafi like a hawk over its prey.

"The Mauvais has the watch? Don't you think that's what you should have led with? The wizard who wants to rule us Magics and enslave the Norms has regained the incredibly powerful, the insanely dangerous object that could allow him to do that very thing. And you send me bloody half-troll Chester with the news? Why are we not on full alert?"

"First off, if I can't call her girl, you can't go around pointing out Chester's impure bloodlines in such a disparaging tone."

Olivia no longer wanted tea. Who cared if it was only ten a.m., she needed scotch.

"Sod the bloody semantics, Rafi. We need to activate all the defensive tactics we have ready."

"No, we don't." Rafi leaned back and put his feet up on the edge of Olivia's desk. He wore a grin that made Olivia want to scream. The only thing holding her back was that she hated revealing the tiny drop of banshee blood she carried in her veins. Well, and the fact that she could kill Rafi with her scream.

Not that she wasn't tempted. Her fingers twitched with the urge to wrap around his long neck. But being frustrating first thing in the morning wasn't a punishable offense, so she restrained herself. Instead, she shoved his feet off her desk.

"Need I remind you I have the authority to set your hair on fire?" Olivia said through tight lips. "Which I will do if you don't explain things more clearly right this very second."

"The Mauvais had disguised himself. He got his hands on the watch, but the watch is useless because the girl absorbed all the power out of the watch. Supposedly she's got a knack for magic, even though she only started training a few weeks ago."

The lurch within Olivia's stomach had nothing to do with hunger. Too many issues, problems, and rumors were snapping together to create a tower of concern.

"Where did this take place?" she asked, although she was willing to bet she already knew.

"Portland community. Busby Tenpenny, he was one of the people she brought back."

"Busby's dead?"

"Not anymore."

"This girl—"

"Young woman," Rafi corrected.

"Whatever. She doesn't happen to be named Starling, does she?"

"No, Black. Cassie Black." With a heavy exhale of relief, Olivia dropped into the chair opposite Rafi. He then added, "But she is the daughter of a couple Starlings. Name got changed somewhere along the way, I guess."

Once again, Olivia pressed her fingers to her temples and worked them in small circles.

"What's her name matter?" Rafi asked, his voice full of confused worry. Olivia was one of those people who were never shaken. She was a steadfast rock who radiated confidence and authority without being overbearing. For her to show this much distress made him wish he'd left Chester to deliver the information.

"Because I just received a stack of reports from various sources indicating Simon and Chloe Starling may still be alive."

345

"She's their kid?" Rafi asked, awe replacing his concern for his boss. "The people who got the watch from the Mauvais in the first place?"

Olivia nodded.

"And based on the information I've just received," she said, tapping the folder in front of her, "they could indeed be alive. If they are, they would be in extreme danger. Until you and Chester came in, I'd been thinking we might put a team together to sift through the files, sort out their exact location, and extract them." Rafi's mahogany skin went a shade more in the direction of pine. Olivia raised a hand as if wiping a slate clean. "Sorry, not extract as in *extraction*. Although, that may have already happened. I mean, *extract* as in get them out. Rescue them. If we can. They deserve our care after what they did for the community at large."

"How can they not be dead after all this time? It's been what? More than twenty years, yes?"

"Twenty-four. If they are alive, it won't have been a thriving existence. They're nothing more than pawns to whoever has them. Likely kept just enough alive. Again, assuming these reports aren't false leads, if the Starlings aren't dead, it's quite likely they wish they were."

"You're thinking the Mauvais has them." Chills went up Rafi's arms.

"I haven't had time to sort out what I'm thinking, but from what you've just said, if this daughter of theirs has tricked the Mauvais and it turns out they're being held by him, he's going to use them to get to her. He'll dangle them in front of her then throw them away once he has what he wants. What I don't understand is why wouldn't he just go after her directly? What good do the parents do him?"

"He tried." Rafi's voice carried a hint of amused pride. "He

346

was trying to get the watch, but she beat him."

"Her years of training have really paid off. Remind me to commend the Portland community." Rafi, an enigmatic grin lighting up his face, shook his head emphatically. "What?"

"I just told you. She wasn't trained. I mean, she was, but only for a couple weeks. Before that, she had no idea she was one of us. Think about it," Rafi said, clearly impressed, "barely trained and she beat him. Of course, she had been hopped up on donuts, but it's still impressive."

Olivia's stomach growled at the mention of food. She stood up, flipped open the report cover, and looked at the photo of a lanky, dark-haired white woman. Barely trained and she had survived going toe to toe with the Mauvais.

"But you said the Mauvais had the watch. That doesn't sound like she won."

Rafi's face beamed like a pre-teen gushing over the latest boy band. "She pulled all the power from the watch into herself. The Mauvais got the watch, but it's nothing more than a decorative trinket now. He'll be fuming once he finds out."

Barely trained and she now held the watch's power within her. Olivia closed the folder. "We need to call her in," she said with stern decisiveness.

"Are we locking her down or inviting her to work with us?"

"We'll see."

The Uncanny Raven Winston is available on most major book retailers in paperback and ebook formats.

Find your copy at Books2Read.com/ CassieBlack2 or by scanning this QR code

THE PART WHERE I BEG FOR A REVIEW
IF YOU ENJOYED THIS BOOK....

You may think your opinion doesn't matter, but believe me, it does…at least as far as this book is concerned. I can't guarantee it mattering in any other aspect of your life. Sorry.

See, reviews are vital to help indie authors (like me) get the word out about their books.

Your kind words not only let other readers know this book is worth spending their hard-earned money and valuable reading time on, but are a vital component for me to join in on some pretty influential promotional opportunities.

Basically, you're a superhero who can help launch this book into stardom!

I know! You're feeling pretty powerful, aren't you?

Well, don't waste that power trip. Head over to your favorite book retailer, Goodreads, and/or Bookbub and share a sentence or two (or more, if you're ambitious). Even a star rating would be appreciated.

And if you could tell just one other person about Cassie Black's story, your superhero powers will absolutely skyrocket.

Thanks!!

By the way, if you didn't like this book, please contact me and let me know what didn't work. I'm always looking to improve.

WANT MORE FROM
CASSIE'S WORLD?

Then perhaps you need your very own Cassie Black Bonus Pack. The pack includes...

- A pretty snazzy, although definitely not-to-scale **map of MagicLand**,
- **Exclusive behind-the scenes glimpses** into the creation of the Cassie Black Trilogy.
- Your very own **Cassie Black Coloring Pages** (in case you need to line your cat's litter box),
- And **a recipe from Spellbound Patisserie** for Sacher Torte...but given you're not a Magic (are you?), I can't guarantee it will come out quite as good as Gwendolyn's.

If you're interested in getting this bonus pack, all you have to do is send in six easy payments of $19.95, plus shipping and handling...Wait, no, that's not right.

You can get the Cassie Black Bonus Pack for free by signing up for my newsletter.

This monthly bit of fun features my writing updates, glimpses into the writing life, my latest discounts, and exclusive freebies when I'm feeling generous (which is fairly often).

Sign up today at *www.subscribepage.com/cassieblackbonus*

ALSO BY THE AUTHOR

THE OSTERIA CHRONICLES

A Six-Book Mythological Fantasy Adventure

Myths and heroes may be reborn, but the whims of the gods never change.

Perfect for fans of the mythological adventure of *Clash of the Titans* and *300,* as well as historical fantasy fiction by Madeline Miller and David Gemmel, the Osteria Chronicles are a captivating fantasy series in which the myths, gods, and heroes of Ancient Greece come to life as you've never seen them before.

The Trials of Hercules
The Voyage of Heroes
The Maze of Minos
The Bonds of Osteria
The Battle of Ares
The Return of Odysseus

THE CIRCUS OF UNUSUAL CREATURES MYSTERIES

It's not every day you meet an amateur sleuth with fangs.

If you like fantastical, cozy mysteries like those by Kim M. Watt and C.K. McDonnell that mix in laughs with murderous mayhem and mythical beasts, you'll love the Circus of Unusual Creatures.

Hoard It All Before
Tipping the Scales
Fangs A Million

DOMNA

Destiny isn't given. It's made by cunning, endurance, and, at times, bloodshed.

If you like the political intrigue, adventure, and love triangles of historical fiction by Philippa Gregory and Bernard Cornwell, or the mythological world-building of fantasy fiction by Madeline Miller and Simon Scarrow, you'll love this exciting story of desire, betrayal and rivalry!!

Part One: The Sun God's Daughter
Part Two: The Solon's Son
Part Three: The Centaur's Gamble
Part Four: The Regent's Edict
Part Five: The Forgotten Heir
Part Six: The Solon's Wife

AND MORE...

To see all my currently available books and short stories, simply scan the QR code or visit

books.bookfunnel.com/tammiepainterbooks

ABOUT THE AUTHOR
THAT'S ME...TAMMIE PAINTER

Many moons ago I was a scientist in a neuroscience lab where I got to play with brains and illegal drugs. Now, I'm an award-winning author who turns wickedly strong tea into imaginative fiction (so, basically still playing with brains and drugs).

My fascination for myths, history, and how they interweave inspired my flagship series, The Osteria Chronicles.

But that all got a bit too serious for someone with a strange sense of humor and odd way of looking at the world. So, while sitting at my grandmother's funeral, my brain came up with an idea for a contemporary fantasy trilogy that's filled with magic, mystery, snarky humor, and the dead who just won't stay dead. That idea turned into The Cassie Black Trilogy.

I keep the laughs and the paranormal antics coming in my latest series, The Circus of Unusual Creatures, which is filled with detecting dragons, murder mysteries, and...omelets.

When I'm not creating worlds or killing off characters, I can be found gardening, planning my next travel adventure, working as an unpaid servant to three cats and two guinea pigs, or wrangling my backyard hive of honeybees.

You can learn more at *TammiePainter.com* or at that QR code, where you'll find probably more info than you could ever want or need.

Printed in Great Britain
by Amazon

24870932R00199